"The most promising and original writer of fantasy to come along since Robin McKinley."
—Peter S. Beagle, author of *The Last Unicorn*

Praise for
Sharon Shinn and the Samaria trilogy . . .

Archangel

"Shinn is a good storyteller. . . . *Archangel* takes advantage of the familiar—goodness, the Bible, *Paradise Lost*—through building its own lively quest narrative with these sure-fire building blocks so that one feels at home in the narrative very quickly; it also has a clean, often wryly funny prose."
—*The New York Review of Science Fiction*

"Taut, inventive, often mesmerizing, with a splendid pair of predestined lovers."
—*Kirkus Reviews*

"Displaying sure command of characterization and vividly imagined settings, Shinn absorbs us in the story . . . an interesting SF-fantasy blend that should please fans of both genres."
—*Booklist*

"Excellent world-building, charming characterizations. A garden of earthly delights."
—*Locus*

Jovah's Angel

"Shinn displays a real flair for [music and romance], giving music a compelling power and complexity, while the developing attraction between Archangel Alleluia and a gifted but eccentric mortal should charm the most dedicated anti-sentimentalist and curmudgeon. . . . [A] book of true grace, wit, and insight into humanity, past and future."
—*Locus*

"Some may raise eyebrows at Sharon Shinn's less-than-saintly angels, but they make for far more interesting characters than the winged paragons of legend. Many will no doubt find her end results quite heavenly."
—*Starlog*

"Romantic . . . delightful. I'm eagerly awaiting her next novel."
—*The Magazine of Fantasy & Science Fiction*

The Alleluia Files

"A warm and triumphant close to Shinn's Samaria trilogy." —*Publishers Weekly*

"A tale that makes for exciting, suspenseful, romantic, frightening, and even amusing reading."
—*St. Louis Post-Dispatch*

Heart of Gold

"An elegant and suspenseful tale."   —*Library Journal*

"A telling story of a racially divided society, and a pretty good love story, too . . . another top-notch outing."   —*Kirkus Reviews*

"Will appeal to readers who enjoy unconventional romances and strong women protagonists."   —*Science Fiction Weekly*

"Smoothly written. Shinn has a talent for creating vivid, sympathetic characters. Nuanced and intelligent. A thoroughly entertaining reading experience."
                    —*SF Site*

"The love story of this book is balanced by deft examination of prejudice, intolerance, and inequality. This book is difficult to put down and will appeal to fantasy readers as well as fans of an intriguing love story."   —*VOYA*

"A tightly woven SF story with touches of romance, intrigue, and fantasy."
                    —*KLIATT*

"Clever plotting, subtle characterization, and just plain good writing will keep readers fascinated from first page to last. Shinn is one of the most intriguing voices in speculative fiction today."   —*Romantic Times*

"Extraordinary. Science fiction of the highest caliber." —*Midwest Book Review*

Summers at Castle Auburn

"Intensely emotional. . . . An exquisitely rendered coming-of-age tale in which Ms. Shinn shines as a powerful storyteller with a depth of feeling that touches the soul."
— *Romantic Times*

"The latest enchantment from Crawford Award–winner Shinn combines romantic spice, a dash of faerie, and a pinch of intrigue to create a hybrid soufflé that is delicious."
— *Publishers Weekly*

✦ Jenna Starborn ✦

SHARON SHINN

ACE BOOKS, NEW YORK

JENNA STARBORN

An Ace Book / published by arrangement with
the author

PRINTING HISTORY
Ace trade paperback edition / April 2002

All rights reserved.
Copyright © 2002 by Sharon Shinn.
Cover art by Jean Pierre Targete.
Text design by Kristin del Rosario.

Visit our website at
www.penguinputnam.com
Check out the ACE Science Fiction & Fantasy newsletter!

Library of Congress Cataloging-in-Publication Data

Shinn, Sharon.
    Jenna Starborn / Sharon Shinn.
        p. cm.
    ISBN 0-441-00900-X
    1. Young women—Fiction. I. Title.

PS3569.H499 J46 2002
813'.54—dc21

                                    2001056051

ACE®
Ace Books are published by The Berkley Publishing Group,
a division of Penguin Putnam Inc., 375 Hudson Street,
New York, New York 10014.
Ace and the "A" design are trademarks
belonging to Penguin Putnam Inc.

PRINTED IN THE UNITED STATES OF AMERICA

10 9 8 7 6 5 4 3 2 1

For Jean,
with whom I had the conversation about tigers

✧ Jenna Starborn ✧

Chapter 1

✦

You would think that if someone commissioned your conception, paid for your gestation, and claimed you immediately after your harvesting, she would love you with her whole heart; but you would be wrong. Aunt Rentley had had me created to fill a void in her existence, which was unexpectedly filled by others. I was quickly made not only redundant but unwelcome, and yet there I was, in her house, under her feet, a constant reminder of how much she had paid to purchase something she no longer wanted.

This was never clearer than on Jerret's ninth birthday, an event celebrated with as much flourish as my aunt could muster. The cooks spent a week baking special dishes for the delectation of the hundred guests. The housemaids cleaned every room in the fifty-room mansion down to the curtains, walls, and floorboards; the gardeners replanted the entire front lawn with a hybrid rose imported from Karian and doomed to die within a month in our unfavorable climate. The walls of the mansion were themselves recharged so they hummed with energy and delighted you with the faintest static shock if you ran your hand too rapidly over the simulated brick. Cold and sunless it might be outside, but inside existed an environment of warmth, light, cheer, and goodwill.

For those welcome in the house, of course.

During all this frenzied activity, I kept to myself as much as possible, for there was nowhere I was particularly wanted. As Aunt Rentley's ward, I was not exactly a servant, so there was no work for me to perform in the kitchen or laundry room; and yet neither Aunt Rentley nor Jerret wanted me to join in their family councils as they planned their guest list and considered activities for the celebration. I was used to being ignored by my aunt and her son, but during these planning stages, I was positively reviled. My briefest appearance caused her to shriek with impatience and order me from the room, stupid girl, did I not see how busy she was with important preparations? Jerret, a born bully, would leap to his feet and point a chubby finger toward the door, bawling at me to get out get out get *out*, he did not want me ruining his party with my sallow face and witch's eyes.

He stopped at verbal abuse if his mother or one of the servants could hear, but if I happened to cross his path when no one else was near, he would fall upon me in physical rage. I was a year older than he was, but he was by far bigger, and more than once he cornered me against some doorway or banister and threw punches into my stomach and raised bruises on my shins. This afternoon, he had wrestled me to the ground and twisted his hand in the collar of my shirt so that I could scarcely breathe. I truly thought I would lose consciousness or suffocate, but then I heard footsteps down the hall.

It was Betista, coming around the corner with her arms piled high with fresh linens. "Master Jerret!" she exclaimed, and suddenly I was free, supine on the cold floor, too faint to immediately raise my head. Through a strange dullness in my ears I heard Jerret scramble to his feet and make his sullen defense.

"It was her fault. She hit me," he growled.

Betista ignored him, dropping to her knees to investigate my condition. I heard the sounds of Jerret's footsteps fleeing down the hall.

"Jenna!" Betista exclaimed. "Jenna, dear girl, are you badly hurt? Do I need to send you to the PhysiChamber?"

I had recovered enough now to push myself to a sitting position. She was still staring down at me, clasping her hands under her full chin, her gray eyes sick with worry. I attempted a smile. "I'll be fine. I feel sick to my stomach, but that will pass."

"Let me take you to the kitchen," she said briskly, hauling her bulk to her feet and reaching out a hand to help me up. "I'll make you some tea."

But the thought of swallowing anything hurt my bruised throat. "No, thank you very much," I said formally. Ignoring her outstretched hand, I pushed myself to my feet. "I'll just go to my room now."

Betista looked undecided. She was the housekeeper, a woman of some influence in the household, and she was the closest to an ally I had ever had. Yet, as she would never overtly defy my aunt Rentley, and she could not protect me from Jerret, there was very little she could do to materially improve my lot. Except not hate me.

"I think you should come sit quietly by me for a while," she said. "I should keep an eye on you. You look pale and a little strange."

"I always look strange," I said, with an attempt at humor.

Betista bristled. "Now, that's not true! You're a lovely girl—a little thin, maybe, and dark, though some consider a dark complexion to be fashionable—you shouldn't listen to what your aunt says, you know she's partial to Master Jerret—"

I let it go; I was not about to discuss my physical merits with the housekeeper here in the hallway when all I wanted to do was go to my room and lie down. "In any case, I'll be fine," I said.

Betista gathered up her linens, which she had dropped helter-skelter on the floor when she came to my aid. I sensed a certain indecision in her manner. "Now, what happened this afternoon," she said slowly, uncertainly. "You're not going to tell on Master Jerret—"

"No," I said tiredly.

"Because she can't help it, he's her son and she loves him. When you tell tales on him, she doesn't believe you."

"I know."

"So it does no good to be reporting stories to your aunt," she finished up in a rush.

I had made my way somewhat shakily to the head of the stairwell; it was the servants' staircase, but it would take me by an indirect route to my own chamber. Over my shoulder, I said curtly, "She's not my aunt," and I began the long climb up to my room.

*I*n point of fact, she was not my aunt; she had intended to be my mother. That was when she was childless, of course, before the doctors had made the miracle of Jerret possible. So she had commissioned me, and I had been grown in the generation tanks of Baldus, and she had come every day to watch my fetus shape itself and uncurl. She had laid her hand on the glass tanks, trying through the impermeable substance to touch my clenched fingers, and she had counted the minutes and the days until I was ready for harvesting.

When did it go wrong for her? When did I lose my hold on her heart? Was there something repulsive in my small, squalling body—was there a timbre in my midnight wail that sent tremors through her sensitive bones? I like to think neither of these things are true; I like to think that any child she had brought home from the gen tanks would have, eventually, seemed to her something foreign and hateful. She is not a happy woman around synthetics; she cannot stand the sight of the cyborgs that labor in the mines, indifferent to the planet's cold and its poisons alike. I like to think that it was the method of my creation, and not the soul inside my body, that made her despise me.

Or perhaps it had nothing to do with me or my conception: Perhaps she was so limited in her love that she had none to spare for me once she could produce her own son. It had been an accepted thing, since some early childhood trauma, that she would be unable to conceive; and among her contemporaries, to bear a child naturally was considered the highest accomplishment a woman could attain. But something happened only two months after she brought me home. The doctors perfected the artificial womb, and her fortune was easily large enough to purchase one, and suddenly she was carrying within her own body that most precious commodity, another life; and there was no room for me in her thoughts, in her house, in her heart.

Naturally, this left me in a most precarious position. Since she had paid for me, she was responsible for me; I was not easily disposed of.

And yet, since she had never formally adopted me, I was not legally her daughter. In fact, I had no legal status at all. I simply was.

The technical term for my condition was half-citizen, and there were many like me, on Baldus and throughout the interstellar system. We were created from many circumstances. Some, like me, were rejected gen-tank babies. Some were legitimately conceived sons and daughters whose parents had decided, for some reason or another, not to acknowledge them. Some were orphans, with no family to care for them and no institution willing to pay for their upkeep and training in a profession that would allow them to earn enough to buy their own citizenship.

Citizenship existed at five grades, from the fifth and lowest rung to the first and highest. Fifth- and fourth-level citizens were accorded such status only on their home worlds; third- and second-class citizens were accepted in more regional districts of federated planets; and first-grade citizens were honored everywhere throughout the Allegiant Planetary Council Worlds.

Citizenship grades had been instituted in the first greedy, brutal days of interstellar exploration. The fractured governments of the planet Earth being unable to sustain any cohesive space-going program, the real advances in technology and colonization had been, at the beginning, financed by extraordinarily wealthy private entrepreneurs who were not willing to share their prizes with the masses back home. As one of the great early merchant princes put it, "Imperialism is incompatible with democracy." Those first families in space risked much, gained everything, and passed on to future generations wealth so fabulous it could hardly be reckoned—and the same disinclination to share their fortunes. As the Allegiance was formed between newly settled planets, social systems grew more codified, and the chance of breaking from a preordained caste grew more and more remote.

There were only three ways to become a citizen of any rank: Be born (or adopted) to the status, marry into it, or buy it. I had been unlucky on the first count. Even at the age of ten, I could see that the other options did not look promising for me, either. I knew I was contemplating a lifetime of half-citizenship.

But it would not be so bleak as all that. Half-cits were allowed to work, and keep their wages (though they generally were employed in menial jobs and taxed at exorbitant rates). They could marry. They could not vote and they could not own extensive property and they were strongly discouraged from reproducing (though these days you heard fewer stories of half-cit children being whisked away from their mothers' arms and disappearing into some unmentionable hell). But they could be productive members of a vast and far-flung society, and I had hopes of one day finding my entrée into that universe. I believed I could gain some useful skills, and find worthwhile employment and support myself in some not wholly distasteful enterprise; and it was this goal that gave me the strength to go on during my darkest days under Aunt Rentley's roof. I was not valued here, but someday, somewhere, in the smallest of positions, someone would value me, and on that slim hope I fed even when I could take in no other sustenance.

That night, dinner was torture. My awkward position in the household made it impossible for me to dine with the servants, so I always took my meals with Aunt Rentley and Jerret. Usually they ignored me, which was easy to do, as the table was long and narrow, and we sat as far from one another as we could. I always ate as quickly and as quietly as possible, though Aunt Rentley invariably remarked on my slurping or chewing sounds, and I excused myself from the table as soon as I was able.

This night, though I ate my soup as noiselessly as I could, my gestures or my appearance or my very presence irritated Aunt Rentley almost at once.

"Sweet Lord Yerni, girl, can't you manage to swallow your food with a little less commotion?" Aunt Rentley exclaimed. "I declare, my son and I can hardly hear each other speak for all the racket you're making."

"I'm sorry," I said, though I did not feel at all sorry; I felt maligned. "I can eat with Betista if you'd rather."

"Eat with Betista! Of course you could not! Eat with the servants, what will you be saying next . . ." Her voice trailed off. Down the length of the table I could feel her eyes examining me. "What in the world have you done to yourself? You've dirt all around your neck."

I took another spoonful of my soup, this time sucking it up with the noisiest inhalation I could manage. "It's not dirt," I said.

"Stop that! Eat like a lady," Aunt Rentley said sharply. "If it's not dirt, then what is it?"

I knew better—and Betista had warned me—but I could not help myself. I was angry, and my face hurt, and my muscles still ached with that remembered brutality. So I said, calmly as you please, "A bruise. Jerret choked me in the hall."

"I did not!" Jerret squealed just as Aunt Rentley uttered a sharp exclamation of disbelief.

"Wicked girl!" she cried. "To lie about your betters in such a way!"

I shrugged. "I'm not lying. He pushed me, and he choked me, and he wanted me to be hurt."

"Lying! She's lying!"

Aunt Rentley was on her feet, pointing a trembling finger at me. "You will go to your room, miss, and you will meditate on your sins, and you will not be allowed back at this table—no, nor shall you have any dinner or any breakfast or any food at all—until you apologize to Jerret."

I pushed my chair back and stood up. This was not the first time I had been banished from the table and told I would skip a meal or two, but this time it looked like starvation to me, for I would not apologize to Jerret if it meant my very death. "I feel sorry for you," I remarked. "To be so blind that you love someone so cruel."

She actually gasped. "*Sorry* for me! You—you—lying, terrible creature, it is yourself you should feel sorry for, for your evil ways will lead you to damnation and hellfire—"

"I'm not the one with evil ways," I said, still in the calm, certain voice that I knew roused her to fury, and yet I could not stop myself. She was wrong; I was right; and though I knew enough of the world to realize that that guaranteed me nothing, still I could not bear to back down from a stance I knew was proper. "Your son is the liar, and your son is the unkind one, and *he* is the one who would face damnation and hellfire, if there were such things awaiting us after death, which there are not—"

I had not thought she could grow angrier or more red-faced, but at this heresy she did both, stamping her foot this time in earnest. "*Godless* child!" she shrieked, for she worshiped most devotedly at the Church of the Five Saviors. "To insult me—and my son—and then to scoff at the Lords themselves—"

Jerret had lost interest in our argument a few strophes ago, for he was now spooning up food with great concentration, but at this he said, "Stupid PanEquist. Now you really will die and go to hell."

"Go! Before I call one of the servants in to *throw* you in your chamber!" Aunt Rentley panted. "To your room! And you will not come out, or speak to a soul, until I grant you permission! Now out! *Out!*"

I laid my fork on the table with great deliberation, stood quite slowly, and nodded my head most gravely in her direction. "I am glad to go," I said, and headed with dignity out the door.

Soon enough I was back in my room, a small, ill-lit chamber on the third floor, a level below the servants but nowhere near the family suites. A few guest bedrooms could be found on this story, though they had never been used in my experience, and a schoolroom, some storage rooms, and an infinite number of closets. There were days mine were the only feet to patter down the corridor—weeks, even. I could be banished here and completely forgotten, and my bones might not be found till a new tenant moved in and began exploring.

I climbed to the middle of my bed and sat, looking around at the forbidding gray walls. This had always been a haven to me, a place where neither Jerret nor Aunt Rentley would bother to come to torment me. But to stay here till I starved . . . even my stubborn soul quailed at that. Surely Betista would not let such a fate befall me. Surely even Aunt Rentley would at some point remember my existence.

I sat for a few moments unmoving, my heart heavy and my thoughts bleak, then I shook my head and looked around me for distractions. Books were my constant solace, for Jerret monopolized the StellarNet computer screen that offered us entertainment and a view on the events of the Allegiance, but he was not much of a reader. Neither was Aunt Rentley, and the only reason the house held any books at all was that the former tenant had left behind an entire library of very rare volumes, and Aunt Rentley had been too selfish to sell them. She knew that people she respected placed a high value on actual books, and so she liked to have them about her, but I was the true beneficiary. I would creep down to the library, steal a volume from its overloaded shelves, and spirit it up to my room to be read at leisure. I had devoured many of the classics of Baldus and the Allegiance, and I considered all the great authors of the day my personal friends.

But when I opened the drawer on my nightstand, the item that I first encountered was not a novel but a treatise on the PanEquist philosophy, which I had been studying for some weeks. Betista had given it to me, whispering an admonition to keep it hidden from my aunt, and we had talked it over with great animation when we had a few moments alone in the kitchen. I had heard of the PanEquists, of course, for on those rare occasions when I did get a chance to browse over the Stellar-Net, they were often to be found on the news sites. But until I had read this tract, I had had no clear idea what their beliefs were and how they viewed the world.

Though I had no real need to refresh my memory, I perused the pamphlet again, starting at the beginning and reading with great pleasure the articles of belief. "Whereas the Goddess is an infinite Goddess, a Goddess of all places, all planets, all peoples; whereas the Goddess created every creature, from the simplest invisible microbe to the most complex member of mankind; whereas the Goddess created not only the animals of the universe, but the trees, the rocks, the soil, and the water; we believe that the Goddess loves each of these things equally, that there is no difference between one being and another, one atom or another; that all things are the same and all things are equal. Thus I am no more important to the Goddess than the spider on the wall or the exploding fire of the nearest star; we are one, and we are the same in the eyes of the Goddess."

Yes—exactly—in so many words were put down the feelings I had had since childhood but not known how to articulate. Aunt Rentley

believed I was inferior because of the manner of my creation; the government believed I was invisible because of my undesirable legal status;
Jerret believed I was insignificant because he could hurt me, and torment me, and buy things I would never be able to own. But I was the
equal to all of them in the Goddess's eyes. I was fully human, fully
alive, fully integrated into the source and flow of the universe. I
belonged here; my breath and my molecules and the blood in my body
were revered by the great spirit of the universe. It was the PanEquists
who saw the truth, and so I was one of them, heart and soul, in secret,
and in exultation.

I was in my room five days before anyone remembered my existence. The first two days I was hungry, and I prowled the room looking
for forgotten cakes and crackers that I might have left carelessly behind
on some more provident day. I had plenty of water, for I had my own
small bathroom where I could refresh myself daily, so thirst was not a
problem; and hunger was only a problem for a while. By the third day,
I was listless but not unhappy. My stomach no longer roared and
pleaded for food—indeed, I was indifferent to the very thought of eating. By the fourth day, I cared even less about the missed meals. I was
feeling light, wispy, fanciful, and odd, but not hungry. I spent a good
deal of time sitting at my single window, watching the foreign roses
shiver in the hostile breezes, and wondering which of us would die first.

I also watched the cars pulling up the long, graded drive, for this was
the day of Jerret's party, and every notable member of Aunt Rentley's
acquaintance was arriving to celebrate. I had a deep interest in things
mechanical, and so I watched with interest as each new model arrived.
There was the Stratten Aircar, a marvel when it had been introduced,
but considered inefficient and cumbersome now; there was the sleeker,
more powerful Killiam version, which could circle the planet without
the need for maintenance or refueling. I pressed my face against the
glass to get a better look at the Organdie Elite and the Vandeventer II,
and for one of the few times in my life I was envious of others.

Sounds and scents of the party drifted up to my level as the hours went by. I heard laughter, music, shrieks of merriment from the children who had been invited, the lower rumble of adult voices in both serious and comical conversation. There were to be games played on the south lawns, but my window faced north, so I could not even watch these activities. And once the sunlight faded, there was nothing to see out my window at all, not even the comings and goings of the great aeromobiles. I sighed, and returned to my bed. I lay there, sniffing with disembodied pleasure the faint smells of the grand banquet being laid out below. I could imagine the fruits, meats, vegetables, pastries, and other fine dishes being sampled and exclaimed over, but I was so far removed from hunger that I did not care that I had no chance to sample them.

The banquet—indeed, the party—seemed to go on well into the night. I lay dreamily on my bed, envisioning the lazy good nature of the guests as they reached the midnight hour of reveling. They would be smiling through their yawns, and patting their full stomachs, and crying out to one another, "By Lord Yerni's bones! It must be time for us to be going!" And yet they would stay for one more slice of cake, another moment's gossip, a final good-bye to the hostess who had presented such an elegant affair. Even when I sensed the house beginning to empty, saw the headlights of the aircars traveling across the ceiling of my room, I could not summon the energy to rise to my feet and cross to the window again. I lay on the bed, imagining the slow exodus, and smiled to myself at the grand sight it must be.

I was still smiling the next morning when they found me, and I was still too weak to rise to my feet, and eventually all the bustle and riot that surrounded me grew too great for my brain to sort out, and so I closed my eyes and slept.

I had not been to a hospital before, and so I was fascinated with the machinery. There was equipment in my room, attached to me; there was equipment down every hallway, connected by cords to other patients or plugged into unfamiliar sockets on the walls. Everything beeped, hummed, flashed, and monitored with such a lovely, brilliant

array of signals that I could not stop watching and trying to understand. My night nurse, a cyborg, caught my interest early on, and
explained the functions of various machines. She even taught me how
to study my own readouts and determine my progress.

Which was unfathomably slow. I had not expected to waken in a
hospital in any case; most household illnesses were diagnosed in the
PhysiChamber, a closet-size computer-controlled room where all the
functions of the body could be scanned and analyzed. In point of fact, I
had rarely had occasion to be tucked inside this room, since I was seldom sick and what few ailments I had succumbed to had never been
deemed serious. Jerret and Aunt Rentley, on the other hand, used it on
an almost weekly basis to check the state of their health.

But a hospital—that bespoke a real state of emergency. I could not
believe a few days without food had reduced me to such a state. Which
I observed to the cyborg.

"Is that what the trigger was?" she asked in her pleasant, neutral
voice. She was nearly eighty percent machine, from what I could tell;
her face was attractive but not particularly expressive, and her touch
was preternaturally gentle. Obviously I was in a half-cit ward; no
cyborg would be allowed to nurse a full citizen. "Starvation?"

"Does five days make starvation?" I wanted to know.

She adjusted one of the dials while I watched. "Not for a healthy
adult, but for a malnourished child, that's a dangerous period of time to
pass without eating."

"I had water," I offered.

She nodded. "That's why you're still alive."

"I've gone hungry before," I said.

She nodded again. "Many times. And been physically mistreated.
The doctors are asking your aunt about these abuses. There is also a
legal representative present."

My eyes opened wide at this. I could not imagine my aunt reacting
kindly to any inquiries about her treatment of me. "I am only a half-
cit," I said.

"That status only prevents you from attaining certain property-oriented goals," she said, still in that precise, unemotional voice. "It does not allow others to harm or neglect you."

"You're a cyborg, aren't you?" I asked. Such creatures had not come my way often, at least not to talk to. Aunt Rentley had a force of maybe eight who maintained the grounds and worked her scant arable fields, but they were never allowed inside the house and I had never had a real conversation with one of them. They were considered lower than the half-cits, and many people were actually afraid of them. Certainly my aunt was.

The nurse nodded. Her hair was more perfectly coiffed than any human's hair would be; her skin had a flawless, elastic look to it that made it appear melted over her bones. If she had bones. Perhaps it was a metal framework beneath the layer of supposed flesh.

"Cyborg, but human enough to be happy," she said, smiling. It was a slow, strange smile, a little dreamy, a little sad, as if thoughts circled through her brain that could not show on her artificial face. Then she patted the pillow upon which my head was resting. "Now it is time for you to sleep. Your aunt will be here in the morning."

Obediently, I lay back on my pillows as if to rest. "And the doctors? Will I be seeing them? I must have been asleep every time they have been here before, for I have never seen them."

She touched my cheek with that soft, kind hand. Again her expression seemed strange, as if her eyes and lips could not convey the emotion that coursed through her. "Oh, yes, the doctors will be here with your aunt," she said. "I think you will be interested in all they have to say."

*I*n fact, the room seemed crowded the next morning when everyone even remotely interested in my well-being gathered around my bed: my aunt, two doctors, a representative from the Social Services Agency, and a tall man I vaguely recognized from his past visits to my aunt's house, whom I believed to be her lawyer. And me.

One of the doctors, a wiry young black-haired woman, seemed furious. "Basic physical records show this child has been systematically mistreated for the whole course of her existence," she said in a cold voice that would have made me shiver had it been directed at me. "There are evidences of broken bones that were not properly set, common childhood diseases that were not treated, recent internal damage to the stomach which I can only suppose was inflicted by some kind of blow, historical malnourishment that has contributed to slow growth and possible deformities that I cannot identify yet—would you like me to go on?"

My aunt was furious as well. "I have treated this girl as if she was my own daughter—I have fed her, clothed her, educated her, watched over her—"

"With the result that she is stunted, bruised, starved, and—"

"I believe we all understand your position," the lawyer intervened. "Mrs. Rentley is very sorry to have caused you distress over the girl's condition. In the future we will—"

"In the future, Jenna should be out of Mrs. Rentley's care," the doctor said shortly.

"And who will care for her, pray, if not me?" my aunt said sharply. "She is not a criminal or a wayward girl, so none of those institutions will take her in. She has cost me no end of trouble and expense, it is true, but I have done my best by her and stand prepared to continue to do so. But not if people say nasty things to me and accuse me of things I have not done—"

"Oh, you have done them—"

"Indeed, doctor, perhaps your tone—"

"There are places she can go," a new voice interceded smoothly, and everyone in the room turned to face the woman from the SSA. She was sleek, compact, and manicured; even her face seemed lacquered on, though she was clearly completely human. Something about her voice made me dislike her instinctively, though I could not have said why. "There are institutions that will take her in."

The black-haired doctor turned on the social agent with as much contempt as she had shown for my aunt. "And be treated no better, would be my guess."

The agent shrugged with a small economical motion. "These places are schools, training facilities that will enable her to learn a career that will in turn enable her to live a full and productive life. They survive on government funds, it is true, so they are not luxurious places to live, but they are adequate, and they have advantages."

"What sort of advantages?" asked the second doctor, a heavyset young man who had not spoken until this point.

"They will feed her. They will clothe her. They will prevent her from being a drain on society by making her a useful professional instead of a petty criminal or a charity case. Or a homicide case, which in her present circumstances she is likely to become."

There was a moment's silence while everyone in the room assimilated that final statement. The doctors looked thoughtful; my aunt grew positively pink with rage.

"Are you actually suggesting—you filthy-minded woman, I will have my lawyer charge you with slander this very instant—"

"A very injudicious comment to have made, particularly before credible witnesses," the lawyer said gravely to the social worker.

The SSA woman turned her hard, uncaring gaze on the lawyer. "I have seen hundreds of cases just like this one result in death," she said. "Hundreds. If you sue me for slander, I will sue you on Jenna's behalf for child endangerment, and the headlines that your client's friends will read will destroy her more surely than any careless remark of mine."

There was another short silence, during which everyone in the room seemed to take a figurative step backward. Even I, listless and unconsulted in my white bed, pressed my head deeper into my pillow and tried to avoid snagging that cool, indifferent gaze.

"What do we need to do," the heavyset doctor asked, "to register Jenna for one of these schools?"

"Determine which school would be most suitable, obtain Mrs. Rentley's consent, obtain Jenna's consent, and send her off."

"What if there is no opening?" the lawyer asked.

The agent smiled faintly. "There are always openings."

There was the sound of soft crying from my aunt's direction. "So she is to be taken away from me, and no one cares what my feelings are," she wailed. The lawyer patted her insincerely on the shoulder. "And no one believes me when I say I have done my best by this child—"

"Because you haven't," the dark doctor said briefly, and then she sat carefully on the edge of my bed. "Hello, Jenna," she said, smiling at me. "You must have heard us all discussing your future just now."

I smiled back. I liked her. "You want to send me away to school somewhere," I said.

"Yes, that's it. We think you might be happier there than at your aunt's house. What do you think?"

I took a deep breath. "I would love to go away to school!" I exclaimed in a rush. "I would love to learn—so many things!— engineering and mathematics and religion and philosophy. Oh, there is so much I do not know. . . ."

The doctor smiled at me again. "What sorts of things do you like best? You mentioned science and math—those are the things I like too."

"Yes, anything with motors or energy or components—my aunt was always angry when I went down to view the generators, but I loved to watch them, I love to think about them spinning and spinning and cre- ating a sort of fire out of nothing but motion—"

"There is a fine tech school on Lora," the agent interposed at this moment. "She could get training there and be equipped to work on any of the space stations in the Allegiance."

"Lora! That's pretty far away," the doctor said, turning her head to survey the agent.

Who gave again that concise, disdainful shrug. "And do you think she would be coming back here for any reason?" she asked softly.

"Now, now," the lawyer said, turning away from my sniffling aunt to rejoin the conversation. "Jenna has strong ties of affection to Mrs. Rentley. I am sure her aunt will be a part of Jenna's life no matter how far from this planet she roams."

Aunt Rentley wiped her cheeks and turned to me with a tremulous smile. "Yes, I'm sure that's true, isn't it, Jenna?"

I met her eyes for the first time since she had entered the room, for the first time since she had banished me from the table for five days of hunger. "No," I said. "I won't care if I go away to Lora and never see you again. Send me away to school, please," I said to the doctor, looking away from my aunt, who cried out and staggered against the wall. "I am ready to begin a new life."

Chapter 2

✦

Classes were cut short that day because of the funeral. We all turned marveling eyes toward Mr. Branson when he gave us that news; never, in the two years that I had been at the Lora Technical and Engineering Academy, had classes been truncated for any occurrence. He caught our wonderment and smiled very slightly, that sad, somewhat guilty smile that seemed to be the only expression he had besides dour abstraction.

"Until then," he said, "work on the problems I have posted to your sites. I expect them all to be completed before we leave the classroom in"—he consulted his watch—"an hour and thirteen minutes."

I glanced briefly around the room, wanting by some silent communication to share my surprise with one of my classmates; but with Harriet dead, I had lost my closest friend at Lora Tech. I bent to my assignment, calling up the indicated page on my desktop monitor and working my way slowly through the required problems. They were advanced astrophysics equations, and although I was better at math than I was at languages, I was better still at scientific application. The theory did not hold as much appeal for me as the practice.

Mr. Branson stopped at my desk, glancing over my solutions. "Yes—

that's right, Jenna—I see you were listening yesterday when you did not appear to be attending."

I looked up at him. He was a kind man, despite his appearance of utter depression, and this made him something of a rarity among the teachers at Lora Tech. "It was hard to pay attention, Mr. Branson," I said.

"Yes. I know. Such a terrible thing . . . Steps have been taken to ensure nothing of the kind ever occurs again."

I nodded, and returned my attention to my keyboard. He watched a few more minutes in silence. "*Very* good, Jenna. I did not realize you understood that theorem. But you are, after all, one of our better mathematics students."

"Not as good as Harriet," I said in a muffled voice.

He was silent a moment. "No," he said at last. "Well. There were not many on this world as good as Harriet."

He moved on to monitor the progress of the others in the class, but I felt my attention slacking again. Harriet had become my fast friend on my very first day at Lora Tech, a day that had been awful in every other detail. The five-week trip to Lora had been wretched in itself, for of course I had no money to command even a second-class berth, and neither my aunt nor the SSA system was willing to pay for luxury accommodations. I traveled in the communal quarters, where food was insufficient, hygienic requirements barely met, and privacy nonexistent. Like the other travelers, I managed to stake out my own space within the first forty-eight hours of our journey, and my boundaries of suitcase and sleeping blanket were scrupulously observed, but I was never comfortable for a single minute of the entire endless voyage. I scraped up a civil acquaintance with my nearest neighbors, watched their twin babies when they needed a few minutes alone to converse or merely walk the ship for exercise, and always observed the necessary courtesies with my other fellow passengers that kept steerage-level travel tolerable. And yet the voyage was miserable.

By the time we docked at one of Lora's twenty off-planet spaceports and took the last of many shuttles to the surface, I was sick, exhausted, and terrified of what lay before me. It proved to be several hours of confusion and despair as it turned out no one from the school had been sent to collect me, and I did not have funds to take a public conveyance to the school—or to pay for my accommodations overnight in a hostel of any acceptable repute. A frantic call to the school elicited the information that one of the professors would be coming to the shuttle station in a few hours to pick up his daughter. I could obtain transportation with Mr. Kelliman.

The trip from the station to the school that afternoon was an exercise in degradation. Mr. Kelliman was a haughty, silent, well-groomed man of level-two citizenship; his daughter was an exotic brunette beauty who had never known an hour's uneasiness; and their opinion of my appearance and my circumstances could not have been more disdainful, and more plainly to be read in their expressions. I told myself I did not care, and I stared stonily out the window at the unending lanes of skyscrapers and city boulevards that covered the entire hundred miles between the shuttle and the school. Even so, I wept silently as we traveled through the dense jungle of commercial buildings, and I could not hold back a brief but profound sense of self-pity.

The first sight of Lora Tech was not designed to reverse my mood. It was a crowded, unappealing campus of perhaps thirty structures, all huddled dispiritedly together under Lora's two pale suns. The architecture was uninspired, the landscaping was sparse, and the air that hung over the overpopulated acreage was dismal. Students hurried between classes with their heads down and their shoulders hunched; the professors strode past them with an uncaring arrogance that was hard to mistake. I did not see a single smile in the short time it took me to be dumped from the Kellimans' car and make my way down a narrow, cracked sidewalk to the junior class dorm.

There, a bored housekeeper registered my name, issued me a series of keys to doors and buildings that I could not remember, and assigned me a room. "Level twelve," she said. "Sorry, but the elevator's broken today. Stairway's over there."

So I trudged up the dozen flights of stairs, almost glad at this moment that I had so few possessions they could be contained in two lightweight bags. I stopped twice to catch my breath and gather my wits. I had not felt so disoriented and disembodied since the night before my hospital stay; I was beginning to think my entire journey, my entire life, had been a fitful dream. Where I would be, who I would be, when I wakened, I could not imagine, but I had to believe it would be to a better life than the one I struggled with now.

Up the endless stairwell—down what appeared to be a coiling, infinite hall—coming finally to a pause before the door that matched the numbers on my key. Fully expecting to find myself balked here, before a door that would not open to my command, I was astonished to find the key a perfect fit, the lock well-oiled, and the door easy to swing open upon my push. The room revealed, though spartan, gray, and cheerless, looked like a haven of mystical beauty to one who had suffered so hard to find it. I stepped inside, let my bags slide to the floor, and leaned my back against the wall for support. I sighed and closed my eyes. Home.

A small rustle from across the room made me leap to an alert position; I had not realized there was another occupant in the room. But she was small, smiling, and unalarming; there was a pale prettiness to her fair hair and features that gave the dull room a certain glancing light.

"Hello," she said, and her voice was soft and soothing. "You must be Jenna. I'm Harriet. I'm so happy to meet you."

My lack of wardrobe was nothing to her. "We are almost the same size. You can borrow my clothes when you like." The tale of my travel elicited quick, easy sympathy. "I came with the pastor who headed our orphanage. He took such good care of me! But you, poor thing, to travel all that way by yourself. You must be so brave!" My confession of apprehension about my new surroundings, my terror that I would not perform well in my classes, she heard out and responded to. "Everyone is afraid when they first come—and they are strict, it is true. But they have classes for every level of student at every grade of intelligence, and they will find the place suited to you. You will learn quickly how it goes, I promise you."

Thus, in a few short sentences, she became the best friend I had ever had; and as the days, weeks, and months passed, she was to become dearer to me than anyone I could imagine. She had such sweetness of temperament, such goodness of heart, that she drew friends wherever she turned; even my stubborn, passionate nature was gentled. I had never met anyone who meted out kindness as a matter of course, unsolicited, unearned. I never again expect to meet anyone as generous as Harriet Fairlawn.

Her companionship was the only thing that made the first six months of my tenure there endurable, for Lora Tech was not an easy place to be. The hours were long, the classes were hard, the teachers were stern, and, since we were a charity school, the amenities were few. I had had no formal schooling, so I was far behind in every subject. But Harriet encouraged me every night, tutoring me patiently and greeting each small gain with extravagant amounts of praise.

"That's it, Jenna! You're making such progress! Soon you'll be elevated to your own grade, I know you will."

And she was right. One day, inexplicably, all the foreign phrases and incomprehensible equations clicked from nonsense to sense in my brain; I understood the conjugated verbs, I could reduce the calculation as required. I graduated up to my proper grade level, and acquired a new set of teachers who seemed less formidable. I began to learn, truly learn, new ideas and new subjects, and my mind began to wake with a desire keener than hunger. I had always been fascinated by science, and now I became good at it. I was becoming what I had always wanted to be: a person with value to the universe.

Thus my life unfolded for the next two years. I never heard from my aunt, though Betista sent me occasional poorly spelled notes and, once in a while, a small present. I wrote her faithfully and told her of my progress. Harriet herself received mail on a sporadic basis, from the pastor of her orphanage and various friends she had made there during her ten-year stay. When she received small gifts of money, we would wait for our rare holidays and take a public aircar to the nearest shopping district. Dressed in our drab gray school coveralls, we would find some vantage point on the busiest streets to watch the fashionable parade hurry by: women in their glittering tunics or their bright short dresses or their long ceremonial gold gowns that signified a position of some rank in the political stratum. The men wore a much less interesting array of clothing, coveralls like ours if they were workers, formal black and gray if they were citizens of any standing.

Because the whole planet of Lora was, essentially, one huge connected city, the parade was absolutely endless; we might watch for hours and not see any two people who looked or dressed exactly alike. Harriet and I pointed out those whose faces we liked, to whom we wished we belonged, and we made up stories about our long-lost relatives whom we would somehow inadvertently discover during these streetside vigils. Our tales became complex and outlandish, and produced much muffled laughter. Those were unquestionably the happiest days of my life.

Much less happy were the hours spent working off some punishment that a professor or headmaster or residential advisor deemed appropriate for misconduct or high spirits. The youngest miscreants were given jobs such as cleaning the toilets and scrubbing the kitchens; the older students, particularly those who excelled in the sciences, were generally assigned the task of stoking the generators. These were located in a central building near the middle of the grim campus; they supplied power to every one of the dorms and classrooms and research facilities at the school.

They were also frightening. There were a dozen different generators, all run on different fuels and principles, which had been installed over the decades as theories of power production and consumption were revised. Many of these old, and even ancient, models could be found installed as primary energy sources on planets throughout the Allegiance. For a strange thing had happened once the high-grade citizens had descended a few generations from their robber baron forebears: They had grown lax and suspicious of technology. They knew it had spawned their own wealth and position, but they did not like tinkering with it and facilitating any fresh spate of change and improvement. They had the current patents and equipment, used throughout the Allegiance. They were not interested in having their own systems super-seded. Thus technological advancement was discouraged unless it occurred in a few carefully controlled environments—the only environ-ments, to tell the truth, where there was enough money to fund the nec-essary research.

Thus, the students at Lora learned how to operate every type of gen-erator, even the obsolete. We did, every couple of years, have a chance to build new ones when some modern model was sanctioned for gen-eral use. Since many of us were being trained to become solo engineers and tech support personnel on frontier planets, space stations, and star-ships, this hands-on experience with the school's machinery was an important part of every student's curriculum.

But Harriet and I were too young to have had much experience with the large, noisy, complex, and variable machines. I, of course, had played around my aunt's generators more times than I could count, and I loved the interplay of power and reaction contained within the huge silver shells. But Harriet—a math genius, but a poor hand at basic sci-ence—was terrified of their noise, emissions, unpredictability, and might. Whenever some alleged infraction sent us down to the generator rooms for the evening, her hands would shake and her voice would tremble as we walked the rounds, checking on output.

It was my one real chance to be stronger than she. I would walk beside her, step for step, taking my own measurements and explaining what they meant. Then I would tell her what each machine was capable of, why it had been built, what its drawbacks were, and where it was most likely to be installed.

I was particularly enamored of the new Arkady Core Converters, which relied on muon-catalyst fusion, and any of the generators that fed off the relatively rare dubronium fuel. I could talk about them for hours, though Harriet would rarely listen that long.

Once I finally stopped speaking, she would sigh. "You're so smart, Jenna. I'll never understand these machines like you do."

"You don't have to. You'll become the logistician for some shipping company, or the actuary for one of the colonizing organizations. If we have six thousand people planning to emigrate to—to—Mazilachistan" (making up the planet name just to hear her laugh) "and three thousand of them are over the age of thirty, and three thousand are under the age of thirty, how many can be expected to survive the journey?"

"But you would need to know so much more than their ages," she said gaily, entering the spirit of the game. "What's the incidence of disease among this population, and what's the general lifespan of non-travelers from the same star system, and what percentage is married and what percentage is not—because, isn't it strange, a married person tends to live longer than an unmarried one—"

"More to live for," I guessed.

"Happier," she said, sighing again. "Just think! To have someone love you, every day of your life. Surely that would make you strive to have the longest life possible?"

"Though I don't think that's why Mr. Wellstat has lived so long," I said, and we both began to giggle. Mr. Wellstat appeared to be a hundred and forty years old. He was the gloomiest, sourest, bitterest teacher at the academy, and by all accounts, he and his wife hated each other.

"Perhaps he has lived so long merely to spite her," Harriet suggested. "He does not want to give her the satisfaction of being alive without him."

"There you have it! Real life once again helps us to interpret dry statistics."

Talking in such a way, we would make our rounds for the appointed number of hours; and even the punishment did not seem so bad.

I cannot even remember what infraction it was that sent us to the generator rooms late one night—a tardy paper, a missed meal, an impertinent reply to a teacher. Yet there we were, once again, Harriet and I, making the long, noisy rounds between the generators. The upperclassmen had been at work there earlier in the day, I could tell, for the Arkady Core Converter had been partially shut down and its protective covers were pried off so the students could study some of the interior mechanisms.

"This is odd," Harriet said, peering into its open cavity. "Look at the light lancing through here. It looks—alive, almost. It's writhing, twisting on and around itself like the craziest kind of snake."

I glanced up from the clipboard where I was recording measurements. "Well, you shouldn't be able to see that at all," I said. "The shield should be up."

She put a hand out as if to stroke the spout of sapphire flame. "Is it safe to reattach the shield while the generator's still running?"

I nodded. "This one, anyway. Do you want to put it in place?"

"In a minute. I want to watch it for a while."

I smiled. "You will even yet be seduced by science," I said, and moved down the great aisle.

The fission generators had been toyed with, too, as I saw immediately, and the water in their tanks glowed with an eerie blue light. Ahead of me I could see the cold fusion tanks sparkling with their own incessant output of power.

"Is it even safe for us to be here?" I wondered aloud, turning to look for Harriet. But she was no longer behind me. She had skipped ahead to the early-model Delta Five reactor and was bending over some open cover that I could not see. "Harriet?" I called, a thread of alarm in my voice. "That one's not safe to touch. Harriet!"

Who knows what combination of colors and magic drew her in? Always before this she had been too frightened of the great tanks to need supervision; always before this they had been properly shielded, and no one would have needed to be afraid. I heard my voice calling her name what seemed like a hundred times in the few seconds it took me to run to her, but I knew before I arrived that I was too late. She pulled her head back from whatever sight had entranced her, and she gave me her usual luminous smile; and perhaps I imagined it, but her skin was already dangerously radiant, her cheekbones and her out-stretched hands incandescent with absorbed fire. I felt my words choke down, I felt my heart coalesce.

"Jenna," she said, happily enough, "I feel so strange."

*I*t took her four days to die, and they would not let me see her. Although Lora Tech was not an institution celebrated for its compassion, I know they did what they could for her, because I was two doors down from her, being treated for a lesser exposure to ionizing radiation. I saw the parade of doctors, nurses, and specialists who clustered around her and attempted to salvage the burned skin, the altered cells. But there was nothing to do. The dosage had been too strong. She suffered, she slept, and she died.

Her body was cremated, but memorial services were to be held two days later. This was because I was not the only one shocked by Harriet's sudden terrible death; I was not the only student who had missed classes on those four days while Harriet lingered, idling along as if enraptured by the scenery on the bleak, dark road to death. She had had many friends. Not one of them could bear to believe she was gone from us.

I returned to my classes for those two days. What else was there for me to do? Those two nights I worked in my room, trying to catch up on the assignments I had missed and unwilling to ask any of the other students for help. I could not bear either their sympathy or their silence. I would rather fail every class than attempt to speak aloud.

But as the night grew later and the silence unbearable, I began to shake and rock myself on the chair where I sat. Tears formed in my eyes and fell, unbidden, down my cheeks. My hands wrapped together of their own accord, squeezing so tightly that I could feel my own bones doing damage to myself, and yet I could not unlock them. With my feet, I pushed myself away from the desk where I sat, and fell to my knees on the hard floor.

"Oh, Goddess," I groaned, "for I know you are there, and listening, pray guard over that one soul with special care. Take every last atom of that precious being, and bless it, and return it to this earth or some other world with its own fresh and lively purpose. Plant her in the gardens of Karian where she can burst delighted into spring. Set her into the heart of a nightingale so she can sing. Fling her into the molten core of your brightest sun, so that she can light up the heavens with her brilliance. I know there is no death—I know we are all one being, the length and breadth of the universe—I know that we are here to be used, and used again, in your grand and glorious design. But Goddess, oh

Goddess, make her beautiful and make her happy, for so she was in her time here on Lora, and I miss her—I miss her—I miss her—"

And I collapsed to the floor, and I wept; and not all the theology ever written could console me.

𝒯he day after the funeral, Mr. Branson drew me aside as math class was ending. "Jenna," he said, "I think I may have something for you. Please come to my office."

So I followed him down the plain hallway to his small, spare office, and sat quietly on the hard-backed chair he offered me. He settled himself behind his narrow black desk.

"A package came for Harriet a few weeks ago," he said. "A birthday gift from the members of her parish, sent here by her pastor. I was saving it to give to her next month, but—now—so. I have notified her pastor of Harriet's death and asked if he would like the package returned, but he said I should give it instead to some other deserving student. I am sure there is no one Harriet would rather have seen it go to than you."

"What is it?" I asked, with only the barest flicker of interest.

He smiled slightly. "I don't know. Let's open it together."

So he rummaged in a desk drawer and pulled out a small, flat package in a brown box. I opened it to find a handheld electronic recorder.

Mr. Branson's sad face lightened to one of pleasure; clearly, he was more familiar with recent commercial technology than I was. "Ah, an 865 Reeder Recorder/Player," he said in a low, satisfied voice. "Not an inexpensive gift at all. Well, Jenna, you should be quite pleased."

I turned the object over to examine it from all angles. It was black and flat, with a silver-gray screen smaller than my palm. It only possessed a few buttons on its sleek front surface, and the slotted openings of its microphone were almost invisible. On the back, it had a few serial ports that I assumed would connect in some fashion to a larger computer terminal.

"What does it do?" I asked.

Mr. Branson took it from me to touch its knobs and dials. "It is merely a lightweight and very transportable recorder that will hold one hundred terrabytes of information. You could leave it on from sunup to sundown every day of your life, record every minute of your waking existence and live to be two hundred, and still you would not have used up all its available memory. You can play back audio, or—see this button here?—have it convert all input to text, which you can have printed out at any terminal. It is small enough that no one will notice if you carry it with you every day, but it is powerful enough to pick up most sounds in a room as large as an auditorium."

I took it back from him, starting to be pleased myself. "It is a diary," I said.

Mr. Branson frowned slightly. "Well—more useful than that, surely. You can record your class lectures, listen to them at night, and print them out so you can study the hard copies. When you take a job, you can use your Reeder to record your employer's instructions to make sure you do not misunderstand—or, even, have a kind of proof of what he's said, in case later the two of you disagree—"

"Yes, that would be very helpful," I said politely. I touched the switch that activated the microphone. "I will make certain I bring this with me to mathematics class. I am sure I will benefit from hearing your lectures more than once."

Mr. Branson gave his dismal smile. "I would be honored to be included in your daily recordings," he said.

I hit the playback button, and our most recent words floated out into the air between us. I could not keep a faint smile from forming on my face; what a fun and silly device to have, after all!

"Thank you so much for thinking of me," I said formally. "I will treasure this always—because it was meant for Harriet, and because you were so kind as to give it to me."

After that, it was rare that I went anywhere without my little recorder, though I did not leave it on constantly to chronicle every minute of my unexciting existence. I took it with me to classes, and found that using it to reinforce the original lecture improved my understanding of everything my teachers had said. I also began to use it to summarize my days, nearly every night speaking softly into it to record my impressions of the world around me.

"Today the sunrise was glorious, after weeks and weeks of rain. I felt my heart lift with such energy that I was sure it would tug me with it into the heady atmosphere. . . . The luncheon meal was dull, but dinner was very good, and we all ate and talked with such gaiety that I almost felt giddy by the time the meal was over. . . . I have made three very good friends this month, and though none of them will ever replace Harriet, their companionship eases some of my loneliness, and that, I know, is something Harriet would have wished. . . . Today we received our grades for the semester. I was at the top of my class in nuclear energy, and even in mathematics my scores were respectable. After a week's holiday, I will begin classes in my new grade, thus beginning my fourth full year here at Lora Tech. . . ."

Such were my comments for the next eight years, sometimes more in depth, seldom more emotional. I began to be—not happy, exactly, but content. This school was familiar to me, I knew my place and my abilities, and upon my graduation, I was offered a job as instructor. I had no other plans, no other place to go, and so I accepted, though a tiny, very quiet voice inside me made a faint protest. So much of the universe left to see and I willing to crouch in this one small corner for the whole of my existence! The calm years here at Lora Tech had made me placid, but they had not entirely subdued my passionate, wondering nature. Even as I lectured, and graded tests, and helped each new student make his or her shaky way up the ladder of knowledge, I found myself growing restless.

So it was that, when I turned twenty-four, I consulted the employment listings that the school kept for its upperclassmen. Lora Tech students were prized all over the Allegiance for their sound training and attention to detail, and there were many openings listed on the terminal. I paged through them carefully, but for one reason or another, few of them appealed to me. I did not want to work on a space-going liner; I had not enjoyed my one experience of interplanetary travel enough to want it to form the whole of my life. Nor was I interested in working at one of the large, impersonal plants that were set up on many of the commercial space routes. I was a small, quiet person; I would be lost in such a large environment. I needed something more intimate, yet not imposing, something that suited my skills *and* my personality.

At last I found it, the position that sounded perfect: There was a need for a generator tech at the outpost holding of an individual who owned property on a world called Fieldstar. I looked this up quickly on the StellarNet and discovered it to be a small, terraformed planet in the Kaybek system, far enough from the nearest sun to require independent energy sources, but successfully settled by a handful of commercial businesses and investor families. Once the planet's thin, poisonous atmosphere had been stabilized by science, its soil had been found to be rich enough to yield self-sustaining crops, while the real business of the planet (mining dubronium) went on. Each landholder was responsible for keeping his own property contained and powered up, so each holding was equipped with its own generator. At Thorrastone Park, a new Arkady Core Converter was the one requiring a knowledgeable tech. The planet was somewhat isolated, the advertisement warned, though the spaceport was adequate and there would be opportunities for any new employee to get off-planet for recreation.

I looked up. Ideal! I loved the Arkady converters, and I had no fear of being marooned on a lonely outpost with few compatriots about. On the contrary, after fourteen years on the crowded streets of Lora, I liked the idea of living somewhere quieter, less populated. Fieldstar was located centrally enough in the Allegiance shipping corridor that I could, if I wanted, take holidays at any of the great metropolitan centers of the universe, though I did not see that being a great attraction to me. I was not yearning for breathless frivolity now. Just something a little different.

I checked the listing again. It had been posted a few weeks ago, which indicated that it was not a popular offer. Most of my classmates and students would be looking for that colorful, spasmodic life that appealed to me so little. But this was good news for me; if the owners had had few applicants, they would be even more inclined to view my résumé with favor.

Calling up the reply screen, I typed in my relevant information and posted my response before I could think about it too long. The instant my finger had left the "send" button, I felt my nerve fail me. Leave Lora! Leave my friends and my familiar, comfortable life! But I heard that small, much-ignored voice inside me say, "Yes," very firmly, and so I went in to dinner with a great conflict of hope and terror raging inside my soul.

And hope and terror, dear Reeder, are exactly what are embattled in my heart right now. For I received today my response from the seneschal at Thorrastone Park on Fieldstar, and it was an offer of employment. The salary is small but adequate, and there is a commercial cruiser leaving in three weeks' time that will take me by a fairly direct route to my destination. I have turned in my resignation to the director of the academy, who has wished me well and already posted notice of my job opening.

I am leaving Lora, I am leaving my old life behind. What lies ahead of me may be as dull and uneventful as what has come so far, but I find myself hoping that there is to be the smallest bit of color and excitement in my life after all. I am ready for it.

Chapter 3

✧

Thorrastone Park on Fieldstar was a neat, pretty compound, well-kept and cared for, but somehow seeming to lack much real personality. I toured it in company with Mrs. Farraday, the seneschal, who took me out in a small hovercar the morning after my arrival.

"Here, now, this is the northernmost boundary of our grounds," she was saying, bringing the little car into an awkward curl with the skittishness of one who did not often handle mechanical controls. She was a middle-aged, comfortably fleshed woman with curly brown hair and faded brown eyes. I had assessed her immediately as kind but not particularly forceful. "You can tell by the airlock mechanism, of course, but there is also the shimmer effect of the forcefield. Which I think is quite pretty, don't you?"

"Yes, quite lovely," I murmured, and it was. The whole of Thorrastone Park—indeed, every similar holding on Fieldstar—was enclosed by just such an artificial wall, holding within the atmosphere necessary for breathing and the warmth required for life.

As my shuttle had, that very morning, brought me into the nearest spaceport, I had gazed out my window at a truly magical sight: the aerial landscape of Fieldstar, seeming to bloom all over with huge, golden, iridescent bubbles of light. The holdings were widely and irregularly spaced, and the random placement of the globes of light gave the planet a charming, artless look—at least from the air. On the ground, it was hard to overlook just how calculated existence was on this small world. The very air inside the domed spaceport and the protected grounds of Thorrastone Park felt stale and processed. This was definitely not a natural world.

Within hours after my arrival, Mrs. Farraday had offered to show me the grounds and I, quite curious about my new home, had accepted. I had only been able to form a guess as to the extent of Thorrastone Park, for Mrs. Farraday had mostly shown me the manor proper and its grounds; we had not investigated the mining area nor the buildings erected there. But they were visible from many vantages of the manor and its gardens, a dark cluster of small buildings and untidy phalanxes of scurrying workers.

"Do the house generators supply power for the entire compound, or do the mine generators perform that function?" I asked.

She had already explained to me how Thorrastone Park was governed by two sets of generators, and how, since the last tech had left, the mining supervisor had overseen the equipment at the manor. These house machines were the only ones I would have any responsibility for, unless some drastic disaster occurred on the mining fields; those generators had their own personnel.

"Actually, the house equipment controls the major forcefield, though the mine equipment can be used as backup," she said. "The failsafe has never had to be used, but it is a comfort to know it is in place."

"Indeed, yes," I said. "And how often do the generators experience a breakdown?"

Her amiable face showed a faint expression of worry. "We have never had a *breakdown*, you realize, but as I understand it, the equipment needs constant maintenance. But you would understand such a thing better than I, would you not, Miss—Miss Starborn?"

I smiled involuntarily at the hesitation in her voice. It was clear the syllables sounded strange to her; she could not imagine what such a plain person was doing with such a fanciful name. "I did not mean to imply that you had completely lost power," I assured her. "But some of the Arkady converters are known to be temperamental, especially the early models, and I wondered how often little—glitches—were known to occur. Don't worry, I will consult the last tech's records. They will tell me all I need to know."

Her face cleared, she smiled again. "Then, if you have no more questions about the compound—"

I gestured in the direction of the mining buildings. "But should I not go over there and make myself known to the other techs? If we are going to provide backup support for each other—"

"Oh, dear me, no," Mrs. Farraday said hastily, accelerating the hovercraft so inexpertly that it jerked and shuddered violently enough to send us both clutching at the door frames. "No, no, you do not want to associate with the miners at all. You must not go there."

"But if I am to be useful to them—"

She had gotten the craft steadied now, and she sent us with its inconsiderable speed back toward the main house. "They have a handful of techs—they can back each other up. It is only we, at the house, who need help from them. No, Miss—Starborn, you do not want to be trafficking with the miners."

Now that I was no longer in fear of being dumped out of the car, I began to be amused. "But, Mrs. Farraday, whatever could be wrong with them? I have been around rough, untutored men and women before."

"They are all of that," she said with a certain grimness. "And some of them are worse."

"Are they cyborgs?" I asked.

She seemed to jump as if scalded. "Cyborgs! What would make you ask such a thing? Mr. Ravenbeck would not have cyborgs on his premises!"

"The more loss to Mr. Ravenbeck, then," I said quietly. "But tell me what the problem is with the miners."

She seemed to stiffen her spine, as if girding herself to say a most unpleasant thing. "You yourself are a half-citizen, Miss—Starborn," she said. There was no way she could avoid knowing this; it had to be included on my résumé. "You know that to be taken seriously in this society, you must behave better than your own class. You must associate upward, not downward. And the miners, for you, would be a step downward. Your behavior must be above reproach for you to look for any advancement at all."

"I do not look for much advancement," I said slowly, "but I do take your point. You are telling me that the workers are not even half-cits, then. Are they criminals? Have they given up all status?"

She nodded unhappily. "Some of them. Not the mine supervisor or his assistant, of course. Now, promise me, Miss Starborn, you will not leave the manor grounds. Promise me you will not mingle where it is against your best interests to go."

I had never met anyone of no status before, and I must admit my curiosity burned far more brightly than my fear, but I had no particular reason to alarm this somewhat simple-minded lady who appeared to have only my well-being at heart. "Certainly I will not seek out trouble, Mrs. Farraday," I said gently. "It is kind of you to warn me."

At that, she relaxed, and allowed the hovercar to drop back to a more reasonable speed. We were nearly at the house, in any case, and she must now begin maneuvering the vehicle through the narrow tunnel that led to the garage. She was not very adept at this task, and so I said very little during this passage so that she could concentrate more fully.

Once we were safely parked and back inside the spacious foyer, Mrs. Farraday seemed to experience a revival of spirits, and asked me quite happily if I would care to join her in an afternoon snack. Soon we were seated in a tastefully decorated blue salon, where I had been told we would take all our informal meals, sipping hot tea and munching on some excellent cookies.

"Tell me, Mrs. Farraday, just who exactly the owner of Thorrastone Park is," I said somewhat boldly, for she was so genteel that I was not sure she could bring herself to gossip. "The name, Everett Ravenbeck, I know from the papers, but of the man I know almost nothing at all."

"He is a level-one citizen," she said earnestly, as if that summed him up completely. In one sense, it did; it told me he had wealth, resources, the right to travel anywhere he chose, and, no doubt, a cosmopolitan outlook on life that I could never hope to understand. On the other hand, it told me nothing.

"But what is he *like?*" I pressed. "Is he kind? Cruel? Indifferent? Patient? Peremptory? Does he like to laugh, or is he a silent man? What are his opinions and philosophies?"

"He is kind—very kind," she said somewhat randomly; clearly she had never before been asked to analyze her employer for his merits. "And—yes!—he is intelligent. I cannot follow half his conversation, but I listen and smile."

"I assume he has several estates?"

"Oh, yes. Perhaps eight."

"How often is he at Thorrastone Park?"

"Not more than three or four times a year. He does not stay long, of course, for he must oversee his other holdings as well. But when he is here, the house becomes quite lively, for he and the other property owners get together to discuss the progress of the mines and the political situation—all sorts of things that I never really bother my head with."

I smiled at that. Such conversation would fascinate me, for I so rarely had a chance to overhear anyone discussing anything of more importance than pressure on a fuel line or the risk inherent in some procedure. A political salon would be quite a welcome change of pace! But I did not say so. Instead, I asked, "And you, Mrs. Farraday? How did you come to be employed by Mr. Ravenbeck?"

"It was quite a stroke of fortune," she said seriously. "I was married to his second cousin, Richard Farraday—the most wonderful man, Miss Starborn, I miss him still. But Richard died, and we did not have enough cash for me to maintain—maintain our lifestyle. And at the same time, I heard that Mr. Ravenbeck was looking for a seneschal for Thorrastone Park. Inquiries were made, and I was installed here, with full family rank and title."

I listened carefully, for there were many gaps in this story. Farraday—yes, I remembered now, that was part of the family name that had appeared on the employment listing: Everett Livingston Farraday Ravenbeck, a man with many connections among the upper strata of Allegiance society. This Richard Farraday must have been some minor offshoot of some distantly related branch of the family, and the woman before me one with no connections herself, who had married for love. Richard's death would have left her in a precarious position if she had no family willing to take her back and no money to support herself. She had, I realized, been in grave danger of sliding backward into half-citizenship, until Mr. Ravenbeck recognized her as a family member and gave her a place and position.

I understood belatedly why she had been so concerned about me fraternizing with the miners; she herself had come so close to a degraded level of life that she wanted to protect anyone else from such horrors. And I could not help noting that, even though it had served him as well, Mr. Ravenbeck had done a kind thing by taking her in.

"That was fortunate indeed," I said gravely. "I imagine that running a household such as Thorrastone Park must be challenging."

"As to that, it is a small enough household until Mr. Ravenbeck is here—but I must be ready at a moment's notice to accommodate him and any guests he might choose to bring," she said with some complacency. "When he is not here, it is just me, and the few indoor servants, and the tech, and Ameletta and her tutor."

"Ameletta?" I repeated, for I had encountered no one by this name.

"Mr. Ravenbeck's ward. You have not met her yet because she is in town with her tutor attending an art show. They will be back tomorrow."

"I look forward to meeting them." I wanted to ask how Mr. Ravenbeck had come to acquire a ward, but since the information was not volunteered, I did not like to be prying too deeply into what might very well be a private matter. "How often and how easily does one get 'to town' from here, Mrs. Farraday?"

I thought it quaint the way she referred to the closest Fieldstar spaceport as "town," but I supposed it did serve as a sort of metropolis to the outlying holdings and manors of the planet. After knowing the unending city streets of Lora for fourteen years, I found the spaceport's few square blocks of commerce rather sparse. It would be a pleasant place to spend an afternoon, but it was no great cultural center.

"Oh, it is a simple enough matter to get there, Miss Starborn," she replied. "There is a public airbus that takes a route past our place three times a day, so that you can come and go at a time that suits you. And if you wished, you could borrow one of the aircars—that is, if you know how to operate an aeromobile, Miss Starborn?"

I smiled. "Not I. I would have more luck repairing it if it malfunctioned than attempting to drive it myself."

She had leaned forward to secure herself another sweet, and she offered the platter to me. "Another cookie, Miss Starborn?"

"No, thank you."

There was a slight pause as she set the plate down, and then she turned toward me with a look of great determination on her face. "Miss Starborn! I must ask. How is it that you come by such an unusual name? I was caught by it when I saw it on the application, but your credentials were so good that I did not hesitate. And yet now, seeing you, I cannot help but wonder—for you seem like a more retiring sort, if you will do not mind my plain speaking."

I smiled again. "No offense. In fact, I am a half-citizen because I was conceived without a name, in the gen tanks of Baldus."

Mrs. Farraday struggled to keep her expression neutral, but it was clear she had not often come across fabricated humans, and she was not sure how to react. "I was meant to be adopted by the woman who had commissioned me, but once she took me into her household, she chose not to complete the transaction," I said steadily. It had been so long since I had thought of my aunt Rentley, so long since I had reviewed her ill treatment of me! I was surprised to learn the memories still stung. "So, essentially, when I left her house, I had no name."

"Poor child," Mrs. Farraday murmured, sympathy winning out over repugnance. "But then, how came you to choose *such* a name? I would think a simple Smithfield or Johnson would have served you better."

"Many of the offspring of the gen tanks found themselves in peculiarly similar circumstances," I said. " 'Starborn' is a common name among those of us created in such a fashion. It gives us a community of sorts, a family name, if you will. It is whimsical, I do admit, but it tells us truly where we are from, since we most certainly were not born of man."

"Yes—I suppose—well, indeed, that makes a kind of sense," she said uncertainly. "Still! A strange name to get used to."

"Call me Jenna, then," I invited. I knew I was taking a risk, because she was clearly a very conventional woman, and our society was a very formal one; the lower-class citizens were required to address their betters by courtesy titles, and the upper-class citizens, as a mark of kindness, usually returned the favor when they spoke to their inferiors.

To my relief, her face relaxed into a smile. "That's what I shall do, then, Jenna, if you do not think it too familiar."

I smiled back. "After the life I have had, I would welcome a little familiarity," I said.

After our meal, I retired to my room for a few hours to unpack and rest. It was something of a trick to find my bedchamber again, for the house—larger even than my aunt's mansion on Baldus—was filled with wandering corridors and unexpected turns. I could only suppose the builders had attempted to emulate the style of ancient estates, which, having been added to over the centuries, presented an erratic charm, though certainly Thorrastone Park had been conceived and constructed over a short, efficient period of time.

The main story consisted of an entrance hall which immediately faced onto a grand stairway. Most of the entertaining would be done on this floor, for here could be found the well-stocked library, the formal dining room, a small sitting room, the kitchen, and the smaller breakfast room which adjoined the kitchen and where most members of the household took their meals. A level above was an assortment of rooms that I had not entirely identified—Mrs. Farraday, on our tour, had spoken briefly of Mr. Ravenbeck's study, Ameletta's schoolroom, her own office, and an informal sunroom.

The third story contained all the bedrooms for residents and guests, though the space was divided into two wings that were accessible by different hallways, so that commingling would be prevented if that were for some reason desirable. The bedroom I had been given was situated in the wing near the rooms of Mrs. Farraday, Ameletta, and the tutor. The cook and two intermittent housemaids had rooms in another quarter of the house. I had been astonished when Mrs. Farraday first spoke of servants—for, with so few people even in residence, I could not imagine what servants could be expected to do to occupy themselves—but when I comprehended how large the house actually was, I realized that a whole battalion of workers would be necessary to keep everything looking reasonably clean and free of dust.

My own room, though small by the mansion's standards, seemed luxurious to me. Its many amenities included a private bathroom, a walk-in closet, a window overlooking the lawns, a computer terminal, and a large four-poster bed supporting an air-filled mattress. After the lumpy bed at Lora Tech—and the hard bunk I had slept in so recently on my voyage here—I found this bed the most comfortable place I had ever laid my body.

I did take a short nap, then showered and changed into a clean pair of coveralls. Going in search of Mrs. Farraday, I found her in the second-story sunroom. We had not exchanged half a dozen sentences, when we heard voices on the stairs, and within minutes, Ameletta and her tutor burst into the room. Well, perhaps the tutor, with her sober face, did nothing so energetic, but little Ameletta skipped forward eagerly, a vision in blond curls and a frilly white frock, and at once turned the place into the vortex of a whirlwind.

"But you must be the new Miss Starborn!" she exclaimed, nearly dancing around my chair in her excitement. I caught a glimpse of blue eyes and a ravishingly fair complexion. "I must say, you look nothing at all like I had pictured, for you are quite young and not in the least grand. Have you been all over Thorrastone Park? That is such a shame, for I meant to take you myself! It is a pretty place, is it not? For a mining outpost, anyway. I have been to Hestell and Corbramb, and they are ever so much nicer—at least, I think they are, for I have seen pictures, but I was so young when I was there that I'm afraid I don't really remember. I'm Ameletta, of course. I'm eight."

Both Mrs. Farraday and the tutor made some attempt to stem this tumbling tide of speech, but I was neither offended nor annoyed. Would that I had been such an open, happy child at the age of eight!

"Hello, Ameletta," I said solemnly. "And where have you been all day?"

"Oh! At the most wonderful show! We saw paintings and holograms and the dearest little dog—not a real dog, of course, it was animated, but it *looked* real, and if it had come up to me on the street, I would have petted its head and called it 'nice doggie,' for I would not have been able to tell the difference. Oh, and Miss Ayerson, what was that piece you liked so much? The one that moved?"

"It was called a 'scenograph,' and it depicted a landscape with living creatures in it," her tutor replied in a composed voice. "Or at least, so that is how they appeared. Good evening, Miss Starborn. I am Ameletta's tutor, Janet Ayerson."

I made a polite hello and a private assessment. Miss Ayerson was a severely dressed, plain-featured young woman a few years younger than myself, bearing all the unmistakable signs of poverty, hardship, and a determination to make her way nonetheless in a not entirely hospitable world. No question that she was a half-cit; this kind of work was not sought by anyone with a pedigree. Indeed, there were some who might have been able to see very little difference between us, our features and our stations in life. I could not decide if this should make me more sympathetic to her—or if it would make me strive, in every small way, to be as different from her as possible.

We all talked generally for the next few minutes, while Ameletta chattered away as if everyone was listening to each of her sunny syllables. Then Mrs. Farraday rose to her feet, quickly smoothing down the front of her expensive pantsuit.

"Goodness, look at the time. I've a few things to do before dinnertime, my dears, so if you will excuse me, I'll just be off for a while. I know it is not strictly proper, socially speaking," she added for my benefit, "but when Mr. Ravenbeck is gone, I usually dine with Ameletta and Miss Ayerson. You may certainly have a tray in your room, if you wish, but I was hoping you would take your meals with us."

I came to my feet as well; there was still much I had left to do in the way of unpacking my bags and reordering my room. "Indeed, I shall be happy to have the company," I said warmly. "I shall see you all tonight at dinner, then. I expect it shall be most pleasant."

*I*t was—that dinner and the dinners that followed, in the nights and weeks that came after. Mrs. Farraday and Ameletta were cheerful if limited companions, intellectually speaking; Miss Ayerson had a scholarly turn of mind that did not entirely track with mine, though we spent much time discussing novels and poetry, and found our tastes remarkably similar; and everyone did her best to be courteous, thoughtful, and interesting. And yet, for me at least, there was something lacking. I would have loved an energetic, emotional debate on the merits and demerits of the Allegiance social system—or the most popular religious trends of the day—or the newest scientific advances which I followed as best I could from the computer terminal installed in my room. Such conversation was not to be had with friends such as these, and I had not often had it in the past, but I nonetheless found myself longing for it with a sort of fierce wistfulness. I tried not to disparage the calm, productive haven I had found, but it was sorely empty of drama.

My days too were mostly uneventful. I spent many of my daylight hours in the underground facility which housed the manor's Arkady converter. Among other things, it was my task daily to monitor the tritium-deuterium mix, activate the waste disposal systems, and check all the electrical lines feeding from the generator. Some small adjustment always had to be made, and I was filled with a sense of accomplishment any time I caught and diagnosed a problem. Because of my vigilance, disaster was averted.

This was, if extrapolated to the direst possible consequences, really true. A malfunctioning generator could poison the whole household, leading to lingering illness and eventual death; a breakdown in the electrical system could compromise the integrity of the forcefields, allowing the thin, toxic atmosphere of the planet to suffocate or poison us all. When I thought about it, it gave me pause: We were here on Fieldstar, all of us, at the sufferance of science. If science failed, or was misused, we would all be dead.

Sometimes I looked around me at the construction of my basement fortress. Imported, every stone, every metal alloy—every drop of water in the hydraulic converter, every atom in the carefully mixed, carefully contained atmosphere. Fieldstar had possessed none of these riches in its natural state. A desirable natural nuclear fuel—yes, that it possessed in abundance, and men had reinvented the planet in order to redistribute that particular fortune. But it had nothing else we needed.

I felt an affinity for the sere, cold ball of insufficient elements, nonetheless, and I liked to spend my afternoons strolling through the park grounds surrounding the manor. Men had ferried in ships full of a renewable topsoil, merely so they could plant it with familiar seeds and grasses, so I walked across a green and pleasant lawn, enjoying commonplace flowers. But I wondered often what lay beneath that manicured surface, what rocky or sticky or completely unfathomable loam was the natural cloak of this world, and what fantastical trees and shrubs it would have produced on its own.

One such example was before me even as I made my afternoon rounds; I never failed to walk by it to express my intense, silent delight. It was a tree, of sorts, gnarled, twisted, and bulky, with massive, knotted limbs so contorted the tree might be supposed to be in agony. Yet its branches could have been made of iron, so impervious were they to axe or chain saw, and its roots must have extended to the center of this unfriendly earth. For the groundskeepers had tried, Mrs. Farraday had told me, to remove the tree with every device they could muster. They had attempted to poison it as a seedling, to hack it down as a sapling, to uproot it, burn it, detonate it. It would not die. It would not even cower back. It bore, to this day, scorch marks on its lower branches and a crisscross of machete tracks along its trunk—bore these marks as proudly and unregenerately as a soldier bears his scars of battle.

Nobody knew what the tree was, though it had been dubbed the oxenheart. Apparently it was a hybrid of sorts, part import, part native, though its indigenous cousins had been cleared away without incident when Fieldstar was first being settled. Some combination of foreign and familiar cells had given it the tenacity to endure any humiliation, any vilification—and not only to survive, but thrive.

I loved the moral implicit in that; I wanted desperately to believe that willpower and chemical makeup could make you stronger than your surroundings. I was a transplant myself, a hybrid sowed in uncertain soil. I hoped to grow just as strong, just as stubborn, just as irrepressible as the oxenheart tree.

Whenever I made my way around the environs of Thorrastone Manor, I did not neglect another significant part of my duties: checking the glimmering edge of the forcefield to make sure it did not show any signs of stress. It should not, if my reactors were functioning properly, but sometimes a lapse in the product was the first sign a tech would have that the machinery itself was experiencing a malfunction. So I strolled down the edge of the property and made sure there were no gaps in the iridescent fencing.

More than once my wanderings took me near the miners' compound, and I stood at the edge of the domestic grounds, looking toward the forbidden property. I did not think I would be doing anyone a disservice if I continued to circle the entire perimeter of the forcefield, checking for trouble. But I held back and did not cross the invisible line into the restricted territory. Mrs. Farraday would hear of my trespass, no doubt, and she would be hurt at my disobedience and frightened of the connections I might make. My curiosity was not a good enough reason for me to cause her anxiety.

So I looked, wished, and turned back to my assigned area. Others, I learned one day, were not so docile.

This was a day as fine as Fieldstar offered, which was to say overcast and gray, but bright with a strange, reflected light that made my eyes squint against the glancing rays. The sun was so far away that its heat was insufficient to sustain human life; it provided adequate light but never achieved the brightness I had become used to on double-sunned Lora. The air, as always within the forcefield, was still and silent, and I fancied that even from a distance I could hear shouts and clanking noises from the mine nearly a mile behind me. I was more surprised to hear sounds coming from *before* me, for the first I noticed that I was not alone in my walk was when I heard the breathy, unmelodic sound of someone singing off tune.

I looked around quickly and finally spied the stranger sitting on a rustic bench installed by one of the hedges. She was badly dressed in a tunic and trousers that neither matched each other nor the oversize boots she had pulled on her feet. Her gray hair appeared to be uncombed, or at least neglected for the better part of the day, and her sallow face bore the evidence of some childhood scar that no one had bothered to pay to mend. All these signs led me to the obvious inferences: poor, underemployed, half-cit. These should not have led me to dislike her on sight, but there was a furtive, measuring expression in her eyes when she first caught my gaze that led me to distrust her instantly.

"Good afternoon," I said, civilly enough, but tersely. "I don't believe I've seen you before."

Her eyes shifted behind me toward the compound. I wondered if she was meeting someone there or if that was where she belonged. "Is that right?" she said. "Well, I don't believe I've seen you either."

"Should we have met?" I asked. "Do you belong here in Thorrastone Park?"

A half-smile split her creased face. It did not make her any more attractive. "As well as I belong anywhere," she said. Her voice had a strange, unplaceable accent, as well as a rusty quality. She did not seem to be a person who often engaged in idle conversation.

"You work here, then? In the mines?"

She nodded in the direction of the compound, though the gesture was so vague that it could have meant she worked down in the spaceport, when she bothered to work at all. "Not in the mines, exactly," she said, "but I do my job over there."

"You're a part of the cooking staff, perhaps?" I pursued.

She emitted a type of laughter I could only characterize as a cackle. "Efghf!" was her next indistinguishable comment. "As if anyone would eat my cooking."

"Laundress, then? What exactly is your position?"

Her smile was secretive and unnerving. I felt apprehension skitter down my spine. "I suppose you might call it tech support," she said.

"*Tech* support!" I exclaimed.

She added, before I could go on to voice my disbelief, "Just like you."

That stopped me with my mouth half open. It had not occurred to me that I would be known to anyone who was a stranger to me, and I could not imagine how this odd creature could have come to hear about me. "Then we have much in common," I said stiffly.

"Efghf," she observed again. "I would doubt it."

I glanced around me at the sheer, effervescent forcefield, and thought it looked just the slightest bit paler than it had. "I check the fields every day," I said, just in case she thought I took my duties lightly. "To make sure everything is holding properly. I never overlook this chore. I hope someone does the same down at the mining compound?"

She shrugged elaborately. "Someone may," she said. "It isn't me. Not my sort of work."

"Yes, well, I'm sure your task, whatever it is, is quite important," I said, and I could not keep the cold tone from my voice. "If you don't mind, I think I'll be on my way, continuing with my *own* work."

She waved a careless hand, as if releasing me from an obligation. "Go along with you. I'll just sit here a while longer, enjoying the fine day."

I nodded curtly and moved off, very deliberately stepping to the edge of the fencing. I did not see what she could have done to harm it; theoretically, it could withstand most limited assaults, from small meteor showers to rapid-fire projectile bullets. Even if she had heaved a rock or a knife at it, and somehow managed to breach its wall, the generator power made the field self-healing; there should be no permanent tear. But systems had failed before this, all because someone did not double-check reality against theory, and she did not look to me like the sort of person who could be trusted not to tamper with a seductive challenge. I examined the forcefield while she watched me, and hoped she realized why I chose to look it over again at just that moment. But I found nothing amiss.

Without saying another word to her, I headed back to the manor house, going immediately to the underground facility to read over the gauges. No disturbances registered; all, apparently, was well.

That night over dinner, I broached the topic with Mrs. Farraday. "I encountered the strangest woman today, as I was out walking through the grounds," I said while the four of us ate our soup. Ameletta was noisily engaged in the act of eating, so her incessant chatter for the moment was silenced.

"Did you, now?" Mrs. Farraday asked comfortably. "Who might that have been?"

"I did not catch her name," I said. "She was poorly dressed, and she was sitting by herself, singing, and she gave every appearance of being a vagrant—though I don't know how one would have gotten on the grounds. She assured me she worked in the mine complex as a—a member of the tech support team."

It might have been my imagination that Mrs. Farraday and Miss Ayerson exchanged quick, alarmed glances. But whatever chagrin Mrs. Farraday may have felt, she instantly mastered. "What did this strange woman look like? Do you recall?"

"She had gray hair and a scar on her face. A bad complexion, like she had not been much cared for in her life."

Mrs. Farraday nodded and touched her napkin to her lips. "That was Gilda Parenon, I expect."

"And she is in fact employed by Mr. Ravenbeck?" I demanded. "As a technician?"

Mrs. Farraday made the smallest gesture of uncertainty. "I suppose that would be the best description of her job. . . . It is very specialized— or so I'm told. Mr. Ravenbeck says it would be difficult to find someone to replace her."

"So he has met her, then? He knows what sort of odd people he employs?"

"Oh, yes, I believe Mr. Ravenbeck is very aware of Gilda Parenon and her services. Now, Jenna, don't let her disturb you. It is unlikely you'll have any reason to run into her again."

I could not escape the notion that I was being lied to, but I could think of no reason Mrs. Farraday would have for withholding the truth about Gilda Parenon—or indeed, any of the workers at Thorrastone Manor. "No, I don't suppose I will," I said slowly, "not if I never tour the mining compound."

"And you won't do *that*," she said, almost playfully. "Here, Miss Ayerson, would you like more bread? Ameletta, dear, you could eat more daintily. A stranger here would believe we had starved you for half the week. Pass me your water glass, Jenna, and I will refill it. Thank you, dear. . . ."

And so, with commonplaces and courtesies, the rest of the meal was passed without real conversation. But it seemed to me that Miss Ayerson studiously avoided meeting my gaze for the rest of the evening, and that Mrs. Farraday, not usually much of a chatterbox, never gave me the opportunity to lead the talk again. And I could not help believing that if there were something stranger about Gilda Parenon than her appearance, I would probably never learn it.

Chapter 4

✦

When I had been at Thorrastone Manor little more than a month, my account was credited with my first paycheck. It was not a fabulous sum by any calculation, but it was more than I had ever earned in a comparable period in my life, and I was elated to receive it. Although I had not yet asked for a holiday, I knew that I was entitled to several during the course of the year. With my precious money finally available, a brief vacation was exactly what I wanted, so I notified Mrs. Farraday of my intent. And the next morning I was gone.

The public buses that serviced the holdings near Thorrastone Park made the circuit between the properties three times daily, once very early in the morning, once near noon, and once late in the day. I was up with the dawn in order to catch the early bus, and I was waiting in the assigned area a good half hour before it was scheduled to appear. Each of the holdings (so I had been told) were equipped, like Thorrastone Park, with a small airlock which would allow buses and closed aero-mobiles and any other vehicles to safely enter their environs. There was, naturally, no forcefield over the uninhabited roadways and regions of the world, so any vehicles traveling between settled points had to be equipped with their own closed atmospheric systems—even the local buses that only covered a few hundred miles at a stretch.

I was used to waiting, but I admit to feeling some impatience by the time the sleek silver airbus darted into view. It eased into the airlock with an interesting suck and exchange of gases, and then it was safe for me to board. Naturally, the two dozen or so other passengers were all strangers to me, but I gave the whole assembled ridership one quick, neutral glance before settling into an unoccupied seat near a window.

The ride in, to me at least, was fascinating, for I had not left Thorrastone Park since my arrival and I had not, on my first journey from the spaceport, paid much attention to the landscape. There had been rough attempts at terraforming the whole surface of Fieldstar, but such work had been only rudimentary in the areas that were not actually supporting human life. Thus the route we followed took us over terrain that bore little resemblance to the manor's thick lawn. The grasses were starved and pitiful, unlike the thick, coarse turf that formed our lawn; they, and the half-naked shrubbery, and the tall, twisted trees, were almost all of a uniform fawn color with no hints of our own familiar green. Against the gray rocky soil from which they sprang, even their fugitive color seemed gay, a vibrant contrast. I found myself wishing I had any skill with paint or pencil so I could catch that bleak and delicate beauty on paper.

The lights of town, when we arrived nearly two hours later, seemed garish and overbright in comparison, and for a moment I was reluctant to disembark from the bus. But soon enough I forgot the minimalist delights of the prairie landscape, and turned with some enthusiasm to the more hedonistic pleasures of commerce.

As I had noted before, Fieldstar's small spaceport was hardly a retailer's dream, but it offered more variety and opportunity than I had seen for a while, and I spent a happy day wandering under its high, glittering dome. I did not have a large number of credits at my disposal, so I spent more time looking than buying. I did eye an apricot-colored silk pantsuit with a great deal of longing, even going to the extent of trying it on and visiting it two more times during the course of the afternoon, but I could envision no possible occasion on which such attire would be appropriate for a half-cit technician in an out-of-the-way holding, and so I resisted. In the end, I contented myself with buying two new serviceable gray tunics, a pair of comfortable shoes, another pair of khaki coveralls, and a length of pink ribbon for Ameletta. I also treated myself to a somewhat expensive lunch, which included a fruit-tart dessert so delicious I almost could not resist ordering a second.

After the meal, I shopped some more, then spent some time viewing a new art show at the tiny museum. My packages, though not many, began to grow heavy, and I was just as glad when it was time for me to catch my bus back to Thorrastone. I waited for a little while in the air-bus terminal till my bus arrived, then I climbed aboard and settled against the cushion with a sigh of satisfied exhaustion.

I was deposited at Thorrastone Park barely an hour before sundown—a time after which any reasonable person did not want to be out of doors. For the planet seemed to make one quick, violent rotation away from its distant sun, plunging the world into sudden and instant blackness; even the presence of artificial lighting strategically placed all over the grounds did not entirely counteract the total bleakness of the Fieldstar night. The airlock lay a little more than a mile from the doorway, a distance I could usually cover in less than half an hour, so I did not worry about being safely inside before total darkness descended. The airlock door closed behind me as I hefted my packages one more time and set off toward the house.

I had not taken five steps when there was a wild disturbance behind me, and a large shape careened through the outer door of the airlock. An awful sound of rending metal echoed through the small enclosure, a counterpoint to the *whoosh* and choke of air exploding outward, then being swiftly contained. I dropped my packages and whirled around in time to see a small aeromobile bounce against one nearly invisible wall, knock backward against another, then come shuddering to a halt on the stony floor of the lock. It did not move again.

For a moment I was motionless with stupefaction, but I soon realized there was probably at least one individual inside the downed car, very possibly seriously hurt. I ran back to the inner door, checked the gauge to make sure the atmosphere was breathable, then hurried into the airlock to see what assistance I could offer.

Even as I approached the craft, the bubble lid was being raised from within, and in seconds, a head and shoulders emerged. I had very little time to assess any particulars of the new arrival except that he was male, dark-complected, and sporting a trickle of blood across his forehead.

"Sir!" I exclaimed, reaching up to catch the weight of the lid with my own hand until I felt it click into place in its upright position. "You're hurt! Can you speak? Can you move? Shall I fetch help from the manor?"

I found myself fixed in the glare of a pair of dark eyes set in a very irate face. "Who the devil are you?" the newcomer growled. "And why would you be out prowling around at such an hour?"

I thought him extremely rude, though perhaps the accident had impaired his natural civility, but I was relieved to note that he at least appeared to have retained his senses. "I suppose anyone may walk around at any hour she pleases, assuming she has a right to be on the property in the first place," I answered. "But tell me—how badly are you injured? There is some blood on your face. Have you sustained any hurt to your head?"

"I have sustained a great deal of hurt," he replied, again in that impatient, rumbling voice. I presumed he meant his tone to sound forbidding, but to me he sounded cross and fretful, like one of my students at Lora Tech who had been balked in his plans because of some homework assignment I had distributed. "My head throbs with a remarkable sharpness, and my ribs feel as if they have each individually cracked and reknitted in a manner not conducive to easy breathing, and I am sure I have twisted my ankle. However, I am most injured in my pride, for only the stupidest, most inexperienced boy would so misjudge his landing speed and angle as to crash headlong into the forcefield. My only excuse is that I caught a glimpse of you heading across the lawn, and I was so amazed that I stared in the wrong direction."

"And that's a poor excuse by any standard," I said cheerfully, "for I have never before caused any vehicle to stutter from the sky nor any pilot to forget where he is going. I am afraid your car may have been damaged, but your rational conversation reassures me that *you* at least are not hurt beyond repair."

He gave a short bark of laughter—not an infectious sound, but one that made me want to smile nonetheless. "Ha! If you consider this rational talk, I'm guessing you've had very little of it recently."

"Not at all," I answered serenely. "My own conversation is always supremely rational. Now, tell me: What can I do to help you? Shall I go to the manor? Or can you walk that far on your own? It will be dark very soon, and I don't think you want to be out here past sundown, tinkering with a disabled vehicle."

"As to that, I don't think it is as disabled as it appears," he said, ducking his head back inside. "There are no frantic lights flickering on my instrument boards. I think it is operational."

"Your right wing is crumpled beyond use," I pointed out. "You cannot fly."

His head emerged again; he was grinning. The expression illuminated his rather grim face, for, now that I had a chance to study him without fearing for his life and sanity, I could form some opinion of his looks. He had bold, strong features, and extremely black hair; in this insufficient light, his eyes appeared to be nearly black as well. He was not a handsome man, but a compelling one. I felt the force of his personality even through the strangeness of our circumstances.

"Why," I asked, "is it amusing to you to learn that you have broken your wing?"

"Because it does not matter," he replied. "It's a convertible hover/land rover, and I can, by pulling a few levers, make it drivable, at least for a short trip to the manor house. There is only one slight problem."

"What is that?"

"The lever requires some strength to engage, and I do not believe my ribs can withstand the effort. Could I ask you to add to your goodness—I was going to say, your officiousness, but since I need a favor, I don't want to offend you—and request you to pull the lever? I am afraid it is a task I cannot manage on my own."

I thought it strange that he expressed a wish not to offend me when it seemed he had expended every effort to accomplish just such an end, but I did not say so. Indeed, I found his brisk, irritated, outspoken masculinity a rather refreshing change from all the considerate femininity I encountered on a daily basis.

"Certainly, sir," I said, stepping forward again. "Show me what I must do."

Groaning a bit, he shifted his position to allow me access to the gears and instruments inside the cockpit. I allowed myself to be distracted for a moment by the array of dials and gauges.

"Ah, a Vandeventer V convertible," I said, for I had not recognized the make by its exterior markings. "A superior vehicle by all the reviews. It has not been available for commercial distribution very long."

"No, I believe I have the first model on Fieldstar," the injured man said, and I caught a note of amusement in his gruff voice. "But how do you come by an interest in short-range planetary vehicles? When it comes to that, how do you come to be at Thorrastone Park at all?"

To myself I thought, *I might well ask you the same question,* but it was not generally encouraged for half-cits to interrogate full citizens—which this man, with his arrogance and his expensive tastes, most assuredly was.

"I have a somewhat scientific turn of mind," I said demurely. "I am employed at Thorrastone Park as a generator technician, but I do know a little about mechanics and machinery."

He reared back as far as the confines of the seat would allow him. "The technician!" he exclaimed. "Of course! I knew there was one expected, but I would never have marked you for the role."

"I do not believe I was hired for my appearance, sir," I said blandly. "Now, may I get to that lever?"

Still watching me with some interest, he shifted cautiously in his seat to allow me the necessary access. He was right; it took a fair amount of strength to move the lever, and I could both feel and hear the wheels engage when I finally locked it in place. A series of dials turned from green to amber on his instrument panel.

"There you are, sir," I said. "I believe you're all set now."

"Thank you," he said, adding, in an abrupt way, "Get in."

"Sir?"

He was resettling himself on the driver's side of the vehicle. "I'll drop you off at the doorway. It's close to dark now, and you can't be looking forward to the hike across the lawn."

In fact, he was right, but my concern for a fellow creature had made me overcome my dislike of roaming the grounds at night. I hesitated, however, for I knew nothing of this man except that he was careless with an aeromobile. How did I know I could trust him to take me where he promised?

He must have read my mind, for he was grinning again. "Come now, technician, you can't suppose I have any evil designs on your person. I scarcely have the strength to steer, let alone attempt assault. I think you're quite safe to travel a mile at my side."

I felt a blush rise, for this was plainer speaking than I was used to, but he spoke nothing but the truth. "I do not want to take you out of your way," I demurred, for I had come to the conclusion that he was headed toward the mining compound. He was an inspector of some sort, perhaps, or a consultant come to discuss efficiency with the engineering techs.

"Not at all," he said. "Hop in."

So I circled the convertible and clambered with less grace than I would have liked into the passenger's side. Detouring only to recover my dropped parcels, we made the brief trip in silence, for he made no effort to talk and I did not feel it was my place to initiate a conversation. He pulled up before the doors with no other mishaps.

"Here you are, technician," he said. "Despite what you may think, I do appreciate your help. I still blame you," he added, though that note of amusement was back in his voice, "but I thank you nonetheless."

I climbed out of the car and retrieved my packages. "Then you are very welcome. I hope you manage to avoid similar accidents in the future."

He laughed. "So do I! Good evening, my friend." And so saying, he drove away.

I stood for a moment or two, watching the Vandeventer speed off in the direction of the mines. *My friend.* An odd thing to call a chance-met stranger on the strength of twenty minutes' acquaintance. Odder still was the little warm glow it gave me, to be so named by such a man.

I shook my head twice, to shake away such thoughts, and went quickly into the house.

It was nearly dinnertime, and I was not sure I was in a presentable state. I had not combed my hair during the long day, nor checked my face for smudges, nor thought to straighten my tunic over my trousers, and the bus had been none too clean, and there was no telling what smears of grease—or blood!—I might have acquired from my adventure in the airlock. So I hurried to my room, grateful that I managed to arrive there unseen by any other residents of the house, and there freshened myself up.

What a day! What a day, indeed.

By dinnertime I was both clean and composed, and I made my way with my usual soberness down to the dining room. But no one there matched my own state of calm. The table was set, but no one was yet sitting in her place. Mrs. Farraday was speaking with a great deal of animation to the cook, Miss Ayerson was examining her reflection in a mirror and attempting to smooth some style into her flat locks, and Ameletta was jumping up and down on one foot as she attempted to circle the table.

Mrs. Farraday broke off when she saw me. "Oh, Jenna! We were getting worried about you. Miss Ayerson saw the bus go by nearly an hour ago, and we were afraid you had somehow missed it. No one saw you come in."

"I'm sorry. I was covered with dirt and wanted a chance to clean myself up, so I went straight to my room. But what is going on here? Everyone seems excited."

"Excited! Yes, I should say so! I learned this afternoon that Mr. Ravenbeck would be coming in tonight, and I am on the verge of being unprepared. Fortunately, he is not expecting any guests—at least, not immediately—so it is just a matter of making sure his rooms are aired and a fit dinner is prepared."

The owner of Thorrastone Park? Arriving here tonight?

"That is wonderful news," I said slowly. "Is there anything I can do to help you?"

"Oh—no—just excuse me from dinner, I fear. I have too much to do to think of eating."

So saying, she disappeared through the door, following the cook. I glanced at Miss Ayerson, who had gone to Ameletta's side to convince her to show her enthusiasm in a more acceptable fashion. She looked up with the cool half-smile that was her warmest expression.

"Well," she said, "we may as well eat."

So the three of us sat down to dinner, but though I ate heartily enough, I did not pay much attention to the food. "Mr. Ravenbeck," I said finally. "What does he look like? I think I may have seen him arriving as I was crossing the lawn."

"He is a dark man, solidly built," she replied.

"Youngish?"

"In his forties, perhaps," she said. "I would not call that young."

"To own such an extensive property," I amended.

"I believe he inherited most of it from his father and his brother," she replied. She spooned more vegetables onto Ameletta's plate and told her to eat. "Who are dead," she added.

"I beg your pardon? Who is dead?"

"His father and brother. All of his family, as far as I'm aware."

"That's unfortunate."

She gave me that cool smile again. "As you and I both know."

"When did he come into his property?"

"Five or six years ago, I believe. I don't know that much about him, actually. He has seldom been to Thorrastone during my tenure."

"So this visit is a rare occurrence."

"Rare and no doubt brief. He will want to meet you," she said, in what seemed to me a sudden change of subject.

"He will? Does he meet all the new staff members?"

She nodded. "He prides himself on knowing the name of everyone in his employ, from servants to miners. I think that is a fairly admirable trait."

"Indeed, yes," I said, thinking, *I believe I have already met him.* Would he want to repeat the introduction under more regular circumstances? I was glad now I had taken the time to restyle my hair and put on a clean overshirt. I did not like to appear so vain as to insist upon changing my clothing *now*, just when I learned I was about to be called into the owner's presence. On the other hand—ah, much more likely!—he might decide to put off the meeting for a day or two, till he had recovered from his accident and rested from his travels. I need not have taken any care with my appearance after all.

Ameletta chose this moment to join in the conversation. "He will have brought me presents," she said. "A pretty doll, and a new computer game, and—"

"Ameletta," Miss Ayerson admonished. "You must not ask Mr. Ravenbeck to shower you with gifts."

"I do not need to ask him!" the girl replied, wide-eyed with innocence. "He chooses to do so! And, yes, I am very, very grateful!"

I could not help smiling at this, but Miss Ayerson did not seem amused. I left her to the instruction of her pupil in social civilities, and bent my attention to finishing my meal.

We had just finished our dessert when Mrs. Farraday bustled back in, looking just as flustered as before, though quite happy in her commotion. This was what she lived for, after all, the chance to show off her housekeeping skills to her employer.

"Ameletta! Miss Ayerson! Mr. Ravenbeck would like you to join him in his study in half an hour. I believe he has some treats for you, hmm, Ameletta? But you must first prove to him that you have been doing your lessons, for I don't believe girls who do not know their math problems will be entitled to any presents."

I smiled at the storm of protest this evoked ("But I do! I know every single multiplication table, and *all* of the addition!") and turned toward the door. Mrs. Farraday called me back.

"And, Jenna! Mr. Ravenbeck asked if you would be willing to meet with him ninety minutes from now. Also in his study."

I turned back to face her, my eyebrows lifted. "Willing? He is my employer. How could I refuse?"

"He thought the hour might be too late for you." In ninety minutes it would be eight o'clock, as time was kept on Fieldstar.

"No, indeed, I will be up for another three or four hours. I will be happy to join him when he wishes."

I said this with my usual calm demeanor, but I must confess my heart was beating just a shade faster than usual. *Silly woman!* I reprimanded myself. *You cannot be so pleased at the thought of seeing such an uncouth man so soon again!* But that was indeed the source of my pleasure. I wandered to the library, to pass the intervening time browsing through the news reports of the day, but I have to confess, very little information registered in my brain. The ninety minutes passed as slowly as ninety days, but at last it was time for me to go and formally meet the master of Thorrastone Park.

The second-story study was a small, pleasant room, too dark with heavy drapery and wood paneling to suit my tastes, but just now brightly lit with an array of high-watt lights that gave the room a rather cheery aspect. Miss Ayerson and her pupil were off in a corner, trying out the new computer game that Ameletta had evidently received, and Mrs. Farraday hovered at the doorway, awaiting my arrival. I walked in exactly on the stroke of eight.

"Punctuality!" a male voice announced from the depths of an armchair turned away from me; I could not see the speaker's face. "I like that in an employee—indeed, in anyone."

Mrs. Farraday smiled at me, but she was still fluttering. "Jenna! Come over here and meet Mr. Ravenbeck. He cannot rise to take your hand," she said in an undervoice that everyone else must have been able to hear, "because he twisted his ankle this afternoon in a dreadful aircar accident."

"I would hardly call it dreadful," that voice said again. "Stupid is more like it. But it has left me, for the moment anyway, a bit unsteady on my feet."

By this time we had strolled forward so that we were standing directly in front of the speaker. It was, as I had guessed from his voice, the man I had aided in the downed aircar only a few hours ago. In the bright room light, I confirmed the impressions I had formed by dusk: Mr. Ravenbeck had full, strong features, masses of dark hair, and snapping black eyes that just now seemed to be shaded with a hint of malice. He was smiling at me, but it was not precisely a welcoming smile—more like a challenging one. I repressed my natural instinct to smile in return, and merely nodded at him.

"Mr. Ravenbeck," Mrs. Farraday said, "this is Jenna Starborn, our new generator technician."

Mr. Ravenbeck held out his hand and grasped mine with all the strength he had claimed he did not have when he said he could not operate his convertible lever. "Miss *Starborn*," he said, emphasizing my surname. "I am pleased to make your acquaintance."

"And I yours, sir," I answered. He released my hand almost immediately and gestured toward another armchair, placed so that it faced his across the distance of a few feet. "Take a seat, please, so that we may talk awhile. I would like to learn a little of my new technician."

Mrs. Farraday said "Oh!" in a small, surprised voice. I therefore realized she had assumed that I would make my curtsy, so to speak, and be instantly out of the room. "Would you like something to drink, sir?" she asked. "Anything more to eat?"

He waved her away somewhat impatiently. "No, no, I'm quite settled, thank you. I will not be interrogating Miss Starborn long enough or with such vigor that I will require additional sustenance."

A small frown flitted across Mrs. Farraday's face—clearly she did not think such banter appropriate—but I confess that a renegade smile came to my own lips. I tried to repress it before my employer could see, and I seated myself where he had indicated. Mrs. Farraday, after a moment's hesitation, crossed the room to join Ameletta and Miss Ayerson.

"So! Miss Starborn. Tell me about yourself," Mr. Ravenbeck said after a short silence.

I raised my eyebrows at this, for that was a rather comprehensive directive. "What exactly is it that you wish to know?" I asked. "My educational background? My qualifications for the job? My opinion of your Arkady Core Converter? Only ask me and I will be happy to oblige."

His face registered a mix of responses—irritation at my deliberate obtuseness but a certain enjoyment of my verbal quickness, as well. At least, so I read the expression on his face. "Those facts I can obtain from your résumé—all except your opinions of my nuclear systems, and that we can get to later. Tell me about yourself. Where you were born, what kind of family you come from."

"I have no family and I was not born," I replied.

"No family! Not born! Then you are some sort of mist-creature, conjured up by the fumes of Fieldstar's buried dubronium mines or the souls of the native creatures who were exorcised from this planet when we settled it."

"I understood that Fieldstar had no native life when the Allegiance took it over for terraforming."

He pointed a finger at me. "Ah! That is what we all understood. But I have seen a strange creature now and then, slinking quickly into shadows when I passed by, and it bears no shape or features I recognize from my domestic textbooks. Thus I must assume it is a product of the planet itself, and resents my presence here, and would harm me if it could. Which is why I am perfectly willing to believe you the embodiment of such a creature, for, as you know, I blame you for my little accident this evening."

I could not hold back a smile at this. "I still deny being even the smallest cause of your misfortune."

"But you do not, I notice, so readily deny being called an agent of Fieldstar out to reclaim your own."

"I have been called worse," I said. "I would be honored to be accepted into the fabric and structure of Fieldstar and deemed a part of the planet."

"Would you, indeed, Miss Starborn? That is a strange thing to say. You have not been here above a month and yet already you experience a kinship with this rather inhospitable rock on the edge of an unfriendly galaxy. How could you so quickly have come to love such an unlovable place?"

"Is Thorrastone Park so unlovable?" I countered.

"To me it is. For more reasons than its dreary skies and unforgiving soil. But you have not answered the question! Why is it you feel any affinity for this world at all?"

"I feel an affinity with all places, all living creatures. I believe each offers its own delights, if we can but find them. But more than that, I believe we all share a commonality that gives us a bond even when we do not immediately sense it."

He threw his head against the back of the chair; had he been a stallion or some other wild beast, he would have reared back. "I cannot believe it! You are one of the PanEquists! For such is their philosophy."

I nodded calmly. From the corner of my eye, I saw Mrs. Farraday look up, for his voice had been loud enough to be heard across the room. I was not sure she knew the term—but if she did know it, I was sure she would not like it.

"Indeed, I am," I said.

"But this is amazing! I have never met one face-to-face—never hoped to have such a chance to debate doctrine with one. For, let me be honest with you, I cannot believe any sensible person could subscribe to such a theory as universal equality among all races and creatures."

"And living organisms and nonliving organisms and synthetic and natural *things*," I added, for the religion makes no distinctions at all.

"But—this is absurd! You are telling me that the people of this faith—that you—that anyone could equate a living, breathing human being with a—with a *rock*? A *tree*? The metal hull of a spaceship? All these things are the same to you?"

"They are made of the same material. The building blocks of their construction are interchangeable. The living, breathing human being, when he dies, is returned to the soil of his world, where his bones and his body decompose into their compound atoms. The rosebush planted over his head draws in the chemicals he releases. Until the plot is razed, and the mine is dug, and the dirt that his body has become is compressed and sifted for its metallic content, and he is turned into that very spacecraft you mentioned. Where is the difference? Where does the man end and the starship begin? I cannot tell. Do you think you can?"

He appeared thunderstruck—but, against his will, intrigued. "But Miss Starborn! I say again, with some stupefaction, Miss *Starborn*! One is a sentient, intellectual creature with some control over his thoughts, actions, and destiny. The others—this rosebush and this ore-struck hull—they cannot think, move, feel, speak, argue, fight, change the course of history—they are not in the same league at all!"

"Do you have to be able to debate philosophy to have some value to the universe? Can an oxygen molecule recite the laws of physics? I think not. But you would not want to try to exist without it."

"But . . ." He put his hand to his forehead as if checking his own reality. "But I would not want to try to exist without brandy, either, and yet I am not going to leave my inheritance to that bottle over there! It is not an—not an entity! Surely you must see the difference."

"Of course I recognize that there are differences in the way all creatures, plants, and objects exist. What I am saying is that those differences do not elevate one over the other." Casting my mind about for some kind of example, I remembered a news story Ameletta had shown me about Old-Earth animals being resurrected and bred for an interplanetary zoo. "The proud man who lords it over his household today may be eaten by a tiger tomorrow, and the essential equations of the universe will not change. Not an atom will have been lost—not a single cell of his body will not be reused."

"His soul will have been lost," Mr. Ravenbeck interjected quickly. "Or do you claim that he has no soul? Or that a soul does not matter?"

"His soul is ineffable and will have been gathered up to the Goddess."

He leaned forward with a sort of pouncing motion. "Aha! But does not his soul in the very first place render him superior to that rosebush, that tiger, and that piece of metal?"

"How do you know they do not have souls as well?" I countered.

"How do I—but of course a spaceship has no soul!"

"But how do you know?"

"Because it does not! Because it does not live!"

"And a rosebush? A tiger? They do not live?" I asked.

"They live, but not as we do. Certainly they do not live at such a level that they espouse a religious doctrine, and surely, if there is any purpose for a soul at all, it is to be converted by faith." He half-smiled as he said this; he knew he was muddling his arguments by this slight introduction of humor.

"I understand that it is difficult for you to accept a soul in a piece of machinery or a flowering bush," I conceded. "But surely even you must acknowledge that animals may be suspected of possessing such a commodity. Why, throughout the history of mankind, animals have been worshiped as gods, or seen as the receptacle of human souls as they make a slow journey from atheism to enlightenment. They meet all your criteria for living creatures—they move, they breathe, they think, they fight. Are you alone to decide that even so, they have no souls?"

"I do not believe they do, but very well! I will admit it is a possibility, though remote. Even so, I will not concede that this—this tiger of yours is any way equal to the man whom he consumes."

"And why not?"

"Why not? What has a tiger achieved in comparison to what man has achieved? Men have continually refined their environments to sustain a greater and greater explosion of population. That is the most remarkable achievement in the human canon. They have moved from caves to continents to galaxies, always adapting their worlds to suit themselves. No tiger has done that. No tiger has replanted his native rainforest with a more salutary crop or bred a food source that more exactly met his requirements. No tiger has been able to expand his population base exponentially and still managed to support his numbers— and mankind has done that, over and over and over."

"And that is a good thing?" I asked gently. "The proliferation of mankind?"

"Well, of course it is!" he exploded, and again I saw both Mrs. Farraday and Miss Ayerson look in our direction. They exchanged puzzled glances, then returned their attention to Ameletta. "What sort of question is that?"

I shrugged. "If mankind's greatest achievement is to produce more spaces for mankind to live in, I do not think I am so impressed," I said. "Particularly since he has continued to *need* those new spaces because he has fouled his old ones. What men have done is found ways to endlessly reproduce themselves—and that is not such an amazing ability. The smallest, least complex amoeba can do that. Men do it on a larger scale, but they do not do it with any more grace. I will not concede superiority on that score. Indeed, I will not concede it on any."

Mr. Ravenbeck again put a hand to his brow, but this time he seemed to be offering his own head a precarious means of support. "You, Miss Starborn, are an anarchist," was his next unexpected observation.

I felt an involuntary smile come to my lips. "I, sir? Merely because I am defending tigers?"

"No. Because you do not recognize social order. That is, in fact, the philosophy that is at the heart of the PanEquist doctrine. If there is no superiority in species or substance, then there is equality throughout the system. The servant is the equal of the master. Everything is level."

I smiled again. "But surely a desire for social equality abides in the heart of every creature who does not have it?"

"Perhaps, but few of them state it so openly!"

"I assure you, I am very well aware of how society works, and I know that I am the employee here, and you the employer. I believe that in the Goddess's eyes, we are all equal. But the Goddess does not deposit my paycheck. You need not worry that I will agitate for a revolution."

"You relieve me," he said, somewhat sardonically. "I was beginning to peg you for just such a radical."

"If it unnerves you to speak of my religious beliefs, we may discuss your own instead," I said in a pacifying voice. "I take it you follow some doctrine?"

He shrugged and made a gesture of uncertainty. "Oh, I know the litany of the Reformed Neo-Christian Church, but I confess that I use that knowledge to do little more than add force to an exclamation," he said. "It is the same with most of my set. Now, Mrs. Farraday is rather more devout than I am, following the evangelistic branch of that same church. You might apply to her if you were looking for a more socially acceptable affiliation."

As if she had caught the mention of her name, Mrs. Farraday came to her feet and headed in our direction. Her pleasant face was puckered with worry, and she looked at me somewhat uncertainly. I doubted she had understood half our rather exhilarating conversation—I at least had found it exhilarating—but it was obvious that the tenor of it had disturbed her.

"Mr. Ravenbeck, surely you must be growing tired? Your long trip—and your accident—I am wondering how much later you should sit up."

"Thank you for your concern, but I am quite hearty," he said. His voice was a bit testy but not, I was happy to hear, unkind. A man who spoke cruelly to his dependents was not to be respected, no matter how quick and fine his mind. "In fact, I am far from tired. Miss Starborn and I have been having the most invigorating conversation on the construction of the universe. Her theories are bizarre, but her rebuttals are good, and she is making me think very hard. Something, to my discredit, I do not often do."

This explanation, though murky, seemed to reassure Mrs. Farraday a little. At any rate, her face cleared, and she bestowed upon us both a shy smile. "Well, I must say, your talk has sounded very strange to me," she said. "I would have thought you would have been asking Jenna all about her schooling and her work so far."

"Indeed! And so I should have!" Mr. Ravenbeck said briskly. "Let us, Miss Starborn, return to those mundane but still important matters. Where did you go to school? And how long have you been out of it?"

Satisfied at the turn our conversation was taking, Mrs. Farraday returned to her own seat again. I answered at once. "I attended Lora Technical and Engineering Academy, where I graduated four years ago. I stayed on as an instructor until I became restless, when I applied for this position."

"So you have seen only two worlds in your short life? Fieldstar and Lora? That does not seem an adequate exposure for anyone."

"Three worlds," I corrected. "I lived on Baldus until I was ten."

"Lived there? With whom? You said you had no family."

"I do not. I was raised in a household by a woman who did not like me, and sent away to school when that option arose."

"She did not like you? Well, if you spouted such radical ideology while you were under her roof, I am not sure I can blame her. Why did she raise you if she did not like you?"

"She felt responsible for me," I said unhelpfully.

That response earned me a quick, sidelong look, but he dropped the line of questioning. "So you relocated to Lora at a tender age and immersed yourself in nuclear physics," he said. "I suppose you also have the usual grasp of languages and history?"

"The courses were required for graduation."

"Which you accomplished four years ago, following that with another stint of mindless existence which they call living on Lora—oh, do not bother to protest! I am familiar with both the world and the academy, and there is nothing exciting or endearing about either. I do not wonder at your desire to escape—I only wonder that you did not feel impelled toward it sooner. And—yes! I wonder one more thing— that of all the places in the inhabited universe you could have wandered to, how you could have managed to end up . . . here."

"Chance—fate—random motion," I said.

"You have no free will?" he retorted. "You could not have selected a more lively venue, more broadly tenanted? There is much less to see on Fieldstar than there was on Lora, which at least had the advantages of a dense population and an unending supply of technology and commerce."

"I am a timid woman and am moving my way upward by slow degrees," I said with a small smile. "Eventually, as I gain confidence, I will migrate to the wilder climates of Karian and Corbramb."

I had named two of the most sophisticated worlds in the Allegiance, and he laughed aloud at this. "You are anything but timid, Miss Starborn, and that I say with certainty after knowing you only a few hours. But I take your point. You would be out of place in a much more frivolous or frenetic environment. And yet someday you must allow yourself to experience something more urbane than this. I assure you, the universe offers far more exotic treats than you have encountered in your travels so far."

Almost upon his words, the clock struck the hour, and I realized with astonishment how long we had been talking. The chime was the signal for Miss Ayerson to gather up Ameletta and her things, and for Mrs. Farraday to fold up her household accounts and prepare to vacate the room. I too came to my feet.

Mr. Ravenbeck looked up at me with a frown. "What? Where are you going? I have not given you leave to go."

"The hour is growing late," I pointed out. "And—forgive my bluntness—but I believe Mrs. Farraday is right. You have had a trying day and you should be tired, even if you are not."

"I think I may be able to judge if I am tired or not," he grumbled, but he did indeed look exhausted. "Very well, then! All of you may go! But I will see you over the following days, I suppose? You do not have some pressing engagements that will prevent you from keeping me company in the next evening or so? I am interested in continuing our conversation."

I nodded serenely, though I felt anything but calm. To look forward to such discussion over and over again in the evenings to come! What a treat to anticipate! "I am at your disposal, sir," I said.

"Good. Tomorrow night, then, after dinner. I will expect to see you here with the others."

I nodded again and then, since I could think of nothing more to say, turned to leave the room. Mrs. Farraday waited for me at the door, smiling but inexorable, and followed me out into the hallway.

"Things are very different when Mr. Ravenbeck is here," she observed as we began walking down the hallway toward the stairs.

"I can see that," I said, laughing inwardly at my own understatement. "It's unfortunate that he is here so rarely."

"Ah, well, it's a pleasant enough life at any time," she said. We had by this time made it to the foot of the stairwell, though she turned toward the kitchens to make a final inspection. "Good night, Jenna. Sleep well."

"Yes, you too," I said, and climbed up the two flights of stairs to my room.

Where I sit at the window, looking out at the ill-lit acres of lawn and expecting no such blessing as a good night's sleep. Instead, I have gotten out my recorder and told it every word I could remember from my extraordinary conversation with Mr. Ravenbeck. My brain feels like it has been turned to tinder for the greediest of fires; thought after thought sparks through my mind, leaving its own trail of brilliance and complexity. Amazing how the chance to express your opinion aloud begets in you opinions you did not know you had and fuels you with a desire to explain the smallest detail of your ideology.

I bent my head over the recorder in my hand and I whispered, "Oh, Reeder, I have met the most remarkable man tonight!"

Chapter 5

✧

*B*ut the next two days did not, to my chagrin, live up to the promise of the first. That was not a reflection on Mr. Ravenbeck; it was not that, by the cold light of day, he seemed more pedestrian and less able-minded. On the contrary, he seemed invisible. We did not see him at all.

This was a blow to Mrs. Farraday, who lamented the fact over every shared meal and during our quiet, feminine gatherings in the evening. "Poor Mr. Ravenbeck! He has been so busy he's scarcely had time to gobble down a breakfast, and I declare he was over at the mine compound until past midnight last night. Such a shame, for it *is* nice to see him on those few occasions he is actually here, and I daresay he'll be going away again any day. Well, I will just have the cook go ahead and prepare that special braised beef. I am sure he will have an opportunity to eat it, even if he doesn't get to sit down at a table like a civilized man."

Ameletta too did much pining over Mr. Ravenbeck's absence, though I had to confess I could not judge the depth of affection that lay between them. They had not seemed to interact at all during the time I had been in the same room with them. Miss Ayerson seemed driven to distraction by the little girl's constant sighing, and spoke a little more sharply than her wont. If she missed Mr. Ravenbeck's presence, she gave no sign.

As for myself, I was conscious of a bitter disappointment, but I conducted myself with all my usual calm dispassion. I had no claim on Mr. Ravenbeck, like Ameletta; no history, like Mrs. Farraday; I had no reason to suppose I would ever lay eyes on him again. Thus, I refused to be sorry that his affairs kept him elsewhere during his brief visit.

"Last time Mr. Ravenbeck was here, he took me for a long ride in his aeromobile," Ameletta was saying wistfully. "We flew past town and on to the Taff holding, and then we went in and had luncheon. And Mr. Ravenbeck told me silly stories and I laughed and laughed, and he said he had more stories to tell, but he would save them for another time— but the time is now and he is not here!"

"Oh, Ameletta, could you please *stop*!" Miss Ayerson exclaimed. "I am sure Mr. Ravenbeck will find a few hours to spend with you, but it is not attractive to be so desperate over any man's attention, even that of your guardian."

That statement told me a lot about Miss Ayerson, though I could not exactly argue with the sentiments. I smiled at Ameletta and held out a hand. "Why don't you spend the day with me, Ameletta?" I suggested. "I am going to walk every inch of the forcefield checking for strains, and I am going to bring a picnic lunch with me, and eat it by the oxen-heart tree, and then I am going to sit outside in the afternoon sun and read from a book of stories. I think you would enjoy spending such an afternoon with me, wouldn't you?"

A look of mingled relief and guilt crossed Miss Ayerson's face. "That would be very kind of you, Miss Starborn, but you do not need to feel compelled—"

"Yes, a wonderful idea, Jenna!" Mrs. Farraday interposed. "Janet has been looking forward to a free day when she can go into town, but I have not been able to spare Mary or Rinda to watch Ameletta." These were the two maids-of-all-work who assisted Mrs. Farraday with the upkeep of the household; they were half-cit teenage girls who only stayed at Thorrastone Manor a few days every week, and I had had scarcely any contact with them. Mrs. Farraday continued, "If you think you can handle her, this will suit everyone. I am very sure it will suit Ameletta."

Indeed, the little girl was bouncing up and down in her seat and mouthing "Please, yes, please, yes" over and over as we debated her fate. I smiled at her again. "I think I will not only handle her, but enjoy her," I said. "It is settled, then. Ameletta, go change into your most comfortable shoes. I will tell the cook to pack enough lunch for two. Meet me in the foyer in fifteen minutes."

"Thank you, Miss Starborn," Miss Ayerson murmured as Ameletta tore from the room.

"A pleasure for me," I said lightly. "You forget, I was a teacher myself for four years. If I can instill any theories of nuclear physics in her head during our outing, I will do so, but I do not have high hopes of making this an educational episode. I am afraid the most you will have to hope for is that she will be exhausted and compliant by bedtime."

A few minutes later, Ameletta and I met in the hallway and headed out for our adventure. She was dressed in a bright pink tunic and leggings; I wore a similar ensemble, though in a more sober gray. She skipped along beside me with so much energy that I thought she might go airborne, like Mr. Ravenbeck's aeromobile. A good thing for both of us to go on a long, brisk walk!

We spent a pleasant day together, once the edge of her excitement was worn off. She chattered incessantly; I needed to do no more than smile, nod, and interject the occasional comment to keep her talking. She loved the holoshows that Miss Ayerson allowed her to watch one day a week, and she described plotlines and character traits to me with so much detail that I would have sworn she was talking about actual acquaintances if I had not known better. A lonely life for a child, I reflected, immured here on this outpost in the company of two spinster women and one who may as well have been. How had she come to be here, anyway? I had never had the opportunity to ask.

At noontime, we spread a thin plastic sheet under the oxenheart tree and unpacked the basket I had carried with me all morning. The cook had catered more to Ameletta's tastes than mine, I saw at once, for there were any number of cakes and cookies tucked inside and very few items of real sustenance. But a diet of pure sugar would not hurt me one day out of the year, I supposed, and so I set out the items with a great flourish. We munched and chatted and munched some more, until Ameletta stretched out on the sheet with a big sigh of contentment.

"That was the best," she said happily. "I'm so full I think my stomach will pop!"

I was sure Miss Ayerson would not approve of such language, but I did not bother to reprimand her; I felt much the same way. "Would you like to take a little nap? Or would you like to return to the house? If you're tired, we can go back now."

She shook her head, tangling her honey-colored curls with the motion. "No, I want you to read to me from your storybook. You said you would bring it."

"And so I did. But perhaps you would like to read to me? And then we could tell Miss Ayerson you have been practicing your vocabulary words."

She shook her head again. "I am feeling too lazy," she said. "You read."

So I smiled and took out my book, a collection of children's stories from across the Allegiance. It was one of the few things I had taken with me from my aunt Rentley's house. "Once, long ago, there was a little girl who lived on the edge of the forest," I began. Ameletta closed her eyes, and kept them shut until I had read the final paragraph. Then she opened her eyes and gave a little bounce—as much as a person who is supine on the lawn can be expected to bounce.

"I liked that very much!" she exclaimed. "Will you read me another?"

I had the entire day to amuse her; reading stories was the least taxing of the activities we might undertake. "Yes, as many as you like," I replied, and began the second one.

We were on the fourth tale when I heard the hum of a motor in the distance and paused in my reading. Ameletta scrambled to an upright position and stared hard in the direction of the mine compound.

"That must be Mr. Ravenbeck, returning to the manor," she exclaimed.

"Now, Ameletta," I admonished. "Mr. Ravenbeck is a busy man. Even if it *is* your guardian, we cannot assume that because he is headed in this direction, he has any time to spend with us."

But I may as well have directed my comments to the tree itself for all the heed she paid me. She leaped to her feet and began jumping up and down, waving her hands wildly to catch the driver's attention. "Mr. Ravenbeck! Mr. Ravenbeck! We are over here!" she called. I sat where I was, making no more attempt to check her. If it was indeed he, and he had a moment to spare, he might stop; if not, he would not. Let the matter be between him and his ward.

Nonetheless, I was a little surprised when the aircar veered from its course and turned our way, coming to a halt a few feet from where our plastic sheeting was spread. The driver was indeed Mr. Ravenbeck, and he swung himself from the seat with all of an athlete's natural ease. I noticed that he did not seem to favor his leg as he strode over to us, and that the three-day old cut on his forehead had healed almost completely.

"Miss Starborn! Ameletta! What a happy chance! I was just thinking I had not seen either of you since I arrived. Ameletta, *chiya*, you need not greet me with quite so much enthusiasm," he added, for the girl had thrown herself at him the way a puppy will leap toward his boy-owner's face. I noticed the endearment—the first I had heard anyone use toward her—and saw also how it made her flush with pleasure. But I wondered why it would occur to him to use a word that came, if my linguistics were correct, from the Corbramb world where an exotic dialect spiced up the Millennial English used by the rest of the Allegiance.

"It is just that I am so happy to see you," she explained somewhat breathlessly. "Everyone tells me that I must not bother you, but it does not bother you to take me for a ride in your aeromobile, does it, or to fly me into town for a piece of cake at the pastry shop?"

"No, not a bother at all," he said, smiling. "In fact, I was wondering if you would like to do just that—ride into town for a bit of a snack." He looked over at me. "Miss Starborn can come too."

I smiled. There was nothing I would have liked better, but Ameletta deserved his notice far more than I did. "I think your ward wishes for a bit of your undivided attention," I said. "She has talked of very little except you for the past three days, and how much she enjoyed your previous outings. I would not like to intrude on that."

"No intrusion," he said with a slight frown just as Ameletta was crying, "Oh, Miss Starborn! Please come with us!"

But I was resolute. I shook my head, smiling still. "Some other time, perhaps," I said, knowing there would probably be no other time. "I have spent the day with this little bundle of energy. I have plenty of things I can accomplish if you are to take over her care for a few hours."

He still did not look entirely pleased, but he did not let that keep him from patting Ameletta's blonde head with an absent-minded though gentle gesture. "Very well," he said. "I shall take full responsibility for my ward. But you," he added, glancing down at that ecstatic creature, "need to run inside and change into something a little more fancy. We will be going to the Mayfair Shop, and I only take the most elegant ladies there."

She giggled and glanced down at her tunic. "I have the prettiest dress I have been saving for weeks and weeks," she said. "It is made of ivory lace and sewn all over with pearl buttons. Shall I wear that? Is it fancy enough for the Mayfair Shop?"

"It sounds ideal," Mr. Ravenbeck said.

"But, Ameletta," I warned. "You have spent the whole afternoon eating sweets and candies. Make sure you order something healthy and nourishing in addition to dessert."

"I will," she promised. "Mr. Ravenbeck, I will be *right back*. Don't move an inch!" And so saying, she took off as fast as her short legs could carry her toward the door of the manor house.

The two of us gazed after her in silence for about thirty seconds. "You could have offered her a ride," I remarked. "It would have been much faster."

He gave a short bark of laughter. "I know. That is why I chose to let her run. I wanted a chance to have at least a brief conversation with my new technician. I have been a bad employer, I know. I have not seen you in three days or checked on your work or inquired if you had any questions to ask me. I would remedy that now."

I took a deep breath. "As to the performance of my duties, I feel reasonably confident," I said. "The questions I do have pertain more to the inhabitants of Thorrastone Manor, and those perhaps are better left unasked."

He threw back his head and laughed. "Miss Starborn, you astonish me. Not one woman in ten thousand would have the nerve to bring up such a subject to her new employer mere days after having met him."

"I have brought up no subject," I pointed out. "I merely commented that there were subjects I would *like* to bring up."

"Let me guess," he said, glancing back toward the manor. "Ameletta."

"I admit to some curiosity about her origin—and her place here."

He nodded. "Shall we stroll, Miss Starborn? I have been sitting in meetings all day, and I think a little exercise would clear the cobwebs from my head. We need not go far—I believe we were strictly adjured not to move an inch."

I nodded and fell in step beside him. "Ameletta?" I prompted as we began a leisurely pacing in a grand circle around the tree.

"Ameletta," he said. "My ward. There was a time in my life, Miss Starborn, when I was not quite the sober and upstanding level-one citizen you see before you now."

I glanced at him sideways, and he smiled. "Ah, and you are wondering just how 'sober and upstanding' I can claim to be now, but you feel your acquaintanceship with me is too short to allow you to judge," he said, almost gaily. I felt a flush come to my cheeks, for that was exactly the thought in my mind. "Nevertheless," he resumed, "I am a far more diligent, responsible, and solemn man than I once was, and that I was ever a dilettante and ne'er-do-well I blame entirely on my family. I was the youngest of several sons, born late to a mother who died shortly after my arrival. My father's estates were vast enough that he could have happily supported twice the number of sons he in fact produced, and yet this was a man for whom the word 'greed' had the ring of virtue, and he did not like the thought of breaking up his property even after he was dead."

We walked on slowly another few yards. Mr. Ravenbeck had clasped his hands behind him, and he gazed down at the ground as he walked. The result was to give the appearance of a squarish, solid man tilted forward in a posture that might eventually make him tumble over. By contrast, I held myself with my usual erectness, my face angled toward the distant sun.

"Thus I was told, when I was a young man, that I had two choices. I could accept a small inheritance which would enable me to retain my status as citizen until the money ran out, or I could perform a service for my family which would bring in enough wealth to render me a profitable asset. The service did not seem so disagreeable—and it was not, as I see by your shocked face, technically illegal—and so I saw no reason not to comply with my family's wishes."

"You did the deed, sir?"

"Oh, I most certainly did the deed. Thought the matter over perhaps two weeks, performed it in less than two hours—and regretted it for the next eighteen years. For there were conditions attached to this action that were not revealed to me until it was far too late—conditions which I would have thought would have turned even a greedy man into a philanthropist, so repulsive were they. And yet, as you say, the deed was done. There was no undoing it. I kept my temper, I bowed— metaphorically speaking—to my family, and I left the estates, for what I vowed would be the rest of my life."

"To embark upon a course of dissolution," I said.

He gave me another sideways glance, amused again. "Now, why would that be the first thought to leap to your mind?"

"It is the natural course for many people who have been violently disappointed," I said.

"For many people," he said. "Not you? You need not reply, for the answer is written clearly in every line and hollow of your face. You are not a woman who would ever give over to debauchery."

"I have not ever been living in circumstances in which debauchery seemed plausible," I remarked. "But I must say the options that I know about have never appealed much to me. Including, as I suppose they do, drinking, gambling, experimenting with hallucinogenics, and consorting with—well, with all sorts of unsavory characters."

"Yes, especially the consorting," he said, his face now brimming over with laughter. "But you mean to tell me that, even in your darkest days at Lora—and those unspeakable early days that were so dreadful you will not even discuss them—you were not attracted to some method of dulling your pain and forgetting your sorrows?"

"If I wanted to make myself feel better, I think I would do a good deed and not a bad one," I said. "I would extend a kind hand to someone in more distress than I. This would make me feel better than all the whiskey and all the hallucinogens you could produce."

"Hmpph. Well. You are almost unique in that attitude, but I must say it does you some credit. You will not be surprised to learn that was not the course I followed—doing good, I mean. I traveled to Corbramb, that place of such luxury that even you have heard of it, and I spent a hedonistic decade. I had funds, so I had friends, and I had no responsibilities, so I had unlimited time. You can imagine what my activities were. I wish that you could not—I would like to have been more creative in my vices, but I was lethargic as well as depraved. For a time, I was involved with a woman who operated what they call 'a pleasure palace,' a virtual reality emporium where you can experience all the gratifications of the flesh without actually exposing yourself to risk. In fact, there was some talk between us of opening our own palace, me to finance it and she to manage it. She had very grand ideas about entertainments—I'm sure it would have been a popular destination."

"But you never did found such a place, did you, sir?"

"No."

"I am glad to hear it."

"Why? Because it allows you to have a higher opinion of me than you would otherwise have?" he said, a strong note of derision in his voice. "I assure you, your opinion of me can be quite as low as you like, despite my not having become a purveyor of electronic fantasies. I have done nothing to earn any special regard."

"Finish your tale, and let me judge for myself afterward," I said quietly.

"As I say, we had our plans, but they were derailed in the most commonplace manner imaginable. I discovered she had a second—shall we say—business partner who was eager to fill each of my several roles in her life. Naturally, I had to sever the connection immediately. I must say, to do so gave me a profound relief on many fronts, and I resolved to be a little more wary before I pledged my heart—or my bank account—to anyone in the future."

"A wise decision," I said, for the pause in his speech seemed to require a comment from me. "But none of this comes any closer to explaining Ameletta's presence in your life."

"I must first explain Coletta before I can explain Ameletta."

"Coletta?"

"The name of my erstwhile companion. Shortly after she and I parted ways, she sent me a message telling me she was pregnant with my child. This was not something she had wanted, mind you, and it was not something she expected to grant her a further hold over my heart. It was merely something she passed along in the way of information."

"And you replied?"

"Well, first I asked her what she intended to do about it. On Cor-bramb, while there are millions of doctors who will perform an abortion for an insignificant fee, there are also hundreds of institutions where a woman can take her unborn fetus and submit herself to operations of a different sort. And those institutions will pay you, instead of the other way around. And Coletta, in case you had not guessed, was a very avaricious woman."

"She took her baby in to be harvested," I said calmly, though I did not feel calm at all. I felt hot, and flushed with rage, and covered in prickles of hatred.

"Exactly. In case I might have some interest in the child's well-being, she told me where she had deposited her little burden. To her credit, she had chosen one of the institutions that will grow a baby to full term and then sell it to an individual desperate for a child. She did not go the less ethical route and leave the fetus with one of the organizations that merely is interested in blood cells and tissues."

He spoke dispassionately, but it was hard to believe he could feel no emotion. As for myself, I was almost faint with it. "What did you do then?" I asked. It was an effort to raise my voice above a whisper.

"I went to the clinic, paid an exorbitant fee to claim the child as mine—though I was not positive, not by any means, that I was the biological father—and I waited until she was harvested. Then I engaged a nurse, installed the two of them in a small home, and went on about my life for the next few years as if I had no daughter or ward or any claim at all upon my life."

I swallowed twice before I was able to choke down the lump that had formed inside my throat. "But—you could have easily had that checked, you know," I said. "Her DNA against your own—"

He nodded. "I know. And that was my original thought, when I went to the clinic to investigate. Why should I support some other man's mistress's child if she had not the smallest claim on my time, resources, or affection? And yet, as I stood in that sterile, unfriendly room, surrounded by indifferent personnel, I could not help but sympathize with that tiny, still almost invisible life. I knew what it was like to be pushed to the brink of abandonment by someone who ought to have had your best interests at heart. I knew what it was like to be rejected by *family*, turned away because you did not fit in with a social or financial scheme. I had never done a good thing in my life, not that I could think of at that moment. But this would be a good thing. I would claim that tiny life, give it my name, accord it status of citizen, and keep it as safe as a negligent nature could do. So I determined, and so I have done, in my careless way. Eventually, when this property came into my hands, I moved her here, as being a less corrupt environment for a child. But I am still reconsidering that. It is a moral place, but a lonely one."

"It would not be so lonely for her if you were around more," I ventured. "She is very fond of you."

"Yes, but I am not so fond of young girls and mindless chatter! I do my best, but I have a finite patience with constant exclamations and artless questions."

He shuddered elaborately and I smiled. "That makes me hesitate to ask my own questions," I said.

"Ask away! Your conversation, whatever else I might call it, is hardly artless. What would you like to know?"

"First, *is* she in fact your daughter?"

He gave me a crooked smile. "I never had the tests done. She is my ward, and in some sense my heir, and because of me she will always be a full citizen of the Allegiance—but I do not know if she is flesh of my weak flesh and bone of my wretched bone. By your own standards, that should not matter at all. By your way of thinking, we are related whether we are the same bloodline or merely the same species."

Very true; that *was* what I believed; and yet it made his actions in adopting her just the slightest bit chivalrous. "Second, does she know her own history?"

"No, and Mrs. Farraday and Miss Ayerson know very little. Merely that I had a connection with her mother at one time and in that way came into possession of the daughter. Unlike you, they do not like to interrogate me, and my demeanor can be forbidding when I choose."

So saying, he turned a most unnerving scowl on me, which would have quite cowed me to silence had we not already had this most revealing of conversations. As it was, I could not hold back a smile, and his own grin returned.

"And is that your final question, Miss Starborn? For I believe I see a small white dot emerging from the manor door, and I am certain it signals the return of my ward dressed in her best finery. All confidences will perforce come to a sudden end."

"One more question," I said, "though this I suppose I could learn from Mrs. Farraday, if she were more inclined to gossip. How did you come into possession of your family's property? For this was once your father's holding, was it not?"

The grim look was back on his face. "Indeed it was. My father's holding, this one and various others on scattered worlds, and destined to be split between my two brothers upon my father's death. But greed, as I mentioned, runs in the Ravenbeck family. As my father lay quite ill, during the last months of his life, my oldest brother began reviewing the advantages to being sole heir to the several holdings. I am not sure whether or not he hastened my father's death, but he secretly arranged for my other brother's murder. And, being not nearly as clever as he was covetous, he was almost instantly found out. Accused, tried, convicted, and incarcerated. And, by the way, stripped of his citizenship. With my father expired, my one brother murdered, and my other brother dead to society, I became the single inheritor. For all property reverted to me in the unlikely event that I was the only family member to survive." He threw his hands wide, figuratively embracing the whole vast expanse of Thorrastone Park. "And see how happy such a fortune has made me! What a place to call my own!"

Before I could demur at his irony, the tumbling little ball of ivory and gold that had grown gradually larger in the past five minutes resolved itself into the panting, glowing figure of Ameletta. "Mr. Ravenbeck! See, I am all ready now! Don't you like this dress? Doesn't it make me look pretty?"

"You always look pretty, *chiya*," he said, chucking her under the chin with an easy affection that made her squeal. "Are you ready? Shall we be on our way?"

"Yes, please, I am *very* ready. Miss Starborn, are you sure you will not accompany us?"

I came to her side and gave her a very tight hug, for the story of her life had filled me with a fierce desire to protect and love her. She looked up at me in astonishment but willingly returned the embrace. "Yes, Ameletta, I am sure. I have the two new Arkady maintenance supplements to read, and I would like to get to them before the day ends. Besides, I want you to have a special day with your guardian. You can come to my room when you get home and tell me all about it. Will that be good enough?"

"Yes, that will make me very happy," she said, disentangling herself with no more ado. "Shall we go, Mr. Ravenbeck? Shall we go?"

He gave her a lazy smile, but I was able to read into it goodness and sentiment and affection. He helped her into the aircar, then climbed in himself. They waved good-bye to me and sped off toward the airlock, and within minutes were out of my sight. But I stared off into the distance where they had disappeared and I thought, as I had thought the first day I met him, *There is a rare and complex and intriguing man indeed.*

*   *   *

The next two days, we again saw almost nothing of Mr. Ravenbeck. I was busy with routine maintenance and the implementation of
the Arkady upgrades, so naturally I had no time to wonder about his
absence. However, if I chose to rise early or go to bed late, I did catch
glimpses of the estate hovercraft making its way toward the mining
compound, or his larger Vandeventer returning from the direction of
the airlock. Mrs. Farraday claimed not to know what his business was,
though I was very grateful to Ameletta for posing the questions I would
not bring myself to ask.

"Oh, *where* is Mr. Ravenbeck today? And *why* does he stay away so
long?" My thoughts exactly, but no one could answer.

Nothing of any note happened during that time until late in the afternoon of the second day. I was making my customary rounds of the
incandescent fencing when I encountered that strange woman Gilda
Parenon hurrying across the lawn, a look of anxiety on her face. I
changed my route to intercept her and called her name rather sharply.

"Is something wrong?" I asked. "You appear distressed."

She gave me one quick, assessing, and somewhat apprehensive look.
"No—nothing wrong. What should be wrong?"

"I merely inquired. If I can offer you assistance—"

"*You'd* not be the one I'd ask for help in this matter."

"Then there is something wrong?"

"Nothing. Nothing at all. Good day, Miss Starborn," she said, and
hurried off without a backward glance. I looked after her thoughtfully,
to see if she exhibited any erratic behavior, but though I distrusted her,
I could not see that she did anything amiss.

Dinner was the usual counterpoint of calm feminine conversation,
intermittent wails from Ameletta asking after Mr. Ravenbeck, and
clinking of china and silver. Miss Ayerson excused herself early and
dragged a complaining Ameletta away, I think to send her to bed
merely to quiet her protesting. Mrs. Farraday and I retired to the
library to read a while in companionable silence, and then I too went
up to my room. I updated my journal and went to sleep.

A few hours later I woke from a strange, depressing dream to a sense of utter terror. My heart was pounding, my head felt like it was wrapped in terrific pressure, and I was gasping for breath as if my lungs had filled with fluid. For a moment I thought I was developing a malevolent virus, and then I felt the mattress under me seem to sway and swell.

The air-filled mattress, more comfortable than any I had ever slept on. Expanding rapidly as the confining weight of atmospheric pressure bled away.

The reactor! Failing in the middle of the night! I forced myself to my feet, for light-headedness was making me lethargic, and threw on a robe over my thin sleep-dress. All the rooms of the house were equipped with small portable oxygen tanks for just such an emergency, and I snatched mine up and clipped the mask over my face. Immediately I felt a return to my normal alertness, the oxygen no doubt aided by a spurt of panic-driven adrenaline.

I rushed out of my room and down the stairs helter-skelter, not pausing to wake any of the other residents. We would have a few hours of barely sufficient air left, for the fact that I was alive at all indicated a slow leak, not a catastrophic one, and I was better off to attend to the equipment than rouse the house. So I was thinking as I leaped down the second flight of stairs . . . to see Mr. Ravenbeck's crumpled body lying half in and half out of the doorway.

My sob could not have been more theatrical had I been Ameletta. I threw myself down the final few steps and flung myself to my knees beside him. "Mr. Ravenbeck! Mr. Ravenbeck!" I cried through the muffling medium of my mask. I shook his shoulder but he did not respond; his face was ashen. Oxygen deprivation—no doubt the atmosphere outside was even thinner than that inside the shielded house, and he had fainted just before he could make it to safety.

I ripped the mask from my face and held it over his nose and mouth, letting him breathe the oxygen until I myself was in danger of fainting. Then I held the apparatus to my mouth, took a few more breaths, then held the device again to his face. He stirred on the floor and his eyelids fluttered. I saw him try to speak through the mask.

I shook my head, and gave myself another breath before returning the mask to him again. "Don't move. Don't speak. I'll get you a tank but I need to take this with me. I'll be back momentarily."

I snatched away the mask and saw his lips form a word: *who* or *what*, I could not be sure. I did not wait to find out, but ran as fast as I could to the nearest room, the library, and grabbed the tank installed there. When I returned to Mr. Ravenbeck's side, he had fainted again. I attached the lines securely to his face, made sure he was breathing, then left him there and ran headlong to my basement workroom.

I was expecting a fouled fuel line, a meltdown in one of the cores, or any number of small emergencies that should have been signaled by an alarm bell that would have roused the house. What I found was sabotage. I stood in the doorway, frozen and appalled, staring. The damage had been crudely done, an instrument panel crushed in, an electrical wiring system ripped from its connector and the alarms themselves smashed in. The reactors had not been touched, but it would take some time to render the whole system operable again.

But who would do such a thing? And why? It was not only homicidal, it was suicidal, for anyone who stayed in this house unprotected would die.

No time to solve that puzzle. I hurried forward and began the task of rerouting the electrical circuits to the secondary generators, which could easily supply enough power to fill our needs, at least for a few days. It was not long before I could feel the eerie pressure on my chest subside as the forcefield reasserted itself and the voracious vacuum of space was forced back outward again.

I was so absorbed in my task that I did not hear Mr. Ravenbeck come in, and only when I had turned to go did I realize he was standing in the lab, watching me. I started, but did not scream. He had laid aside his mask and tank, though he leaned against the door frame like a drunkard and his color still was not good. He was watching me with a great and analytical intensity.

"Will we live?" he asked. There was an undertone of sarcasm to his voice that let me know he was not really afraid of the answer, but I was not in a mood just now to banter.

"I believe so, though I would like to check on the others," I said sharply. "And I think you or someone should call out to the mining compound to make sure all is well there."

"They are independent systems," he said. "Theirs will not fail just because ours has."

"It will if its failure is triggered by the same event."

"Which would be what?"

I gestured at the smashed instrument panel. "Willful destruction. Someone took a hammer to the board and slashed through the wiring. The intent was clearly to disrupt the forcefield, and, I must assume, to kill us all."

He stared at me in sheer incredulity. "Unbelievable! That would be an act of madness. Whoever would do such a thing would have to expect to die as well."

I shrugged. "Take a look for yourself. I assure you, such destruction does not spontaneously occur even on the most ill-maintained machinery."

But his eye had followed my first gesture, and a look of grim comprehension was tightening his features. "I see. Yes . . . you must be right. But—then—the awful question arises—"

"As to the identity of the vandal," I said, somewhat eagerly, "I believe I may have a clue. In fact, I think I encountered her this afternoon, acting strangely out on the lawn."

"You saw her! Impossible! Whom did you see?"

I thought his tone of voice a bit extreme even for the situation, for he seemed almost thunderstruck at the notion that I might be able to identify the culprit. "A woman named Gilda Parenon. She claims to be a tech support worker in the dubronium mine compound."

"Ah," he said, on a low, thoughtful tone, and his whole body seemed to relax. "Gilda Parenon is the one you saw. Well. I see. It is true she is subject to fits of—strangeness—but I hardly think this is her handiwork."

"I think you should go investigate, sir," I said urgently. "For if not Gilda Parenon, then who? And if Gilda Parenon, then why? I think you cannot trust her to stay in your employ—not when Ameletta and so many others are depending on you to keep them safe."

"Gilda is well enough. You do not have to fear for her," he said somewhat absently. Completely ignoring my advice to go look for answers, he strolled deeper into the room, his gaze running over the jury-rigged equipment and the merrily flashing lights on the instrument panels. "But why were we not alerted to danger? Is there not an alarm that should have woken us all before our lives began to ebb away?"

"There is," I said shortly. "It was disabled. Chance alone led me to wake up in time to save the house—but it was almost too late to save you."

His perambulations had brought him quite near me, and now he turned on me the full force of his regard. His eyes were so dark they appeared devil-black, and just now they were focused on me with an unnerving intensity.

"Yes. I have not forgotten. You need not remind me that you saved my life. I doubt I will forget from now till the day I die. I am not used to owing anything to anyone—I never borrow a dollar because I hate debt so much that it leads me to despise my lender. But, is it not strange? I am happy to be your debtor in this. There is nothing I can think of that I would rather owe you."

I was a little embarrassed at this speech. "I merely happened to wake, and I happened to find you. Anyone could have done as much."

"But no one else in the house has stirred," he said quietly. "What supreme delicacy of constitution led you to wake when everyone else has merely slumbered more deeply? What small voice whispered 'Danger!' in your ear and roused your fierce protective instincts to safeguard the ones you love? For there are many in this house you love, are there not, Miss Starborn? When you worked with such concentrated efficiency—I know, I watched you a good half hour—you were laboring to save Ameletta and Mrs. Farraday and Miss Ayerson and . . . others. You would have worked just as hard to save strangers, I know—that is the kind of woman you are—but knowing that a slip on your part could result in the deaths of people you care for—that must have given your fingers greater quickness, must have sent the mental orders sizzling through the synapses of your brain."

"I did not want anyone to die, sir," I said quietly, for his talk was strange and made me uneasy, and I thought a sober answer might soothe him. "As I am one of the inhabitants in the house, some of my liveliness may be attributed to a sense of self-preservation."

That made him smile, but the expression erased little of the intensity on his face. "That is the Miss Starborn I have gotten to know over the past week—valiant in such an unpretentious way that you cannot even get her to admit her heroism. Very well, we shall tell none of the others how close they were to oblivion, so that you need not suffer their gratitude as well. But I at least insist on thanking you—with all my heart, Miss Starborn."

He held out his hand and, wondering, I put mine in his. I could not recite a dozen times in my life when a level-one citizen had touched me of his own accord; it was the highest mark of favor. He clasped my hand with a grip so firm it drew me a pace nearer to him, and he peered down at me from those black eyes as if he would devour my own soul to light his darkness.

"The first moment I laid eyes on you, when I saw your small figure stealing across my lawn, I knew you would exert some amazing and terrifying influence on my life," he said, very softly and very rapidly. "I was trying to argue myself out of this conviction when I lost control of my aircar, so you see, you instantly fulfilled my dark predictions. You and I are destined to meet in confrontations more strange and violent than this one, Miss Starborn—that I tell you with no fear of contradiction. You are my good angel or my bad angel, I know that for sure, but I could not say for certain which you will prove to be."

"I hope I am no man's bad angel, Mr. Ravenbeck," I said, as calmly as I could, though his wild talk made it hard to speak without agitation.

His hand squeezed on mine so painfully I thought he had forgotten that I was, in fact, flesh and bone. "Then good angel you shall be," he said, his voice barely above a whisper. "I take that as your promise."

I could scarcely think of a reply to this mad declaration. "I will do what I can, sir," was all I could come up with.

Again, he squeezed my hand. "And so you shall, Jenna, and so you shall."

What I could have replied to that—addressed as I was by my given name!—I could never have guessed. Just at that moment there was a ringing at the upstairs door loud enough to rouse the whole unnaturally sleeping house.

"The mine superintendent, no doubt," Mr. Ravenbeck said, dropping my hand and swiveling around to glance toward the exit. "I surmise you were correct in thinking damage was done at the compound as well as the manor. I must go and make sure all is well there."

"I will check on the others," I managed to say in a cool voice.

He glanced at me once and nodded briskly. "Do that," he said, and strode for the door without another word. I stared after him blankly a moment before turning back to make sure I had successfully completed all the repairs I could manage at this hour of the night.

Once satisfied that the generators would get us safely to dawn, I climbed wearily back upstairs. I went silently from room to room, making sure all the residents were alive and breathing. I kissed Ameletta on the cheek before leaving her room and finally making my way back to my own chamber. There I sat on my bed and stared at my hand for a good half hour before climbing back under the covers and commanding my stupefied brain to relax itself into slumber.

Chapter 6

✦

$\mathcal{P}$erhaps it was no surprise that I slept late the next morning, something I do so rarely I can count the occasions on my two hands. As soon as I woke, my thoughts instantly went to the place they had stayed so stubbornly the night before, when I could not will myself to sleep. The whole night had been so strange, from the powerful dreams to the terror of seeing Mr. Ravenbeck unconscious to the frantic working in the generator room to repair the malicious damage. But my thoughts lingered only briefly on those events. What I considered, again and again, was the feel of his hand commandeering mine and the dark look in his dark eyes as he watched me.

I shivered, and got out of my bed and dressed.

Down in the breakfast room, there was some of the chaos I was beginning to expect during the days of Mr. Ravenbeck's visit. Miss Ayerson was eating tidily enough, but Ameletta was doing some kind of twirl around the room, and Mrs. Farraday was half in, half out of the doorway, talking to an invisible person on the other side. I gathered a plateful of food and seated myself at the table.

"Is something amiss?" I inquired.

"Apparently there was some excitement last night," Miss Ayerson said with her usual serenity. "We have not yet learned all the details, but there was some trouble at the mine compound."

I poured myself some coffee and looked interested. "Oh? What kind of trouble? A brawl between workers, you mean?"

The look she flicked in my direction was very cool. "Nothing like that. One of the generators failed, and there is some suspicion it was sabotage. Mr. Ravenbeck was summoned in the dead of night."

Mrs. Farraday stuck her head back in the room to address us. "Yes, did you not hear the ringing at the door, Jenna? I did, but I declare I was so tired I could not force myself to move! And eventually I convinced myself it was just a part of my dream, for I was having very gloomy dreams—things I'm sure I don't like to think about in bright daylight."

"The doorbell?" I repeated, not sure how to answer, for indeed I had heard it but under circumstances I was loath to repeat. It seemed Mr. Ravenbeck had kept his promise and refrained from telling the others what danger they too had been in.

"Yes, it rang and rang, but I slept through it and didn't hear a thing," Ameletta said mournfully. She twirled over in my direction for her morning kiss, a custom we had begun in recent days.

"Just as well, for a good night's sleep is what a child of your age needs," Mrs. Farraday declared. "Though I must say, for having slept as deeply as I did last night, I do not feel particularly rested."

No answer to that either. I sipped my coffee. "So Mr. Ravenbeck was called away to deal with the crisis? Did they find the individual who vandalized the equipment?"

"Mr. Ravenbeck seemed to think he was quite certain who was responsible and would take immediate steps," Mrs. Farraday said. Someone from the other side of the door addressed her at that moment, and her face again turned from us as she made her reply.

I raised my eyebrows at the tutor. Mr. Ravenbeck had showed no such certainty to me last night—indeed, had rejected out of hand my one very good suspect. "Really!" I said. "I wonder who?"

"Even if we had the name, we are unlikely to recognize the staff at the mining compound," Miss Ayerson said. "No doubt it was some malcontent Mr. Ravenbeck had already heard of."

"Well! This is all very exciting," I said. "I shall have to ask Mr. Ravenbeck for more details if I see him today."

Mrs. Farraday's head swung around in our direction again. "Oh, you won't see him today. He's left."

"Left?" I said blankly. I felt my stomach quite irrationally dissolve at the news. "For good?"

"No, just for a few days. He's gone to the holding of the Ingersolls, half the continent away, to consult about—some new mining process, I believe he said, but I simply have no head for matters like that. He and Bianca Ingersoll have always been allies here on Fieldstar, and they frequently share information about—new markets or new techniques, or whatever it is. I sometimes think Mr. Ravenbeck would not come to Fieldstar half so often if Bianca Ingersoll was not just a day's flight away."

It was not just my stomach; it was my bones and muscles and arteries that were liquefying beneath my skin. "She sounds like a good friend to him," I said in a hollow voice.

"Yes—perhaps more than friend one day. No! Rinda! Not *that* serving tray!" Mrs. Farraday exclaimed, and dove through the door to disappear into the kitchen.

I was left staring blindly at the plate on the table before me. My fingers could not support the weight of my coffee cup, so I sloppily set it down. The smell of my food left me nauseated, and for a moment I thought I might be sick.

"I do wonder what will become of us if Mr. Ravenbeck marries Bianca Ingersoll," Miss Ayerson observed in such a casual voice it was clear she neither noticed my distress nor suffered from any herself. "Obviously, both mines would still be in operation, but I cannot imagine that they would want to maintain two households, and Sollbrook Manor is much finer than Thorrastone Park. Perhaps they would relocate all of us there—or some of us. I cannot imagine that I would still have a position here. And Mrs. Farraday . . ." Miss Ayerson shook her head. "Well, we shall just have to await the outcome of events."

I looked over at her, though my eyes were having trouble settling on anything, and certainly her pale, closed face did not give me much to focus on.

"And, of course, if they closed the manor, you would have no work here either," she pursued. "But technicians are wanted everywhere. Perhaps they would even need you at Sollbrook Manor. So I would not despair, if I were you, Miss Starborn. I cannot think your life would change at all for the worse if Mr. Ravenbeck were to marry."

I could not later remember how I escaped the breakfast room and Miss Ayerson's knifelike conversation. I performed my duties that day as one in a dream, skimmed the technical bulletins on the StellarNet without registering any of the words, and walked the grounds of Thorrastone Park for hours. I knew that my reaction was not only extreme, it was ridiculous, for there was nothing, could be nothing, between my employer and me. The fact that he had held my hand and gazed down at me with something like infatuation last night did not change the facts of the case. Which were: He was a level-one citizen, I a half-cit, and our worlds could only with great violence intersect. I did not expect them to; I had never even shaped that plotline in my dreams. I just had not expected—so quickly and so abruptly—that my ability to fantasize over him freely would be taken away. For you can, with some forgiveness, moon over an unattached man who has shown you some kindness. Only a fool or a scoundrel will pine after someone who is married, or about to be.

It took me most of the day, and a great deal of vigorous walking, before I had full command over myself again, but by and by my natural composure reasserted itself. When I joined the others at dinner, I was able to talk with about the same level of coherence I thought I usually managed. Just give me a day or two to adjust to the idea, and I would be even more unconcerned than now I pretended to be.

Still, this hard-won calm did not prevent me from engaging in a shameful exercise that night when I returned to my room. I went to my private StellarNet terminal, which heretofore I had only used to check on the day's news events or Arkady updates, and I activated one of the search engines. Narrowing down my inquiry by degrees, I entered in the following sequence of names: *Fieldstar, Ingersoll, Sollbrook Manor* and *Bianca Ingersoll*. Then I waited for the information to leap to the screen.

It arrived in seconds, complete with graphics. Sollbrook Manor was, as Miss Ayerson had said, a splendid place, a rolling, multistoried mansion of simulated gray brick on lawns more festooned with gardens than Thorrastone Park. The upkeep of the imported roses must in itself cost a small fortune. It was hard to imagine why, on such an inhospitable and not particularly sociable planet, any property holder would need such a huge house. I had had that thought more than once about Thorrastone Park. The expansive grounds—yes, that I could understand, and the mining operations themselves required a great deal of space. But why build such a large manor for a handful of inhabitants; would that not serve to emphasize your loneliness rather than erase it? But I was not one who delighted in grand displays. My idea of true happiness was a small crowded hearth, not a great empty one. Perhaps this was how citizens and half-cits differed. We craved closeness and they craved ostentation.

The text gave me details of the manor's founding, the name of the architect and the year the building was completed. But I did not care much for that information. I pressed on to the next screen, grimly curious to see the face of Bianca Ingersoll.

And there she was, laughing back at me from her electronic storage. She had fine, patrician features, high sculpted cheekbones that looked arrogant enough to be natural but perfect enough to have been purchased. Her eyes were a sunny blue, unclouded by any troubles, and her full mouth was turned up in a smile of pure happiness. But her true glory was her hair, a sparkling champagne blonde that cascaded over her shoulders with great abandon. In this image, it was impossible to judge its length, for it seemed to tumble down past her waist and out of range of the camera.

Only a full citizen would have hair like that. Only someone who did not have to rise early in the dark, dress herself quickly, tie back whatever stray tresses might fall in her way during the hours of her labor. Only a full citizen could be that beautiful, that carefree. Who would not love to look upon such a countenance, unwearied by stress, by worry, by fear? Who would not want to come to rest inside the circle of such beauty?

Leaving Bianca Ingersoll's image on my screen, I fetched a small round mirror from my dressing table and propped it up against a stack of books, right beside the monitor. Now my own face peered back at me, side by side with Miss Ingersoll's. Oh, here was a contrast! Here was a study in contradictions! The skin of my own face was dark and sallow, while my narrow mouth showed no inclination toward merriment. My cheekbones were firm but unremarkable, and my eyes were shaded and secretive. Even when I attempted to smile—to laugh, like the beautiful woman on the screen—my expression remained watchful, as if I expected whatever event amused me now to turn in a flash to something that would destroy me.

And my hair! Short, straight, brown, severe, it framed my face in a dark halo as if to further contain any thoughts, any expressions, that my features might otherwise give away. This was a working woman's coiffure, cut in such a way that it would not impede my vision or fall into a set of gears and get wound around a working mechanism. This was the hairstyle, this was the face, this was the expression of a half-citizen.

Who would ever love a woman like me? Could Mr. Ravenbeck? Could anyone?

Three more days passed with no additional mishaps or even significant events. I took Ameletta with me one of those days, more for her companionship than to gratify Miss Ayerson, and again we picnicked under the mighty oxenheart tree and read fables aloud. We did not encounter Mr. Ravenbeck on this particular outing, nor Gilda Parenon, nor anyone else. We had the whole park to ourselves.

That evening was yet another of those meals in which Mrs. Farraday seemed beside herself with excitement. She fluttered in late, took her seat, jumped up to go confer with the cook, returned, helped herself to the main meal, ran to the kitchen again, and, upon rejoining us, settled herself with a breathless little laugh.

"Oh, my! I don't know when I've been so flustered!" she exclaimed. "Jenna, could you pass me the potatoes, please? Yes, and the gravy, too. Ameletta, love, the meat platter. Careful—now—"

"Has something happened to upset you?" I asked, though she did not seem unhappy, just agitated.

"Upset me! No! Though the house may very well be turned upside down. Mr. Ravenbeck is returning tomorrow—and bringing a houseful of guests with him! I declare, the last time we had five or ten people staying here was—was—well, I can't recall!"

"Guests? Really? From Sollbrook Manor?" Miss Ayerson said, for I was incapable of framing the question.

"Indeed, yes, Bianca Ingersoll and her sister and her mother, and several houseguests who have been staying with *them*—Mr. Fulsome and Mr. Taff, I believe, and perhaps one or two more—it's very exciting, but I must confess to a little onset of nerves—"

"Is there anything I can do to help you?" I started to ask, but my question was interrupted by a squeal from Ameletta, who had leaped to her feet upon the first mention of a party.

"Ooooh, may I dress up in my pearl-white dress and sit at the table with Mr. Ravenbeck?" she cried. "May I have luncheon with the ladies? May I stay up late every night and—"

"Ameletta," Miss Ayerson reprimanded. "This is a party for adults. I am sure Mr. Ravenbeck will want to show you off once or twice, but he will not want you attending every event. You must be very good, or he will not want you present at all."

"But last time Miss Ingersoll came to visit, the two of them took me to town in the aeromobile and we ate little pastries at the Mayfair Shop! And she said I was the most delightful child and she wished I was her very own! She will want me there, I know it!"

The last time Bianca Ingersoll had visited? When was that? How long had the stopover lasted? And how many other visits had preceded that one?

"That was when Miss Ingersoll came all by herself," Mrs. Farraday said in an admonishing tone. "This time she will have many others to entertain, and she cannot be wasting her time on one little girl."

"Never mind, Ameletta," I said, as the child's face fell pathetically. "You and I shall have another picnic under the tree, and we shall dress up every night and hold our own parties in the schoolroom."

"As for that, I think your attendance will be wanted once or twice, Jenna," Mrs. Farraday said.

"*Mine?* I am hardly in a position—"

"Yes, and mine, and Miss Ayerson's," Mrs. Farraday pursued. "Mr. Ravenbeck has always been very good about including those of us in the—the *intermediate* ranks at his gatherings. He knows it is a treat for us, and I do appreciate the thoughtfulness."

"I have passed many interesting evenings here at Thorrastone Park when Mr. Ravenbeck had guests," Miss Ayerson added helpfully.

"But I—I have nothing suitable to wear and I—I am not comfortable in grand company. I am sure he will allow me to be excused."

"Well, he seemed most set on it before he left the house," Mrs. Farraday said doubtfully. "He said, 'Make sure both Miss Ayerson and Miss Starborn know they are to be included in our evenings, and do not let them come up with paltry excuses for denying themselves this enjoyment.' So you see, I am sure he wants you there."

I felt as if mercury was running through my veins, quick and poisonous. It was true that I was never at ease around full citizens of any level in society, but I was even more terrified of spending an evening in the same room with Mr. Ravenbeck and the dazzling Bianca Ingersoll. Bad enough that I had had to stare at our two countenances, side by side; I certainly did not want him making the live comparison and coming to the inevitable conclusion.

"I will think about it," I said faintly, and came shakily to my feet. "But I cannot believe he will insist."

Miss Ayerson also stood. "You will see, Jenna," she said, using my given name for almost the first time. "It will be very pleasant."

* * *

The guests did not arrive for another full day and half, and during that period of time I worked as determinedly as I could to forget the summons I had received by proxy. I installed new shields in the generator room; I entertained Ameletta whenever I could; I provided some trifling help to Mrs. Farraday; and I spent a great deal of time looking over my limited wardrobe and realizing that I had not a single piece of clothing that would not disgrace me utterly.

Nearly everything I owned was plain, somber, and serviceable. I had a selection of cloth coveralls, which suited me admirably for working on the generators or strolling through the lawns; and several sets of tunics and leggings, which I considered good enough for my infrequent trips to town and other public outings. Neither of these could be worn in the social setting I would be facing in a few hours' time.

The wealthy citizens of the Allegiance wore a range of clothing so diverse and inclusive as to make it hard for any historian to come up with a standard style of dress for the era. At social functions, women could be seen in anything from bejeweled street-length velvet gowns to form-fitting transparent gauzes that moved with their bodies like second skins. If anything could be said to be the current fashion, it was color, the brighter the better. Since everything I owned was a dull hue like gray or navy, I could not have fit in even if I had had clothing in the proper cut.

The only thing I could possibly wear to the evenings Mr. Ravenbeck had devised was a gray silk pant suit that owned the quietest air of elegance. I had purchased it in a shop on Lora shortly after I accepted a position at the academy, and I had only worn it twice, to formal school functions. There it had been proper; here it would be disastrous. The top was high-necked and long-waisted, falling in loose folds halfway to my knees; its pearl buttons were simple but pretty. The pants themselves were more tailored than the tight-fitting cotton leggings I usually wore, though there was nothing particularly distinguished about them. A pair of unobtrusive black shoes, and I would complete my ensemble.

And be laughed from the room, silently at least. Not that it mattered. Not that I thought I belonged there anyway.

How could a Goddess who knew I was the equal of every creature on the planet conspire to put me in a situation that would prove to me I was not?

*H*aving given up on my wardrobe dilemma, I joined Mrs. Farraday in her task of assigning rooms to the arriving guests. Large as it was, Thorrastone Park did not boast more than a dozen bedchambers, and residents were already installed in some. She and I toured the remaining rooms to determine who should sleep where.

This was an education to me, for I had seldom been in this wing of the house. It was on the third story, directly above the main entrance, overlooking the most beautiful sweep of garden and lawn. The sunlight arrived here first every morning, slanting in sweetly past the curtained glass and giving each room a festive glow. Each room was decorated in its own theme—one very modern and stark, another very gilded and ornate, one an explosion of abstract colors, another a study in ivory and lace.

"This is the room I think we should put Miss Ingersoll in," I said, when we had come to the latter.

"Why, and how did you know this is the room she prefers?" Mrs. Farraday exclaimed. "This is where we always put her."

"It seems to suit the great beauty she was described to me as being," I said. "And is very feminine besides."

"And it is as far from Mr. Ravenbeck's room as it can be and still be in this hallway," Mrs. Farraday added. "I know it is old-fashioned of me, but I always think company should be separated very carefully—the single women in one quarter, the single men in another, and the married couples and families all grouped together. But Mr. Ravenbeck doesn't care about that—none of these modern people do."

"Mr. Ravenbeck's room is down this hall?" I asked, for I had not, till this moment, ever envisioned his sleeping quarters at all.

"Yes, and let us take a quick peek in there to make sure everything is in order."

It was; the whole room was fresh, spartan, tidy as if no one had ever set foot to carpet or laid head on pillow. The furnishings were done in an indeterminate masculine hue, the bed was properly made, the bathroom gleamed as if every faucet and marble surface had been left untouched since the house was built. I spied no portraits on the walls, open books on the table, scattered items of clothing, stray shoes, crumpled letters. It was as if the man did not live there at all.

"Not a room which shows much of its owner's personality," I remarked.

"He is here so little," Mrs. Farraday excused him. "He cannot be expected to leave behind objects that hold much value to him."

"Where does he leave those objects, then?" I demanded. "Where does he spend his time?"

She looked at me somewhat blankly. "Why—his other holdings—he has several other properties, you know. . . ."

I glanced around the room again. "All of them, I would venture to say, as devoid of character as this one. I am not sure that Mr. Ravenbeck actually owns much that is of any value to him at all."

"Nonsense, he has many fine and expensive possessions," Mrs. Farraday said firmly as she ushered me back in to the hallway. It was clear she had no idea what I was talking about.

𝓛ate in the afternoon, the company arrived. Ameletta and Miss Ayerson, giggling and whispering, had invited me to watch the arrival on the security camera monitors that were installed, though seldom watched, in a small room on the upper story of the mansion. Indeed, Miss Ayerson said, she believed Mr. Ravenbeck had had them disconnected when he inherited the property, for they had not been in use since she arrived. Although I knew Mrs. Farraday would not approve of such an illicit activity—and I knew I therefore should not participate in it—I could not resist indulging my curiosity in such a harmless way, and I joined the other two in stealth.

Miss Ayerson was fiddling with the camera controls when I entered the room. "I cannot get the focus adjusted—we shall see nothing but blurry faces and splotchy colors at this rate," she remarked. "Here, Jenna, you are the technician. See if there is something you can do."

"These are a far cry from nuclear generators, but I'll give it a try," I said. Every dial and panel was covered in a layer of dust; I touched them with some caution. I could not help but wonder what images they would have shown us if they had been recording a few days back. The sinister image of Gilda Parenon making a destructive midnight visit to the house, perhaps?

"Well, I think—oh, I see what the—now maybe this will do it. . . ." I muttered to myself as I jiggled a few connectors and twisted a few dials. Ameletta's shriek of excitement let me know before I looked back at the monitor that I had done something right.

"Look! Look! That is her, that is Miss Ingersoll. Isn't she just the most beautiful lady?"

I quickly turned my attention back to the screen, to see this beautiful lady entering the mansion on the arm of the master of the estate. She was dressed in a clinging silver sheath that was only a few shades icier than her champagne hair, and below the hem her ivory legs were bare and shapely. She was laughing carelessly at something someone behind her had said, but I saw her eyes dart with an appraising possessiveness around the treasures in the foyer. She knew that she was considered a likely bride for the owner of Thorrastone Park, and she was tallying up her inheritance.

"Oh! And her sister! Melanie! She is not quite as pretty as Miss Ingersoll, but she is very nice."

"Is she older or younger than Bianca Ingersoll?" I asked.

"Younger by a year or two, I think," Miss Ayerson replied. "Mrs. Farraday would know."

Melanie Ingersoll was a darker, less vivacious version of her sister, with a vapid expression on her face, though I could not but help feel her lack of predatory interest gave her a few points in amiability. She was making an observation to the older woman beside her, a faded beauty who looked so much like Bianca she had to be the mother of the two. Like her eldest daughter, Mrs. Ingersoll seemed to be estimating the worth of the antiques and silver immediately on view in the hallway, and comparing them to pieces she had at Sollbrook Manor.

"They're all quite lovely," Miss Ayerson said with a certain wistfulness. I had scarcely ever heard her speak with anything other than complete indifference, so this change of tone caught my attention. I looked up at her with a little smile.

"In the eyes of the Goddess, we are just as beautiful and certainly as valuable," I said, "although I admit at the moment I am having a hard time convincing myself."

She smiled back, gave the tiniest of shrugs, and said nothing.

"Look! Mr. Taff—and Mr. Fulsome—oh, and Mr.— Mr.—I cannot remember his name, can you, Miss Ayerson? He came here that one time with Miss Ingersoll and he took you and me riding in his convertible craft—"

"Mr. Luxton, I believe," Miss Ayerson said coolly. "Joseph Luxton. He must be one of the houseguests Mrs. Farraday mentioned."

Joseph Luxton was a man so good-looking it was almost sinful. He had lustrous black hair and chiseled features, with lips so full and dramatic that they could only be called sultry. His eyes—startling in such a dark face—were an electric green that seemed to create an energy of their own. They could have powered every generator in the underground facility and still singed our skin if they turned our way. Though he would never look our way; he was bored even with the exalted company he was keeping, as his slouching posture and half-sneering expression attested.

"Oh, my," I said comically, and gave Janet Ayerson another rueful smile. Again, she returned my expression and gave a little nod. Not much more we could say in front of Ameletta, but our glances spoke volumes. "With that so near at hand, one wonders what the attraction is for Miss Ingersoll in other quarters."

"I have often thought the same thing," Miss Ayerson replied.

The other two men in the party had passed under my camera view before I had gotten much chance to study them. They appeared good-natured enough, if not particularly intelligent, and I would have had a hard time telling them apart without a little study. Both were fair-haired and fair-skinned, athletic, well-cared for, smiling. More than that I could not determine.

"Well! And this is the company we shall be keeping this evening!" I said as I turned back to my fellow watchers once the parade was over. "Offhand, I cannot think of a single thing I could have to say that would interest any of them in the slightest."

"You need not worry—they will talk to each other and not realize you are at the table," Miss Ayerson said with a touch more dryness than she was used to exhibiting. "Mr. Ravenbeck will from time to time address a remark to you, to let you know that he at least realizes you are a human being, and you will answer, and then you will become invisible again. But it is still entertaining to listen to them talk and, later, to play games. I would not miss it."

"Oh, no!" Ameletta breathed. "I would not miss it for the world!"

I would have gladly missed it—except a certain perversity of spirit had cropped up in me as the afternoon had worn on and told me that I *should* attend this dinner, attend it, enjoy it, and learn from it. If I truly believed I was as good as any other man or woman at the table—if my religion and my philosophies were not to fail me at some more critical juncture in my life—then I needed to prove it to myself and not shy away from a convivial evening because of wholly unmerited feelings of inferiority. I might not be Bianca Ingersoll's equal in looks, live-liness, or social standing, but I was willing to bet my intellect surpassed hers. And I could match her, atom for atom and soul for soul, on the Great Mother's delicate scales, and I would not be found wanting.

Miss Ayerson and I had agreed that she and Ameletta and I would go down to dinner together so that we could provide one another other moral and physical support. Accordingly, I dressed in my gray silk suit and set a small pearl barrette in my hair and then waited patiently in my room for the knock to fall on the door. It came precisely at the agreed-upon hour.

I opened it to find Ameletta, as expected, in her pearl and ivory dress, her blond hair caught in a butterfly flurry of ribbons. But Janet Ayerson looked as I had never seen her look before. Gone was the quiet, scarcely noticeable black tunic; in its place was an embroidered crimson jacket over a long, pleated silk skirt of the same color, and on her pale face she had brushed the lightest combination of cosmetics.

"Janet!" I exclaimed, startled into using her given name, though she had been experimenting with mine for the past few days. "You look magnificent!"

She looked self-conscious as well, but I could tell my genuine approval pleased her. "Hardly that," she said, with a semblance of her usual calm. "But it is the best I could do. You look very nice as well."

"I look *dreadful*," I said with a grimace. "But I am glad one of us at least shows some elegance. Ameletta, you look charming. How pretty your hair is!"

"Miss Ayerson styled it for me," she replied. "Oh, please, can we hurry downstairs?"

Janet and I laughed, and we made some haste as we went down the hallway and the main stairwell. The group was to gather in a midsize drawing room adjacent to the formal dining room so that we could all go in to dinner together. Not surprisingly, my party was the first to arrive. Janet convinced Ameletta to sit quietly beside her on a pretty little love seat and practice the words to a poem she had been taught, as a way to distract the girl from impatience. I wandered idly through the room, inspecting the art on the walls as if I had never seen the prints before.

Thus we were separated by the width of the room when the first of the grand visitors arrived. Mrs. Ingersoll and her daughter Melanie swept in together, followed by Mr. Fulsome and Mr. Taff. I turned to greet them, and Janet and Ameletta came to their feet, but we might have been pieces of animatronic sculpture for all the heed they paid to us.

"My dearest, it is not worth worrying about. You shall have the surgery done, and you will be recovered by the Dominion Ball, and it will not matter at all," Mrs. Ingersoll was saying to her daughter. The two looked like a study in the life cycle of a rose, for Melanie wore a bright fuschia dress, short and sparkly, and her mother wore the same color, several degrees paler, in soft pleated folds like discarded petals.

"But, Mother, if I have the surgery even next *week* I shall still have a swollen face by the time of the ball and I cannot possibly go out in public looking like that."

"Have it after the ball, then. The bump is so small, no one will notice—"

"What, that little nudger on your left nostril? I didn't notice a thing till Bianca mentioned it to me," was the gallant remark of the man I had decided was Mr. Taff.

Melanie whirled on him with a muffled shriek. "Bianca *told* you about it? What did she *say*? Oh, that spiteful cat—"

"Just that you weren't satisfied with the work at the Roberson Clinic. She thought the doctors were inferior and the PhysiChambers substandard. I'm thinking of having a little mole removed myself," he added by way of extenuation, "and she just thought it would help me decide between that and the Hopeton Clinic."

Melanie had her hand over her nose, where the offending knot was located. "Oh, if she told you, she told all of you—I'm so embarrassed—"

"Nothing at all to be embarrassed about," spoke up Mr. Fulsome. "Had a scar bleached out just last year. Best thing I ever did. Right under my hairline. Couldn't run a comb through my hair without shuddering—never liked to be out anywhere I might encounter a strong wind, for fear my hair would rise and the scar would show."

I glanced at Melanie for signs of a laugh, for this sounded like a joke to me, but she looked neither amused nor distracted. "I'm going to kill her, Mother, I swear I will."

Her mother patted her absently on the shoulder. "Nonsense, sweetheart, she wasn't trying to make you look ridiculous. You're so sensitive, Melanie. You shouldn't let things affect you so."

Mr. Fulsome had strolled over to the rose-girl's side and was pulling up the fall of hair that laid a romantic blonde patch across his forehead. "See? Well, of course, can't see a thing now because nothing *to* see. All gone. Man was a genius."

Melanie turned away, but Mr. Taff came over to inspect the site. "Really? Where'd you have it done? I've this little—it's a nothing, really, this mole, there by my ear—can you see it?—I've thought for ages about having it removed."

Mr. Fulsome dutifully glanced behind the other man's ear. "Oh! That! Yes, sort of thing you'd want to get rid of eventually."

"And you went where? Roberson? Hopeton?"

"No, a new place, on Brierly. Combination spa-surgical facility-recreational place. Athletic leagues and so on. There nearly a month, liked it so much. Try it."

I could not help noticing that Mr. Fulsome dropped his articles and predicates from his speech with some regularity, almost as if he was too lazy to form the words "you" and "I" and "the." But this laziness paled beside the triflingness of their very lives, that they could spend so much time discussing the merest of vanities as if there were no more important matters in the world.

Melanie flounced over to the other side of the room, her arms crossed and her pretty face drawn into a sulky frown. "Well, I don't want to go to any spa on Brierly," she said. "*I* like the Roberson Clinic, and that's where *I* shall go, and I hope Bianca gets all sorts of warts and moles and ugly things all over her face and no one thinks her pretty anymore."

This was a speech worthy of Ameletta, but I was astonished to hear it uttered by a grown woman, in the presence of her mother (who should have taught her better) and two eligible young men (whom I would expect her to be trying to impress, not disgust). Yet no one in the room except me seemed embarrassed for her. Except perhaps Janet Ayerson, and so many people separated us that I could not see her face.

The next two people to arrive were Bianca Ingersoll and Mr. Ravenbeck, who must have met on the way from their not-quite-separate-enough bedrooms. Once again, she entered the room on the arm of the master, her arm linked through his so casually it was as if she did not notice she was tethered to a package of male energy. I could not imagine ever touching this man without a sense of caution and portent; I did not think I could ever overlook his combustibility.

"Oh, are we late?" Bianca Ingersoll sang out, and her voice matched her countenance, so full was it of silver and luxury. "I was afraid I would be the last one down, as I so often am, but no, here was Everett, leaving his room just as I was."

"Ah, but I was delayed by business, and you were delayed by vanity," Mr. Ravenbeck said. The light tone made it unlikely that this was an actual rebuke, though I would not have liked to have had such a thing said to me, however gaily. "Thus my behavior is excusable and yours is merely rude."

"Oh, you cruel man!" Bianca Ingersoll cried, but in such exaggerated tones that it was clear she was flirting, not protesting. "Mother, call for the aircar. I will not stay even for one dinner in a house where I am being insulted."

Mr. Ravenbeck resecured her hand, which she had snatched away from him, and planted a solemn kiss on her knuckles. "And yet the result you have achieved is so perfect that I cannot but forgive the rudeness," he added. "I would not have had you ready one second earlier if it would have detracted by one iota from your beauty."

There was a general laugh from the assembled company—half laugh, I amend, and half sigh at the really quite exaggerated compliment. I did not think I would like something so patently insincere to be said to me either, but Bianca Ingersoll seemed to accept such heavy-handed gallantry as her due. And, in fact, she was quite stunning, dressed as she was in a strapless, floor-length gown of emerald silk, with that frothing blonde hair trained to run over one shoulder and down the front of her dress like a cascade of spidery lace.

"Well, she can have dawdled as long as she likes beautifying herself, but she's still not the last one down," Mr. Taff commented. "Luxton hasn't made his appearance, so we still can't sit down to eat."

A quick frown pulled down Miss Ingersoll's faint, delicate brows; I supposed she had planned to make the final appearance of the evening and did not like to be beaten out for that honor.

"And as he has neither business nor beauty to delay him, we must ascribe his sole motivation to discourtesy," Mr. Ravenbeck said. "So let us vilify him one and all when he makes his way into our presence."

They had not long to wait before falling in with this admirable plan, for almost as the words left Mr. Ravenbeck's mouth, the handsome Mr. Luxton slouched in. If possible, he looked even more attractive than he had on the security monitor that afternoon, for he exuded an almost feral charisma that was both mesmerizing and seductive. He was dressed all in black, which emphasized both his extraordinary green eyes and his dark complexion, and his arrogant cheekbones tilted back in surprise when his entrance was greeted with howls of derision and disapproval.

"That's a strange reception. I thought I was welcome here," he said in a sleepy, drawling speech whose rhythms were infinitely attractive. "Shall I go away again?"

I thought it strange that fully one third of Mr. Ravenbeck's guests had, in a few short minutes, offered to leave before their first meal was ever served; but he, like Bianca, was not serious.

"Our disapproval stems from our hunger, and not your existence," Mr. Ravenbeck explained. "You have kept us waiting and we cannot love you for that."

"Surely Bianca is still behind me," Luxton said in that lazy voice. "I can't have held you up at all." A movement of that blonde head caught his attention, and he let loose a low, irresistible laugh. "Oho, I see she has arrived on the scene already! Why so eager, Bianca? You must find the company extraordinarily agreeable."

He was smiling, though rather unpleasantly, and she was frowning, and I had to wonder what sort of ill will existed between the Ingersoll heiress and this gorgeous man. A little jealousy, perhaps? For Mrs. Farraday had distinctly told us that the Ingersolls had already been entertaining guests when they decided to journey to Thorrastone Park. Perhaps Mr. Luxton had come wooing and his suit had appeared to prosper until Mr. Ravenbeck made his reappearance on the scene.

Not that I would ever know any of it.

Miss Ingersoll did not bother to reply to Mr. Luxton's comment, but merely turned her back on him. "I believe we are all assembled," she said. "Shall we go in to dinner?"

"Certainly, but first let me make you known to a few of the members of my household who will be joining us tonight," Mr. Ravenbeck said. "Mrs. Farraday I believe is already in the dining room, making sure the china does not slide to the floor while we are engaged in conversation elsewhere. And you have all met her on many occasions. Also, I believe some of you are familiar with my ward, Ameletta."

At that, Ameletta skipped forward out of the shadows, a little dancing moonbeam of a girl. She was too cowed by her company to indulge in her usual chatter, but she was smiling like summer itself as she held out her hand to Bianca Ingersoll.

"But of course! The charming child I spent such a delightful day with the last time you were on Fieldstar!" Bianca exclaimed. She bent down to give Ameletta an airy kiss on the cheek. "Don't you look beautiful tonight, Ameletta! How lovely to see you again."

Ameletta pirouetted to give the whole company a chance to glimpse her face, and the others nodded or smiled or waved as the mood took them. "And Miss Ayerson, her tutor," Mr. Ravenbeck continued, motioning Janet to step forward.

She did so, laying her hand unobtrusively on Ameletta's shoulder, as if to contain the child by the weight of her own presence. But I knew better; I knew she was using Ameletta as an anchor, and I wished I was standing close enough to grasp even such a frail savior myself. The women gave her the most cursory of looks, then dismissed her, but the men all smiled more enthusiastically than they had at Ameletta. Even the indifferent Mr. Luxton let his emerald gaze linger for a moment or two on the tall, crimson-robed figure standing so quietly in the center of the room.

"And Miss Starborn, our nuclear technician," Mr. Ravenbeck said finally. I forced myself to take one step away from the wall so that the others could, by my movement, locate me. I knew otherwise they would not have been able to make out my indeterminate shape and color. Bianca and Melanie Ingersoll and their mother brushed their glances across my face and looked elsewhere; Taff and Fulsome nodded brusquely; but Luxton held my gaze for an electrifying moment that reminded me, even if briefly, that I was alive and female. It was one of the most peculiar, though shortest-lived, moments of my life.

"Very well, now that we are all friends, let us go in for dinner," Mr. Ravenbeck said. We all turned in one body toward the door, and I followed Mr. Fulsome's blonde head into the other room.

Mrs. Farraday was already fluttering about the guests, directing each of us to our seats and dropping an absentminded kiss on Ameletta's head. Not to my surprise, I found that Mrs. Farraday, Janet, Ameletta, and I were grouped together at the foot of the table, while the more exalted guests were ranged toward the head of the table, closer to Mr. Ravenbeck. Large centerpieces of flowers and ivy had been strategically placed between those of us on the lower half of the table and those on the upper, so that it was hard to peer through the foliage. Thus the half-citizens and less desirable residents would be present but invisible. I wondered if the arrangement had been Mrs. Farraday's idea or Mr. Ravenbeck's.

Conversation was desultory as we waited for Rinda and Mary to bring out the first course. From much browsing over the StellarNet, I was familiar enough with the news of the day to have followed any conversation about current events, but most of their talk consisted of idle chatter about people and social venues that were mysteries to me. Many of the observations about absent friends were rather slyly spoken and elicited muffled or outright laughter. It occurred to me I would not want to be an acquaintance of any of these people and missing from one of their congregations, for to have my character so blithely blackened seemed disagreeable in the extreme.

Eventually, the meal commenced as Mary and Rinda brought out platters of steaming vegetables. We always had decent meals at the manor, but for this evening, Mrs. Farraday and the cook had assembled a truly magnificent repast. Courses of salads, meats, pastas, and fruits followed the first one, and a fine array of desserts capped off our culinary adventure. I knew better, but I could not stop myself from sampling portions of every dish, and eating till I literally thought my body would explode. Everything was so good! And I was not used to indulgence. I ate, and was sorry for it, but ate again.

The four of us situated below the greenery did not make much attempt to talk to one another, though Ameletta did crane her neck

almost continually, trying to get a glimpse of the faces on the other side
of the dividers. Most of Janet Ayerson's conversation consisted of low
admonitions to the young girl, telling her to be still, sit quietly, eat some
more of her carrots, did she want to spill chocolate on her dress? Mrs.
Farraday, though she filled her plate several times, seemed always to be
straining toward the kitchen, awaiting the sounds of some disaster
unfolding just beyond the door. Yet nothing untoward occurred.

It must have taken us two hours to finish our meal in a leisurely fashion. I was relieved when Mr. Ravenbeck finally put down his fork and
exclaimed, "Well! That was a splendid example of the advantages of
modern civilization! An excellent dinner, Mrs. Farraday. Thank you so
much for putting it together."

The other guests murmured vague thanks, glancing through the
leaves in her direction and looking quickly away. Mrs. Farraday
appeared flustered but delighted. "Oh—no trouble—well, I'm so
pleased that you enjoyed it. Thank you, yes, thank you."

*Good. Now it is time for us all to separate, my confederates and I to
go up to our rooms, and Mr. Ravenbeck and his guests to indulge in
some other pursuits.* This was my innocent thought as the meal came to
its close; imagine what dismay I felt in the next few minutes!

Mr. Ravenbeck came to his feet and glanced down at his guests. "So!
Taff, I understand you are quite a hand at SpaceShot," he said. "Miss
Ingersoll tells me you and she have played every week for six months
and she has never bested you."

SpaceShot was an electronic game played over computer terminal
screens, and many of the students at Lora Tech had been proficient at it.
Not one to have much interest in games, I had never attempted to play
it, but my students assured me it could be quite thrilling.

"I'm a master of the sport!" Taff replied, smiling enough to make the
immodest boast less annoying. "I'll challenge any of you to beat me at
the game."

"SpaceShot? That's *my* best game," Luxton said in his dreamy voice.
"I'll take you on."

"Oh, such fun for the rest of us," Bianca said with a little pout.
"Watching the two of you shoot imaginary torpedoes at each other."

"We'll play teams," Mr. Ravenbeck said. "I ordered the upgraded version the other day. Four players to a screen. I am assured the action is much faster and the kills more satisfying."

Everyone laughed except Janet Ayerson and me. We were staring at each other in dawning horror as a quick review of the company present, combined with the most rudimentary mathematical exercises, warned us who might be asked to play on these teams.

"But we don't have enough people to fill your crews," Mr. Fulsome complained. "For you don't have to tell me that Mrs. Ingersoll does not excel at simulation games—"

"Oh! Don't be ridiculous," that lady said in rather sharp accents. "I'd rather be thrown alive into the vacuum than attempt to learn something so pointless."

"Well, then. Can we play three to a team?" Taff inquired. "Each lady to serve as captain and choose her men?"

"I would be happy to take the role of captain," Bianca Ingersoll said with purring satisfaction. "May I punish any of my crew members who do not perform to my standards?"

"Only if you reward those crew members who exceed them," Luxton said. "Though I have to admit, you are handier with a rebuke than a reward."

"One is merited so much more often than the other," the beauty replied.

"Well, that settles it, you two cannot play on a team," Mr. Taff said merrily. "Melanie, will you be captain and choose your men? For it looks like we will have one girl and two boys to each side."

"I am perfectly willing to be captain if I am not expected to play very well," Melanie said with a coquettish smile. "And surely I may be allowed to be decorative if I am only one of two?"

"But we have four ladies," Mr. Ravenbeck said. On his feet, he was tall enough to see over the greenery, and his eyes, wickedly mocking, were fixed on mine. "Miss Ayerson and Miss Starborn would both be pleased to play."

"Oh! Of course. Tutor and technician," Mr. Fulsome said, looking around in some bewilderment, as if he had forgotten exactly where we had been placed. "Can't believe you slipped my mind. Happy to play on any team they're on."

Melanie looked less than pleased, and Bianca actually raised her eyebrows. "But, Everett, surely they are not interested in wasting their time on such frivolity?" she asked. "And perhaps they are not familiar with the game and would find it embarrassing to try to play in front of strangers."

"They could hardly be any worse at it than you and Melanie," Mr. Ravenbeck said cheerfully. "You forget, I've seen you play. Come! Miss Ayerson! Miss Starborn! On your feet, and come join us."

Predictably, Ameletta had jumped up before either of us had moved a muscle. "Oh, Mr. Ravenbeck! May I play too? I am ever so good at SpaceShot—Miss Ayerson and I play it all the time!"

This was news to me, but the dread on Janet Ayerson's face intensified to such a degree that I realized it was true, and that she would now be expected to perform with some skill on her team. Mr. Ravenbeck laughed and held his arms out in a welcoming gesture.

"You can play on my team—you shall be my hands some of the time," he said, as she hurried down the length of the table to hurl herself into his arms. "Will that be good enough?"

"But, Everett," Bianca Ingersoll said in a rather dangerous voice. "A *child*? Are you sure? And your friends have not said they would actually like to join us."

"I want them to join us, and that should be good enough for them—and for all of you," he replied. He spoke smilingly, but there was a certain stubbornness in his delivery that made Bianca Ingersoll draw back slightly in her chair. "Come! Let us repair to the library. The games have already been set up."

Everyone stood, some of us more slowly than others, and in a ragged group began to make our way to the appointed room. Mrs. Farraday had bustled off to the kitchen before Janet and I had gone more than a few steps, and I turned to my fellow sufferer with a look of marveling apprehension.

"Can this really be happening? Is there no way to refuse?" I asked.

She shook her head. Her cheeks were pale, but the smallest smile was beginning to work its way across her face. "He believes it is a treat for us—a rare privilege—to be allowed to socialize with citizens as equals," she said. Myself, I doubted the purity of his motives, but I didn't like to say so. "It would hurt his feelings for you to reject this offer. You cannot disappoint him."

"Then quickly tell me the rules, for I have never tried my hand at this or any similar game."

"Well, I have not played the expanded version, but it cannot be much different. There will be two screens, and to each screen, I assume, will be attached four consoles, each player to be assigned to a console. It is a role-playing game that simulates a space battle, so you will be, perhaps, the second gunman, with the ability to shoot torpedoes in a certain range. You only have a finite amount of ammunition, and if you do not spend it wisely, you will not be able to protect your side of the ship when the battle becomes fierce, so hold your fire until you have a clear shot."

"But—how pointless and inane!" I exclaimed. "Why would anyone enjoy such a pastime?"

Janet smiled more widely now. "Well, the screens are very realistic, and the sound effects are remarkable. And I must say it can be exhilarating to be the winner and watch your opponent's ship explode. But is there any intrinsic social, moral, or intellectual virtue to this game? None whatsoever. I cannot imagine you will enjoy yourself at all."

I was about to retort that I could not imagine she had ever passed any time in such a diversion, as Ameletta had claimed she had, but we had by this time made our way to the library, where the rest of the company had already assembled. And, as we learned in minutes, divided into teams.

"Ah, Miss Ayerson! Arrived in good time!" was Mr. Ravenbeck's greeting as we entered the room. "You are to play on the team with me, Joseph Luxton, and Bianca Ingersoll. Miss Starborn, the others are to be your companions. Quickly, now, we are all grown impatient."

Before joining my crewmates, I took a moment to assess the setup of the game. The library had been transformed into the mirror images of two starship command centers. Each ship bridge consisted of one over-size monitor, perhaps fifty inches in diameter, with an array of authentic-looking consoles laid before it. Each console contained a keyboard, a joystick, a bank of blinking lights, and a variety of sound mikes and headphones that might have been merely props to add to the air of realism. Before each console was a highly ergonomic chair, such as I imagined ship's captains to find comfortable for a long space journey. All the other members of my team were already seated in their assigned places.

"Miss Starborn! Come quickly!" Mr. Taff called, waving me over. "We are ready to begin."

"Been ready for a long time," Mr. Fulsome observed. My captain said nothing, just gave me one quick sulky glance. It occurred to me that my team consisted of all the least colorful, least dramatic individuals of the octet; Bianca overmatched her sister in both impact and intelligence, while Miss Ayerson was far more brilliant than I this evening. And there was no question that both Everett Ravenbeck and Joseph Luxton had much more personality than either Mr. Taff or Mr. Fulsome. I did not see much hope for my team to overwhelm the other.

Nonetheless, I hurried over and seated myself just to the right of Mr. Taff. I was amused to learn that I must buckle myself into my chair, as if to prevent myself from being dashed to the ground by a stray blast of laser fire. A quick review of the command board revealed that its functions were obvious even for a novice—this button called up the protective shield, this button retracted it, this button loosed the weaponry. I assumed I could not fire through the shield, and a quick whispered question to Mr. Taff confirmed this.

"And don't worry about navigation—Melanie will handle that part as captain," he added. In fact, I had not given navigation a thought, but I supposed this meant she would be responsible for trying to weave us through the hazardous channels of imaginary space. I did not expect she would do a very good job of it.

"Are we all ready?" Mr. Ravenbeck demanded. Ameletta, seated on his lap, bounced with impatience. Bianca Ingersoll, next to him, gave him one long, languid look before returning her attention to her screen. Mr. Ravenbeck continued, "Miss Ayerson, you are strapped in? Miss Starborn, you are acquainted with your equipment? Very well! Mrs. Ingersoll, will you give the order to commence?"

Mrs. Ingersoll, ensconced in a chair with a book open before her, seemed taken by surprise. "Oh! Me? Oh, very well. Let your silly game begin!"

It all began to unfold very quickly after that. Within minutes, the air was filled with the sounds of battle—or at least, the sounds that one might expect to hear aboard a ship which had just been fired upon. A siren blast nearly split my ears, and the clatter of doors slamming and footsteps running and voices shouting out cries of warning nearly made me leap from my chair and run for the door to see who was outside raising the alarm. I realized I must focus more completely than that. I concentrated on the story being enacted on the large screen—an armed spaceship, heading our way—then checked that against the individual grid laid out on my console. Ah, now I understood. The three-dimensional grid highlighted areas of the enemy ship that were vulnerable to the firepower in my particular weapons. The numerical displays flashing on my monitors must be estimates of time needed to elapse before my missiles could be expected to hit home, and the percentage chance I had of making the shot. As the oncoming ship shifted and altered course on the photorealistic screen, my numbers fluctuated in response. Our own position in space, as determined by Melanie's unsteady hands, must also be affecting my ratios.

Well, this seemed clear enough. Janet had warned me not to waste firepower, so I should wait till my numbers made my position look advantageous, and then attempt to destroy my enemy.

Consequently, I resisted any—very faint—impulse to fire while I listened to the energetic banter of the players around me. My team members seemed to be dropping shields and firing at a reckless pace, though I could not see that they had achieved any damage, and they cried out encouragement to one another with every shot fired. Mr. Ravenbeck and Mr. Luxton also seemed to be busily engaged in attempting to attack us, for Ameletta was frantically pushing buttons at Mr. Ravenbeck's behest, and Mr. Luxton was calling advice to Bianca Ingersoll in a very excited tone of voice. Bianca herself was tightly gripping her steering mechanisms, and her eyes were so focused on the image on the screen that she seemed to have no attention for anyone in the room. She was busy maneuvering her craft into a position that would allow her guns to annihilate us.

"Miss Starborn! You haven't fired a single weapon!" Mr. Taff's voice sounded with some agitation over the renewed looping of the siren. "Don't you understand the equipment?"

"I have not gotten a clear shot," I explained.

"No! And you will not! You can only hope to do a little damage and wear them down! Really, you must do your part or the game will be over in fifteen minutes."

"Well, I'm doing my best," I said, and to placate him, I loosed a bolt that clearly had no hope of achieving any damage. It hit its mark, however, and caused the oncoming ship to hesitate a moment, and Mr. Taff gave me a wide smile.

"You see?" he cried. "Very good!"

I shrugged and settled back into my chair, my eyes flicking between my readouts and the large screen. Once or twice in the next twenty minutes, I thought I saw an opening and I hazarded some of my firepower, always with at least a little effect. I did not fire as frequently or as enthusiastically as my teammates, however, or as often as my adversaries, who seemed prepared to empty their whole guns on us in one frenetic maneuver. Stifling a yawn, I wondered to myself how long this particular engagement should be expected to endure, and what would be the next entertainment when it was over.

So distracted, I was unprepared for the sudden loud *boom*! that came seconds later, a noise so great that it literally rocked us in our chairs and caused several of the ladies to scream. The initial bewilderment was followed by a series of shrieks from Melanie as she tried to right our ship, which had been blown disastrously off course by a well-aimed missile. Around me, my fellow gunnars were throwing their shields back up and shouting encouragement to our captain. Across from me, howls of victory and congratulations were being tossed about by Mr. Luxton, Mr. Ravenbeck, Bianca Ingersoll, and Janet. Mr. Ravenbeck even leaned over Ameletta to slap Mr. Luxton vigorously on the back.

My teammates were frantically calling out status reports—"Shields very low, only fifteen percent." "Guns almost exhausted, two rounds left."—without bothering to ask me what my capabilities still were. Meanwhile, our disabled ship drifted in a wide arc toward the opponent, which, on my screen, showed a whole unprotected grid that was vulnerable to my attack. Shrugging again, I dialed my power up to maximum and fired.

The noise was astonishing. I have never, indoors, heard anything so loud and so frightening. Glasses rattled on the table and books tumbled from their shelves. The lights flickered—or perhaps my eyes dimmed from the terrific pressure exerted against my skull. I would not have been surprised to learn the forcefield was briefly compromised, or destroyed altogether.

A profound silence followed in its wake, broken only by the small whimpering sounds of somebody crying. As if recovering from a dreadful tragedy, the people in the room straightened in their chairs, looked dazedly around them, and began to ask one another quietly if they were all right.

"Lord of all the suns and planets," Mr. Taff swore, recovering his company voice sooner than any of the rest of us. "What in the seven hells was *that*?"

A sudden babble of voices rose as everyone talked, asked, and explained at once—till the slow, infectious sound of Mr. Ravenbeck's laughter broke through the talk. He was pointing across the room at Melanie's screen, where the burning hulk of Bianca's ship could be seen cartwheeling into a starry distance.

"I believe we have been outgunned, my friends!" he cried. "Taken unawares when victory was in our grasp, and blasted from the sky. My congratulations to the enemy! Who on your team was patient enough to save nearly every ounce of firepower for this surprise final attack?"

I preserved a discreet silence, but Mr. Taff instantly bent an accusing glance my way, and soon everyone in the room was staring at me. I folded my hands in my lap.

"Did I do something wrong?" I inquired.

Mr. Ravenbeck laughed again, though everyone else on his team was scowling. My cohorts, however, were beginning to chuckle and grin, as it became clear to them that we had actually won the encounter.

"Not at all! Very good strategy!" Mr. Fulsome approved. "Wait till the very last. Won't know what hit them."

"I thought you had never played this game before," Bianca said coldly.

"I haven't. I was merely trying to make sense of it."

"And a splendid job you did!" Mr. Taff said. "Let's play again, Everett, and keep the same teams."

Bianca stood up so quickly her chair spun. "I think not," she said, still in that frigid voice. "The—excessive—enthusiasm of Miss Starborn's attack has given me a headache. I don't believe I could bear such a great noise one more time in the same evening."

"Well, we'll play teams of three, then," Mr. Taff suggested. "Melanie, you'd like to sit out a round, wouldn't you?"

Melanie gave him a look every bit as frosty as one her sister might muster. "I will play as long as anyone else does," she said.

Mr. Ravenbeck was on his feet too, gently setting Ameletta on hers. "No, no, I quite agree with Bianca. That was plenty of excitement for one evening. Besides, I don't think we could ever best that level of playing. Let's turn to simpler entertainments."

Whatever these were to be, they required the company to redispose itself around the room. The Ingersoll sisters found seats near their mother, while Mr. Ravenbeck and Mr. Fulsome leaned against the wall near the women. A few stalwarts stayed seated at their consoles, fiddling with the dials or playing back the readouts to see where they had gone wrong. At least, that appeared to be Mr. Taff's activity. Mr. Luxton and Janet Ayerson stayed seated, carrying on a quiet, if what appeared to be somewhat stilted, conversation. I had risen to my feet but now stood indecisively, not sure where to position myself. Unobtrusively, picking up fallen books and knickknacks, I moved away from the group and closer to the door.

"What shall it be?" Mr. Ravenbeck was asking. "We can play Continents and Capitals for those who think they know their current history.

Or there's a very good trivia game I subscribed to the other day—we can access it here on the library monitor."

"Or we could take turns traipsing down to the PhysiChamber for comforting massages," Bianca retorted. "I think I need something to soothe my nerves."

"Will a glass of wine aid you there?" Mr. Ravenbeck asked. "Or something more unusual? I was on Corbramb last month, you know, and I picked up a case of sweet redbark."

That caused Mr. Taff to look up from his calculations. "Redbark? Really? I've been wanting to try some for ages, but I couldn't find any-one who would handle the shipping."

The others in the room added their approval to this plan. I edged closer to the door. Even less than playing pointless aggressive military games was I interested in sampling the dangerous, potent liquors of one of the most decadent planets in the star system. Two more steps, another book retrieved from the floor and replaced on its shelf, three more steps, a glance around—and I melted through the door.

Reprieved from near damnation!

I had not gone half a dozen steps down the hall, however, when I heard quick footsteps behind and whirled around to see who approached. It was Mr. Ravenbeck, headed toward the cellar for his liquor, but making a quick detour to confront me in the corridor.

"Miss Starborn! But where are you going? The evening is not half over yet, with many treats still in store."

He came so close so rapidly that I felt a moment's panic, like a small furry animal cornered by a bird of prey. It had been five days since I had seen him, and our last solitary encounter had been strange, wonderful, charged with tension . . . and a half-cit's foolish imaginings. I had not known what I would say when I would see him again—but I had not known I would see him as a member of a frivolous, socially superior party, where I had no right to be, and no interest either.

"I find myself in agreement with Miss Bianca Ingersoll," I said steadily, over the stupidly rapid beating of my heart. "The noise of the game has given me a headache, and I cannot think sweet redbark wine will have anything but an adverse effect on me."

"You are merely tired of the company," he said, unimpressed. "You find them shallow and exhausting, and you do not want to waste any of your valuable time trying to sort them out."

I forced a smile, though I was surprised to hear him so exactly put my thoughts into words. "Even if I felt that way, I would not say so, and neither should you," I said. "They are your guests—you should treat them with respect even when they cannot overhear you."

"That's my Jenna," he said admiringly. "Never missing an opportunity to correct me or put me in the wrong! But if I must respect them, so must you! Come back and do them honor with your presence."

"They are not *my* guests," I pointed out. "I would not have invited them. If I were looking for congenial company, I would have limited myself to—" I snapped my mouth shut on the words.

"To whom?" he demanded, pouncing on my unfinished sentence. "To—Mrs. Farraday and Janet Ayerson? Or perhaps you would include Mr. Taff? He seemed to speak to you agreeably enough during your recent battle. Or even Joseph Luxton? He has a face all the women adore, or so I've been told. Do you agree? Is he a handsome man?"

"I don't think anyone could dispute that, sir," I said frankly.

My answer clearly surprised him. He seemed to have expected a negative or, at the least, an equivocation. "Hunh," he grunted, eying me with a touch of disfavor. "And how would you describe me? As a very unhandsome man? A dark, glowering sort with irregular features that are not in the exact exquisite proportions?"

I could not help a small smile from forming on my face. "As I understand it, such imperfections can be readily corrected by surgeons in clinics on several nearby worlds," I said helpfully. "Melanie Ingersoll and Mr. Taff had an extended conversation on that topic just this evening."

"Hunh!" he said again, even more forcefully, even less delighted at my reply, for he surely thought I would take that occasion to compliment his looks or at least his personality. But I was not happy with his treatment of me this evening, and I saw no reason to please him with my behavior. "That's answered me very well, I think! Just don't ask me for any valuation of your assets in the future, for I might be disposed to respond in kind."

"I never ask questions unless I want a true answer," I said calmly. "And I only seek an opinion when I value the person who might give it. I have a very clear picture of my face, my figure, my intellect, and my other 'assets,' as you call them. I do not need you to point out my flaws in order to become aware of them."

Now his face softened, and he watched me with something like warmth in those dark eyes. "I would not necessarily be cataloging your flaws—unless you had just done something to irritate me," he amended. "I could list your virtues as easily."

I knew I should not say it, but I did anyway: "Then someday you shall do so," I said. "Not here and now, however."

"No, for I—" he began, but was interrupted by the sound of a door opening behind us.

"Everett? Are you still talking in the hallway?" called the voice of Bianca Ingersoll. "The wastrels are getting restless and questioning the very existence of your promised treat."

"In a moment! A little problem to clear up here."

"Well—do hurry. I don't know how long I can placate them," she said, and withdrew into the library.

Grinning, I had turned to leave, but he shifted position to block my escape. "Your ordeal is not yet ended, Jenna Starborn, nuclear technician," he said, leaning forward just enough to let me know he intended intimidation. Yet he was smiling, so I was not alarmed. "While my guests are here, I expect you to join us in the evenings for dinner and such amusements as we are able to agree upon."

"I cannot imagine that my presence will significantly add to anyone else's enjoyment of the evening, and it certainly will not add to mine," I said rather boldly. "I wish you would excuse me."

"It may serve to educate you about how little you need to envy those who, by the law of society, may be considered more exalted than you, or at least more fortunate," he said.

"I do not envy them even now."

"And it may serve to educate them about the quick wit and resourcefulness of those they are used to considering inferior," he said, grinning now. "I refer of course to your brilliant and audacious use of weaponry in our late military encounter."

"Such education cannot serve to endear me to them, however, so their enjoyment of my company is likely to be even more impaired."

"I, however, will enjoy your presence at these gatherings," he said decisively. "And that should be reason enough for you to attend."

I made a brief deferential nod of my head. "Very well. I shall do as you ask. I will not participate in any more games, however, but will merely sit quietly observing the foibles of you and your guests. Will that content you?"

"It will do perfectly," he said, and without another word, turned and strode toward the cellar.

I stared after him a moment, then shook my head in amazement. An abrupt, changeable, difficult, and altogether unpredictable man—and yet he fascinated me. Merely to be in the same room with him—to see his live flame ignite the slumbering souls of the ridiculous creatures he chose to surround himself with—made my own soul catch fire. I would join their revels, as he asked, since he asked it of me. Even though I must watch his flirtation with the cold, gorgeous Bianca Ingersoll, still I might watch him; and fool that I was, this seemed a treat and a blessing to me.

All of this I recorded in my diary, every word that I could remember, every impression of the evening. "Oh, Reeder," I whispered as I concluded, "with no encouragement at all, I could fall in love with this man."

Chapter 7

✧

The next few days passed in similar, though rather less spectacular, fashion. During the days, I managed to keep mostly clear of the grand company, adjusting the generators in the basement and only circling the lawns when I was fairly certain the others were not outside. They were not the athletic sorts who would engage in some kind of energetic outdoor play—at least the ladies were not—so I only had to worry about encountering them as they assembled for some excursion elsewhere—to town, for instance. This they did almost every afternoon, for they were easily bored and the amusements offered at Thorrastone Park were relatively limited. Once or twice I caught a glimpse of their Strattens and Vandeventers leaving or arriving, but I was always far enough away that I did not even need to wave.

In the evenings, we had dinner followed by some sort of electronic entertainment. One night, Mr. Ravenbeck showed a holofilm in the library and we all crowded in to watch. It was some paltry romance which made the women sigh and the men groan; I did not think it very worth watching, but at least it obviated the possibility of any interaction with Mr. Ravenbeck's guests, and that made it a welcome diversion to me. I appeared to be the only member of the female sex who found it silly, however, for I discovered Mrs. Farraday and Janet Ayerson in tears once the room lights came back on, and even Ameletta seemed moved by the story. The Ingersoll women, of course, were all openly sobbing, Bianca Ingersoll leaning on Mr. Ravenbeck's chest to do so. Melanie Ingersoll was wiping her eyes and hunting frantically in her pockets for a tissue, when Joseph Luxton came to his feet, pulling a handkerchief from the back recesses of his jacket. I saw Melanie form a pretty look of gratitude on her face, but she was unable to bestow it upon Mr. Luxton—for he stepped past her to offer the cloth to Janet.

"Crying over something like this," he said in his sleepy, seductive voice. He softened the words with a smile. "I would think there would be so much else to cry over."

My thoughts entirely. Certainly Janet instantly wished she had been able to contain her emotion, for suddenly she was the cynosure of all eyes. The handsomest man in the room showing a slight kindness to one of the most invisible females in the manor? It was almost shocking. Even I felt a moment's disapprobation, and I believed she was every bit his equal.

"Th-thank you," she said, stammering somewhat over the words, and taking the handkerchief. "Perhaps it is easier to cry over things that do not really matter. The other tears are too difficult to shed."

"But why should anyone cry at all?" Mr. Ravenbeck demanded. "Let's play some happy music, so everyone is smiling again."

So that evening ended with a sort of impromptu dance, though neither Janet nor I participated in it. Mrs. Farraday did one stately turn around the room with Mr. Ravenbeck (their calm demeanor at wild variance with the almost abhorrently lively beat of the music), and Ameletta danced several times with each of the men. The little blonde girl only came up to their navels, but she had a great deal of style and skill, and she enjoyed herself so much that her delight reflected back on her partners, who each begged her for another turn. Yes, she was a little flirt, and I could not help thinking of her unprincipled mother, wondering what tendencies this little one might have inherited; but what harm could she come to in such a setting, with such guardians around her? Janet and I watched her enjoy herself, and we smiled.

The fourth night of the Ingersolls' stay, Mr. Ravenbeck had planned a new entertainment, which we discovered when we all trooped into the library upon his request. But there were no monitors set up, no holoscreens, no special toys immediately visible.

"Looks like a great deal of fun," Mr. Fulsome said, glancing elaborately around. "Should have thought of this myself."

"I hope you do not expect us to amuse ourselves with conversation, Everett," Bianca said, smiling, though her voice held an edge. "I think we've quite exhausted our available topics over dinner, and I for one can't think of a single additional malicious thing to say about anyone I've ever met in my life."

"My dear Bianca, I'm sure you underestimate yourself," Mr. Ravenbeck said genially. "But don't worry. I don't expect any of you to tax your conversational abilities any longer. This night you shall have an opportunity to listen instead of speak."

"Oh, of course, that's always so much more interesting," said Mr. Taff. Even his amiable voice sounded ironic.

Mr. Ravenbeck pointed toward the ceiling, which, I assumed, was meant to indicate his study on the level above us. "Just for tonight, I've subscribed to one of the online psychic services. It's very expensive, by the way, though I was able to convince myself that nothing was too good for my guests. We can each go in there, one at a time, and ask our clairvoyant consultant the questions that—shall we say—trouble our hearts. I've been told the accuracy rate is remarkably high. Of course, I was told that by the saleswoman with whom I conferred this morning, but I suppose that is no reason not to believe it."

Mrs. Ingersoll looked up from where she was sitting, a book open on her lap. "Oh, but they *are* accurate!" she said with great earnestness. "I have had my aura scanned many times, and I was always amazed by how completely the computer program analyzed my personality and predicted my future. Quite eerie, I assure you, but fascinating."

This was the longest speech I had ever heard the Ingersoll matriarch make, and her testimony obviously had some effect on the others. Her two daughters—always fairly impressionable—looked intrigued, and even the men looked curious, or at least willing.

"Is it a computer program, then, or is it a remote link to a psychic based elsewhere?" Mr. Taff wanted to know.

"Both, I believe," Mr. Ravenbeck replied. "There is a scanner attached to the computer, and it reads your face and presumably takes in other data, which is fed to the psychic on the other end. Using this physical evidence, and asking you a series of questions, the psychic herself—or himself, I am not sure which gender we have secured—will then do a reading for you. You may also ask it specific questions and receive clear answers—or so I am told. I have never indulged in this particular parlor game before."

Mrs. Ingersoll was on her feet. "Well, I am quite ready to try it now!" she said. "Shall we draw lots? Or may I volunteer to be first?"

"You may of course be first," Mr. Ravenbeck said graciously. "The rest of us will devise some method of deciding who shall follow in what order."

"And the monitor is set up in a room upstairs?"

"I will show you the way," he said, and escorted her out the door.

"Well! I must say, this seems very unlike Everett," Bianca said, sinking gracefully into a chair and propping her head upon her hand. She was wearing a bodysuit of indigo velvet sewn with sequins; with her pale hair, she looked like the first intimation of dawn over a stormy sky. "Romantic almost, don't you think? I cannot see him caring too much about someone else's opinion, or putting too much stock in a computer's predictions about his future."

"Still, if it's as accurate in its analysis as your mother suggested," Mr. Taff said in a somewhat excited tone of voice, "I would find it very hard to discount what such a psychic might have to say."

Mr. Fulsome shrugged. "Simple enough to do," he said. "Physical scan gives your basic height, age, weight, condition. Actuarial tables supply some of the possible outcomes. Fact that you're buying the service at all means you're probably wealthy and idle. And the questions you ask"—he shrugged again—"bound to give away all sorts of clues."

"I won't ask it any questions, then," Mr. Taff promised.

Bianca laughed. "Well, I will! I have things I want to know! And I'll be sure and ask it a few qualifying questions before I pose the real ones, just to see if I can really trust its answers."

"Oh, yes, that's what I'll do too," Melanie decided.

"Wonder what your mother's asking," Mr. Fulsome said. "Seemed to be pretty eager to go in and talk."

"Why, she's asking about her daughters' futures, of course," Bianca replied flirtatiously. "What else would she want to know?"

Conversation continued on in this meaningless way for the next hour or so as, one by one, the guests left the room to consult the computer-aided medium. After Mr. Ravenbeck had deposited Mrs. Ingersoll before the psychic screen, he had returned to help decide who should go next, and who should follow that lucky individual. Mr. Ravenbeck thought perhaps the company should go alphabetically, which pleased Bianca but was not agreeable to Melanie, whose name fell so much later than that of half the company. Then Mr. Ravenbeck proposed to set forth a series of riddles, and whoever answered the first one correctly would go next, and whoever answered the second one would follow, and so forth. But everyone rejected this as being too taxing. Going by age was clearly ineligible, since Bianca would not want to admit to being older than anyone in the room, even her sister, and letting Ameletta choose would obviously be an exercise in disaster.

"We shall draw lots, then," Mr. Ravenbeck decreed. "It is the only truly fair arrangement."

Accordingly, he tore up sheets of paper, numbered them, folded them, and scooped them all up in the palm of his hand. "No one is to glance at his number until we have all drawn papers," he ordered, and he offered his hand to Bianca.

"Thank you, Everett," she said with a warm smile, as if certain he had positioned the number one scrap on the top of the pile just for her. He smiled back, and moved to her sister, and then to Ameletta.

"Oh! I am number two! I am number two!" the little girl squealed.

Her guardian frowned at her. "You were not supposed to look until all the pieces had been distributed," he scolded.

Her face fell; she looked as if she might cry. "Must I give it back?" she asked.

He could not keep from smiling at her; indeed, none of us could. "No, you may remain number two—though you are really number one in my heart," he added in a loud whisper. "Just try to be good next time."

"I will. *So* good."

After Mr. Ravenbeck had allowed the society women to pick from his palm, he approached Janet Ayerson where she sat quietly typing into a handheld monitor. She looked up in confusion when he held his palm out.

"Miss Ayerson," he said. "Surely you would like to know what your future holds."

"I have a fair guess," she said, recovering her composure.

"Perhaps you will be surprised. Come! I already paid the subscription price. We should all enjoy the novelty."

"Thank you, Mr. Ravenbeck," she said, and selected a number.

After this exchange, I could hardly be astonished when he came my way next, and I did not bother to protest. "This should be instructive," I remarked. "I will be interested indeed to learn how such a program assesses my life and its possibilities."

"Perhaps you will share with me what the psychic predicts for you," he said in a low voice.

"It depends upon her commentary. If she foresees a life of ignominy and wretchedness, I don't believe I shall tell you. If, however, she sees me raised to some high station, mistress of some vast establishment and doing good works—why, yes, I will be happy to convey the news."

He tried to discipline a smile. "I can see you do not have much faith in my electronic mystic."

"More faith in my own analytic powers, that is true," I said. "But I will reserve judgment until I see this program in action."

After this exchange, he moved on to hand out slips of paper to the men. Then, upon his signal, we all unfolded our numbers at once. Mine was eight—which, since I had noticed Mr. Ravenbeck did not reserve a piece of paper for himself, meant I would be the last in the group to be summoned.

"Ah, I am first," Bianca said, making no attempt to disguise her pleasure. "I wish Mother would hurry."

The others called out their numbers as well, and there was a great deal of good-natured grumbling when they realized that Mr. Ravenbeck did not plan to submit himself to the clairvoyant's powers.

"I would rather be surprised by my future," he said. "For I remain continually surprised by my past."

This caused everyone to laugh and forgive him for his omission. In a few minutes, Mrs. Ingersoll returned to the room, looking thoughtful but not unhappy. Bianca immediately jumped to her feet.

"My turn!" she exclaimed. "Everett, should you escort me to show me what I must do?"

"Happily," he said, and took her arm to lead her from the room.

"Well, Mother? What did you learn?" Melanie demanded.

Mrs. Ingersoll seated herself in her customary chair and took up her book again, though her eyes retained a faraway look that made me think she might have trouble concentrating on the pages. "Many interesting things," she replied regally. "I don't think we are supposed to discuss them."

"Takes some of the fun out of it," Mr. Fulsome observed. "Think I might be inclined to talk about it, myself."

"You," Mrs. Ingersoll said, bending her head to read, "may do as you choose."

Not unexpectedly, this put something of a damper on general conversation for a few minutes, though Melanie managed to move her chair next to Joseph Luxton's and engage him in a quiet discussion. Mr. Taff and Mr. Fulsome took out a board game and argued halfheartedly over the rules, and Janet returned to her monitor. Ameletta skipped over to my side.

"Oh, Miss Starborn, what do you think I should ask the sidekick?" she inquired.

"Psychic," I corrected, though inwardly I was laughing. "You might ask if you will grow up to be a good, happy woman who makes others around her happy as well."

"I think I shall ask if I will marry a handsome man. Or a rich one," she said. "And if I will be very beautiful when I grow up."

She was vain and ridiculous, but she was eight years old, and I stroked her pretty blonde curls. "How could you not be a beautiful woman?" I murmured. "You are such a lovely child."

I noticed that Mr. Ravenbeck did not return while Bianca was out of the room, and concluded that he was helping her frame her questions or interpret the replies she was given. I wondered if he would be quite so assiduous with all the rest of his guests. Ameletta, plainly, would need some guidance, but I fancied most of the rest of the party could handle the computer interface on our own.

When Bianca returned, some twenty minutes later, she looked pensive and not entirely pleased. She was not clinging to Mr. Ravenbeck's arm, as she usually did, though he stepped into the room right behind her looking remarkably cheerful. In fact, she did not spare him another glance as she crossed the room to draw up a chair beside her mother and began whispering in the older lady's ear.

If he noticed this rather ominous turn of events, the host gave no sign. "Ameletta, I believe you are the next one to consult the fortune-teller," he said. "Do you have your questions ready?"

She hurled herself across the room and fairly towed him out the door. "Yes, I have so many questions! Do let us hurry!"

The rest of the evening continued in this fashion, Mr. Ravenbeck escorting his guests to the study, the rest of us continuing our own quiet pursuits while we waited for our turns. From my place on the sidelines, I observed the face of each supplicant as he or she returned from a visit to the oracle, and I was surprised to note that none of them looked ecstatic. None showed the same degree of instant unhappiness that Bianca had displayed, but all the others looked pensive, uncertain, or worried when they came back into the room. I began to wonder what sort of bad news our medium was handing out, and if I would be offered a similarly unpalatable forecast.

I questioned those I thought I had some right to interrogate, beginning with Ameletta, who dropped back to my chair looking positively woeful. "Why, *chiya*, what is wrong?" I asked as she came dragging back to my chair, for I had adopted Mr. Ravenbeck's pet name for her. "What did the psychic tell you?"

"She said I must study very hard and learn all my mathematics, for someday I would be the mistress of a large holding, and I would have to know how to do my accounts."

"But that is hardly bad news! Mistress of your own property—why, many young girls would be thrilled to know that was their fate!"

"Yes, but I don't *want* to learn my mathematics! I don't want to know my accounts. I want to marry a rich man, and wear pretty dresses, and eat pastries whenever I wish."

I hid a smile. "Well, perhaps you will marry a rich man, and it will be his estates you will be looking over."

Ameletta heaved a sigh. "She didn't think so."

"You asked her whom you were to marry?"

"Yes, and I asked if he would be rich and handsome, and she said that she was unable to foretell, but that he would most assuredly be kind and considerate."

"But those are excellent qualities! Why are you so depressed?"

"Because he sounds so boring! I did not want to marry a boring man!"

This time I could not smother my laugh, though I did think, even at eight, a girl should have some respect for kindness and consideration. I gave her a little hug and said, "Well, you never know. The mystic could be wrong. You may yet marry a handsome devil who will treat you very badly."

She eyed me suspiciously at that. "Miss Starborn, are you trying to be funny?"

I laughed again. "All I am saying is that you should not put too much stock in the words of a fortune-teller. They are notorious for being wrong, you know. And you have within you the power to make your own fate, no matter what it seems the universe has assigned you."

This speech was clearly over her head; besides, she was beginning to lose interest. She picked up one of her little handheld games and, in a few moments, was absorbed in sending her virtual heroine off on a quest for treasure.

Miss Ayerson's turn came perhaps forty-five minutes later, and she also reentered the room looking slightly shaken. When she saw my eyes lift to her face as she came through the door, she immediately crossed the room to my side.

"That was a strange experience," she remarked, taking the seat beside me.

"In what manner? You look unnerved," I replied.

She laughed slightly. "I'm not surprised. I went in expecting the usual array of pretty promises and sweeping generalities, the sorts of things that could be applied to any half-cit woman working to support herself. But this mystic's observations were uncannily accurate, and the predictions it made were so near the things I have been wishing for that I truly felt as if the machine had scanned my brain and read from the printed transcript."

"That would be unsettling," I agreed. "Do you wish to share with me any of the forecasts it made?"

She laughed again, with even less mirth. "Oh, the psychic warned me against following an inclination I would live to regret. I do not wish to be more specific, although *she* was. And I cannot help wondering: How could she know my heart so thoroughly—and how can she be sure I would regret it?"

From the staid Janet Ayerson, this was wild talk indeed, and I could not imagine what sort of radical behavior she would indulge in that would cause her a moment's distress in the future. She had always seemed too serene and contained for rashness. Too much like me.

"Of course she can be sure of nothing," I said, almost mechanically. "She is a charlatan, and this is a highly sophisticated parlor game. Take none of it to heart."

"I wish I had your unwearied good sense, Jenna," she said, and rose hurriedly to her feet. "Ameletta! It is well past your bedtime. Come, you and I must go upstairs." They were out the door a few minutes later, Ameletta uncharacteristically offering no protest. I realized that Janet's confidences, such as they were, were at an end.

To tell the truth, I was beginning to get a little tired myself, and had Mr. Ravenbeck not made such a point of including me in the event, I would have slipped away also and made my way to my room. But there was still Mr. Luxton to be returned and Mr. Taff to have his session before I would be called before the psychic. Sighing quietly, I returned to my reading, scarcely looking up when Mr. Ravenbeck brought back the one man and left again with the other.

Mr. Taff had not been gone five minutes when Mrs. Farraday came to the door, a look of perturbation on her amiable face. She cast a quick glance around the room, obviously seeking Mr. Ravenbeck, and then motioned for me to come over. I did.

"There is a visitor here for Mr. Ravenbeck," she said in a whisper. "I offered to show him to this room, but he said he preferred to see Mr. Ravenbeck in private. Do you know where he is?"

"He is leading each guest by turn to the upstairs study—and then, apparently, staying to guide them through a complex computer program interface. I am scheduled to go in next—would you like me to alert him? Or would you like to go tell him now, yourself?"

"Oh, no, no, I hate to interrupt him when he is enjoying himself with his friends! Would you be willing to give him the news? The visitor said it was not urgent, but I cannot help thinking—if someone comes to call so late at night—well, perhaps it is not an *emergency*, but it is something one ought to address as soon as one can."

"Certainly. What is the man's name? Why has he come?"

"I don't know why he's here—he wouldn't say. All he told me is that his name is Merrick and he comes from Wesleyan-Imrae."

I knew very little about this exotic world on the far edges of the settled galaxy, except that it was famous for its export crops of spice and hallucinogenics. As far as I knew, Mr. Ravenbeck did not deal in either.

"Don't worry," I said. "I shall inform him as soon as I see him."

"You're so good, Jenna," she said. "Tell him I have put Mr. Merrick in the breakfast room and given him a meal. I hope that was the right thing to do."

"I'm sure it was. I shall tell him."

She withdrew, and I found myself finally impatient for my turn to come. It seemed to take eons for Mr. Taff to hear his fortune, but at last he reentered the room. Whatever news he had been given seemed to sit fairly well with him, for a change, for he was smiling with great energy and he cast a benevolent look at his friends sitting around the library. But he did not pause to speak to any of them; he came directly to me.

"Your turn, I believe, Miss Starborn," he said, and bent his arm as though to escort me from the room.

I stood. "Yes—but I was expecting Mr. Ravenbeck. I have rather important news to tell him."

Mr. Taff shrugged. "He asked me to fetch you and said he had business elsewhere. Perhaps he already has heard your news."

"Did Mrs. Farraday seek him out, then?"

"I did not see her, but she may have encountered him in the hall. Come! I think you'll enjoy this."

I allowed him to lead me from the room. "You seem to have enjoyed it, at any rate," I observed.

"Oh, it was great fun! And I received the best news! I can hardly wait now for my future to unfold."

It seemed pointless to warn him that this future might well be manufactured, so I was silent while we climbed the steps to the study. Mr. Taff entered with me to explain the mechanism. I was astonished to find that the room, normally quite pleasant and cheerful, had been altered to suit the mysterious circumstances of the event. Only a few lights were on, and these were turned very low, so that the brightest source of illumination came from the terminal in the middle of the room. This was not an ordinary screen, but a great crystal ball, bigger than my head, sitting on a base that appeared to be onyx but which was, no doubt, its electronic connection. It had been set up on a table, over which hung yards of dark velvet, so that it appeared to be situated inside a small curtained tent. The back of the room was in utter darkness. I was surprised to find my skin starting to prickle; I was usually not so susceptible to a staged mood.

"I take it I am to sit here," I said, seating myself in a straight-backed chair pulled up to the table. I took a moment to glance over the crystal ball. I could detect no mechanisms for collecting or relaying data, but I was sure such devices had been installed in the base. Nor was there a keyboard, nor any way that I could determine to control any of the proceedings.

In the depths of the round glass, there appeared only a slowly turning image of a constellation on a blue-black sky. "And this is whom I am to speak to?" I asked with a note of derision in my voice. "I am not sure I can take a star cluster very seriously."

"The psychic's face will appear once the program is activated," he assured me. "It's stylized, of course, but not at all repulsive."

"How do I activate the program?"

"You speak your name aloud and say you want your reading. There will be a short delay, and then the session will begin."

"And how do I know when the program is ended?"

"She will tell you so, and the screen will revert to this."

"It sounds simple enough. If you see Mr. Ravenbeck—"

"I know. I will tell him you need to speak with him. Enjoy yourself, Miss Starborn! I think you will find this an amazing venture."

I waited until the door had shut behind him before I opened my mouth again. Then, reminding myself that I believed in none of this, I stared at the celestial image and spoke in a firm voice. "My name is Jenna Starborn, and I have come to have my fortune told."

There was a moment's complete silence while the constellation continued to rotate on its field. Then suddenly the globe went absolutely blank, and the air thrummed with a faint background music. Just as suddenly, the interior lights of the ball flashed again, and resolved themselves into the image of a woman's face. It was a virtual woman, with flowing dark hair, snapping eyes, and so many necklaces and amulets wound around her throat that I could not begin to count them. She looked to be an amalgam of every gypsy and tarot reader produced in the last ten centuries.

"Well, Miss Starborn," she said in a pleasing, husky voice. "What is it you would like to know about yourself?"

I smiled. "I already know everything I need to know about myself, though I am curious to know how much of that you may have discovered."

"Ah! A skeptic. Have you come to seek a reading against your will?"

"Not unwillingly, but with very low expectations that you will be able to tell me much of the truth—or the future."

"I know your past well enough, though, even you will agree," she said in that gravelly voice. "Your name *Starborn* suits you very well, though you might almost have been called Jenna *Unborn*. For you were not delivered as an ordinary child might be, but generated by science and harvested through technology. You were raised, though not loved, by the Rentley family on Baldus, until you left for an education on Lora. Where you stayed fourteen years until taking your position here as technician. Do you agree that I know the details of your history?"

"They would not be hard to discover with a database and a little research," I said calmly enough, though I admit to being somewhat shaken. My existence at Lora was a documented thing and I had, after all, sent my résumé through the StellarNet, but I had told only Mrs. Farraday of my conception. I would not have expected her to repeat the tale, certainly not to a conjured mystic. Still, the records were there for anyone who had the time and leisure to track them down.

"True enough, and research is a valuable tool for someone in my profession," she said—which I considered a very odd admission for someone labeling herself as a sensitive. "Let me go on to say that your strange origins have engendered in you a passionate belief in the equality of all persons, regardless of race, gender, status, or ability, and that—more than most people who hold such beliefs—you try to live by them."

"I am a PanEquist. I suppose you could have gotten that information from any member of this household," I said. I still found it difficult to believe that Mrs. Farraday—or Janet Ayerson or Ameletta—would have gossiped about such things to such a listener, which rather confirmed some of my earlier suspicions. The master of the house had had a hand in supplying background information to the medium about all his guests, the better to provide her with a chance of reading their fortunes aright.

"Further," she said, as though I had not spoken, "this belief in your equality creates a great well of tension in your soul, as you struggle with the disparity between what you *want* and what you realize you can *have*."

"I would presume that is a common dilemma for many in my situation," I said. "But I do not agonize over that disparity, as you suggest. I see it, I acknowledge it, I go on."

"The disparity need not exist," she said in a low, whispering voice.

"What?"

"The gulf you perceive, between what you want and what you are entitled to—that gulf can be crossed with the frailest bridge that you yourself can construct."

"I have no idea what you're talking about," I said calmly, though I could feel my pulse begin to quicken.

"Do you not? What image that you are afraid to gaze on in broad day is imprinted in secret on your heart? What name do you practice in silence that you would not dare to speak aloud? What future do you envision, knowing it will not be realized? I tell you, gaze on that face. Speak that name. Imagine that future—and it will be yours."

Now my heart was beating so radically that I was afraid to make the smallest movement for fear my violent shaking would be betrayed. She whispered of hopes so impossible I had not even dared articulate them to myself. "I have no need to build bridges," I said, making my voice steady by sheer force of will. "I am content where I am."

"Are you? In that cold, sterile environment where there is sufficient but there is not plenty?"

"Coming as I do from the life you have already described, you must realize that for me, sufficient is a blessing. It is so much better than nothing at all. I would rather sip from the glass half full than have the empty glass shattered on the floor before me."

"You would rather be ill-fed than starving."

"Exactly."

"You would rather read by a few faint bulbs than sit, alone and impoverished, in the dark."

"Yes, of course."

"You would rather have friendship than lose that friendship by trying to convert it to love."

I was silent.

"Ah! So there are some things for which your desires may overcome your fears."

"It is not fear that keeps me from running through the darkness, seeking a blazing fire instead of my few flickering lamps," I said, roused to something like anger; she was baiting me, and I could not understand why, nor could I let all her innuendo pass without protest. "It is gratitude that I have got so much. I have sat, many a night, in full darkness, with no distraction and no solace to hurry the hours along. I have been given a source of light, and a great text to read by it. Why should I complain? Why should I jeopardize that by complaining that it is not enough?"

"Exactly! The reluctance to damage the future by tampering with the present is the precise definition of fear."

"You speak in riddles," I said coldly.

"And you walk through your days, quaking with unspoken dread," she replied. "You are afraid that the little you have will be taken away from you, and you know there is nothing you can to do prevent that."

"So that is the fortune you predict for me? That I shall lose my job here, and my friends here, and be sent off into the universe alone?"

"Is that what you fear most?"

"You are the one who claims to have all the answers."

"I think there are other things you fear even more, but that leaving Thorrastone Park would in any event be a grave blow to you. And you see it as a possibility before you—you know that there is talk of your employer marrying, and the household being broken up. And you think you are powerless to reach out a hand and alter the course of events or stay the cataclysm."

"If Mr. Ravenbeck chooses to marry and close down Thorrastone Park, I do not see that any gesture of mine will be able to stop him," I said with a composure that seemed to me remarkable. "He is a capable and intelligent man. No advice of mine might sway him."

"Advice—perhaps not. But entreaty? Supplication? He might be moved by those."

"So that is your counsel to me? To beg my employer to cancel his nuptials so that I might have a place to live and work? I believe in the equality of the classes, madam, but I do not believe in such a level field as that."

"You misunderstand," she said—or at least, I thought those were her words. Her image in the globe had started to crumble and distort, and her voice had started to climb to a higher range. "You should not implore him as employee to employer but as—"

And here the sound degraded altogether into a squeaky incomprehensible whine. "As a what?" I asked, leaning closer to the crystal ball, now filled with an array of random color dots. "In what role should I approach him?"

The next sound to issue from the speaker was completely different and altogether familiar. "Lord of the seven hells!" it said in the voice of the master of the house. "What's happened to the damned transmission?"

I scooted my chair back and glanced around the darkened room. "Mr. Ravenbeck? Are you in here?"

"No—yes—I'm next door, or actually, in the hall closet. The damned connection's been broken, or something. I don't suppose you'd want to come in here and fix it?"

His voice was still issuing from the speakers, and I assumed the microphone was still carrying mine to him. I returned my chair to its place before the table. "I don't see the point," I said. "Now that you are discovered, you may as well talk to me as yourself and dispense with this ridiculous disguise."

The glass fizzled and cleared, and in an instant it showed me Mr. Ravenbeck's grinning face. He did not look at all abashed at being caught out in a deception—and such an ignoble deception!—but rather looked as though he had been enjoying himself mightily for the past few hours. "Well, Jenna?" he demanded. "How do you rate my performance? Were you even a little thrilled or discomposed? Don't you think my comments were very close to the mark?"

"I think it was very bad of you to have played such a trick on me and your other guests," I said severely. "Who knows what secrets they may have told you, thinking you were a stranger? Who knows what terrible truths you may have uncovered?"

"Well, I learned nothing from you, that's for certain," he said, unimpressed. "Not that I expected to—but I did hope to rattle you more than I seem to have. You are so impassive! Why would you not reveal a bit more of yourself to my inviting creation?"

"Why should I be tempted to do so?" I retorted. "And I did not find her so inviting. She was judgmental and autocratic and would not let me say two words without contradicting me—much like you, sir, now that I think about it."

He gave that sharp grunt of irritation that greeted so many of my speeches and looked a little less pleased with himself. "The others were not all so reticent, I assure you."

"And did you play the gypsy with each of them as you did with me? I thought you had subscribed to a service. Were you in fact the psychic for all your guests?"

"No, only for half of you," he said. "I let the program read what fortune it would for Mrs. Ingersoll and Ameletta and Melanie and Mr. Luxton. It was only for you, Miss Ayerson, Bianca, and Mr. Taff that I intervened."

"And why the four of us? Why were we singled out?"

"I have more of an interest in your fortunes."

"More in mine than in Ameletta's? More in Mr. *Taff's*?"

"It is not easily explained."

"No, I would not think it could be explained at all!" I exclaimed. "I hope you did not, in this illegal manner, obtain any information that would embarrass any of the others. I was on my guard against you, but the other three might have come with more open hearts and told you things they should not have revealed."

"I assure you, I was more interested in dispensing wisdom than collecting secrets," he said. "Nothing they said to me could not have been found in the public record of their hopes and wishes—and I burst a few bubbles with my observations. I don't think my words will hurt any of them. In fact, I think I may have done some good. Tell me how they all reacted. When they reentered the room, what expressions did they wear?"

"Miss Bianca Ingersoll looked pensive and unhappy, and she went straight to her mother for a serious conference. Most of the others—even the ones for whom you *say* you did not intervene—looked thoughtful or disgruntled. Except for Mr. Taff, who appeared quite jubilant."

"Ah, that's because I explained to him how his fortunes will change in the next few months. He will make an advantageous marriage, you see," Mr. Ravenbeck confided. "*And* to a woman he has despaired of ever winning."

"Indeed? How is it you are privileged to know the state of this woman's heart?"

"I know this woman, and she has no heart. And I know the currents and fluxes of the human condition, which make a great deal of individual behavior as predictable as the equations of science. You mock me now, but in six months when his engagement is announced, you will be awed by my perspicacity."

"And Miss Ayerson?" I demanded. "What did you tell her to make her so restless and insecure?"

"I told her what any friend would tell her—you yourself, if you had the knowledge I have. Unfortunately, I cannot repeat it—I may trick my guests and make a game of my friends, but I do have some sense of decency, and that confidence I will not break. Suffice it to say that I wish the best for Miss Ayerson, and would say or do nothing to cause her any grief."

That I did believe; while there might be an edge of malice to Mr. Ravenbeck, a certain sarcastic mockery, there was no cruelty in him, and he was certainly not the man to abuse or terrify anyone more vulnerable than he. However, I would not give him the satisfaction of thinking I in any way tolerated his actions.

"Well, let us hope there are no unexpected repercussions from this evening," I said darkly. "For there is no—oh! Your antics made me forget the most important news!"

His face smiled at me from the globe. "And what news is that,

Jenna? The forcefield has fallen? Vandals have been sabotaging our generators again? Mrs. Farraday has failed to lay in a supply of groceries and we shall all go hungry at breakfast tomorrow?"

"I have no way of judging if this event is anywhere near as calamitous as any of those," I replied with dignity. "But you have received a visitor. Mrs. Farraday put him in the breakfast room and fed him a meal, for he refused to join the rest of us in the library."

"And who is this wayfarer? Or did she give you a name?"

"Yes. Mr. Merrick of Wesleyan-Imrae."

The electronic representation of his face blanched and grew slack; I almost thought the circuits were failing again, so strange and un-lifelike did his image become. I could not see the rest of his body, but I almost thought he lifted a hand to press his leaping heart back in his chest.

"Merrick! Wesleyan-Imrae!" he repeated, so faintly that the speakers almost did not relay his voice. "*That* name strikes a nearly fatal blow."

I leaped to my feet. "I shall come to you! Keep to your seat!"

He waved a languid hand so that I saw it brush across the interior of the glass. "Stay where you are, I am not faint. Merely—stricken. Merrick. I never thought to see him here."

I had remained standing. "I shall go to him and tell him you are not well. No—I shall tell him you left this evening on urgent business and we don't know when you will return. And if he protests, I will turn him from the house—Mrs. Farraday and I, and Janet Ayerson, and even Mary and Rinda. Together we can put him out."

Some color seemed to be seeping back into his face, at least by the monitor's rendition. "Such a display of strength and loyalty is not called for. I shall go to him—I shall even be civil. He has done me no wrong, no harm. He is merely a part of my life I do not like to think of."

"Some connection to Ameletta's mother?" I said, sitting back in my chair and losing a little of my zeal.

He smiled faintly. "Only in the most indirect way. Only because the—excesses—I indulged in when I knew Merrick in some small way drove me to that woman's arms. But he cannot be blamed either for my errors or their aftermath. But, Lord, I wish he were not here!"

He fell into a sort of brooding fit after this passionately delivered speech, and I watched him a moment in silence. I felt strange, stirred up, ready to fight and yet completely helpless. I wanted to comfort him as I would have comforted Ameletta had she come running into my room after a nightmare, and by Mr. Ravenbeck's expression, Mr. Merrick was indeed a nightmare in the flesh. And yet I could not offer such solace to Mr. Ravenbeck—it was laughable—and I could not go into battle for him, and I could not even advise him, for I did not know what the trouble was. So I waited.

Presently he spoke again, lifting his eyes again to meet mine through the medium of the glass. His face was still chalky, making the black fire of his eyes all the more remarkable. Resolution had returned to his features, and yet at the same time his expression was forlorn. "Jenna," he said, "if I were to walk back into the library and all the Ingersoll women turned their backs on me, and Luxton and Taff and Fulsome pointed their fingers and laughed—if I were to go to the spaceport tomorrow and be denied a place at the finest restaurant, a chance to shop in the most elegant shops—if people on the street were to look at me and whisper 'Half-cit!'—would you laugh and point and whisper with them? Would you turn away from me as well?"

"I would not turn away from you no matter what you had done," I said, though I had to wonder what crime he may have committed that would cause his citizenship to be stripped away from him and all his friends to deride him. "You are a good man, Mr. Ravenbeck, I know that in my heart. And whatever gauge society uses to measure goodness is not the same one I carry. I do not judge a man's worth by his pocketbook and his standing in the world, as you know."

He smiled faintly, though his eyes still remained sad. "No, you judge him by the weight of his atoms and the chemical compounds he can return to the earth when he is dead."

"And you, being such a solid, well-built man, will have quite a healthy number of molecules to return to the soil," I said in a comforting voice. The ridiculous sally was meant to make him laugh, and it did. He even straightened a bit in his chair, and smoothed a hand over his dark hair.

"Very well! I will go to Merrick. You must tell my guests that I will not be back for the rest of the evening—I have been called away to attend matters of business. I should, however, be available again in the morning."

"Is there nothing more I can do for you?"

"Not at present. If your services become necessary, I will call you, no matter how late the hour."

Strange what a glow that gave me, that he should consider me worthy to offer him assistance! "I shall see you in the morning, then."

"In the morning."

I made my way with care through the darkened room, which presented many hazards, and was relieved to finally gain the well-lit hall. In a few minutes I was back downstairs in the library. Mr. Taff, still jovial, had drawn up a chair beside Bianca and her mother, and was regaling them with some tale which seemed to hold interest for neither. Fulsome and Luxton were still playing their game while Melanie looked on, pretending an interest so false as to fool no one. None of them even glanced up when I came through the door.

"Mr. Ravenbeck has asked me to tell you all that he has been called away to urgent business," I said in a clear voice that I pitched to carry through the room. A few sullen faces turned my way. None of them seemed to be enjoying themselves this evening, and my announcement only capped the dreary mood. "He will be at your service again tomorrow."

Only Mr. Taff seemed genuinely interested in my news. "Some problem down at the dubronium mine, perhaps?" he asked.

That seemed as likely an answer as anything, though I did not like to lie. "He was not specific," I said.

Bianca Ingersoll flung herself to her feet. "*Lord*, but this has been a dreadful day!" she exclaimed. "Someone fetch me a drink, and then I am off to bed. Nothing could be worse than this."

"You have already had a drink, my love," her mother said.

"Well, then, I shall have another—or another and another—for when there is no entertainment offered, you must make your own."

Mr. Taff was also on his feet, much more assiduous in her service than he had been during the preceding days of his visit. Or perhaps it was just that I had never seen him in a room that did not also contain Mr. Ravenbeck. "What would you like? I'll get it for you."

She gave him a sideways look, so cutting and calculating that I was surprised it did not slit his throat right open. "Would you, Harley?" she said in a sly, purring voice. "I cannot tell you how very much I would appreciate that."

I did not stay to watch any more of the drama play out, but turned on my heel and left the room. Truth to tell, the events of the evening had exhausted me, and I climbed the stairs and went directly to bed. I had much to think about—the strange things Mr. Ravenbeck had said to me under the guise of the electronic gypsy, the strange mien he had exhibited when he learned of the arrival of Mr. Merrick—but none of these thoughts could keep me awake for long. I shifted position once or twice on my mattress; I closed my eyes, opened them again, closed them; and I slept.

Chapter 8

✦

Two hours later the house was roused by sirens. I sat bolt upright in bed, my heart bounding along to the rise and fall of that sinister wail, then I jumped up and dressed. The nearest thing to hand was one of my nondescript working coveralls, so I stepped into this, zipped it up, crammed my feet into a pair of shoes, and ran out the door. In less than a minute I was down all three flights of stairs to my basement workroom, checking my monitors. Nothing. I did a quick visual scan of the instrument boards, which showed no sign of fresh damage; indeed, nothing in the room appeared to have been disturbed.

Then I thought to check the grid that showed the systems for the whole park, even the mine, and sure enough, the red flashing danger light was located in a small building just to the left of the main compound. "Gilda Parenon," I whispered.

They had plenty of technicians in the mining compound, but there might be something I could do. I ran back up to the ground level of the manor, to find nearly the whole house roused. The male guests were all half dressed and milling about the foyer, looking ready to go off and do battle. The women, including Mrs. Farraday, were all positioned at various stations on the stairwell, clinging to the rail or leaning weakly against the wall, peering down toward the front door and calling out faint, mewling questions. I did not see Janet or Ameletta; I presumed the tutor had gone immediately to the little girl's room and was keeping her company there.

Mrs. Farraday was the first one to see me, and the first one to realize that I might have some specialized knowledge. "Oh! Jenna! There you are! This terrible noise—Jenna, are we in any danger?"

Much as the others might despise me, they all fell silent to listen to my reply. "The trouble is isolated in one small building at the mining compound," I replied. "Our shields are intact, and we are completely safe. You may all return to your beds to sleep."

"How could anyone possibly sleep with such a racket as this?" Mrs. Ingersoll cried.

"I imagine the alarms will be turned off at any moment," I said calmly. "They are merely there to alert someone to the emergency. Once a technician begins to address the problem, the alarms will stop."

Indeed, just as I finished my sentence, the sirens quit with an abruptness that made the silence seem ominous. We all stood uncertainly for a moment, as if, one plague lifted, another one would be certain to descend, and in the absolute quiet all we heard was the sound of our own feet shifting. Till there was a sudden external roar of a powerful motor rapidly approaching, coming so close to the door it seemed it would crash right through. Melanie Ingersoll screamed. Then the engine halted, a heavy metal door opened and slammed shut, and Mr. Ravenbeck burst into the foyer.

His eyes swept the assembled company and found me. "Good, you are awake," he said briskly. "We need you."

There was a moment's agonizing silence. "Me, sir?" I said.

"Yes, yes, of course you," he said impatiently. "Come! We have no time to waste."

"But, Everett!" Bianca Ingersoll cried, running down the last few steps and placing her hand upon his arm. "What is the matter? Are the fields down? Are we in danger?"

"No danger," he said briefly. "But there is a problem, and I need a technician's help. Jenna must come with me now. I am sorry to be so harsh, but the situation is grave."

I had, with these few words, recovered my equanimity. "I am ready, sir," I said, crossing the foyer to stand at his side. "Let us go."

In seconds we were out in the strange night air of Thorrastone Park. Under the protected forcefield, there was no great change of temperature, and the well-placed lights made a valiant attempt to push back the utter blackness, so it should not have been particularly eerie and unsettling to be abroad in the late-night hours. And yet, it was. What few stars were visible seemed sinister and random, and even they were obliterated from time to time by great washes of light caused by intermittent solar flares. There was something menacing about the austere night skies of Fieldstar—some cosmic reminder of how small and isolated and unnatural this planet was, forced by the will of man to produce what men wanted—and biding its time till an hour dark enough, cold enough, remote enough, to revert to its indigenous state.

I tried not to think about it. Instead, I hopped nimbly into the vehicle upon which Mr. Ravenbeck had arrived. It was not his Vandeventer or even the sturdy little hovercraft that Mrs. Farraday used to tour the grounds. Instead it was, I presumed, one of the mining cars, a bullet-shaped unadorned cartridge of metal with two uncomfortable seats and no enclosed top. No airborne capabilities, either, for as we went forward at an alarming pace, I realized we were bumping and jostling over the ruts and rocks of the ground on actual tires.

"What is the situation?" I called out over the noise of the unfiltered motor. Shaken by the rough ride, my voice seemed to tremble, though I was at this time quite calm.

"I will explain when we arrive," he said.

"Has someone been hurt?"

"Yes."

"Badly?"

"It is too soon to tell."

Hurt by what agent? would have been my next question had he seemed disposed to answer inquiries; but clearly I would learn nothing till we arrived at our destination. I clung to the door of the vehicle and maintained my silence.

In a few minutes we pulled up in front of a small bungalow built of the same indeterminate gray brick that had been used to construct most of the other buildings in the mining compound. I would have thought, simply by its location, that it had been intended as the housing unit for the mine supervisor or some other person of authority—though, indeed, I had no idea how the personnel were lodged in this quarter of Thorrastone Park. The lot of them might sleep in underground barracks, for all I knew.

I had my hand on the door, ready to exit at once, when Mr. Ravenbeck turned to look at me. "Jenna," he said in a very sober voice.

"Sir?"

"What you see tonight—you are not to talk of to anyone. Not to Janet Ayerson, not to Mrs. Farraday. No one. Do you understand?"

"I am able to keep my own counsel, sir, and I am not one to spread gossip."

He gave the smallest smile. "I know. I have been so fortunate to find you—" He stopped abruptly, as if there was more to that sentence. Then without another word, he thrust open his side door and leaped from the car. I followed more slowly. At the front of the building, he was bending over an electronic keypad inlaid on the sturdy metal door. The code seemed long and complicated; he certainly did not want unexpected intruders breaking into this facility.

We stepped inside a wide, half lit room that under normal circumstances would have seemed comfortable—its furnishings were quiet and well-made, its proportions were pleasing, its green and blue colors were easy on the eyes. But tonight it was anything but welcoming. Two of the chairs were overturned, crockery had been broken and scattered across the woven rug, and a man lay, bleeding and moaning, on the pretty tapestried sofa.

While I stood at the doorway gaping, Mr. Ravenbeck crossed the floor in a few strides and knelt by the injured man. "Merrick! Can you hear me? Are you better?"

"Everett," a faint voice whispered back. "I cannot breathe."

"Don't be ridiculous, of course you can breathe," was the brisk response. "If you could not, you would be dead by now. I have been gone a good fifteen minutes."

"My throat—she has broken my windpipe—my God, she is so strong—"

"Your throat may be bruised. There is nothing I can do about that. What about your arm? Has the bleeding stopped?"

"I don't know, I can't—I can hardly feel it, it is pain but it is numbness too, like the nerves have failed—Oh, God, Everett, will I lose my arm? Will I lose my life?"

"You most certainly are not going to die, and if you lose a limb, well, there are very fine clinics on Brierly and Corbramb where you can get a replacement, you know. It is nothing to be so fretful about."

I thought Mr. Ravenbeck spoke with great callousness to a man who was clearly in great distress and, perhaps, mortal danger. It occurred to me, however, that Mr. Ravenbeck was also blazingly, blindly furious with Mr. Merrick, and that some of his lack of sympathy sprang from that fact. I wondered what the poor man had done to deserve such wrath, and I took a step into the room. "Perhaps, the PhysiChamber back at the manor—" I began.

Mr. Ravenbeck did not even look at me. "No! On no account is he to go anywhere he might be seen. Which eliminates the PhysiChamber at the compound as well."

"But he seems most dreadfully hurt, sir," I pointed out.

"No more than he deserves for his stupidity," Mr. Ravenbeck muttered. "I told him not to—" He stopped, and shook his head violently.

"No matter how stupid he has been, you cannot wish him to die here," I said, coming closer. "We must get him some care."

Mr. Ravenbeck nodded. "I have given him drugs that will ease his pain, and when they have taken effect, I will fly him to the spaceport. He has a small, private craft docked there which, no doubt, has its own medical systems. He will be fine once he is installed there."

"If he survives the trip!"

"He will survive it."

I knew a moment's flash of anger myself. "Why did you call me here, then, if it was not to help you administer to this poor injured man? Certainly it was not to accept my advice."

"No—it was your expertise I wanted, not your opinion. This building is protected by the fields of the mining compound, but it has its own generator system on the next level down. Something went awry there, which is why the sirens sounded. I need you to check for any glitches in the system—make sure the inhabitants of this cabin are not in danger."

"Inhabitants?" I said sharply, for I had seen no one except the unfortunate Mr. Merrick. "Who might they be?"

"Persons who will not trouble you," he said tersely. "My job is to stabilize Merrick, then fly him to town. Yours is to study the systems below and make whatever repairs might be necessary. I will return for you as swiftly as I can, but I warn you, it will be a matter of hours. I want you to stay downstairs, no matter what noises might sound above you. Do you understand? Go below, and wait for me there, no matter what else you think you hear."

"Mr. Ravenbeck, is someone else in this house in trouble?"

He hesitated a moment, as if contemplating a lie. "There is someone else in this house who is not fit company," he said at last. "I swear to you on my life you are in no danger. The guards are in place, the locks are secured, no harm threatens you. But I am uneasy about the systems below, or I would not have dragged you out of your bed so late at night."

I brushed this aside. "I am happy to render to you any service that I can. I am willing to do more, if more is required."

He smiled so briefly I thought I might have imagined the faint lightening of his features. "Someday you may be called upon to redeem that promise," he said. "For now, it is your professional skill I require."

"Everett!" Mr. Merrick gasped from his couch. "I am dying! Do not leave me here!"

Mr. Ravenbeck glanced back at the injured man. "In a moment. Five more minutes and the drugs will take hold. Then you will feel much better, and I will take you away." He looked back at me. "Can you find your way downstairs? I do not like to leave him."

"I believe so. I will look for you when you return, no sooner."

I turned to go, but he stopped me with a hand on my shoulder. "Do PanEquists believe in angels, Jenna?"

I smiled. "No, sir."

"For you cannot be what you do not believe in. But *I* believe in angels, Jenna, and you most assuredly are one. Now go. Be good—and do not stir until I fetch you."

I left the room and made my way to the hallway, where a series of three doors could be found. The first one I tried was a closet, but the second one led belowstairs, and a simple wall switch illuminated my way. In a few moments I was down in the small generator room, looking around to assess the situation.

At first glance, there was nothing amiss here—nothing so overt as the destruction that had been inflicted on the systems at the manor. But upon closer inspection, I found that a few crucial switches had been thrown—nothing to cause profound damage, but certainly enough to trigger the alarms. Since they were still in the alarm position, I concluded that an override had been engaged somewhere in the mining compound, and that none of my tasks here would be urgent. Nonetheless, I was here and charged with safety; best I should look around and see what else I could do to make the systems functional again.

I had not been long in investigating the layout when I heard Mr. Ravenbeck hauling Mr. Merrick from the room. At first I thought the sounds of his hearty swearing were drifting down the stairwell, but then I realized that an air vent of some kind was carrying noises from the ground-level floor to the basement. I could quite clearly catch Mr. Merrick's pants of pain and Mr. Ravenbeck's responsive oaths, as well as what sounded like heels being dragged across a hardboard floor. Then the door slammed, and I heard the faint beeping sound of the lock being reset. A few minutes later, the muffled roar of the motor, and then silence.

Back to my work. It seemed to me that this generator room was ill-maintained and rarely serviced, for the waste disposal system was flashing a steady "near-full" message and a few of the safety breakers had blown and not been replaced. Secondary systems had apparently self-activated to keep the energy flow continuous, but there was no reason for me not to fix the breakers while I was there. I could also start the waste-disposal mechanism that would carry the radioactive byproducts into the underground storage units where the waste from the manor was also stored; it was a simple enough process, though it required a series of well-timed steps, and whoever was watching over this system seemed to have never found the time to perform the task.

Well, I had plenty of time. Hours and hours. I could clean the whole basement by hand with a bucket and a rag, if I wanted.

I had been absorbed in my work for perhaps an hour when I heard the first inexplicable noises from upstairs. There was a heavy thud, as if a sofa had been overturned, and then a series of frantic grunts and clicks and squeaks that came in such rapid, planned patterns that I almost believed they had to represent speech. Did Mr. Ravenbeck keep some kind of wild animal locked up here—something part bird, part ape, part native life-form? Was that what had slipped its leash, assaulted Mr. Merrick, and scrambled downstairs to toy with sophisti-cated machinery? No—that last supposition, at least, made no sense. The switches had been thrown with intent; their deployment had not been the random act of a savage mind. More likely would be the sort of havoc I had seen wreaked upon our systems in the manor basement, unthinking and undifferentiated violence.

The passionate, incomprehensible voice spoke again, its tone simul-taneously so mad and so pleading that I began to feel the skin on my back wrinkle in horror. Softer, more muffled, another voice answered, and I could not tell if this individual spoke true words or responded in kind. My hands began to tremble; I had to stop a moment to compose myself. Another sudden *stomp*, as if the creature above were throwing a tantrum, and this time the other voice spoke more clearly.

"Enough, then. Quiet, you. You've already caused enough trouble for one night, don't you think?"

My arms, my face, my stomach prickled with unease. For that was a voice I knew. That was Gilda Parenon.

Whom was she watching, in this unused, ill-kept house on the fringes of the manor, and what kind of threat was posed to us all by her charge?

For a few moments I stood, tensely listening, almost refusing to breathe in order that I might hear more of the strange conversation transpiring above me, but there were no more sounds. My thoughts were racing. If the creature herself (Mr. Merrick had called her a "she") had not flown downstairs to meddle with the machinery, had Gilda Parenon performed that task? How had the scenario gone? Perhaps Mr. Merrick had arrived unannounced on the doorstep—perhaps he, like Mr. Ravenbeck, had some emotional or financial stake in this beast upstairs—and he had let himself in without sufficient warning. And the animal had broken loose and attempted to brutalize him with so much ferocity that Gilda Parenon could not with her own strength save him. So she ran to the basement and flipped the switches that would cause the sirens to howl, hoping only to draw enough attention to receive aid. Yes, that seemed likely enough to me—if any of this could be called likely, if any of it could be *possible*, if I was not having some strange delusional dream of my own.

Unfreezing from my watchful stance, I moved more slowly around the room, continuing to listen over the faint sounds of my own progress. So quietly that I first did not realize what I was hearing, the thing upstairs began a weird clicking and panting sequence that sounded less like true breathing than a faulty motor trying to cough itself to a functional revolution. I stopped again, feeling once more that unpleasant premonitory shiver down my back. Click-click-click-*pant*-click-click-click-*pant*-click . . . click . . . click . . .

Then a rattling, jolting sound as if someone smashed a crowbar along a metal grate. Gilda Parenon heaving a pipe across the bars of a cage? "Quiet, I said! Be still! You shall not get out again tonight, oh no, no matter who else is abroad."

And then I heard a sound that reversed the blood in my veins, and caused my scalp to lift a quarter inch from my skull. For the creature began a high, steady keening, faint but piteous, that went on and on and on and on. She did not pause to breathe—not for five minutes, not for ten—not for the hour that followed. Unbroken, unvarying, inhuman, the thin heartbroken wail continued, as tireless and unstoppable as a siren with a shattered failsafe. I sat petrified in my basement stronghold, made stupid with fear, and listened forever to the sound of that alien cry.

* * *

$\mathcal{M}$r. Ravenbeck found me sleeping four hours later. Reeder, you may ask (no one else will, since no one else will hear this story) how I could possibly have slept under such bizarre circumstances. I cannot answer this myself. I suppose my exhausted body could not endure its tightly coiled posture for longer than an hour or two; adrenaline sucked every ounce of alertness from my brain and turned my fatigued muscles to jelly. I fell asleep alone and in darkness, the sound of that hopeless whimper bleating in my ears. I woke to weak daylight clawing in through the small high windows and Mr. Ravenbeck shaking me by the shoulder.

"Jenna! Are you awake? Jenna!"

I gasped and leaped to my feet, terrified lest that animal abovestairs had gotten loose and come searching for me. My fear must have been plain to read, for Mr. Ravenbeck's face was instantly flooded with remorse and concern.

"It is only I, Jenna, come back from the spaceport to relieve you," he said kindly. "What demons were you expecting?"

I tried to catch my breath and calm my heart. "Whichever ones are lurking in the bedrooms above me."

He gave me a sharp look. "Ah! And what did you hear during your vigils?"

"The voice of Gilda Parenon trying to soothe—some creature who would not be comforted. Mr. Ravenbeck, what is it you keep here?"

He shook his head. "I cannot answer that, Jenna. Not now, at any rate. Someday. Suffice it to say that I am struggling to act for that creature's good—that I would let nothing harm it as I would strain every nerve to keep it from harming others. There is a story so long it cannot be told, and so brief I could say it in a sentence—but it is not a story I can tell. The words will not cross my lips. Will you accept that? Will you believe in me, and trust in me, till a later day, when I gather my strength to offer you the truth?"

I was speechless. His words were spoken with such solemnity and such desperation that I could doubt neither his sincerity nor his agony.

I had never seen a man so near to complete despair. Yet he still kept a quiet dignity, a pride borne of much grief. I should have asked him a million questions—I should have recounted for him the nightmares I had just endured. And yet I nodded dumbly, too moved to speak.

He smiled, as if it cost him reserves of energy he did not have to make that brave effort. "That's my Jenna," he said. "You are a rare angel, indeed. Someday—when I can—someday—" He shook his head, unable to complete his thought.

Impulsively I put out a hand, to silence him or comfort him or comfort myself, I do not know. "Tell me at that distant time," I said. "For now, we both need to return to the manor and sleep."

"I have guests to entertain."

"If you do not plan to entertain them with news of this night's escapade, I do not know that you will have much to say," I retorted with some of my usual asperity. "How is Mr. Merrick, by the way? Did he survive your rough handling?"

"He did, and now is safely ensconced upon his own vessel. And let me tell you, I was not half so rough with him as I would have liked to have been! But that too is part of the story that will come at a later date."

"Come," I said, urging him upstairs with my hand still upon his arm. "I am exhausted if you are not. Return me to the manor."

There were no noises except those we made as we climbed the steps and let ourselves out the door. Mr. Ravenbeck conscientiously reset the lock, then helped me into his vehicle. Somewhere—perhaps on his journey to the spaceport—he had abandoned the mining car and retrieved his own aeromobile. I leaned against its luxurious seat and willed myself not to sleep until I was safely back in my room. We did not speak again until we had pulled up at the rear of the manor.

I gave him a sideways look; he smiled. "I thought we might encounter fewer people if we came in the back way, so that we might have fewer questions to answer," he explained.

"Mrs. Farraday—the cook—Mary and Rinda," I enumerated. "We are likely to run into all of them."

"Yes, and they may feel free to interrogate *you*, but they would not question me so boldly," he said, his smile growing.

"That is a comfort," I said dryly. "Since I have done you such a great favor this day, I have one to ask in return."

"Granted."

I nodded. "Then I will not see you at dinner tonight, for my request is that I be excused from further interaction with your guests."

"I see that I spoke too hastily," he said. "I will give you this night free, but I will expect you at the table with us tomorrow."

I opened the vehicle door and stepped out. "No, you granted the gift unheard, and now you cannot rescind it. And I thank you. Almost the dreadful evening was worth it if it has rescued me from worse torture in the future."

And on the sound of his low laughter, I entered the back door of the manor and escaped into the lower reaches of the halls.

Chapter 9

✧

*W*hen I woke that afternoon, it was to a sense of well-being that I could neither justify nor explain. Perhaps the hours of unbroken sleep had something to do with my feeling of quiet exhilaration, but I did not think so. What a night! A terrible night! And yet what a chance to prove my worth to Mr. Ravenbeck and spend precious moments alone in his company. I had acquitted myself well, and he had been grateful to me, and so even such a wretched adventure must be counted a success.

Still, I had to admit to a slight embarrassment when, once clean and dressed, I ventured downstairs to see if I could find food. It was well past the lunch hour, so I did not expect to find Mrs. Farraday or my other usual companions at the table, but I was not surprised to find the seneschal in the kitchen going over the evening's meal.

"Jenna! My gracious! I had begun to think you would never waken! Mr. Ravenbeck told us you returned early this morning and that I was not to disturb you on any account, but I had begun to fear you had fallen ill, and I was just wondering if I should come in and check on you."

"No, I am perfectly fine. I do not know that I have ever slept so long, however."

"And what was the cause of the alarm being raised last night? Do you know? I did not like to ask Mr. Ravenbeck."

"Genevieve, could I have some bread and cheese perhaps? Oh, yes, the fruit compote would be delicious," I said to the cook, stalling for time while I mentally reviewed my story. It seemed likely that she would not be able to follow me if I gravely answered her in technical jargon. "Yes, there was a problem in one of the outbuildings in the mining compound. An electrical malfunction in one of the switches. We had to rely on the mine tech's override command to keep the forcefields whole, which of course is just a temporary measure, so I worked to repair the damage with a few reinforced cables—"

She looked confused. "But couldn't one of the mine technicians have handled the repairs?"

"Under normal circumstances, yes, but there was also a malfunction in one of the nuclear generators at the compound, and—"

"Well, I see, I'm glad we had you to spare," she said, waving a hand politely to stop my explanation. "It does seem hard on you, though, to have to spend your whole night bent over some—some machine instead of sleeping in your bed."

I smiled. "That is what I came to Fieldstar for. To bend over malfunctioning machines. It was quite exciting, I assure you."

"Really. Well. I'm glad."

"Mr. Ravenbeck did say I could be excused from the evening entertainments for the next few days, as a payment for my extra work."

"Oh, but Jenna! You were having so much fun!"

"I do believe I need the quiet for a few days," I said.

She would have protested again, but Genevieve called on her attention. I managed to eat my food quickly and escape from the room.

The rest of the afternoon was quiet as, with an economy of motion necessitated by my shortened workday, I checked all my generators and cleaned out waste-disposal systems and did a quick survey of the forcefield wall. Everything seemed in order in our corner of the world.

Toward dinnertime, I made my way to the part of the manor dedicated to Ameletta, consisting as it did of a schoolroom and a connected playroom. In the latter, I found Ameletta and Janet Ayerson practicing a poem that Ameletta was to recite for Mr. Ravenbeck's guests that evening.

"There you are, Jenna. We heard you had quite a thrilling time of it last night," Janet greeted me.

"I'm not sure that is the word I would use, but it certainly was eventful," I said with a little laugh. "And now I have been the most slothful woman alive and slept half the day away. I am sure I do not know how I will persuade myself to fall asleep tonight."

"Oh, I fancy boredom may lull you into a dreamlike state," Janet said somewhat dryly. "Give yourself half an hour in the company of our guests, and you shall be quite ready for bed."

"Ah, but I have been excused for a few days," I said.

"How did you manage that?"

I manufactured a delicate shudder. "The strain on my nerves last night. Too much for me to bear. I need a respite."

She laughed. "Then I shall hope for another emergency tonight that will require my special services!"

Ameletta looked from her tutor to me and back to her tutor. "But Miss Starborn is not to join us tonight? She will not hear me recite my poem!"

"I will listen to you right now, before you go down to dinner," I offered. "That way you can practice your elocution."

"But it will not be the same! I wanted you there with us!"

"Ameletta," Janet reprimanded.

"I think you will find you perform quite well without my participation," I said, touched but completely unmovable. "Come! Speak your poem for me now."

After a few more moments of sulking, she complied, reeling off an animated rendition of a few verses about a child explorer who discovered gold on a distant planet. Janet and I both applauded and praised her when she was finished—and she did an excellent job, for she was a born actress—and this served to rescue her from the sullens.

Just as I was complimenting her again on her memory and her delivery, the little girl interrupted me. "But Miss Starborn! I forgot! What was in the package that arrived for you today?"

I glanced at Janet. "Package?"

The tutor nodded. "Did you not receive it? It was delivered by special courier this morning."

"In the bustle of preparing the meal, Mrs. Farraday must have forgotten," I said. "I cannot imagine who would have any reason to contact me here."

"One of your friends from Lora?" Janet guessed.

"All of them send mail by stel-route. I access all my letters on the terminal in my room."

"A gift from one of them, perhaps."

I smiled. "We are not so close that we exchange presents. I must find Mrs. Farraday at once."

But that task was easier set out upon than achieved. At first I could not locate the housekeeper; then, when I tracked her down in the wine cellar, she was deep in conversation with the cook and Mr. Ravenbeck, discussing the liquors to accompany the evening's meal. I did not like to disturb such a conference, so I returned upstairs to await her—and ended up missing her again as she slipped by me up the back stairwell to search out a special tablecloth in the linen storerooms. Soon, of course, the frenzy of serving the meal began, and once she was settled at the table with the other guests, I certainly could not approach her. I ate a quick meal in the kitchen with Mary, Rinda, and Genevieve, the whole time feeling my soul seethe with impatience.

Thus it was rather late into the evening, and Mrs. Farraday was still in her bustling mode as she oversaw the evening cleanup, before I had a chance to ask the seneschal about my parcel.

"Oh, my heavens! I forgot to give it to you!" she exclaimed. "I put it in my room for safekeeping. It is on my dresser, a small brown envelope. Just go in and retrieve it."

"Thank you, Mrs. Farraday."

Ordinarily I would not have liked to enter anyone's bedchamber unaccompanied—I have such a deep need for privacy myself that I hesitate to intrude upon anyone else's—but under the circumstances I felt justified. So I went to her room, crossed directly to the dresser without glancing curiously about me, and snatched up the parcel without pausing to look at more than my name on the label. Not until I had marched down the hall and closed the door on my own room did I really examine it to see where it might be from.

I did not immediately recognize the handwriting, though the return address, as Janet had expected, was Lora. I ripped open the package to discover, inside, another envelope with a letter wrapped around it. The note was from my old tutor, Mr. Branson, and it was brief:

"Jenna: This arrived for you yesterday, and I am sending it on to you as quickly as I can. I hope all is well with you in your new position. Noah Branson."

I was glad now that I had conscientiously informed my previous employers of my new address, or otherwise this mysterious envelope never would have made its way into my hands. Or was I glad? For the envelope itself bore the return address of Baldus.

My only thought was that my aunt Rentley was dead.

Slowly I opened the envelope and spread out the single typed sheet inside. It read: "Miss Starborn: I regret to inform you that your aunt Sofia Rentley is quite ill, and may in fact be dead by the time you receive this missive. Although everything has been done to ease her from this life, she has been unable to rest completely. Again and again she has expressed a desire to see you once more. I have told her I would look for you and, on her behalf, beg you to come to her bedside. I do not believe you have long to deliberate over this matter, and I urge you to come quickly if you can come at all." That stark message and a scrawled, nearly indecipherable signature, were the only words written on the page. Embossed on the top of the sheet were gold letters proclaiming that the message was sent from the law offices of Kafster & Macking.

I read the letter again.

I had not seen my aunt, my harvester, my commissioner, since I was ten years old. I had thought of her so rarely in the intervening years that now I had a hard time conjuring up her face, her voice, her mannerisms. At one time I had thought I would hate her so fiercely that my final words would be a malediction upon her soul, and now I found myself surprised to learn, or be reminded of, her given name. Sofia. No one had ever addressed her by that term in my hearing.

It is hard to either despise or forgive a woman you do not even know.

I sat for a long time in the gathering dark, not bothering to get up and turn on the lights of the room when the exterior light of the sun dimmed and disappeared. I was not so much remembering as testing, sending tendrils of inquiry through my muscles, to my brain, seeking the bruise or the injury. There were places I shied away from, experiences I refused to relive, even for this exercise, but most of those shadowed places were blurred and indefinite, too insubstantial to support nightmares. My aunt would die tortured by guilt and remorse if I did not go to her bedside; she would suffer, she would grieve. Her pain would escalate as the hour of her death grew nearer, while my own indifference would slowly erase even the troublesome images in my memory. She would grow darker as I grew lighter, and her death would not trouble me in the slightest.

But I had it in my power to bring a fellow human being rest and comfort. And only I, of all the people living in the universe, could bring such gifts to her side.

I have a great capacity for enduring cruelty, but none for inflicting it. I stood, flicked on the room lights, and turned on the computer in the corner of the room. In a few moments I had checked the cost and availability of passage to Baldus. Tomorrow morning, quite early, a transport left Fieldstar for the great shipping hub of Hestell. From there, I could catch a commercial liner straight for Baldus, a semi-direct route that would get me to Aunt Rentley's bedside within three weeks. I punched in the requests that would hold my place, and went downstairs to seek out Mr. Ravenbeck.

I came upon a scene of much noise and merriment. Someone had brought in a music-sim machine and hooked this up in the library. When I entered, Mr. Fulsome and Melanie Ingersoll were performing an upbeat duet that seemed to require them to also perform some sloppy dance steps, their arms about each other's waists and their feet moving in sync. Bianca Ingersoll looked bored by the exhibition, but everyone else in the room was laughing, clapping, and urging them on. Mr. Taff, in fact, had jumped to the top of a sturdy table the better to convey his enthusiasm, and was shaking both fists over his head in a gesture of congratulations.

I paused in the doorway, hoping to discover Mr. Ravenbeck without having to venture deep into the room. Unfortunately, he was all the way across the room from me, leaning over Mrs. Ingersoll's chair and apparently confiding some secret in her ear. She did not look pleased at whatever news he had to impart; her gaze, wandering around the room, actually came to rest on me. I pointed at Mr. Ravenbeck then pointed at myself. For a moment she stared at me, as if debating whether or not to convey my silent request, then she tugged on his arm and gestured in my direction. He spun around, evinced great surprise, and bounded across the room to join me.

"Well, Jenna? Have you recanted? The delightful sounds issuing from the room have made you regret your hasty decision to abandon our evening entertainments and come in to offer us your own rendition of some suitably tasteless cabaret melody?"

I smiled faintly. "Hardly that. May we go someplace where we can speak with some hope of hearing each other?"

In a few moments, we were installed in the breakfast room. We could still hear the music from down the hall, but muffled and at a distance, it had a sweeter, more wistful sound.

"You alarm me," Mr. Ravenbeck said, when I declined his suggestion that we each take a seat. "I fear you come on serious business."

"Not calamitous, but certainly not frivolous," I acknowledged. "Mr. Ravenbeck, I must go away for a month or two."

He had turned away as if to straighten an errant chair, but at that he swiveled back in astonishment. "What! Go away! Where? Why? For so long! I do not know that I can allow it."

"I do not know that you can stop me," I said gravely. "My aunt is ill, in fact dying, and I must be there to ease the end of her life."

"Your aunt! You have no aunt. You have no one, you told me so yourself."

"Well, I have her, and she needs me, and I must go to her."

He peered down at me. "And if I accede to this request, will you at some point in the future produce sisters and brothers and parents who also need you at some inappropriate hour? For in my experience, once you have found one relative, you invariably are petitioned by hundreds."

I accorded this sally the faint smile it deserved. "There is my aunt's son, but I don't believe he could exert any claim on me that would move me to action. She is the only one."

"And what does she need from you that you alone can provide?"

"Absolution," I said.

He started back in the manner of an edgy horse come suddenly upon a snake in the road. "And this is something you are capable of dispensing? Like fever medicine and good advice? I thought it was the province of priests and deities."

"She needs me and I must go to her," I said again, suddenly tiring of all these word games designed to make me doubt my resolution. "It now remains for you to tell me whether or not there will still be a position open to me when I am free again. Such knowledge," I added with a certain coldness, "will aid me in my packing."

He gazed down at me a moment in silence, his face grown serious and a little sad. "Why, Jenna, I am only teasing," he said softly. "It is just that I learn so little *of* you *from* you that I take every occasion to see what I can needle out of you, quiet closed little thing that you are. Of course you may go—and of course your post will be held for you. We could not manage without you. I do not know how we will manage these two or three months that you plan to be gone."

"The mine technicians will cover for me, I am sure."

"That is not what I meant," he said.

There was another small silence.

"When do you leave?" Mr. Ravenbeck asked finally. "How will you travel? What is your destination?"

"There is a shuttle from the spaceport tomorrow morning. I will take that to Hestell, and go by commercial liner from there to Baldus. The length of the voyage is what will take so much of my time. I do not anticipate that the visit will be long."

"And how will you pay for your ticket?" he asked next. "It cannot be an inexpensive journey."

I tilted my head up; I was not about to ask for charity. "I will draw upon the salary that has been deposited to my account."

"An advance could be made to you," he suggested. "Against your future earnings."

"I believe I have enough to cover my expenses," I said stiffly.

"But not much more than that, I would guess," he said shrewdly. "In fact, this unplanned trip must come close to wiping you out."

This was very nearly true, so I said nothing.

"If you will not take an advance, I have very little hope of persuading you to take a loan," he said, reading me quite rightly. "And yet, I cannot understand why not! According to your philosophy, if we are all equal, you have as much right to my money as I do—or as a dog does, or that oxenheart tree outside."

Again, he managed to elicit from me a faint smile. "I believe we are equal in our souls and our bodies," I said. "I do not believe we are equal in material possessions."

"Well, I can't see why not, since that's the only useful way to be equal," he said, unimpressed. "Give me as much money as the next man any day! And I'll be content to know that his soul sits on a much higher dais than mine in heaven."

"And yet, it is not your philosophy that rules my behavior, but mine," I said. "And I require nothing from you."

An idea had occurred to him. "But what if—what if—yes, I have it! What if I commission you to bring back something for me from Baldus? Then, since I am sending you on a job-related excursion, I must naturally incur all or at least some of your costs. Very well, then! Jenna, as your employer I command you to journey to Baldus, leaving immediately, and there procure for me—something. I shall think of it in a moment. And in pursuit of this task I shall pay for your passage to Baldus and all of your meals, besides."

"This might be more believable if there were anything on Baldus that any reasonable man might wish to acquire," I replied. "But since there is nothing that *I* can think of, I cannot imagine that *you* will be able to simulate a desire for anything it cultivates or exports."

"Nonsense, people must live there for some reason. You were only a child when you left—what could you possibly have known about agriculture or commerce? Let me think a moment. Baldus, Baldus—for what is it well-known?"

He frowned down at me ferociously while he cudgeled his brain. I kept an impassive countenance, certain he would not be able to come up with anything. But suddenly his face cleared and he looked down at me with a beatific smile.

"I have thought of it! I need a bottle of their aprifresel wine," he said triumphantly.

"Their what?"

"Aprifresel wine. It's hideous, actually, very sweet, made of some local plant crossed with apricots or some such nonsense. But I must have a bottle. I cannot live another day without it."

"Well, even if I carry out this commission for you, you will have to live deprived for at least two months, since I will not be back with it before then," I observed. "But if it is so dreadful, I cannot believe you actually desire it, and I will not purchase it, and I will not accept your money."

"No, I do want it, I want it above all things. I can sell it for two or three times its worth to Harley Taff, for he collects such things. His wine cellar contains an amazing variety of vintages collected from all over the civilized universe. He does not care about drinkability, only rarity. And I can assure you, there are very few individuals on Fieldstar who have bottles of aprifresel wine."

"Then perhaps it is Mr. Taff I should be going to, for he might be willing to pay me an even higher salary for fetching such a treasure for him," I said solemnly.

Mr. Ravenbeck looked ludicrously crestfallen. "Jenna! You would not do that! And rob me of the chance to play the gallant! It was my solution, after all. I ought to be allowed the satisfaction of acting upon it."

I smiled again. "You have no need to be gallant, or solve the dilemmas in my life. But I do appreciate the offer."

"Which you are telling me you refuse to accept?"

"Which I am refusing to accept. But I will bring you back some of this apricot concoction, if you wish. My only stipulation is that you share it with me. I have grown curious about its taste."

"That is a bargain," he promised. "We will stay up late one night and drink it together in celebration of some event. Your homecoming, for instance."

"Something more momentous, surely," I said. "The announcement of your engagement, perhaps."

He laughed. "Or the night before my wedding. For that is a night upon which I will surely need some fortification! And you would really sit up with me, drinking madly, on such an occasion, Jenna? If you promise me now, I will hold you to it in the future."

"I do not suppose that even I can get too madly drunk upon half of one bottle of wine," I said. "And yes, I would be happy to see you through such an evening, if you think my presence would be a comfort to you."

His eyes rested on me with an unfathomable expression. "You do not know how great a comfort, Jenna," he said.

"Very well, then, that is settled," I said briskly. "You have given me permission to leave and permission to return, which is what I came for, and now I have your commission as well. I have much to do tonight, still, and so I must return to my room now."

"And you will be gone in the morning before we all waken?" he asked.

"Most likely, unless you rise before the dawn."

"I doubt it. Then say good-bye now."

"Good-bye, Mr. Ravenbeck. I hope you enjoy the rest of your visit with your guests."

"Less so with you gone," he said.

"I know, for your teams will be uneven when you play SpaceShot."

He smiled, but rather forlornly. "I don't think I can manage it," he said.

"Manage what? To win at simulated military battles without my aid? I assure you, it will be amazingly easy."

"To say good-bye. I will miss you while you're gone. It will be strange to wake up in this house and know you are not under its roof."

"Think of the many days, the many years, you slept here, and I was sleeping on a planet whose only claim to glory was the production of a bad fruit wine," I said cheerfully. "That should get you through the dreary mornings."

Another sad smile; I began to think he was truly dismayed at my leaving, and my heart began to race, though I showed no outward signs of excitement. "But I think I missed you even then," he said. "For I never cared for Thorrastone Park till you were here. I hated to spend even a week in its confines. It must have been, as you say, those dreary mornings that made me avoid it. And now you force me to endure them again."

"I am sure you can find other consolations," I said, keeping my voice steady, though it was an effort. "Mr. Ravenbeck, I truly must go."

"Yes, you must," he said, but as he spoke, he lifted both hands and set them upon my shoulders, as if to hold me to the spot. His grip was not tight—in fact, he merely rested his palms upon my bones, almost weightlessly, as one might seek to hold in place a shadow that had no substance—and yet I was as effectively anchored to the floor as if he had wrapped me in chains and anvils. Again, he looked down at me with that serious, melancholy, searching gaze, as if somewhere on my face was printed the text to a secret he absolutely must know and had no hope of discovering.

"You will come back, Jenna?" he asked in a woeful voice.

"Nothing could prevent me, sir."

"You will not forget us?"

"In such a short time? Impossible."

He opened his mouth as if to say one more thing, then shut it again without speaking. He leaned infinitesimally closer; for one wild moment I thought he might kiss my cheek. And then suddenly, he lifted his hands, whirled aside, and vanished from the room without speaking. I stared after him, more startled and unnerved by this abrupt exit than I had been by any of the previous times he had left me in a hasty fashion. He was not happy that I was to leave Fieldstar, that much was clear, but what that unhappiness signified was incomprehensible to me. I slowly dragged myself back upstairs and began the sad business of packing for a journey toward death.

*I*n the morning, I caught the dawn bus at the Thorrastone Park airlock. I was one of only three surly passengers, and none of us attempted conversation. Once we arrived at the spaceport, we disembarked, and I carried my luggage through the quiet streets toward the huge, hulking hangars where the space-going craft awaited their next takeoff. I had some trouble finding which section of which hangar would serve as my port of exit, but eventually I located the proper service desk and caught the attention of a clerk who could issue me the tickets I had reserved. I was prepared to recite my credit account number and was astonished when he shook his head.

"Paid for," he said, his speech just as clipped though less genteel than Mr. Fulsome's. "Over the StellarNet last night. You're free to board."

Astonishment saw me silently through the gray corridors of the ship and into the tiny cabin I would share with two other strangers for our one-week voyage to Hestell. Indignation and rage struggled to find a way through my amazement, but they were puny and short-lived compared to the gratitude that sprang up weed-tall and indestructible alongside the shock. Mr. Ravenbeck had trampled on my independence, the very prize of my emotional garden, and yet his motive was so kind and his spirit so generous that I felt beautified, not betrayed.

I chose a bunk at random, installed my belongings in a featureless polystyrene armoire, and left the cabin to check out the amenities of the ship upon which I would spend the next seven days. I needed something real to distract me from the dangerous romantic fantasies in my head.

Chapter 10

✧

*A*unt Rentley clutched my hand for perhaps the third time in an hour. "Do not go, Jenna," she whispered.

"I am not leaving. I was merely resettling myself on my chair."

"I cannot breathe when you are not in the room."

"I know. You told me that yesterday."

"At night—there is no air in the room. None at all."

"Would you like me to bring in a cot and sleep beside you?"

She wheezed heavily, a deeply unattractive sound that yet roused my sympathy. She was skeletal, gray, unrecognizable either as the woman I had once known or, I was sorry to say, even a human member of the parade of species. I thought of the aprifresel wine, the oxenheart tree, things that had been created from two barely compatible organisms. She seemed now a hybrid herself, a discordant crossbreed of life and death.

"Oh, Jenna, if you would do that," she gasped. "That would be so good of you."

"Then I will. Tonight."

The assurance seemed to calm her as nothing else I had said all day had managed to do, and she settled back onto her bed and appeared to sleep. I resigned myself to another few hours of unmitigated boredom.

I imagined if you were watching over the deathbed of someone you truly loved, such a vigil as mine would be anything but boring. Painful, heartrending, each broken breath a cause for unparalleled terror—*No, not now, not this breath, it cannot be the last.* But tedium is all you are aware of when you are overseeing the death of someone you only pity.

My aunt had been pathetically happy to see me when I arrived three days previously. She had thrashed in her bed till she achieved a sitting position, and reached out her one free arm as if to throw it about my neck. I had bent down to allow her to hug me as well as she could, and listened to her choked, rasping words of welcome and apology. I could not tell exactly what she was saying to me and it did not matter. That my presence had given her a lift, a sweet extension of life, was evident. My long, dull, expensive journey had been worth it for this.

Since then, we had had nothing that would pass for real conversation. During her waking hours, she was fretful, suffering, and at times delirious, but she was rarely awake. Her left arm was encased in a PhysIV, a metallic gauntlet that completely swallowed her bones from her fingertips to the bend of her elbow. This neat little contraption performed a variety of functions, both to monitor her vital systems and inject her with necessary drugs and nutrients. I imagined that, on the interior surface of the hard glove, various needles were inserted into her skin at immovable points, offering either an entrance for the essential fluids or an exit for the blood and plasmas that must be tested. The PhysIV was attached by great opaque cables to an ambulatory stand so that, if she really desired mobility, she could merely come to her feet and waltz her self-contained monitors down the halls with her.

But it was clear that, by the time I arrived, her days of climbing from her bed were over. In fact, I could almost fancy that my appearance was the signal for her to begin the final descent into oblivion. For the first day I walked into her room, before she caught sight of me, I saw her lying tense and rigid on the bed, every muscle gathered taut, as though she fought off invisible foes through mental kinesis that required great concentration. Once she saw me, once she had thrown her arm about my shoulders and, in a misguided attempt to kiss my forehead, nuzzled my cheek with her thin, dry lips, she relaxed as completely as a child does upon falling asleep at the end of an exhausting day. Every time I saw her thereafter, she was slack, she was supine; she was wax and water, melting under ethereal heat and evaporating away.

When she was awake, no matter how incoherent, she wanted me near her. When she slept, I could escape down to the kitchens. Of the servants who had been here when I had left more than fourteen years ago, only Betista remained. She had been even more delighted to see me than my aunt had been, and more articulate too, and I enjoyed the chances we had for long, informative conversations. She had aged, naturally—she looked thinner, grayer, more resolute than I remembered—but she was happy to see me.

"So tell me of your exciting life!" she had demanded on that first afternoon as I sat in her kitchen, sipping tea and eating pastries. "Traveling all over the universe like a regular adventurer, you've been."

I smiled. "Hardly that. I've only been to Lora and Fieldstar—oh, and Hestell, to change shuttles, but since I was just there a day, I did not get to see much."

"Hestell!" she exclaimed enviously. "And is it as beautiful as they say? I've seen it on the 'Net news, of course, but that's not the same as being there."

"I took a tour of the capital city while I was waiting," I admitted. "But I was almost frightened! Do you know that one hundred million people live in that one tiny city? Even on Lora, there were not so many people in one small place. I found it hard to deal with, I must say. So many emotions packed down and made that much more intense—hatred, happiness, grief, desire. They are hard enough to handle when they are allowed space to breathe and dissipate, but when they are clamped down tightly like a gas under pressure, you know that there must be explosions every day."

"Oh, Miss Jenna, how you do talk!" Betista said, laughing. "Most people don't have time for such emotions every day. It's a matter of getting up, struggling through the chores as best they can, and falling into bed each night, glad the effort is over."

"Most days," I agreed, thinking of my placid, undifferentiated routine on Lora, and my easy, undemanding weeks on Fieldstar—until Mr.

Ravenbeck had arrived. "But when those combustible elements are added to even the most inert mixture—watch out! Things you never expected to react will prove the most colorful and violent."

She asked me then how I liked Fieldstar, and I told her a little of the inhabitants. Although I did not dwell long on Mr. Ravenbeck and his many virtues, I described in some detail the members of his house party, since I knew she would enjoy some of their absurdities. Having overseen years of Aunt Rentley's entertainments, she could not help but be well-acquainted with the vanities of the upper stratum of citizenship.

"But I have not come here to talk about me," I said finally. "What of my aunt? How long has she been ill? How has Jerret taken the news of her impending death? And what made her think of me at this dark hour of her life?"

Betista, who had been laughing at one of my stories, instantly grew more serious. "She has been sick for four or five months now, though it is only in the past few weeks that her condition has grown so bad. At first it seemed to be nothing that could not be handled by the PhysiChamber, though she made frequent visits there. But when she got no better, she called in live doctors, who ordered all sorts of tests. In the beginning they thought there was a problem with her heart, so they replaced that, and then they thought it was her blood, so they did a transfusion—took out all her own blood, put new blood in. The most amazing thing. But that did no good either. It seems to be something that cannot be fixed. She is just dying. I do not think it will be very much longer now."

"And Jerret? What has he said?"

She grew even more grave. "He has said nothing. We are not even sure he is aware of her illness. We have sent messages by courier and stel-route to all his last several addresses, but he has not replied. The lawyer has posted announcements on all the legal channels, and embedded notices in the mail systems of the StellarNet which should pop up on his screen when he logs on under his own name, but he has not responded. We believe he is still alive, for money from his account continues to be spent—but if he is, he has shown no interest in his mother's fate. I cannot tell you how sad it makes me, that a son should treat his mother so poorly."

"And a mother who loved him so well," I added. "But tell me, when was the last time you saw Jerret? How was he then?"

Betista thought a moment. "Three or four years ago, I believe. Oh, he was a fine-looking, dashing young man then! Wearing the most incredible clothes—though I believe they were the height of fashion— all bright colors and swirling patterns and tight-fitting garments that I—well, I hated to look at too closely for how revealing they were. He came to visit one day completely without notice, and turned the house upside down, and borrowed a good deal of money from his mother, and was gone the next day without waiting to attend the dinner party she had thrown together in his honor. I think it broke her heart. I think that was when she began to get sick and could not get better."

"So Jerret has not turned out well, I take it."

She shook her head. "Nasty, ill-tempered, greedy, idle. And he has been in more kinds of trouble—! There was the half-cit girl who claimed he'd fathered her child, though no one believed her, of course, and I have no idea whatever happened to her. But then there was a level-three citizen—a good eight years older than Jerret—who claimed the same thing a year later, and she had the money and the tests to prove it. Then there have been the scandals over debts and strange illegal deals and I don't know what all. I don't hear the half of it, and I wouldn't want to repeat it if I did. He's been a terrible disappointment to his mother, is all I can say, and now she'll die and he doesn't even care. It's broken her heart, and I swear some days it will break mine."

"She loved him too much," I said softly.

"She loved him *wrong*," Betista said flatly. "Never taught him right from wrong, good from bad. Never taught him to be a good man."

"Does one have to be taught that, I wonder?" I mused. "Are we not born knowing good and evil—and knowing to run toward the one and hide from the other?"

"Maybe—some of us, at any rate," Betista said, watching me closely. "You, for instance. You seemed to have had it all sorted out pretty clearly in your head, and no one was showing you the true path from the false."

I reached out a hand to lay it affectionately on her forearm. "You," I said.

She made a small noise, composed half of satisfaction and half of dissent. "You had those things in your heart, for I didn't have the time to show you much," she said. "Never met anyone with a stronger sense of justice in my life. Whatever happens to you, you won't make foolish mistakes and pretend you didn't know the difference. You'll choose wisely, and you'll choose honestly, and no amount of persuasion will change your mind."

I liked to think that was so; I had always believed it. But these days I was beginning to wonder. "So if they cannot find Jerret," I said, reverting to the original topic, "what happens to all of Aunt Rentley's property? Will it be auctioned off?"

"It's my belief that the minute the notice of her death is posted on the StellarNet, Jerret will be knocking at the door claiming his rights," Betista said darkly. "I shouldn't know what's in her will, but I do. If Jerret's not found within a year, all her property goes to that baby I told you about. The citizen's girl. She has the next legal claim."

I did not even ask if there was a bequest for me. Aunt Rentley loved Jerret too much, even Jerret's unclaimed offspring, to put him aside for me or anyone else. Besides, as a half-cit, I could not inherit property. Some small monetary gift she could leave me, if she had a mind to, but I was not expecting this either. With my visit here, we were canceling all spiritual debts between us; nothing more solid would change hands.

"I always hated Jerret, and I never liked my aunt much, but for her sake I wish he would appear here a day or so before she dies," I commented. "For I think it would ease her journey into that other world to have him at her bedside."

"She would be overjoyed to see him, but it is you who have made her easy, Jenna," Betista said. "You have done a great good deed by coming here. You are the one she has wanted to see the most."

"Yes, but I still don't know why. If she had something to tell me, she has forgotten what it is, or cannot say the words."

"It is you who must say the words, Jenna, and you know what they are."

I smiled a little and nodded, for I did indeed know. "I forgive you, Aunt Rentley," I said. And Betista nodded, and patted my arm as if I were again a child and had learned the most difficult lesson of all.

Two days later, my aunt died. I was sleeping in her room, as I had promised her I would, and I was roused from sleep by one great cry. I leaped to my feet and was instantly at her side, to see her eyes wide, terrified, fixed on some visitor imperceptible to my eye.

"Jenna!" she cried, clutching at my arm with a strength I could not believe she still possessed.

"Yes, Aunt, I am here."

"Jenna, they want you!"

"No one wants me, Aunt. I am quite safe."

"They do, they do, they asked me for you, but I would not give you over to them," she said, moving her head imperiously on her pillow. "Oh, Jenna, I am so sorry! I have treated you so badly! But you were so hard to love—so hard, and dark, and small, and I wanted something soft and beautiful. Why could you not have been soft and beautiful?"

It is no easy thing to be called unlovable even by someone as pitiable as my aunt, and I felt a small part of my sympathy leak away. "I am who I am, born that way, and will die that way," I said, though I was instantly sorry to have brought up the topic of death. "It does not matter now that you could not love me then. I do not hold it against you anymore. I have made my own life, and I am stronger for it, and I forgive you for any sins you think you may have committed."

Her grip on my arm grew even fiercer to the point where I almost could not tolerate it. "You forgive me? All of it?"

"Every slur," I said, smiling. "Every crime."

"But I—I should have—"

"Yes, but it does not matter now. Go in peace."

She opened her mouth as if to speak again, but the words eluded her. Again, she tossed her head on the pillow; her eyes pinched shut and she seemed to be concentrating now on interior visions. I waited for her to speak again, but she did not. Her grip on my arm loosened, and she seemed to sigh. A long time later, she sighed again. I realized she had not breathed once between those intervals.

Two more sighs, after long, long intermissions, and she took in no more breath. Her hand was still curved over mine, but its desperate pressure was relieved. Her whole body seemed caught in one moment of apprehension, the shoulders hunched forward to ward off blows, the knees slightly updrawn to protect the abdomen. But there were no more blows to fall, no more damage to be done. The PhysIV began a small, steady keening, so soft I would not have heard it if I had not been so close. The sound was so plaintive that I thought to myself, *The machine is grieving*. I was glad that something in the room, in the house, in the universe, would make the effort.

I had planned to leave the very day my aunt died, but the following morning, I discovered there was too much to do in the house for me to reasonably leave it all to Betista. So I agreed to stay two more days, but no longer, and I booked my return passage on an outbound cruiser. Then I joined with the housekeeper and the lawyer in tying up the details that even the tidiest soul leaves undone.

It was on the afternoon of this second day that I thought to check my stel-mail, which I had neglected for the whole of my visit. I never received a great volume of correspondence, it was true, so the fact that I had overlooked it for the better part of a week was not a particular sin. And it might not have occurred to me even now had I not been working on my aunt's computer, trying once more to find Jerret and send him the sad news. But terminals could be used for more than seeking out negligent sons, and I logged onto my own account to see what messages might have accumulated during my period of inattention.

In fact, there was only one post directed at me—but this one held a world's worth of shock and woe. It came from Mrs. Farraday and was dreadful indeed.

"Oh, Jenna, I do wish you were here," it began without preamble. "Janet Ayerson has run off with Joseph Luxton."

I looked up from the screen and tried to assimilate the words. *Impossible. No one would be that foolish! Perhaps I had read the words wrong.* My mind still in a state of incomprehension, I struggled through the rest of the missive.

The whole party was scheduled to break up three days ago, and they all planned one last outing to town. Janet told me privately she would stay late, for she had some shopping to do, so I was not worried when she did not return with the others. And I thought nothing of it when Mr. Ravenbeck told me Mr. Luxton had stayed on to confer with his bankers! But the last shuttle came in, and neither of them was on it, and his friends began to ask for him at dinner. No one but me knew that Janet was missing also.

"Perhaps something's gone amiss in town," Mr. Ravenbeck said as they finished up their meal. "A fire or some disaster. I'll take the Vandeventer in and see. Anyone care to join me?" Bianca Ingersoll immediately volunteered, but then her mother claimed to need her help on some project back in her room, and I had a chance to get Mr. Ravenbeck alone.

"Janet is still in town as well," I whispered to him. "Look for her too—I am afraid something dreadful has happened to her."

He looked thunderstruck. "Janet Ayerson and Joseph Luxton both missing!" he exclaimed. "Then it is even more dreadful than I supposed."

"Surely there can be no connection between their absences," I said, for it had not even crossed my mind. "Unless they both have been caught in an accident."

"Oh, it is no accident that has befallen them," he said so grimly that I trembled. "Damnation! I have worked so hard to avert this!"

I was still bewildered and tried to question him, but he strode away from me, into his study where the terminal is always turned on. I followed him, for I did not know what else to do. He quickly called up his messages, and sure enough, there was a new one posted that very afternoon from Mr. Luxton. He had taken his personal cruiser and fled with Janet. He did not say where they were going or when they might return—or anything—and Jenna, Mr. Ravenbeck was in such a rage that I almost forgot my own sadness and horror.

"Mrs. Farraday, we must not breathe a word of this to anyone," he said to me without even looking in my direction. "No one must hear of it, do you understand? If we can retrieve her, we may yet save her reputation. If we can discover where they have gone, I can go after her. She will be safe here, as she will be safe few places."

"Oh, but Mr. Ravenbeck, what does he intend?" I cried. "Janet is a good, moral girl—surely she would not have left with him if he had not promised marriage and citizenship!"

"He may have promised it, but he will not perform," the master said, still in that deadly calm voice. "This is not the first half-cit girl he has charmed from a decent situation, then cast off when he grew bored. I dare not think what may happen to her, on some strange planet, with no friends, no funds, no references—no hopes. We must find them somehow—and we must keep her secret."

As you can imagine, I was happy enough to promise the latter, though I had no idea how to help with the former. He bade me tell the others that he had received a message from Mr. Luxton, saying he had been called home on urgent business, and he settled himself in at the monitor like a man with great purpose. I believe he was trying to contact the central control tower to find if Mr. Luxton had filed a flight plan, and he may have been attempting other methods to follow the cruiser. I did not stay—I do not understand computer tactics. I went to the library to pass on the false story.

But I should have saved my effort. Mr. Luxton had also sent a message to Mr. Fulsome, who had shared its contents with the rest of the company. They were speaking of it excitedly even as I entered. Oh, the awful things they said about poor Janet! Their cruel comments about greedy half-cit girls and foolish wealthy men! Mrs. Ingersoll declared that the whole thing was Mr. Ravenbeck's fault for allowing his staff to mingle with his guests; she declared that the classes should be constantly and irrevocably separated to prevent such misalliances. And they all condemned our dear Janet, every one. Not a one of them realized that her life was ruined, that she was a lost girl now—realized nor cared.

They all left the very next day, and I at least was relieved to see them go. Mr. Ravenbeck left with them, apparently off on the hunt to find the runaways. He says he will be back, no matter what he discovers, but I have not heard from him since. The household has fallen into stark disarray. I am completely incapable of functioning, and Ameletta roams the grounds at will, frightened and unsupervised.

Oh, Jenna, come back to us! We need you so desperately.

Antoinette Farraday

Could a letter ever have been so unwelcome? I read it with my heart climbing up in my throat, and my hand clenched over my mouth to keep that organ from escaping. Janet! Lost! For Mr. Ravenbeck's words were true. Without references, no half-cit girl could get a job, certainly not as tutor to a small child. If Mr. Luxton did not marry her, or make some sort of provision, she would starve to death on whatever city street he abandoned her. Unless she had relatives who would take her in, unless she was not too proud to return to Thorrastone Manor where—I was encouraged by Mr. Ravenbeck's behavior to hope—she would be received again with loving, forgiving arms.

I dropped to my knees on the floor, my hands resting on the edge of the computer desk, my eyes still directed at the monitor, though my gaze was unfocused. This, then, was the culmination of the sidelong looks and halting conversations I had witnessed between Janet and the handsome Joseph Luxton. This, then, was what Mr. Ravenbeck—in his guise as fortune-teller—had warned the tutor against, when he looked into her future and saw her following a course she would regret. She had met the man before, she had told me so herself. That must have been the beginning of their illicit relationship, though I could not guess how far it may have proceeded at that time. But from this point, there was no walking backward, no retracing of steps, no undoing of actions.

Unless, against all odds and all personal history, Mr. Luxton truly loved Janet, she was as good as lost to us forever.

"Dear Goddess, great Mother, take her to your heart now and cradle her," I whispered, the words barely forcing their way through my frozen lips. "She has committed no sin in your eyes, only the eyes of society. Now it is up to you to love her and protect her as mortal beings cannot. Give her courage, give her strength, give her hope, give her love. Let no harm come to her through anything she may have done."

As I spoke, I knew I prayed not just for Janet, but for myself. For what one weak girl could do, might not another? Who was watching over me, caring for me, keeping my blistered feet on the steep and stony path of righteousness? Could not Jenna Starborn become just as easily Jenna Errant? Who would love me if I faltered or failed? Who would save me if I stumbled?

I dropped my hands from the desk, hung my head low over my chest, wrapped my arms around my body, and rocked where I knelt. "Watch over us all," I whispered. "Amen."

Three weeks later, I disembarked from the commercial shuttle into the small spaceport on Fieldstar. I had been gone barely eight weeks, yet it felt like eight years. I kept glancing up and down the crowded streets, noticing buildings I had not seen before and faces that were wholly unfamiliar, hoping against hope some favorite storefront would be found to be still standing, as though I feared that, during my absence, some physical or financial disaster had brought about its ruin. In short, I behaved like some kind of prodigal returned after a long separation, both glad to be home and dreading the consequences of my arrival.

I had missed the noon airbus, so I shopped a bit until it was time for the evening run. I had picked up a bottle of aprifresel wine for Mr. Ravenbeck on Baldus, and some seeds for Mrs. Farraday, who liked to grow her own spices for the kitchen, but I had not found anything I particularly thought Ameletta would like. She was not especially demanding; any trifle or toy would do, and I could as easily find something here in the spaceport as in any commercial venue across the universe. I bought her some hair ribbons in a little shop and considered my mission done.

I still had some time to pass, but less energy to waste, so I sat in the shuttle station for another hour and merely let my mind wander. As always these days, my thoughts turned swiftly to Janet Ayerson. Mrs. Farraday had sent me daily updates, but there was no real news. Mr. Ravenbeck had traced the runaways to Corbramb, but could not induce either of them to return his messages, and he was fairly certain if he traveled all that way to confront them, they would be gone before he arrived. He had contacted Mr. Luxton's family, who refused to discuss the situation with him; even so, he tried to make plain to them that he would bear Mr. Luxton no ill will if he would only pass along to Janet the information that she had a refuge, should she need one, at Thorrastone Manor. He also contacted Janet's family, giving this same information, but was coldly informed that they had no daughter, no sister, by the name of Janet, and they therefore could pass along to her no news at all.

I myself had tried to contact Janet via stel-route, for I had an old address for her that I believed was still active. I was encouraged in that my posts were not blindly returned to me, but if she received them, she did not reply. My messages were full of love and forgiveness and offers of charity, for I did not know what else to send, but I could not blame her for failing to answer. If she was still in love and happy, if Mr. Luxton had not yet cast her off, she would scorn to read such mail; she would laugh at us and think herself the luckiest girl alive. If she was already betrayed and solitary, she would be too mortified to reply; she would think herself so far below the notice of any moral person that she would not be able to accept the simplest expression of goodwill. And yet I wrote because there was nothing else I could do.

Finally, after what seemed like years of waiting, the sundown shuttle pulled into the station. The driver, a strongly built young man, threw my bags into the storage compartment with so much ease that I was tempted to ask him, when we arrived at the Thorrastone gate, to walk me all the way to the door. Naturally, I said nothing of the sort. I took a seat, glanced at my dozen or so fellow passengers, and endured the trip in silence.

I arrived at the Thorrastone airlock just as true dark was settling over the park and the artificial lights were coming on. I tried not to shiver, but something about that cold, unwavering illumination made the vista seem inhospitable and alien to me—seemed to throw the whole terraformed landscape into harsh and realistic relief so that I remembered, what was so easily forgotten, that we were grafted onto this place by sheer force of will, that we did not belong, that the smallest error could send us skating off into the black outer vacuum.

I shook my head to dispel the thoughts and determinedly shouldered my bags. I had not packed any more than I could carry, but even so, I was not looking forward to the mile-long hike back to the manor house. I might rest on my way halfway there, under the oxenheart branches.

I had not made it nearly so far when a slight noise and a sleek movement caught my attention, and I turned my head sharply to the left. Yes—a small hovercraft coming my way at a speed a little too great for our confined space. I dropped my bags and held my ground, for I was sure the driver had seen me, and I had a fairly good guess as to who the driver might be.

Soon enough the craft came to a halt directly before me—indeed, deliberately intersecting my course so that, had I been attempting to walk forward, my path would have been impeded. Mr. Ravenbeck sat very still in the driver's side, watching me seriously and making no move to step from the vehicle. I stared back at him, and refused to be the one to break the silence.

At last he said, in a fairly normal voice, "Did it not occur to you that, if you had sent word of your arrival, someone would have come to the spaceport to pick you up? One of the servants could have been spared—or even I, busy man that I am, could have taken the requisite hours to see you safely to the end of your long journey."

I smiled under the peculiar light and felt the shadows play oddly across my skin. I was very sure that I looked gaunt or eerie or otherwise fey, but no matter how I tilted my face, I could still feel that unflattering light across my cheekbones. "I need expend very little effort to climb aboard a shuttle that will take me precisely to my destination. Why should someone else be inconvenienced when I face no hardship? Now, if it were a very difficult thing to make it from town to Thorrastone Manor, be sure I would have announced my arrival days ago and been imperiously demanding an escort from hangar to hall."

He smiled at this, and I noticed his own features looked more natural than mine felt, or perhaps it was the smile that eased them back into familiarity. "I wish I believed that were so, but, Jenna, your idea of what would inconvenience you, and *my* idea, are so radically different that I do not believe you can be entirely trusted to decide."

"Well, I am here now, and ready to be fussed over," I said. "I will accept a ride to the manor, if you are willing to offer it."

"I have come this way for that very purpose," he said, climbing nimbly from the car.

"Oh? And how did you know I was to return this day?" I scoffed, clearly not believing him.

He had hoisted both bags into an open trunk in the back of the hovercraft while I climbed as daintily as I could into the passenger's seat. "I have come this way every night for the past two weeks," he said, "timing my circuit for the arrival of the sundown shuttle."

This news caused my face to run with a rapid heat, though I hoped the color was not so visible under the bleaching light. I hoped this even more passionately when Mr. Ravenbeck came around to my side of the car and laid his hands on the edge of the door.

"That was kind of you," I said, as calmly as I could manage. "Had I known you would go to so much trouble, I would have given you the details of my arrival, and spared you two weeks of aimlessness."

"Eight weeks of aimlessness," he retorted. "For just so long have you been gone."

"I know for a fact you have not been without occupation for many of those weeks," I said in a low voice. "For Mrs. Farraday has told me of your efforts for Janet Ayerson."

He moved one hand from the door frame to pass it over his face, but I caught its expression before he hid it. He looked sad, shamed, weary unto death. "I have not done enough for her even so," he said. "But I cannot think of what to do next. They have eluded me—they have left Corbramb and moved elsewhere, and I cannot track them. I know neither how to find them nor how to contact her."

"Are they yet together?"

"As far as I can determine."

"Then perhaps he will not abandon her. Perhaps we do him a disservice in assigning the role of villain to him."

He dropped his hand and stared at me a moment. "Am I to understand," he asked at last, "that you condone this runaway act? That you believe love is stronger than disgrace and that a few hours of happiness, however tainted, are worth whatever price an individual might have to pay? For let me tell you, if so, out of my hovercraft at once. This is not the Jenna Starborn I know—this is an imposter, arrived on my lawn at night to trick me."

I smiled faintly. "You must not be surprised to learn that I believe love transcends class, at any rate," I said mildly. "If Mr. Luxton and Janet Ayerson truly loved each other, if that love was equal on both sides, if she did not love him for his money and he did not love her for her dependency—why, then, yes, I would say I would condone their act, I would bless their union. But I am very much afraid this is not so. I am afraid he will abandon her, and society will scorn her, and she will be utterly lost, and I am as afraid for her as I have ever been for anyone."

He was still watching me with intent, serious eyes. "You would not make such a mistake, would you, Jenna?" he asked gravely. "You would not run off with an attractive scoundrel, believing his protestations of affection, if he did not offer you his name as well as his heart?"

"I would not like to say what I would have done had I been Janet Ayerson," I said, dropping my eyes because the look in his troubled me. "I don't believe any of us knows what we would do if we were living another's life. I only know that I *try* to do good and *try* to be strong. The rest is chance and mischance."

"Well, we shall hope your mischances are few," he said, and abruptly lifted his hands from the door. In a few moments, he had circled the car and hopped in beside me, though he did not immediately start up the vehicle again.

"The house has been very quiet while you were gone, Jenna," he remarked now. "All our houseguests left a few days after you did, and of course we were grieving for Janet as well. There has been very little to help pass the long quiet evenings. I have missed you."

"And perhaps missed your guests as well?" I could not help asking. "One or two in particular?"

He smiled at me oddly. "Do you mean Bianca Ingersoll? Rumor has it she will be returning to Thorrastone very soon."

"Indeed? In what capacity? Guest again, or something more substantial—more nearly related to the organization of the household?"

His smile grew wider. "You must ask the servants. I believe they talk of nothing else. It was from them that I first heard the rumor of my impending marriage—or, more precisely, from Mrs. Farraday, who told me that Mary and Rinda and Genevieve expect to be invited to the ceremony, for they consider themselves part of my family and want to be included in any event that deeply touches my life."

"I understand exactly how they feel," I said quite calmly, though my heart was cracking in two like a brittle stone.

"You do? You would want to be present at my wedding?"

"Indeed, yes, and I will keep you company the night beforehand, or do you not remember my promise? I have brought you back the wine you requested, so that we may share it on just such an evening. So if I can celebrate with you the night before, surely I can bear witness for you at the actual event. In fact, I insist upon it."

He smiled again, even more oddly, and finally touched the button that started the motor. "You *will* be present at my wedding, Jenna. I will not be wed if you are not there, and that is a promise I will not break. So stay near me until that great day arrives, or I will remain a solitary man until I die."

It was tempting, I must admit, to lay plans to run off the very next morning in secret, for if my presence was required to consummate Mr. Ravenbeck's marriage to Bianca Ingersoll, I was willing to remove my

person from the vicinity immediately. But that was cowardly and foolish—and fanciful beside. He would marry whomever he would marry,
no matter where in the universe I might be stationed.

"It is a promise, Mr. Ravenbeck," I said. We rode thereafter in
silence until we arrived at the manor door.

Oh, how small and sad and desolate that house seemed to me
tonight! The day I had left, the walls had been crammed with life and
laughter—somewhat empty-headed life and careless laughter, to be
sure, but still invested with an animal vitality and restlessness that
caused the bricks to thrum with a random energy. Now the manor
seemed uninhabited, ransacked, visited by tragedy. The foyer and stairway echoed with the consciousness of loneliness. There were not
enough souls within the entire building to reasonably tenant the rooms,
and the dark doorways seemed to suck greedily at me as I passed, hoping to draw me in. I felt watched by hollowness, and the scrutiny rendered me hollow in turn.

Mr. Ravenbeck paced wordlessly beside me, seeming as oppressed by
the silence as I was. He carried all of my bags, though I had offered to
shoulder one of them myself, so I was very conscious of my hands and
my relative weightlessness as we made our way up two flights of stairs.
He had never, since I had taken possession of it, stepped inside my
room, and I felt oddly nervous as we approached my door. But he was
not a man to overstep boundaries; no doubt he would deposit my luggage on the floor, speak a simple good-bye, and dash from the room.

A few steps—we were there—the handle turned—and sudden turmoil! A cry, a small sobbing body hurtling my way, a confusion of voices
and words, and Ameletta weeping against my stomach. Distantly I
heard a voice—Mrs. Farraday's—explaining that Ameletta had missed
me so much that she had slept in my room every night since I had been
gone, hoping by that method to make sure I did not spend one minute
under this roof without her knowledge. Mrs. Farraday hoped I did not
mind, it had seemed the only thing that would soothe the child, and she
herself was so glad to see me she almost could not get the words out.

"Oh, Jenna, we have missed you so much," she said, coming closer
as she spoke, until she too was embracing me in a hold less fervent but

just as sincere as Ameletta's. "I have never in my life been so glad to see someone again."

I returned her hug, then bent down to scoop Ameletta into my arms and cover her wet face with kisses. "And I have missed all of you just as much—even more," I said into the tousled blonde hair. "You will sleep in my room again tonight, won't you, Ameletta? I should like to wake up tomorrow morning and see your pretty face the very first thing. It will remind me that my travels are now over and that I am finally home."

"I am glad to hear you think of this as home," Mr. Ravenbeck said, surprising me, for I had almost forgotten he was in the room. I turned quickly, Ameletta still in my arms, and saw him smiling at the domestic picture we made. He added, "We are all glad to have you back. I look forward to seeing you again in the morning."

And with that, he left. Mrs. Farraday stayed rather longer, fussing over me, helping me unpack, whispering additional details about Janet's ill-fated flight. She need not have whispered; Ameletta was already fast asleep on my bed, where I could not wait to lay my own tired head. Mrs. Farraday did realize this, for soon enough she kissed my cheek, repeated her thanks that I was back at last, and bustled out the door. In a few minutes, I had climbed into bed beside the sleeping child and curled myself protectively around her.

Home. Oh, that I wished it were. But if Mr. Ravenbeck was to marry Bianca Ingersoll in the near future, how long would Thorrastone Park be a true home to me? He might wish to keep me on, performing my technical duties and acting as sometime watcher for Ameletta, but could I bear to live in the same house with the man I loved and his smug new bride? Yes, the man I loved—I knew it, I acknowledged it, I dreaded it, but the reckoning would have to come, and soon.

Chapter 11

✧

The next few days passed quietly, in something like contentment, though it was more like the suspended silence between an infant's first intimation of injury and its subsequent howl of outrage. I felt as if events were about to break, courses were to be set or altered, and no few hours of peace and calm would convince me otherwise.

During those days, I divided my time between my assigned duties and my assumed ones, when I could not combine them. That is, I spent part of my time watching over my machines and part of my time guarding Ameletta, and sometimes doing both. To the extent that I could, I took over Ameletta's education during this week. Janet had been following a computerized series of courses which I was able to call up and analyze, and once I determined what Ameletta's skill level was, I was able to assign her lessons. In the mornings I set her at this task down in the library, where she would not be totally alone, for Rinda and Mary and Mrs. Farraday wandered in and out of the room once or twice an hour.

After lunch, I would quiz her on what she'd learned, and then I would take her with me on a long walk around the grounds. I would use these occasions to cover the topics that I knew best—specifically, math and science—and I would set her to working arithmetic problems in her head or explaining to me some of the concepts by which we lived on Fieldstar. Thus we covered, in their most basic form, the principles of gravity, sunlight, interstellar travel, and nuclear physics. She did not particularly have a head for the hard sciences, but she preferred this method of learning to laboring over a computer monitor all day, and she did her best to listen, understand, and please me.

In the evenings, she and Mrs. Farraday and I had quiet dinners in which we all tried very hard to be cheerful, though the effort was as visible as the lace in the tablecloth. Sometimes Rinda, Genevieve, and Mary ate with us, just for the comfort we drew from expanded companionship, though Rinda was not much of a talker and Mary's conversation was limited. Still, the goodwill we felt toward one another brightened the dinner hour and lessened some of the loneliness we all felt.

After the meal, Ameletta and Mrs. Farraday and I joined Mr. Ravenbeck in his study. He had begun to teach Ameletta a rather complicated computer game, and every night they sat together while he gave her further instruction. It seemed clear to me from his repeated explanations that she had no real grasp of the game, but that she wanted to learn it from him was obvious; she glowed with the delight of achieving his undivided attention, and she tried very hard to sit still and pay attention. Frequently Mrs. Farraday and I would exchange looks of indulgent satisfaction to see them sitting so close, dark head bent over blonde, as the patient lecture went on.

Those were quiet days, as I said, but happy in a strange, desperate way. Later I would look back at them and marvel, and sigh, and wish I could return to them for only an hour.

A week after my return, I was putting Ameletta to bed when she suddenly sat up under the covers with a stricken look on her face.

"Oh, Miss Starborn! Oh, no! I have forgotten! I have left my pretty ribbons under the tree and they will be out all night and eaten by wild animals! Oh, please, can I go for them now? I will run ever so fast and be back before you even notice I am gone."

It took a few minutes for me to sort out what had happened, and when I did, I confess I did not think it the tragedy that Ameletta did. She had been carrying around the packet of ribbons I'd given her as if they were some sort of unformed doll; she had not braided them together, or knotted them into any sort of figure, but she liked to have them with her to toy with the dangling edges when she concentrated on some problem I had set her. I am sure she also liked to carry them because I had given them to her, for she was a child who reveled in tangible proofs of affection. At any rate, this day she had accidentally left them under the oxenheart tree, where we had paused during our daily walk around the lawn.

"Ameletta, *chiya*, they will come to no harm there. There are no wild animals here in the compound—no one will take them."

"But the birds! And the little squirrels—they will steal my ribbons to line their nests. I will go out tomorrow and they will be gone!"

It was true that Thorrastone Park, through some odd quirk of evolution, harbored a few small creatures that looked like armored squirrels and birds, though Mr. Ravenbeck had told me once that when the forcefield was first erected, no such animals lived inside its walls. They seemed to exist equally well inside the compound or outside in the toxic air, so they could tunnel under the walls to freedom or sneak in and out when the airlock opened. I am sure their wandering across the face of the planet was one of the contributing factors to the cross-pollination of imported and native plant species.

In any case, Ameletta was right. One of these little animals could very easily be attracted to her row of ribbons, and run off with the treasure.

"Very well, Ameletta, I will go after the ribbons. You, in any case, are not to climb from this bed, not to watch me out the window nor to sneak down to my room tonight and make sure I have recovered your prize. I will go for them now, and you can believe me, but you must go to sleep now."

I had never reneged on a promise, so she believed me and instantly snuggled back down into her covers. "Thank you *very* much, Miss Starborn," she said, so sweetly that I bent and kissed her cheek, though I had already kissed her good night. "You are so good to me!"

I patted her blonde hair and rose to my feet. "It is easy to be good to you, for you are a lovable girl," I said. "Now do as I say, and sleep."

I left her room and went straight downstairs, having no great desire to walk half a mile to the oxenheart tree under the ghostly artificial lighting. But a promise was a promise, and I did not hesitate as I opened the door and stepped determinedly out into the falsely lit night.

As I made my way toward the tree—large, ugly, hunkering down under the arched forcefield—I noticed a strange quality in the air itself, as if the very molecules of the atmosphere were bunching together in angry clusters. So did air feel on a natural world when the currents were coalescing for a storm, but I could not imagine what the sensation presaged in a closed environment surrounded by a windless void.

I glanced up at the distant stars, just now bleached out by a run of that frequent nighttime aurora caused by the sun's constant flaring. The streaks of light seemed hotter and more vibrant tonight. Perhaps that solar wind was causing a faint disturbance in the magnetic forcefields that surrounded and sheltered us. Nothing more sinister than that.

I had almost made it to the dark shelter of the tree, and was congratulating myself on my coolness and fortitude, when a shadow detached itself from the main bulk of the trunk and stepped in my direction. I emitted a small scream and would have dashed back toward the house had my feet not inexplicably frozen themselves to the ground. My terror, though intense, was short-lived, for in seconds the shadow stepped closer and resolved itself into the master of Thorrastone Park.

"Great Goddess! Mr. Ravenbeck, how you startled me!" I exclaimed, pressing a hand against my racing heart and hearing the tremolo in my voice. "I did not realize anyone else was abroad at this hour, let alone lurking in darkness at my very destination."

"Did I frighten you, Jenna?" he asked, his voice mild but amused. "Did you think I was a dryad stepping forth to utter a proclamation?"

"No, I thought you were a murderer given a lucky chance to strike me dead," I retorted.

"But there are no killers in Thorrastone Park," he objected. "No one here bears you any ill will—you or any other inhabitant."

"The name Gilda Parenon springs to mind," I said somewhat grimly.

"And if not her, whatever mysterious agent wreaked havoc in my generator room and savaged poor Mr. Merrick."

"Unfortunate incidents, not to be repeated," he said dismissively. "But you, Jenna! If not to be murdered, why did you steal out here in the dead of night?"

"Ameletta left some lengths of ribbon behind this afternoon, and would not be consoled until I promised to fetch them, keeping them safe from rodents and birds and other hazards." As I spoke, I moved forward and bent toward the ground, seeking the packet. The strange light reduced everything to a graduated scale of gray; I would not be able to discern the ribbons by their bright colors. Indeed, in the long grass coiled under the tree, I might not be able to find them at all.

"Ah! Well, that is a quest well worth undertaking," he said, moving back under the spreading branches of the tree and starting to search beside me. "Making a little girl happy."

At first, however, we did not look like we would have much luck in our endeavor, for the grail eluded us for nearly fifteen minutes. Finally I came to my knees and let my fingers go searching through the grass, hoping to discover by texture what was invisible to the sight. "Victory!" I cried, when I finally felt the smooth, slim lengths of satin glide under my fingertips, and I held up the swatch of ribbons in a triumphant gesture.

"Bravo, Jenna! Glorious deed well-done! Now go home and write ballads about your prowess," Mr. Ravenbeck said. He came a step closer and held out a hand. I laid my fingers in his and allowed him to pull me to my feet—just as a low, ominous, grumbling noise gathered momentum at the walls around us.

I dropped Mr. Ravenbeck's hand and glanced apprehensively over my shoulder. "What was that? It sounds like nothing so much as thunder."

"That's just what it is, or something very like. This time of year, we tilt into the solar winds and there's no end of trouble. The by-products we release mingle with what thin layer of atmosphere Fieldstar can muster on its own, and we get these incredible rushes of energy and friction. They're not really dangerous, or haven't been yet, but at Sollbrook Manor one year, they had a fireball ride the whole length of the forcefield and shut down the complex for a day. Everyone had to be outfitted with oxygen masks and evacuated. Which is one of the reasons," he added, "most of the landowners here have installed backup systems on their forcefields. The whole property could have been ruined, and many lives could have been lost, if Bianca had not reacted as quickly as she did and gotten everyone safely out."

I was not particularly eager to hear stories of Bianca Ingersoll's wit and resourcefulness, and in fact I was fairly certain anyone with a modicum of intelligence would have made whatever decisions she had. But her name had been introduced, and her name had laid between us for days now, and recklessly I decided to ask now some of the questions that would determine the course of my existence.

"I'm sure she is a very quick thinker!" I said in an admiring voice. "You must be looking forward to installing her here as mistress of Thorrastone Park. She will bring all sorts of glamour to your quiet home."

He gave me a sideways look; I could have sworn he was laughing at me, though the combination of poor light and dappling shadows made it hard to tell. "Do you think so?" he said. "My guess is that her idea of glamour is much more expensive and uncomfortable than mine, and that whatever gorgeousness she brings to my life will cost me more energy and patience than I have to spare."

"I have never heard a love match described so well," I said in a cordial tone of voice, and at that he laughed aloud.

"Yes, but we were made for each other! Everyone says so!" he exclaimed. "She is avaricious, I have money. She is the picture of loveliness, I appreciate beauty. She is bright, charming, elegant, vivacious—very well, I am none of those things, but my surly swarthiness makes her appear even more charming and elegant by contrast. Plus everyone expects us to marry. What can I do?"

What could he do? Every fiber of my body shouted out the answer, but I would not let the words pass my lips. Instead I said, "So, when you marry Bianca Ingersoll, I expect she will be wanting to make changes in your household."

He was glancing out from under the tree, toward the faintly glowing lines of the forcefield, which seemed to be trembling in a ghostly wind. "Yes, she's already made that abundantly clear," he said in a rather absent voice. "Ameletta, for instance. Bianca does not feel she is up to the task of supervising a child who is, as she put it, so emotionally needy. So she has been investigating schools on other planets—far from here, I'm afraid—where Ameletta can acquire both an education and a certain veneer of sophistication. They are not inexpensive, of course— nothing that appeals to Bianca is—but I think they may provide Ameletta with the stability that has been sadly lacking at Thorrastone Park in the past few months."

"So you will send Ameletta away," I said in an even voice, though I felt a surge of animosity toward his intended bride for her selfishness, and toward him for his easy ability to toss aside a small being who loved him with her whole heart. "I assume you will thus break up the rest of the household? Search for new servants, new seneschals, new technicians—new everyone?"

"I don't know. I haven't looked that far into the future," he admitted. "Certainly Bianca intends to import a whole cadre of servants of her own—cook, housekeeper, butler, gardeners—for she hopes to change the whole look and feel of the manor. I have made it plain that no matter what she does, Mrs. Farraday has a home here till she dies, and Bianca has agreed to that condition."

I took a deep breath. "It would seem," I said, "that there will not be much place for me in this new home."

Now he looked at me again, seeming to peer down at me through the lacelike shadow thrown by the tree. I could not read the expression on his face, though his voice, when he spoke, was serious.

"No, I am sure once Bianca Ingersoll is mistress of Thorrastone Park, Jenna Starborn would not be at ease there," he said slowly. "You came to this place for its quiet and its self-containment—you came to a place much like yourself—and you will not want to stay here when it becomes restless and full of change."

"Then I will look for a new situation," I said, still in that incredibly calm voice I had produced from some still, small, hollow core. "I shall consult the StellarNet right away. Tomorrow morning."

"That will not be necessary," he said. "I have taken it upon myself to find work for all the members of my household who are displaced. I have given a great deal of thought to where you should go, for your talents are extraordinary and should not be wasted."

"My talents are ordinary and can be employed almost anywhere," I said. "But I would just as soon go to a friend of yours."

"Yes—though I am not sure I would call her a friend, just an acquaintance who lives much as we do here, only more so. She and her family have been homesteaders on a new planet called Billalogia on what seems to be the far edge of the galaxy. There are only a few thousand pioneers there so far, so the community is small, but, from what I can tell, very tight-knit and social. The world is incredibly isolated, for the supply ships only come once every six months, and they have no shipyard of their own. Thus they must manufacture or hoard everything they need, and from what I understand, the labor is quite demanding. And yet my friend seems exultant to have found a place that she can farm, and claim, and turn into something of her very own, for until she went homesteading, she had almost nothing. As you can imagine, technicians are in high demand but short supply on such a world, and I'm sure you would be prized like the diamond you are."

Every word turned my soul bleaker; every sentence painted a picture of a world more dreary than I thought the human heart could support. "Is your friend a half-cit, then?" I asked. "Is this her passport to full citizenship?"

"Yes—they all are—a world of half-cits who will, by proving up their claims, become level-two members of society. You must admit it is an exciting opportunity. The same chance would be open to you, if you took this job, to become a full citizen within five or ten years of relocating. I believe the citizenship status transfers to other worlds should you move from Billalogia, but I cannot recall. I must ask her, before I send you so very far away."

"Yes, it does seem far away," I said, and for the life of me, I could not keep the quaver from my voice. "Farther than the human mind can stretch itself to conceive of—farther than the soul can bear to journey from—from—"

"From what, Jenna?" he asked in a tender voice.

"From companionship—and valued friends—and—and—affection."

"Friends—who feel affection for each other—is that what we are, you and I?" he asked, and again I could not tell what emotion hummed in his voice, though he spoke with a certain passion.

"I have believed so, Mr. Ravenbeck."

"Like you, I am nervous at the thought of this great separation, Jenna," he said. "If you are so many light-years distant from me, regulating your hours by the clock of a foreign sun and offering your faithful, sensible cheer to strangers, what becomes of me? What sun orders my days, what smiling face supports me through the heaviest hours? I begin to think I might unravel, and turn into so many yards of ribbon and stuffing, like one of Ameletta's dolls. You, of course, would have no such troubles. Industrious and happy on some alien planet, you'd forget all about me."

"No, sir, not for a minute," I choked out, and then could say nothing more. My iron will was turned to rust; I did not have the strength any longer to hold back my tears. I turned from him, as if randomly surveying the night, and began weeping silently. Whatever low sounds I might be making were conveniently covered by another round of that strange, ominous thunder rolling outside our walls.

But he was attuned to me, as I was to him, and he sensed my distress. With a hand on my shoulder, he turned me back to face him, though I kept my head lowered and would not look up.

"Why, Jenna, such sadness at such a common thing," he said, and again his voice was so tender it only made me weep the harder. "Partings and farewells are the customary coin of life. We could not pay our way to heaven without a little grief at a good-bye we did not want to make."

"Yes—but it is not a common thing to me," I sobbed. "When I previously have left places behind, I did not leave behind anyone or anything that mattered to me. I was glad to go—I was eager. Now, to be torn from Thorrastone Park, where there are friends close to me, people I love—it hurts me, it is breaking my heart."

"People you love," he said, catching up my own words with a certain quickness. "You mean—Ameletta—and Janet, who is already gone—and Mrs. Farraday—"

"And you, sir," I said, quieting my sobs, and finally looking up at him. "All of you."

"Then do not go," he said abruptly. "Stay. There will be a place for you at Thorrastone Park until you die."

"I cannot stay!" I cried. "Even you must realize how impossible that is!"

"Impossible! Why?"

"Your bride will not have me here, and I would not stay where she is mistress."

"I have no bride—there is no mistress of Thorrastone Park."

"One is to be installed any day now."

"Yes—absolutely—I will not rest until that end is attained," he said, and his voice sounded almost feverish with resolve.

"Then I must go," I said, and turned away from him as if to take my first steps off-planet at that very moment. But his hand was still on my shoulder, and he turned me back before I had gone more than two paces.

"No—you shall not go—you shall stay. I shall make it right," he declared.

"You cannot make it right!" I exclaimed, and now I pulled free of him and glared up at him, and I could feel my whole body washed with a righteous fury. "You cannot be so obtuse that you do not understand me. I love you, Mr. Ravenbeck—love you with all the intensity, all the joy, all the intelligence, all the nerves and muscles and atoms of my body. I cannot unlove you just because you take a wife—I cannot unlove you just because, by the laws of our society, I am not your peer and have no claim on your notice. My love for you is elemental and immutable, and it will sustain me until I die. But it will not sustain me through your marriage to Bianca Ingersoll, a woman so unworthy of you that you could as easily have thrown yourself away on Coletta or some other avaricious creature and not debased yourself so completely. I do not blame you for not loving me, because you must, after all, live in your world and accept its dictates—but I do blame you for choosing to love Bianca Ingersoll instead. I will not compromise my principles for false laws and man-made ethics—I will not love or pretend to love someone who is not at my level. But you have done it, and I cannot watch you demean yourself, and I will leave this place as soon as I am able."

"No—you shall not leave," he said in a suddenly imperious voice, reaching again to catch my shoulder. I moved away.

"I am nearly packed already. You cannot hold me."

He came forward swiftly for every step I backed away. "I can—I will—I must. I love you, Jenna, as you love me—even more so, I think, though I do not have the gift for expressing it as you do."

This time I took three steps backward, powered by amazement. "What are you saying? Do not reach for me again, or I will scream to wake the manor house."

But he disregarded me; he caught my shoulders and held me so I could not run away, and held me at arm's length, gazing down at me. "You, Jenna, I love you with all my heart. And with my atoms and molecules and electrons and whatever further breakdown you require. You are right—I have no love for Bianca Ingersoll, and she none for me. I have no intention of marrying her—have had none, since you entered my life. I will have no mistress of Thorrastone Park but you."

"What!" I exclaimed, for this turnabout was too sudden and unexpected for me to credit. "First you toyed with her affections, under the full gaze of everyone in her family and everyone in your own household, and now you think to cast her off and engage my heart instead! Mr. Ravenbeck, that is despicable. It is unconscionable. I cannot be a party to this—let me go this instant!"

His hold became rather tighter; his face became almost boyish in his eagerness to explain. "No—you misunderstand—very well, I admit it looks bad for me, but my motives were pure and my behavior almost blameless. I have never cared for Bianca Ingersoll, as you so easily surmised, but for years now it has been an accepted thing that we will marry. We seem to be a good match, financially at any rate, and every-

one in our circle has expected it. Certainly Bianca has, and I had no reason—until recently—to fight the force of expectation with anything like
real energy."

"With the result that everyone of your acquaintance now believes
you to be engaged," I said tartly.

"A fiction merely—a convenience," he said. "She no longer wants to
marry me either, but she does not want her consequence to suffer by
having our relationship so suddenly cool."

"And why has she changed her mind about you?" I demanded.

"Because of the fortune-teller who spoke to her one night while she
was visiting my home," he said. "You remember the computerized
gypsy, Jenna? And you know I had some hand in the gypsy's comments.
Well, I spoke for the medium while Bianca was in the study, and I
warned her that my fortune was much lower than she had been led to
believe. I explained that my dubronium mines were nearly stripped and
my financial concerns on other worlds in jeopardy. She was deeply distressed to hear this information, I assure you, and she treated me coldly
for some days. Until we discussed our situation, and agreed we would
not suit, but also agreed that it would look better for her if everyone
still believed I yearned for her. So she went away happy enough, and
plotting to ensnare her next victim—and if I am not mistaken, Harley
Taff will be announced as her fiancé in the very near future. He's a good
man, Harley—deserves better than Bianca Ingersoll, but he seems to
love her, and he will treat her well. A happy ending all around,
wouldn't you say?"

I gazed up at him through the latticework of shadow and saw the
hopeful, sincere look on his face, but I was not yet ready to be convinced. "And you still agreed to play the part of pursuing suitor, to save
the reputation of a greedy, shallow woman who did not care for you in
the slightest? You have made a fool of yourself before your friends and
your own household, merely to minister to her vanity?"

"It served some purpose of my own as well."

"Indeed? What purpose?"

"It made you jealous. It made you examine your own feelings
toward me, and realize their strength. My charade made you speak out,

as otherwise you would never have had the courage to do. It made you declare your equality and your love—it made you mine."

As he spoke, he attempted to gather me closer, into a true embrace, but I pulled back with some force. "You played this game merely to make me show my hand?" I demanded. "Mr. Ravenbeck—"

"Call me Everett."

"Mr. Ravenbeck, that is contemptible."

"No, no, not contemptible. Desperate," he amended, drawing me against his chest and squeezing me so tightly I felt the air dance from my lungs. I struggled still, though I admit, some of my indignation was melting before a fire of joy and excitement. "I did not know how to make you love me—I did not know how to make you realize that a love such as ours was possible, except by showing you a love that was impossible, a supposed love that did not truly exist. I knew you would see my engagement to Bianca Ingersoll as the mockery it would have been, and I counted on you to compare it to the genuine manifestation of love. And you see? I was right—for you have admitted all, and now by your own words I have you. You are caught in a net of your own making, and such a net cannot be sliced or unknotted. I have you now—and you are mine—"

I looked up to make one final rejoinder, and his mouth came down to cover mine. Such a shock as went through me then! My whole body came alive with delight and wonder; I felt emotions coursing through my veins like scattered lights and colors. I was Amazement—I was Desire—I was Ecstasy and Rapture and the slightest bit of Greed. He crushed me closer, and I was Breathless, and I made a small, wordless sound of protest designed to signal my need for air.

His hold loosened slightly, though he did not release me. Indeed, he merely shifted his grip on me so my head was buried against his chest and his cheek lay on top of my hair. I panted against his shoulder, full of wonder and strangeness, and a little frightened at the wild exultation that made me feel expanded to twice my size.

His own voice, when it came, was scored with an exultation of its own, but so fierce and unbridled was it that it sounded almost more like rage. "The gods of the universe may gather to hurl what storms they may, but this is my course, my goal, my great achievement, and I will not falter or veer away now!" he cried, but in a voice so low I could not believe he was addressing me. "I have her, I will keep her, and no sanction, human or divine, will ever part us."

I looked up to reply, but before I could speak, a great boom of thunder pealed through the night. The faintly glowing walls of the forcefield suddenly blossomed with yellow light; the air crackled around us with latent danger. I felt my hair lift and swirl, while the skin on my arms ran with an electric energy. The thunder snarled again, and a great *snap!* killed the feverish light of the fence, leaving it vaguely iridescent as before.

"We must get inside!" Mr. Ravenbeck called over the continued low protest of sound. "I have no idea what trouble this portends!"

"Let us run for the house!" I cried, and on the words, we were dashing back across the lawn, hand in hand, half laughing and half fearful as thunder chased us back toward safety. We flung ourselves inside the foyer, still laughing and now gasping for air, and stood for a moment on the flagged floor, leaning against each other for support and trying to regain our equilibrium. Outside, the rolling, growling sounds went on, and even the air inside the house seemed charged with expectation.

"Home and safe," Mr. Ravenbeck said into my hair, the words part observation and part kiss. "Though I almost expect the sirens to sound at any moment."

I closed my eyes and experienced fresh marvel at the feel of his arms casually about me. "I will go downstairs and check the systems."

"You will do no such thing. You will immediately haul yourself upstairs to dream of your future life—which will involve no such drudgery as monitoring generators and securing the house from radioactive trash."

I smiled against his coat. "Well, I hope to make myself useful no matter what other role I may take on in your household," I said. "I may as well employ the skills I already have."

He pulled back and I reluctantly straightened to a normal posture. "I can see this argument will take more time than I have at present," he said. "But I warn you now—your life is about to change in all its small details, for you have been visited with an unexpected glamour. I know much more about this life than you do, so you should resign yourself now to being entirely guided by me."

I smiled up at him. "I am willing to be guided by you in *some things*, but I do not trust your judgment completely, no matter how much I love you," I said. "We may join our lives together, but I will still choose my own course."

He sighed theatrically. "Stubborn, obstinate, intractable Jenna Starborn!" he exclaimed. "I will yet see you melting in my arms."

"Ah, but your arms were made for melting," I said, and leaned forward again for one quick kiss. This was bold of me, yet the moment seemed to call for such action, and he obliged quite heartily.

"No more, Jenna, not tonight, anyway," he said, pulling away with no real enthusiasm. "Now you must go to your room and fill your head with dreams of incredible sweetness—while I go to mine and try to learn the ways of patience."

"I think I am like to have more success than you are," I said saucily, and earned myself another quick kiss.

"Good night, then," he said, and ushered me toward the stairwell. "In the morning we will talk again."

And so we parted, though from the corner of my eye I watched him head to the library where I thought he might indulge in a celebratory glass of liqueur. I hurried up the stairs, practically humming to myself—till I reached the first landing, where a figure stood half cloaked in darkness. I stopped short, not for an instant recognizing Mrs. Farraday—who, by the horrified expression on her face, appeared not to have recognized me. Or—no—I suddenly understood. She had witnessed my last interlude in the hall with the master of Thorrastone Park, and she feared my fate would be as dreadful as Janet Ayerson's.

It was not up to me, a half-cit, to claim to have been offered marriage by a full citizen. There was nothing I could say to reassure her. I merely paused a moment before her and tried to sustain a look of purity and conscience on my face. "Good night, Mrs. Farraday," I said gently. "All will seem much better in the morning."

And with those words I ran away to hide myself in my room till dawn might arrive.

Soon enough, however, I was beginning to think that hour might never come. The intermittent thunder had grown nearly continuous, accented at jarring moments by loud spats of crackling light. These jagged flares always struck somewhere along the forcefield, making me worry about its ability to withstand the stress. It was possible we would all, like the Ingersolls, be cast into a vacuum before night's end, and I made sure my oxygen canister was nearby and ready for use. Then I began fretting about Ameletta, small and solitary in her room, and wondered if I would make it to her side soon enough to save her if something happened to compromise the walls. So, after changing into my nightclothes, I hefted my oxygen tank over my shoulder and took the short trip down the hall to the little girl's room.

Not to my surprise, I found her still awake. "Miss Starborn!" she greeted me in a penetrating whisper. "Have you found my ribbons? Have you rescued them from the squirrels?"

"Yes, I have found them, but I did not come merely to return them to you," I said. "I thought you might be afraid of the storm."

Give her credit for her good points, she was quick to capitalize on any situation. "Yes, so afraid—the very loud noise is keeping me awake," she said instantly. "I am frightened and do not want to stay in my room all alone."

I smiled in the dark. "No, I thought you might not. Shall I stay with you, then? Would you promise to go to sleep right away and not chatter all night?"

"Oh, yes, I will be the quietest thing in the house," she vowed.

"Very well, I shall stay with you. But first I must find your oxygen container and make sure it is primed. You lie down—I will climb in beside you shortly."

During the five minutes it took me to locate and review the safety device in her room, Ameletta talked without ceasing. I thought it unlikely she would ever sleep this night—then again, sometimes it was hard to imagine the little bundle of energy ever closing her eyes, relaxing, and drifting off to dreamland, and surely she must sleep *sometime*.

I answered her absently, situated the two canisters close to my hand at the side of the bed, and then climbed in under the covers beside her.

She gave a long sigh of pure satisfaction and curled up beside me. "*Now* I am no longer afraid," she said. "I wish it would thunder every night!"

I smiled at this disingenuous remark. "Go to sleep, Ameletta. No more talking."

"But I have stopped talking!"

"Yes, well, you shall prove that by not saying another word."

Naturally, this request elicited a few more protestations of innocence, but gradually, as the night grew later, she grew quieter, and eventually did drop off to sleep.

I lay awake longer, listening to the grumble and mutter of the storm—which at one point was punctuated by the loudest thunderclap yet. This was followed by a slow, ominous groaning as if some structure was suffering an agonizing dissolution. I stifled a gasp and slipped from the bed to run to the window. But I could see nothing on the lawn outside, for the power surge had shorted out the circuits that controlled the artificial lights. From this distance, I could not tell if the fence itself was still intact, and I balanced on my feet a good fifteen minutes, awaiting the alarm.

But all was quiet; the sirens did not rise and whine. Even the storm seemed to have completely expended itself with that last ferocious attack, for the thunder abated and, within that quarter hour, ceased altogether. Some damage seemed to have been done, but it did not look as though we would suffer for it, and so I climbed back into bed beside Ameletta, and let myself fall asleep.

In the morning I learned what the storm had destroyed, and I could not help feeling a deep though perhaps overstated grief: Some fireball of energy had ripped past the forcefield and across the lawn, exploding in the very center of the oxenheart tree. And that mighty entity, resistant to all malice and misadventure for so many years, had cracked in two and lay dying on the lawn.

Chapter 12

✦

The next few days were strange ones for me—full of more love and happiness than I had ever expected to experience, but also limned with an odd sense of displacement and apology. The morning after the storm, I waited in my room as long as I reasonably could, hoping by this stratagem to allow Mr. Ravenbeck plenty of time to tell Mrs. Farraday our news. When I finally descended to breakfast, I found that he had indeed had a chance to speak with her, but the conversation did not appear to have allayed all her fears.

"Oh—my goodness—Jenna, there you are," she greeted me with more than her usual look of distraction. "I have just heard—the master has told me—this really does explain what I just happened to observe last night, though of course it is no place of mine—"

I smiled, though I felt a certain painfulness around my heart. I suppose I had been expecting her to welcome me effusively, exclaim at how well I suited Mr. Ravenbeck, and wish me joy. But she seemed nervous and ill at ease, and I could only suppose she disapproved of the union. "Yes—Mr. Ravenbeck and I are to be married," I said, for I wanted to say the words aloud to someone, no matter how displeased she might be.

"It is very sudden," she observed. "For only recently—well, of course, you were here also—and he has known Bianca Ingersoll so long—"

"It might appear sudden," I said, determinedly ignoring this reference to the woman I despised. "But I have felt a great affection for Mr. Ravenbeck since the day I first met him, and that affection has only grown over time. And he has felt the same way about me. And so we have decided to marry."

"Your stations in life are very different," she said. "And I am not sure—it is possible you might not understand—it might be hard on you," she ended in a rush.

Only then did it occur to me that some of her unease might be on my behalf, and I felt my heart leap up in gratitude. "Yes—I fear I might be exposed to the mockery of some society people who do not believe I deserve this good fortune," I said. "My hope is to avoid those people as much as I can."

She looked even more worried. "But you can't, Jenna. You are used to the company of servants and cooks and workers from all walks of life, and those are the people you like," she said, and her sentences became more coherent as she tried to explain. "Now those people will be beneath your notice—or only noticeable when you have an order to give them, or a report to hear. They will not be your friends. You will draw *friends* from the ranks of the Ingersolls and the Taffs and the Fulsomes—and I do not know that you will find them much to your taste."

"It will be a challenge, I know," I said.

"And you are a strong woman who has faced many challenges," she said, though her expression did not lighten. "And yet I fear for you. But I am so happy to know that you are not following the path poor Janet went down. That was a relief to learn when Mr. Ravenbeck came to me this morning."

"I am sorry to have worried you," I said. "I did not know what to say."

"No, nor I. What kind of household would people say I preside over, if my two young women both ran off scandalously with men?" she exclaimed. I had not previously considered this point of view, and I have to admit it made me chuckle.

"I at least will not do so," I promised her, patting her arm. "I do not say I would not have been tempted, but I am safe from all blandishments now."

She covered my hand with hers and attempted a smile. "I am happy for you, Jenna, truly I am," she said, though the tears starting in her eyes somewhat belied this assertion. "I just hope your life does not change in ways you did not expect."

I wanted to ask who among us could ever anticipate the changes that would be wrought in our lives, but I merely accepted her weak congratulations and went about making up a breakfast plate.

I thought the worst of it was gotten through with that interview, but I soon found out I was wrong. Mary, Rinda, and Genevieve, with whom I had been on cordial terms in the past, began instantly treating me with a distant courtesy while addressing me from rigid, masklike faces. They knew I was to be the new mistress of Thorrastone Park, and they knew they were no longer my equals—though *I* did not know such a thing and made every attempt to treat them with the friendliness I had shown before. Their remoteness hurt me, but I knew it was only a precursor to the other cool receptions I would encounter.

Well, I had courage and, as Mrs. Farraday had pointed out, I had faced many challenges in the past. I could endure the iciness of friends and the hauteur of acquaintances as long as I did not lose the one thing that really mattered—the affection of the man I loved.

But Mr. Ravenbeck's behavior, it turned out, was much different than I had anticipated as well, and somewhat troublesome. Whereas he had formerly treated me with a rather avuncular humor, teasing me and trying me but always offering me dignity and respect, now he seemed to think I had become some kind of delightful doll that had been designed expressly for his entertainment. He wanted me to sit with him over lunch and read from a book of romantic poetry he had unearthed; he wanted me to perform duets with him on the music-sim machine because, he declared, my singing voice must be among the most beautiful instruments in the galaxy. (It was not.) He wanted me to go for long walks with him around the manor grounds, so he could hold my hand and whisper nonsense in my ear without the fear of Ameletta or Mrs. Farraday bursting in on us unexpectedly. I was content enough to do that, but I insisted on combining the exercise with a basic inspection of the fences, and this displeased him greatly.

"I told you, Jenna, you are done with such work," he said, pulling me back from the forcefield when I would have taken a closer look at a suspiciously pulsating link. I calmly pried his fingers from my wrist and approached the fence again, bending down to examine the problem.

"And I told you, Mr. Ravenbeck, I will be done with it when there is someone here to take my position," I said. "As of yet—"

"Everett," he corrected.

"You have not—what?" I ended up confused.

"Everett. You are to marry me—I would assume that gives you liberty to address me by my proper name."

I was silent a moment, frozen in my stance by the glowing fence. "I suppose it does. Yes, of course it does. It's just that—you see—many times, even the half-cits do not address one another by their given names. I am not used to such a privilege."

"A right, in this case. And one I am eager to see you exercise. Call me Everett—say the name now. 'Everett, I will leave off this foolish desire to slave in your basement facility and inspect your precious forcefields—' "

I smiled and turned away from him, once more gazing down at the questionable section. "Everett, I will continue to work at my assigned duties until you have replaced me, which I cannot imagine will be any time soon. Meanwhile, there is work to be done, and I am the most qualified candidate. I need to get a GRC conductor out here to see if this link is failing. It looks sturdy enough, but I do not like the way it flickers."

"I will bring over someone from the mines to handle such details," he said, catching at the waistband of my coveralls and trying to drag me backward. I dug my feet into the soil and continued with my examination.

"You will not," I said. "I came to Thorrastone Park to be useful, and useful I will be, no matter how my situation alters."

Satisfied that I could learn no more by observation, I straightened and allowed Mr. Ravenbeck—Everett—to tow me back from the fence and onto our former course. "Ah, but that is the trick of it, Jenna," he said, slipping an arm about my waist, which I decided to permit. "Your 'usefulness,' as you call it, is about to change drastically. You must learn the new skills of entertaining company and advising me on investments and being my lovely, empty-headed escort at vacuous shareholder dinners, one of which is coming up in the not too distant future—"

"What? Shareholder dinner? What's that?" I demanded, instantly alarmed, for it sounded quite formal.

"The one we will be attending in a few weeks will be held on Salvie Major," he said, naming a planet so close to Fieldstar that many residents traveled there frequently for recreation. "Others are farther afield. Most of the companies in which I own an interest hold annual meetings which turn out to be more play than work. There are sumptuous dinners and lavish balls and all sorts of entertainments. Very crème de la crème, my dear," he added, allowing his voice to take on an exaggeratedly haughty tone. "You will mingle with the finest—or at least, the richest—members of society."

"I have no wish to do so," I said firmly, though my voice was underscored by panic. "I will not attend."

"But you must. As my wife, you will need to appear beside me and give me consequence."

"I am not the type whose presence confers consequence on anyone. I shall not go."

"But you must, Jenna," he said, more seriously this time. "For—again, as my wife—you immediately become my heir. If I die before you, my property and my investments will fall into your hands, and you must have an understanding of how to administer them. You must be conversant with the people to whom your financial fate is tied."

I stared at him, for this had never previously occurred to me—none of it, not the financial nor the social obligations. "I become your heir?" I repeated. "But Ameletta is your heir."

He shrugged. "She will inherit some of my property, that is true. But my wife—and, if I have them, the children of my body—will inherit the bulk of it. You *must* learn to oversee my business concerns. It is a responsibility you cannot walk away from."

On the words, however, I did walk away from him. I was highly perturbed and had trouble seeing myself in this new light. "I am not prepared for this—I had not thought this far ahead," I said, striding very fast and brushing away his hands when he would have reached for me again. "I thought only of how my heart would be richer, not my purse."

He laughed and managed to catch hold of my hand, which he then refused to let go. "Yes, and that is one of the many things I love about you, that you gave no consideration to improving your station in life when you agreed to marry me," he said. "By the way, Jenna, when are we to be married? I thought next week sometime."

I scarcely heard what he said; I was still thinking about this dreadful dinner. "I have no dress," I said abruptly. "Nothing at all suitable to wear."

"To be married in? Wear your working clothes, for all I care. This outfit, for instance. I like it very much," he said, tugging again at the elastic waist and laughing aloud.

"Stop it. No, I have nothing to be married in *either*, but what I was talking about was your threatened dinner! With all your society peers in attendance! I cannot wear my gray pants to *that*."

"We will go on a shopping trip," he said, suddenly inspired. "Right now! To the spaceport! And if nothing there is suitable, we will take a quick jaunt to Salvie Major and stay until we have amassed for you an entire wardrobe of silk and gauze and sequins."

"No—do not speak of such extravagances for me," I exclaimed, backing away. "A nice dress or two, these will see me through many wretched evenings, but I cannot be acquiring a whole closetful of fancy clothes. I would feel strange and foolish—I would feel like I was pretending to be some exotic creature, when I am really a very ordinary one. It would make me behave oddly, you will see—I would not be the woman you have fallen in love with, but some tricked out, tarted up Virtual Jenna for whom you could feel no affection at all."

"I think I am not so easily beguiled *or* blinded by outward accoutrements," he said, in no way impressed. "But we will start with an outfit or two, and work our way up to a wardrobe. I look forward to seeing you tricked out and tarted up! Thus will one of my many fantasies be coming true."

It took a moment for the meaning of this to sink in, and then I blushed a deep red as bright as the dress I hoped to buy in town. "What! Oh—you debased creature—see if I go to the spaceport with you after all! Or anywhere! Clearly it is not safe to be alone with you, even meekly dressed as I am. I do not know that I wish, by my ensemble alone, to incite you to further indiscretions."

He laughed aloud at this and we did, I confess, spend a little time trying out a few of the milder indiscretions an affianced couple might be expected to indulge in. Usually I was the one to call these sessions to a halt, but this time he pulled back most unexpectedly, leaving me feeling rather deprived and somewhat surprised.

"No time for this if we're to have any time at all for shopping," he said. "Quick, let's go find the Vandeventer and be off."

But this I could not allow, since I first had to continue my circuit of the yard, and if I were to leave, I would want to apprise both Mrs. Farraday and Ameletta of my intentions. These conditions made Everett somewhat impatient—and he grew even more so when Mrs. Farraday asked for time to put together a list of things she would like from the shops and Ameletta begged to be allowed to accompany us.

"For it has been ever so long since I have had a chance to sit in the Mayfair Shop and eat pastries!" Ameletta said pathetically. "And I have not worn my pretty dress in days and days and I am feeling so sad about that."

"This is not an excursion for little girls," Everett said with what appeared to be a real frown. "This is for adults—engaged adults, at that, and they do not need the chaperonage of children."

On his last words, it occurred to me that such supervision was exactly what I *did* require, for Ameletta's presence might make it easier for me to behave with decorum when there might otherwise be no checks to my enthusiasm at being alone with the man I loved. My gaze lifted involuntarily to Mrs. Farraday's face, and I could see the same thought was flashing through her mind, and so I made my decision.

"Actually, Ameletta, I would like to have you with me," I said, bending down and catching her frail body in a quick hug. "For you have a much keener eye for fashion than I have, and I would find your advice invaluable as I am choosing colors and fabrics for my wardrobe."

Everett's frown grew even blacker, but Mrs. Farraday's expression lightened, and my resolve grew solid as steel. "Now, Jenna, let us rethink this," he began in a blustery voice, but Ameletta's squeal of delight and my steady avowals soon convinced him that he had no hope of gainsaying me.

"I understand your game, little trickster," he said to me at last in a low voice pitched to carry under Ameletta's continued prattling. "You seek to restrain the lover by calling upon the guardian. Very good! Excellent move! But it will not serve for long. My day is coming—very soon, I hope—and then there will be no barricades, and no grounds, for keeping me at bay. You take this round, but my time is at hand. I shall win all and carry home the prize at last."

After all the arguing, it soon became clear to us that we had wasted most of the day and had better postpone our trip till the morrow. This was good on many counts, not the least being that it gave me time to calm Ameletta enough to make her promise to be at her most docile the next day. In fact, she and I stole away together to spend a most pleasurable hour before the computer monitor in my room, browsing through the fashion sites and discussing what styles would look best on me. I had not been jesting earlier; she had a most discerning eye for cut and color, and she insisted that I look at several outfits that ordinarily I would have passed by as too daring or too unusual. But the more I studied them, the more I liked them, and I agreed that—were anything like these to be found in town—I would try them on.

Dinner that evening was anything but quiet, with Ameletta bouncing in her chair and describing to Mrs. Farraday all the items we would be seeking at the spaceport, but it was quite enjoyable too. I felt a buzz of excitement running through me like a subcutaneous current of energy; I was sure that if I were to touch anything metallic, I would send sparks flying. It was a rather delicious sensation.

The next morning, we set out on our expedition at a relatively early hour, Ameletta dressed in a blue and saffron dress and me in my trusty gray jacket and pants. Everett had the Vandeventer waiting for us at the front door, and with exaggerated ceremony, he made sure his ward and his fiancée were safely strapped in. Then we took off for town.

I must say, this style of travel was far superior to the shuttle bus that had served me on my previous jaunts to the spaceport. The vehicle was superbly maintained and soared so smoothly through the air that there was almost no perception of movement at all. It was much easier to view the landscape through the half-dome of the circular lid than it was through the grimy windows of the public conveyance, and Everett set himself up to be an excellent tour guide.

"There, that is the first settlement made outside the spaceport on Fieldstar. You can see it has been abandoned—the soil mix was faulty and everything planted in it died."

"But weren't the mines still operational?"

He shook his head. "That property had been set aside for experimental agriculture, so it never had a working quarry. There's another property much like it halfway around the globe, and there they got the soil mix right. They grow all sorts of things there—fruits, vegetables, flowers, things you'd never want to eat if you were starving to death and blossoms you wouldn't even want to throw on the grave of your worst enemy. You'd like it, Jenna. We'll have to go visit some day."

"Oh, may I come?" Ameletta exclaimed.

"Yes," I said just as Everett scowled and said, "No." Ameletta looked in some dismay between the two of us. I smiled and kissed her on the head.

"Yes," I said into her ear. "Wherever I go, you are always welcome."

Everett slanted me a wicked look from the corner of his eyes. Ameletta sat between us on the narrow front seat, or I imagined he would have reached over to give my hand a warning squeeze. "There are some journeys small girls are not going to be allowed to go on no matter how much they beg and plead," he said in a meaningful voice. "And one of those journeys is coming up very soon. Next week, I do believe."

I smiled again and hugged Ameletta closer to me. "Where are you going? Why can I not come with you and Miss Starborn?" she demanded.

"Where we are going is a secret, because I am taking Miss Starborn there on our honeymoon, and I want the whole trip to be a surprise for her," Everett said. "But let me assure you that it will be a most magical and wonderful place."

"Next week? You are marrying so quickly?" Ameletta cried. "Oh, but that is too soon! No one will have time to buy you gifts! No one will even be able to attend, for you will scarcely have time to send out invitations, and Miss Ingersoll and Mr. Taff and all your friends live so far away—"

"We do not want them to attend," Everett interrupted. "They are not really our friends, anyway. The only ones we want present are you and Mrs. Farraday and the staff. And I will perhaps invite the mine superintendent and the assistant mine supervisor and their wives, but you will not have to talk to them, Jenna. They know their place—but they have been good friends to me, and I would like to include them."

"If they have been friends to you, they are friends to me, and I would be happy to talk to them," I said quietly. "Even if they are half-cits, as your tone implies."

He gave me one quick, comical look, for he realized he had offended my sense of pride, but he decided against an apology. "So is it settled?" he asked me over Ameletta's head. "We have our guest list and we have our date—"

"We do not have a date, for *I* have never been consulted on the topic, and *you* have only mentioned 'next week' as some vaguely appropriate time to hold a wedding," I said severely. "It is not that I am not willing to be married with all haste, it is just that I find it hard to believe you can find a magistrate to perform the deed on such short notice."

"Well, there you're wrong," he retorted. "I contacted the people at the Registry Office two days ago to inquire into their calendar. They handle all sorts of legal transactions," he explained, "including mergers and business dissolutions, and they're equipped to handle marriages as well. I assumed, being a PanEquist as you are, that you would have no particular yearning to be married inside a faith, but I am willing to be overruled in this if you have strong feelings. My only stipulation is that, whatever denomination you choose, it be prepared to conduct the ceremony within weeks, if not days."

"I am content at the Registry Office," I said serenely. "As you suspect, all venues are equal to me."

"But Miss Starborn, what will you *wear*?" inquired the ever-romantic Ameletta.

I smiled at her. "That, *chiya*, is one of the things we must determine during our expedition today."

And indeed, during the next several hours, a wedding dress was one of the outfits we looked for in the shopping outlets of the spaceport. Everett declined to accompany us into the bridal boutiques, choosing instead to stroll outside and talk to his many acquaintances, but Ameletta and I had a grand time. Although we looked at a great many dresses, the one she finally selected for me was a creamy off-white gown of a severe but classic cut. Indeed, the stiffly ruffled front resembled a tuxedo shirt, complete with high pointed collars and three-inch cuffs on the sleeves. The floor-length skirt was made of yards and yards of heavy satin that fell from a deep V at the waist; the material did not swirl, but it had a lovely drape, and the whole presentation of the dress gave me the classical dignity of a marble garden statue. Even my grave face looked suitable above this austere pattern; the fabric was so rich that I looked, not my usual pinched self, but luxurious and pampered.

"I like it," I decided.

"Yes—of course you do—but you must wear a hat," Ameletta said. She was already hunting through the racks of premade caps and veils, impatiently putting aside the ones she felt were inappropriate.

"I don't need a hat," I protested.

"Yes, and shoes. I know exactly what will be best."

In the end, hard as it is to believe, I was dressed from head to toe in my wedding finery on the advice of an eight-year-old girl. She had selected a small beaded headband that curved over my dark hair like a subtle halo, lightening my features and softening the lines of my face. For shoes, she had chosen plain but high-heeled pumps that caused the lines of the dress to fall in an even more flattering arrangement down my hips.

"And you are so short—a little heel like this is just what you need," she said, when I claimed I could not walk without stumbling. She spoke with such authority that I began to wonder exactly how she and Janet Ayerson had passed all their time together when they should have been practicing math and vocabulary. "It gives you distinctive."

"Distinction," I corrected automatically. "What it will give me is bunions."

"You will not have to wear the shoes very long," she pointed out. "And they so very perfectly complete the ensemble."

The tone did me in; I laughed, and then I capitulated. We purchased everything, using some of my last remaining credit, and directed everything to be delivered to Thorrastone Park.

When we rejoined Everett on the street, he exclaimed, "Well? Success or failure? I believe there are half a dozen other shops where you can seek your bridal dress."

"No, we found exactly what we were looking for," Ameletta said briskly. "We have so much more shopping to do! But now it is time for a pastry."

We laughed and agreed with her, stopping for a light snack at a fabulously expensive restaurant to fortify ourselves for further shopping. Then it was back to the mercantile district to look for additional clothes. This time Everett insisted on accompanying us and offering his opinion on all the outfits I tried on. I must say, it made me rather nervous to parade before not only Ameletta and the shopkeepers, but my critical fiancée, in a succession of costumes so daring and so costly that I could not imagine even trying them on under other circumstances. It was he who insisted I attempt the red velvet skintight pantsuit, though anyone could tell I did not have the figure for such nonsense and even he agreed once I emerged, scarlet-faced, from the dressing room. But the royal blue tunic over the harem-cut trousers suited me surprisingly well, and two more sober dresses in shades of green proved to be the best choices yet.

"Yes—that is nice—that is very good," Everett approved as I sashayed around the public area in the second of these two gowns. "I see you are not the peacock of women, but more truly the swan. You require elegance, not garishness, to show off your sleekness and style."

"I am more like a wren or a sparrow, common and colorless," I retorted. "My best hues are the natural background shades against which I can blend in with my surroundings."

He disputed this, and then he disputed even more hotly my intent to pay for my new acquisitions myself. Indeed, we had quite a bitter, though quietly conducted, argument on the topic, which escalated when he realized I had purchased my bridal gown with my own money.

"Do you not understand?" he demanded in a piercing whisper that even Ameletta and the salesclerk, on the far side of the store, had to be able to overhear. "It is my job now—my duty and my pride—to care for you in all things. I want to shower you with gifts, not merely because I can afford it, but because you have gone for so long with so little, and it is my delight to indulge you. But even if I was a poor man with very little money, it would be my task now to provide for you. That is one of the obligations I took on—just as the privilege of loving you in every fashion is also something I have assumed with the vow to marry you."

"Well, you have not married me yet," I said. "I am still an independent woman, not a dependent bride, and I would rather come to you penniless than dressed in rags. I am responsible for myself until I do marry you—and even then, I will be responsible for myself in spiritual and emotional matters—and you must honor my wishes now or I will suspect that you will not honor any of them in the future."

Thus I convinced him, but barely, and spent nearly the last of my hoarded credit. I could not be sorry, though, for I had meant every word. I might be poor in purse, but I was rich in pride, and he would have to learn that now or bruise himself against it for the rest of our lives together.

After we had finished shopping for my trousseau, we spent a couple of happy hours merely playing. Everett purchased a large, gaily dressed stuffed animal for Ameletta (it was not as familiar as a bear nor as foreign as an alien species, but it certainly did not look like any creature that I knew in the universe). We also strolled through a holo exhibit, one of Ameletta's favorite activities, and paid the admission at the Scientific House. This, to me, was a rather weak collection of demonstrations of gravity, light, and motion, but Ameletta ran around happily experiencing weightlessness and centrifugal force.

"The best part is outside," Everett told us when the little girl had finally had her fill of the zero-g chambers and light meters. We waited in line till it was our turn to climb into a small spheroid car that took us up an impressive tower to an open-air landing. The three of us climbed out and were almost instantly knocked over by a whirling wind. Ameletta cried out and grabbed for Everett's hand; I gasped and clutched at the chest-high railing.

"What is this?" I called to Everett over the rushing sound of animated air. I had to brush the hair back from my face and repeat my words even louder for him to hear me.

"Solar tower," he shouted back. "We're still protected by a forcefield, but a porous one, and we're up high enough that we can feel the effects of the atmospheric pressure. Breathtaking, isn't it? Makes you feel like you're standing on the very threshold of space."

Indeed it did. I clung to the rail with even more determination, and turned my face deliberately back into the wind, tilting my closed eyes heavenward. I had the most physical sense of oceans of black space pressing down on me, a great void opening up before me, the limitless miles of the universe piled in spangled constellations above, below, before me. The whistling of the powerful wind seemed to be the whisper of the Great Mother, calming her restless children or adjuring them to behave. The tendrils of breeze across my face—surely no more than my own hair whipping across my cheek—felt like her loving fingertips smoothing away a tear. I felt her presence; I sensed her great and deeply personal interest in me, Jenna Starborn—in all her children. Indeed, as I stood there with my eyes shut and my whole body tense with exaltation, I swear I sensed the life force of every other soul in the universe, embedded in the consciousness of that divine being, who knew us all and forgot none of us and carried us with her wherever her seeking spirit sent her.

"Jenna." But the concerned voice was male, and human, and called me back from the brink of communal ecstasy. "Jenna. Are you going to swoon? You appear to be in a trance."

The hand shaking my shoulder was just as urgent and even harder to ignore. I opened my eyes and turned back to him with a wide smile. "I am quite all right. I am just listening to the Goddess."

This admission earned me a skeptical look and caused him to drop his hand. "And what did she have to say?"

"Merely that she is here and she loves me. Loves us all."

"Who loves us?" Ameletta wanted to know. She still had not released Everett's hand, and she looked very small and windblown, and not entirely happy. I bent to kiss her cheek.

"The Goddess. The unifying spirit of the universe."

"I did not hear her say anything," Ameletta said.

"How odd. Neither did I," Everett murmured.

I smiled again and opened the door to our round little car. "I heard enough for all of us," I said serenely. "You will simply have to take my word."

This event was clearly designed to cap what had been a successful but very long day, and soon we were back in the Vandeventer, heading toward home. Ameletta fell asleep between us almost as soon as we were strapped in, and Everett and I talked in quiet, comfortable voices during the whole trip. I enjoyed those final hours nearly as much as I had enjoyed the entire rest of the outing, and I returned to the manor house as happy and content as I had ever been in my life.

Chapter 13

✧

The next week flew by. Everett and I had, with very little more discussion, settled on a day in the middle of the following week as our wedding date, which gave us exactly seven days to prepare. I, of course, had little to do except fold my new clothes and await the delivery of my wedding dress. Everett was much more occupied, for he had to notify lawyers and financial institutions of his impending change of status, and he had to advertise for my replacement, and he had to make arrangements for Ameletta's care while we were gone. Mrs. Farraday, of course, could watch the little girl some of the time, but she had duties of her own, and auxiliary help was required.

"And then we must come up with a plan for her once we have returned to Thorrastone Park," I told him on the evening before our wedding, as we sat together quietly in his study. "For I don't imagine I will be free to tutor her as she should be tutored, and—"

Everett looked up from where he was sitting in front of his computer monitor, entering computations. "Return to Thorrastone Park!" he repeated. "But we will not be living here. This is not my primary home—indeed, I have already stayed here much longer than is my wont."

"Oh? And where will we live?" I asked calmly, though I felt a certain nervousness jolt through me. I had known this, of course, but I had not really considered it. The place that I had come to consider *home* was to him no more than a stopping place, a seasonal house, a property to be maintained.

"On Salvie Major much of the time, and Corbramb, but we will be traveling as well," he said. "There is so much I want to show you, Jenna! So much you have not seen! We could wander for five years and not see all the wonders of the universe."

"Keep in mind that I am not much of a sojourner," I said. "I like a settled place, and a familiar roof, and faces that I grow to love. And Ameletta will require such things as well."

"Ameletta! She will be enrolled in school very soon. I shall look into that as soon as we are returned from our honeymoon."

"But I thought you had only agreed to send her to school to appease Bianca Ingersoll," I said, troubled. "I had thought we would keep her with us always, or at least near us. I am very attached to her—and I cannot help but look on her as your daughter."

He seemed somewhat exasperated by this, but he threw up his hands and laughed. "We shall discuss this further," he promised, turning back to his computer screen. "I will make no plans for her of which you do not wholeheartedly approve."

And I believed him; therefore, I was certain Ameletta's future would be as happy as I could make it. "What are you engaged upon so industriously?" I inquired then. "I can leave the room if I distract you."

"No, stay—I enjoy having you nearby, and this is not work that requires much concentration," he said. "I am informing all my acquaintances of my coming change of status. I imagine by the time we return, we will have a backlog of congratulatory messages awaiting us—and perhaps a stack of gifts as well." He glanced at me over his shoulder. "Feel free to send the news to all of your friends, Jenna. I assumed you had done so, but in case you thought you needed my permission, I tell you to go ahead now."

I smiled. "No, indeed, I did not think enough of your consequence to keep this news a secret," I said. "Though, in fact, I had very few people to tell. I sent a message to my aunt's estate, in case they would have some need to look for me, and letters to a few friends from Lora. Also my aunt's housekeeper, Betista, who was always kind to me. But no one else would think to wonder where I was or what had happened to me if Jenna Starborn, transformed to Jenna Ravenbeck, were to disappear from the folds of the universe."

Once again he turned to look at me, and the expression on his face was most serious. "I would know," he said quietly. "If you were to disappear into the black mystery of the galaxy, I would feel the loss."

I smiled again. "Yes, but you are the person with whom I am going to disappear," I pointed out. "So you will not need to wonder where I am."

He worked perhaps an hour more in silence, then shut down his monitor and came to sit beside me on the sofa. "And so, Jenna, our last night together before we are husband and wife," he said, taking my fingers in his hand and playing with them as if they were separate and distinct toys that he could roll together to make a bony, hollow music. "Are you nervous? Hopeful? Frightened? Jubilant? You are so quiet I cannot always tell, but sometimes a fugitive joy fizzes behind those earnest eyes and I think, 'Aha! Jenna is happy!' "

I took his restless hand and laid it against my cheek, and I turned my earnest eyes on him with all the soulfulness I could muster. "I *am* happy, Everett, for I love you with all my heart," I said simply.

He turned his head quickly to plant a kiss in my palm. "Sweet Jenna!" he whispered. "I pray every night that I will be a good husband to you—that you have not misplaced your trust by giving yourself into my care."

"I need no such prayers," I said. "I have no fears."

He was silent a moment, as if mulling over something else he might say, and then he gave a short, rather strange laugh, and stood up abruptly. "But I forgot! This is our night to celebrate! You promised long ago to wait up with me the night before I wed, and I promised to share with you that bottle of aprifresel wine. I put it in here somewhere—now where the devil has it gone?"

He searched for perhaps five minutes before locating his prize, and

236 of Sharon Shinn

shortly the two of us were sitting on the sofa, toasting each other with the wine. Mr. Ravenbeck tossed his back with every appearance of a man swallowing poison as quickly as possible; I sipped mine more cautiously. And immediately coughed on the sweet, syrupy stuff.

"Everett! This is dreadful!" I exclaimed.

"Yes, but you must drink it anyway," he said, pouring himself another glass. "That is why you brought it back from Baldus, and a bargain is a bargain, no matter how distasteful. Drink-drink-drink— there you go," he said admiringly as I managed to choke down a few more mouthfuls. "You worried that you would be drunk on the stuff, but you're more likely to contract a stomach disorder."

"I am likely to be both sick and hungover in the morning," I observed through watery eyes as I held out my glass for another portion. "This is positively the last time I will allow you to make me drink a liquor I do not like—but since we *did* make a bargain, I will stick to it. And by that you can judge the extent of my loyalty in future endeavors."

"Done," he said, touching his glass to mine again. Again we drank, and again filled our goblets, and drank again. Soon enough we were both groaning and laughing, and the evening ended on a note of rather disorderly merriment. I stumbled to my feet as the clock struck midnight and gave him an exaggerated (and somewhat unsteady) curtsy.

"Everett Ravenbeck, I will see you in the morning," I said formally.

He bowed in return. "And Jenna Starborn, in the morning I will make you my bride," he said. "Sleep deeply, my beloved. Dream of me."

"I always do," I said, curtsied again, and left the room.

The morning dawned as all mornings on Fieldstar did, to a cold, filtered light, but to me the day was washed with iridescence and suffused with magic. I had slept very little, but woke feeling light and brittle, almost weightless, buoyed by an indescribable joy. Mrs. Farraday had told me the day before that I should keep to my room until the travel vehicles had assembled at the door to convey us to the Registry Office in town; among the elite on Fieldstar, as in many societies, it was customary for bride and groom to not view each other on their wedding day until the very moment the ceremony was to begin. Of course, it was rare that bride and groom shared the same household—thus my confinement to my room.

So I lay abed lazily long after I should have been up, bustling about, and then I took a lengthy shower. I washed with perfumed soap that Mrs. Farraday had given me, and shampooed my hair with an herbal-scented concoction that had also been a gift from her. I was touched at these evidences of her affection—and at her realization that a hardworking half-cit girl would never have thought to indulge in such extravagances. But I loved the luxuriant feel of my washed hair and the silken texture of my pampered skin, and I silently blessed her.

Mary brought my breakfast tray and set it on my little desk, then burst into tears and hugged me. "Congratulations, Miss Starborn," she said. "What a grand day for you!"

"Why, thank you, Mary! It means so much to me that you and the others wish me well."

But then she recollected that I was now to become mistress of Thorrastone Park and that we were not really friends, and she flushed, bobbed her head, and backed out of the door with some haste. I felt a moment's sadness at this, but I strove to banish it. Nothing, as far as I was concerned, would occur to dim the brilliance of this day.

Ameletta joined me as I was finishing my meal, and she sat at the desk and bombarded me with questions. Was I happy? Was I scared? Did I know the things a bride should know? (I hoped devoutly that she knew less about those mysteries than I did, though, given the worldliness she exhibited in other instances, I was not prepared to be certain of this. In any case, I merely answered "Yes" and turned the subject.) Could she come to my room and be dressed alongside me? Could we ride together in the estate car?

At this last question, I laughed and said, "You know, I'm not certain what the travel arrangements are. I know that Mr. Ravenbeck can fit three into his Vandeventer—but only if one of those three is a small person like yourself."

"Mr. Ravenbeck said he would fly the aeromobile and that Mrs. Farraday would ride with him. He said I could accompany them, but I would much rather be with you in the estate bus, Miss Starborn."

"I don't believe I've ever been in this bus. How many will it seat?"

"Oh, ten or twenty people! Sometimes the miners take it into town for a little holiday. Mr. Ravenbeck was not happy that you were to ride in the bus, for he said it was probably dirty, but Mr. Soshone promised to clean it very, very well, and Mrs. Farraday looked it over yesterday just to be sure. And anyway, you cannot ride in the aeromobile, because Mr. Ravenbeck is not to see you. But you can ride with him on the way back. He was very plain about that."

I smiled. "Who is Mr. Soshone?"

"He is the assistant mine supervisor. He and his wife *and* Mr. Cartell and his wife will all be coming to the wedding."

"Yes, Mr. Cartell's name I knew. So in the van it will be you and me, and Rinda and Genevieve and Mary, and the Cartells and the Soshones? One of the men will fly the van, I suppose. Yes, Ameletta, certainly I will want you with me in the bus. Rinda and Mary are very quiet these days, and I do not know the others at all. I will need a friend to hold my hand and remind me to breathe."

"Well, I shall always be your friend, Miss Starborn," Ameletta said, patting me on the arm. "Don't you worry about that."

We had agreed to leave the manor house at ten in the morning, which would get us into the spaceport right around noon. The ceremony would only take fifteen minutes or so, and then Everett had made reservations for us to have a sumptuous bridal banquet at one of the more expensive restaurants in town. I thought this would be a lovely treat for the guests and a warm memory for me as I set off for a new, unfamiliar life.

For Everett and I were to leave Fieldstar a few short hours after the ceremony. My luggage and Everett's would be loaded onto the estate bus; after the meal, the whole small caravan would make its way into the docking area of the spaceport, where our bags would be transferred to Everett's private cruiser. Then we would wave good-bye and climb aboard the space-going craft, and my new life would truly begin.

I found it almost impossible to believe. And yet I longed for it so intensely that at times I felt faint. I had not been entirely joking when I told Ameletta she would have to remind me to breathe.

Ameletta and I were still talking over my breakfast tray when Mrs. Farraday came bustling in. She was dressed in a handsome burgundy pantsuit and had done her hair and makeup with care, and she looked just as proud and maternal as the mother I would wish to have with me on such a day.

"Heavens, are you two still eating? I had hoped to find you halfway dressed by now," she exclaimed.

"I must run to my room and get my clothes!" Ameletta cried. "I will be back oh so quickly!" And she dashed out the door.

I rose to my feet, smiling. "It will not take me long to dress, never fear. We will be ready in time."

"I have insisted Mr. Ravenbeck wait for me at the back entrance, for we don't want him catching a glimpse of you as you come down the stairs," Mrs. Farraday said. She was at my closet door already, and she reverently pulled out the ivory-colored satin dress. "There, now. Isn't that pretty? I can't believe that child picked it out for you."

"I can't believe I am ever in my life wearing anything so beautiful."

"And you will look beautiful in it."

Ameletta returned, breathless, her own clothing thrown over her arm. She was to wear a delicate blue outfit of some sort of floating lace that created a kind of turquoise bubble about her when she moved. It sounds quite odd, I know, but the effect was charming; she looked like a fairy out of legend come drifting down to the planet to bestow good wishes. She had purchased this ensemble during our last trip to town and had been almost unable to endure the wait until she could wear it.

"I am here!" she announced. "Let us get ready!"

Mrs. Farraday frowned, but I laughed, and soon enough we were both busily engaged in beautifying ourselves. My hair required very little more than a quick brush and an application of modeling spray once the headpiece was in place. My cosmetics required a bit more time. I allowed Mrs. Farraday to do the painting, for I had rarely applied makeup before and had no real idea how to go about it. When she was done, I gazed at myself in the mirror for a few moments, quite astonished. My eyes looked much larger than usual, liquid and unfathomable; my cheekbones had acquired enough prominence to make me remember I actually had them; and my mouth looked full enough to kiss.

"Gracious," I said faintly. "Had I known you could make me look this beautiful, I would have come to you for help much sooner."

Mrs. Farraday smiled. "I will teach you how to apply your own makeup, and once you practice a while, you will find it quite easy. Do not forget you will need to look your best in your new life."

"I always try to look my best," Ameletta said, and we glanced over to see her studiously brushing rouge onto her own fair cheeks. My mouth dropped open and Mrs. Farraday gasped.

"Ameletta! Stop that this instant!" the seneschal cried, stalking over and whisking the brush from the little girl's hand. "You are much too young to be wearing cosmetics! For shame!"

Ameletta looked up at us, big eyes luminous with tears, the rather skillfully applied makeup turning her child's face into something much older than it should be. "But I want to look beautiful for Miss Starborn's wedding!"

"You will look beautiful enough in your own skin, missy, and don't you start to argue with me!"

But of course it was not an argument we got, but tears, and it took the two of us the better part of ten minutes to calm her down, convince her that we were serious, and convince her that a child's most exquisite ornament was her clear, natural complexion and fresh, unused skin.

"But I don't want to be a child!" she sobbed into my arms. "I want to be a woman—and have lots of clothes—and wear whatever I feel like—"

I kissed her on the top of her head and tried not to laugh, though Mrs. Farraday did not show much patience for this exhibition. "You will be a woman so quickly you will wonder how it happened," I whispered into her ear. "Be a child for as long as you can, *chiya*."

This little diversion took more time than we'd expected, so once we had Ameletta composed, we had to hurry to finish dressing me. Luckily there was little left for me to do but put on my expensive silken undergarments, step into my high-heeled shoes, and stand still so that Mrs. Farraday could carefully lower my wedding gown over my head. Then the housekeeper fastened the buttons in the back while Ameletta fastened the ones on the sleeves—and I was dressed.

"Oh, Jenna," Mrs. Farraday said, coming around to view me from the front. "Oh, child, don't you look lovely. I couldn't be prouder if you were my own girl."

I pivoted to gaze at myself in the mirror one more time. I am not one to brag about myself, and I know that my physical beauty is not impressive—and I know that physical beauty is fleeting and worthless in any case—but, Reeder, I did look beautiful at that hour. My face, my hair, my gown, and my happiness all combined to give me a look of rare magnificence. I looked like a small queen ready to set sail on the journey of her life.

"Ladies, I believe we're ready to go," I said in a remarkably firm voice. "Mrs. Farraday, you go on ahead and find Mr. Ravenbeck, and make sure the two of you are instantly in motion. Ameletta, in a few minutes you and I will go downstairs."

Very shortly, we were on our way. The estate bus—a rather modest, utilitarian vehicle—had been garlanded with white ribbon and nosegays of white flowers that had no scent. The Cartells and the Soshones were dressed in their excruciating best. They were ordinary, plain-featured folk who did not look at all comfortable in their fancy clothes, but they greeted me with respect and sincerity and thanked me for inviting them to my wedding. I liked all of them at once and wished I had had a chance to get to know them before this day. Even Mary and Rinda and Genevieve, so distant these past days, greeted me with smiles and shy embraces.

I was installed in a cushioned seat that had clearly been fixed up just for me, for an arrangement of ribbon had been erected over this one chair to create a sort of makeshift bower. The others climbed in and situated themselves, and then Mr. Soshone took off for the airlock. Once we were free of the manor, he accelerated to a good pace, and we were on our way to town. This "bus" did not ride as smoothly as Everett's

Vandeventer, but it was much less noisy and more comfortable than the public shuttle, and I did not see a speck of dirt. Mrs. Farraday's diligence, I was sure.

As promised, Ameletta sat beside me and held my hand. She chattered quite unself-consciously during the whole of the ride, discussing what she would do with her time while I was on my honeymoon and how friendly she would be to the interim tutor who was to arrive in two days. "I will show her all my treasures and let her play with my dolls, but only if I like her. If I do not like her, I will not do any of the homework she assigns me, and I will not talk to her either."

"That is not a very nice attitude, Ameletta," I said.

"But I will probably like her," she added hastily. "Why, I nearly always like everybody. Are you remembering to breathe, Miss Starborn? You said I was to remind you."

I took a deep breath and exhaled it loudly. "No, I had quite forgotten. Thank you, Ameletta!"

She giggled and returned to her prattling. In just under two hours, we had come into sight of the spaceport's silver spires. The air above the town was thick with incoming traffic, bright sleek arrows suspended above the terrain or making slow spirals downward. The invisible dome that protected the whole city from the outer vacuum seemed, on this special day, almost perceptible; I fancied I could detect a chrome-colored veil flung over the spindly buildings, dancing with reflected light. But then, everything seemed brushed with opalescence— the buildings before us, the cruisers above us—even the sun, usually so sullen in Fieldstar's sky, seemed to shimmer with a golden munificence. The world not only smiled upon me, it sparkled for me; it blessed me with its silent effervescence.

"Are you breathing, Miss Starborn?"

"Yes, Ameletta, I am."

Finally we pulled up in front of a squat, unattractive building that appeared to have been constructed of mud bricks, and we all disembarked. I felt myself moving as in a dream; never had reality seemed so unlikely. I wished with all my heart that Mrs. Farraday or—for so many reasons!—Janet Ayerson were beside me, but I had no real solace except Ameletta, and I clung to her as we entered. Mrs. Soshone went to the information terminal and requested information; its automated voice told us which elevator and which hallway to use. By now I was fairly faint with fright and anticipation, and I could only follow the others as they set off down the corridor toward the elevators.

We were lifted in a quick sickening lurch up several stories—I could not count—but once the doors opened onto our designated floor, I was relieved beyond measure to see Mrs. Farraday awaiting us.

"There you are, Jenna! We were beginning to wonder if you were lost. Mr. Ravenbeck has been so impatient! But I assured him everything was fine. Are you ready? Do you need a moment to compose yourself?"

"A moment," I said faintly.

She shooed the others down the hall, which was wider and more brightly lit than I had expected from the exterior of the building, and talked to me so cheerfully for a few moments that I began to regain some of my equilibrium.

"I don't know exactly what has come over me," I said, fanning myself with my hand as if that would do any good at all. "I am so happy! And yet just as we pulled up in front of the Registry Office, I began to feel as if I could not move or breathe or think—"

"Yes, the exact same thing happened to me," she said briskly. "I believe it is required of a bride. Your wedding completely changes the direction of your life, you know, no matter how greatly you desire it. I think that moment of doubt and faintness comes from all those imagined and now impossible futures all pressing in on you at once. It is your last chance to experience them, you see, and they all want to be lived at that moment."

This fanciful analysis from the so-practical Mrs. Farraday made me laugh out loud, which for the most part restored me to myself. I was still a bit shaky, but my limbs seemed to have regained their normal function, and my lungs appeared capable of inhaling and exhaling without a direct command from me.

"Is our room prepared?" I asked, taking her arm.

"Everything is ready," she said.

"Then let us proceed."

A few short steps and we entered the room that was to be my wedding chapel. I took a brief, comprehensive look around. It was painted white, and filled with white cushioned chairs, and hung with white curtains, and so it seemed lit with an internal radiance that was very appropriate to the circumstances. Our small coterie of friends had gathered in the front few rows of seats, near to the dark-paneled podium that would appear to serve a multitude of uses. Everett Ravenbeck was standing right before this lectern, staring with some impatience at the doorway. Beside him stood a small, gray-haired man with a pleasant demeanor and a book in his hand.

Everett's face lightened at the sight of me and added its own considerable radiance to the room. "Ah!" was all he said, but it was so heartfelt that it made me smile. I continued to cling to Mrs. Farraday as we walked slowly down the aisle between the rows of seats. When we reached Everett's side, she rather ceremoniously transferred my hand to his, and took her seat somewhere behind us.

"Miss Starborn, I take it?" the registrar asked me in a kind way. Up close, he looked older than seventy, weary and wise, and I liked the sound of his voice.

"Jenna Starborn," I said, my own voice surprising me with its firmness.

"Good. Unless anyone has any questions, I am ready to start."

"No questions," Everett said with a certain arrogance. "Let us begin the ceremony."

The gray-haired man opened his book, glanced inside it, and then looked up at us again. "It is customary before performing the marriage," he said, "to first ask the participants if there are any legal impediments to their union."

"There are none," Everett said.

Ignoring him, the clerk turned to me and said, "Miss Starborn, are there any reasons why you could not be lawfully joined in marriage to Everett Ravenbeck? Are you married already to someone else?"

"No," I said.

"Are you a class-A felon who has been denied a range of societal privileges, including the right to marry?"

"No."

"Are you possessed of a gene flaw that has been determined to produce heinous offspring and thus caused you to be interdicted from procreation?"

"No."

"Are you of an alien race that has been forbidden to intermarry with humans?"

"No."

"Then you are free to marry?"

"I am free to marry."

The clerk then turned to Everett and repeated this series of questions, to which he received identical responses although in a much less docile voice than I had been able to summon. I squeezed his hand in an effort to counsel patience, but this failed somewhat of its intended effect as, in return, he gripped my hand so tightly that I felt the bones protest.

"I am free to marry," at last Everett said—growled, more like.

"Very well. Inasmuch as the state of marriage is a complex one involving financial, social, emotional, spiritual, and physical bonds, and inasmuch as marriage is—"

"Stop the ceremony!" cried a voice from the back of the room.

I turned to a satin-draped pillar of ice.

"Continue," Everett ordered the clerk.

"I think I must see—"

"*Continue*, damn you!"

"Stop the ceremony, I tell you!" the voice repeated, sounding greatly agitated and growing breathlessly louder as the speaker rushed forward. "There is an impediment to this marriage!"

There was a commotion behind me—I think Mr. Cartell and Mr. Soshone leaped up to intercept the intruder—but I could not turn to see. I could not think. I could not see. I could not move. This time, for real, I could not breathe. I heard Everett shout something at the registrar and the registrar answer somewhat heatedly. I felt hands flailing about, beside me, behind me, causing a dark disturbance in the luster of the room. I heard the sounds of blows landing and chairs overturning. Everett continued arguing with the clerk, who ignored him, and who peered around our two bodies to watch the scuffle going on behind us.

"Stop the wedding, I say!" that stranger's voice cried again, but this time I fancied he was not a total stranger. I thought I had heard that voice before, and I thought I could identify him if I must. He sounded even more winded now, as if he had been involved in some athletic contest and now were struggling against forcible restraint. "This man cannot be married—he has a wife already."

At this, I felt myself dissolve. The personal forcefield that kept my atoms in place gave way and loosed the particles of my body into the undifferentiated air. I could not sway or swoon; I did not have enough mass to react with such purpose. I disintegrated into the white light without a trace.

But still I could hear.

"Married already!" I heard the clerk exclaim. "But then he cannot be legally wed today!"

"Exactly! He must be stopped!" the stranger panted.

"Oh, Mr. Ravenbeck! Shall someone call the civil guard?" This from Mrs. Farraday.

"He's a liar! We'll take him outside and take care of him, sir." Mr. Cartell or Mr. Soshone, I could not tell.

"Beat me—kill me—it does not matter! It does not alter the truth. This man is a married man, and he attempts today to become a bigamist. His wife is still living, and I know her whereabouts, and I can prove her existence."

The more he spoke, the more certain I became. This intruder, this man who had come to destroy my life, was Mr. Merrick of Wesleyan-Imrae, a man Everett Ravenbeck had seemed to both despise and fear. I knew, absolutely and without question, that he spoke the truth.

"Mr. Ravenbeck, I asked you once before, but this time I beg that you answer me honestly," the clerk said soberly to the man beside me. "*Are* you legally free to marry? *Do* you already have a wife?"

There was a moment's electric silence while the whole room suspended breathing in order to hear the reply. I could feel Everett Raven-beck's eyes upon me, but I could not turn to look at him; I would not have been able to see him even if I tried.

He did not answer either question. Instead, with an abrupt, jerky motion, he slewed his body away from the registrar and gruffly addressed his small crowd of well-wishers. "There will be no wedding today," he said in a black voice. "Let us all return to Thorrastone Park."

We traveled back in the same configuration in which we had journeyed into town, except that Mrs. Farraday rode in the estate bus, and Mr. Merrick took her place in the Vandeventer. I would not have liked to be in that car at that time; I could not imagine what vitriol would be exchanged between those two men. As for myself, I could feel nothing except surprise that my limbs had moved, my body had obeyed me, and I had been able to walk with any kind of steadiness from the building to the street. There had been a long, horrible wait while the vehicles were fetched from wherever they had been docked. Everett had several times tried to take my hand or catch my eye, but I could not see him; I could not feel his touch. I believe it was Mrs. Farraday who stepped between us, turning me away from him.

"Jenna," I heard him say, but I did not look at him.

And then we boarded and we endured the interminable trip back, and I did not know if my fellow passengers were utterly silent or if the coach was rife with whispering. I sat on my cushioned bridal seat, under my canopy of white ribbon, and felt nothing.

The stop at the airlock seemed to jolt me back to consciousness. I felt my blood surge forward in a rapid race, and all the color of the world seemed to lock back into focus. My arms tingled as they regained feeling, and a sense of complete dread tightened my ribs in my chest.

"Oh, Mrs. Farraday," I breathed, "what will we discover now?"

Our bus was following the Vandeventer, and it went straight toward the bungalow where, one fateful night, Mr. Merrick had been mauled by an unknown creature and I had kept a fearful vigil in the basement.

Gilda Parenon's place. Somehow, from the first day I had met her, I had known she would be a malevolent influence on my life. I could not, even now, see how that could be so, but I felt it for a certainty.

Everett was at the bus door, rather impatiently handing down each passenger as we disembarked. I could not help but put my fingers in his when he reached for me, and once possessed of my hand, he would not let it go.

"We do not need all of you," he said in his rough way. "Someone take the little girl back to the manor house. You, Merrick, and you, Mrs. Farraday—come with us. And Jenna, of course. The rest of you be gone to tell what tales you will."

And with that ungracious dismissal he hauled me to the front door as the others fell helplessly in step behind us. At the door, he assaulted the keypad, punching in numbers as though he hated them, and then he dragged me through the open door.

We entered the same wide, comfortable room I had first seen on that midnight visit here nearly three months ago. Gilda Parenon, who was sitting in front of a viewing monitor, scrambled to her feet at the sight of so many uninvited visitors crowding into her domain.

"Sir!" was all she said.

Everett nodded at her. "You know all these people, I believe—Merrick, Mrs. Farraday, Miss Starborn. They have come to see your charge."

"Sir?" she repeated, puzzled now.

"Your charge, your patient, your project—my wife," he said in a foul, bitter voice. "They have come to view her."

Of all the people in the room, only the two of them could speak. The rest of us were dumb. "It's a good time for it, sir. She's quiet, and the new circuit suppressor seems to be working just fine. I haven't needed to jolt her for two or three days now."

"Excellent. Her brother will be happy to hear it."

"So you'd like to see her now, sir?"

"This instant."

Gilda Parenon led the way down a broad corridor to a room on the far end of the house. Everett followed her and I, still in his merciless grip, followed, with the others behind me. My brain was in a painful whirl. Jolts and circuit suppressors were expressions commonly used to describe electrical projects, not human beings. And human beings, even the maddest and most intractable, were rarely confined to such ferociously solitary quarters, without benefit of therapy or reconstructive socialization.

Gilda Parenon paused at this inner door long enough to enter yet another complicated sequence onto the keypad. This door, like the one to the outside, like the walls to this otherwise homey cottage, was built of a sturdy steel alloy that could scarcely be breached—certainly not by mere human strength. A deadly cold was beginning to settle in my stomach, but my mind refused to put together the pieces.

We stepped in a single huddle through the door into the room beyond. I caught a quick glimpse of a windowless, nearly featureless chamber before my eye fell on the central attraction of the room—a fortyish, pretty, vacant-looking woman sitting serenely in a straight-backed chair. She was dressed in rose-colored cotton coveralls, her hands were neatly folded in her lap, and her eyes, which were fixed on an invisible object at about the height of Everett's face, showed no change when we entered. Her head was banded with a blue electrical glow that emanated from two posts embedded on either side of the chairback—the circuit suppressor, I knew immediately.

"Everett! How inhumane!" Mr. Merrick burst out. He broke free of our group and made straight for the chair as if to find the switch and cut off the power. Everett stopped him with a single violent shove that sent him stumbling away from the motionless woman.

"Humane—because otherwise she hurts herself and those around her," Everett said brusquely. "Never fear, she is released several times a day for exercise and variety. You can see the steadiness of the routine suits her. Her color is good and her readings, when you check them, will show all her systems stable."

"Yes, but—to chain her to one spot like this, like some kind of wretched animal—"

"She *is* wretched," Everett interrupted. "But she is safe, and she is cared for, and that is all you need to worry about."

Mr. Merrick took a step toward the woman—his sister, as I supposed, since Mr. Everett had declared the creature had a brother. "Can she hear me? Will she respond? Can I touch her?"

Gilda Parenon volunteered the answer. "She can hear, all right, but the suppressor keeps her from talking. She'll remember anything you say, though, if you talk to her now."

Mr. Merrick came to a stop directly before the statue-silent woman. "Beatrice," he said, in a soft, almost crooning voice. "I see you're better than you were last time I was here. Do you remember me? I brought you some of those games you like—new ones, very fast." He glanced over his shoulder at Everett. "I suppose you let her play such things now and then?"

Gilda Parenon answered for him. "On her good days. She does love those games you bring her."

Mr. Merrick turned back to his sister. "And some of the candies from Hestell. They were always your favorites. I suppose you still like them—I saw them the other day in the shop window, and I remembered—so much—and I thought—" He came to a stammering stop and covered his face with his hand. I could not tell if he were crying.

Everett had no patience with such sentimentality. "Yes, she still craves sweet things, and we give her a share of those too, every day, though we have to measure her intake or she'll have a bad spell."

"Sugar stirs her up the way it does a child," Gilda Parenon remarked. "You wouldn't think it, seeing as she's hardly human—"

Mr. Merrick whirled on her, fury and desperation on his mild face. "She is so human! If you knew her—if you could remember her—no one was ever more real or lovable—"

"But I don't understand." The new, bewildered voice came from Mrs. Farraday, who, like me, had remained completely mute up until this point. "If she is your sister—and Mr. Ravenbeck's wife—but then, of course she must be human. Why would Miss Parenon say such a thing?"

There was a sudden charged silence in the room, as Everett was too proud, Mr. Merrick too sad, and Gilda Parenon too prudent to speak the truth. It was, strangely, I who answered the seneschal in a voice quite calm and authoritative.

"She is only part human," I said. "She is a cyborg."

*   *   *

*V*ery little of the rest of that day passed for me in anything like coherent sequence. We lingered several more minutes in Gilda Parenon's bungalow as Mr. Merrick made a few more despairing attempts to connect with his sister, whose perfectly still, perfectly placid face did not change in the slightest. I found myself looking from her face to her hands and back to her face, wondering what expression she wore when she slipped into her fits of rage and violence. What caused them? An electrical malfunction seemed the most obvious—a kink in the circuits that could not be repaired, that fed directly into the neural passageways and caused erratic behavior. Androids with such flaws were routinely deprogrammed and cannibalized for parts—but a cyborg presented a whole new set of ethical problems. For, as Mr. Merrick had pointed out, a cyborg *was,* indeed, part human; and our society had rejected capital punishment even for felons, so it could not routinely take the life of a creature whose only crime was a form of uncontrollable madness.

Thus she lived, and suffered, and wreaked damage, and forgot her brother, and railed against her confined environment, and destroyed my life.

As I say, we stayed a few more minutes before returning to the manor. Everett would have drawn me beside him into the Vandeventer, but I would not go. I discovered reserves of physical strength and detached my hand from his, then I climbed unassisted into the bus. Mr. Soshone had taken the others to their various destinations around the park, then returned to wait outside the bungalow for us. Once Mrs. Farraday and I were seated, he flew us at a slow pace to the house, where Mrs. Farraday and I disembarked, then he took off back toward the estate hangar.

Everett scrambled from his aeromobile just as we were alighting from the bus, but I took Mrs. Farraday's arm for support as we entered the foyer. "I believe I need assistance to my room," I said in a low voice, but loud enough for the master of the house to hear. "Could you help me upstairs?"

"Oh, Jenna, you poor child, of course I shall help you! Lean on me, poor girl. There now, once I've got you settled, I shall bring you some hot soup and tea. That will make everything better—well, no, I suppose not everything—dear me—"

Her voice trailing off into embarrassment and I making no attempt to speak, we completed the rest of the climb in silence. I did not even look back to see if Everett watched from the foot of the stairs. I made it to my room, which seemed a haven out of all proportion to its physical amenities, and thanked Mrs. Farraday gravely at the door. Locking it between us, I stood for a moment, eying the great distance between the threshold and my bed, and wondering if I could cross so much space without falling. I did not think so. Carefully, so as not to bruise myself, I lowered myself to the floor, and on hands and knees crawled across the room to my bed.

But I could not summon the energy to raise myself to the mattress; I could not pull myself so high. So there, at the foot of the bed, in a pillow of ivory satin, I lay for the next few hours, and I did not move at all.

Chapter 14

✦

*I*t was sometime past midnight when I lifted my head from the floor. Every bone in my body had compacted during these past few hours; every muscle had coiled into a stiff, unyielding knot. It hurt to shift position, and it was agony to stand, but the physical discomfort was almost a relief—a distraction from the soundless, soulless interior desolation that had robbed me of thought and volition.

I managed to stand—and once standing, managed to undo enough buttons of my dress that I could strip it from my body. I stepped from its crushed satin carcass, left it mournfully at the foot of the bed, and toed off my shoes one by one as I crossed the room. All of my new clothes were in suitcases somewhere—I had no idea where—but there were a few old pieces of clothing left hanging dispiritedly in the closet. I pulled on battered gray coveralls and slipped into a pair of worn-out flats. Running a hand through my hair, I found the bridal headband still in place. I yanked it from my head and dropped it on the floor, and stepped away.

What now? Where to?

I had not eaten since breakfast. I had ignored Mrs. Farraday when she had knocked on the door shortly after our return, for at the time I had believed I would never eat again. I would die of starvation if my stubborn heart were so ruthless as to fail to break. But now, some fifteen or sixteen hours past my last meal, I found my stomach as stubborn and impossible to direct as my heart. It too clung to life and the needs thereof; it demanded sustenance. If Mrs. Farraday had not left the tray at my door, I must go downstairs to seek out whatever food I might find at this hour.

I opened the door and nearly fell over Everett Ravenbeck.

He had wedged himself into the door frame and sat on the floor, immovable, intractable, awaiting my decision to exit. As I stumbled over his unexpected body, he scrambled to his feet and caught me, restoring my balance.

"Jenna!" he exclaimed, peering down at me. "Thank God! I had begun to think you would never emerge, and I had grown so worried. I don't know how much longer I could have endured the silence before I broke down the door and ascertained that you were still alive."

"Alive," I repeated, for somehow the word did not seem to describe my state. "Yes—"

His hold on me tightened; the expression on his face (which I looked at most fleetingly) was all apprehension. "But barely so," he added in a grim voice. "You look so ill, Jenna—not that that is to be wondered at, but you look so pale! As if you have half determined to cross over into the realm of death, and only the faintest memory of what it means to be corporeal has kept your face solid and your limbs from dissolution."

I had no idea how to respond to this, so I said nothing. Perhaps I swayed a little in his hold, for the anxiety on his face grew sharper, and he bent over me again as if to read some script in my expression.

"Yes—I have got it exactly—you would be willing to die, right now, this instant, except that your body does not know how to go about it," he said. "It is your spirit that is sick, not your flesh, and the spirit is not used to death blows. It cannot translate them into action."

I could not answer that either; all I could do was enunciate my most pressing need. "I must eat something," I whispered. "I feel faint."

Without another word, he scooped me into his arms and carried me down the hall. My own weakened condition made his strength seem so much more impressive; he seemed alive with energy. By contrast, I felt even smaller and more frail than ever. How could I gainsay him, what would my pitiful negatives be in defiance of his raw animal power?

He brought me to the breakfast room and propped me up on two chairs drawn close together, and bade me "Be good and sit still now." I did not have the will to do otherwise. He bounded through the connecting door into the kitchen, and I heard him rattle around looking through cabinets and refrigeration units for suitable menu items. Soon enough he emerged with a plateful of food I could not have consumed had I sat at this table for a solid week, eating without pause, and set this before me.

"Would you like wine, Jenna? Or tea? Water if you like. What can I get for you?"

"Water will be fine," I said in a low voice. "Thank you."

I swallowed a few bites of bread and cheese, and this revived me enough that I could sit up straighter and eat more heartily. Everett set a glass of water before me, then sat across from me and watched every single forkful I took. He seemed hungry himself—not for food, but for reassurance—and my willingness to eat was only part of the reassurance he craved. I knew what else he starved for, but that I could not give him.

When I at last pushed my plate away, he leaped to his feet again. "Done, Jenna? Not another bite? Then let us go into the library, where it is more comfortable. We must talk."

Yes—we must—but, oh, how I dreaded the things that would be said in this conversation!

I did not allow him to pick me up again, but walked to the library under my own power, albeit somewhat unsteadily. Here, he attempted to install me on the sofa, where he could sit beside me, but I chose instead a narrow high-backed chair with carved wooden arms where I could rest my hands. He settled himself in a similar chair, and drew it as close to me as its construction would allow.

"I do not know where to begin, Jenna," he said at last, in a quiet though somewhat hopeful voice. "There is no apology, there are no words strong enough to convey to you the depth of my remorse, the strength of my assurance that I did not mean, could never mean, any

harm to come to you. That the harm has been spiritual instead of physical does not make it any less real. You must believe me, Jenna. Had I
had any inkling of the way events would transpire—of how you would
be humiliated and horrified and emotionally brutalized—I would never
have embarked on this course of action. I would have kept quiet till my
days ended, hugging to myself the great joy of this love I have for you.
I would have sacrificed any chance I had at happiness rather than bring
a moment's distress to your life. You must know that, Jenna."

"I do know it, Everett," I said, and relapsed into silence.

That I spoke at all encouraged him; he tried to hitch his chair
another inch or two closer. "Yes—but you only understand part of it.
You do not know how it all came about."

"I will listen, if you care to tell me the story."

"Yes! I must tell you! It has been more than fifteen years since the
tale was enacted, let alone recited. There was a day I could not fathom
of my own will giving the details to another living creature. But *you*—I
want to tell you everything, Jenna. I want nothing to be hid."

I glanced up at him, thinking, *A little late for honesty now*, but he
looked so eager that I could not say the words. "Then be frank" were
the only words I could muster. He nodded twice, decisively, and began
his story.

"I have told you before how matters stood between my relations and
myself. Specifically, I told you that I had two brothers and a father, and
that they had determined to keep the Ravenbeck property between the
three of them, excluding me. I was young and resentful when all of this
became clear to me. I did not see any reason I should have to work hard
for my bread and board when others so near to me did not. So I committed some foolish excesses and showed my anger to my family and
delayed pursuing any kind of meaningful career.

"Then one day my father and my oldest brother approached me, saying they had found a way to secure an inheritance for me. Would I be
interested in hearing the details? Well, of course I would! It turned out
that one of their business partners—a Fordyce Merrick of Wesleyan-
Imrae—had a daughter whom he wished to marry off to someone of
level-one citizenship. Merrick himself was rich enough to have bought

himself a pedigree, but he did not have much polish—at least, this was the story that was told to me—and he wanted to marry his daughter into a family of high rank.

"The rewards seemed great all around. I would inherit a sizable property from Merrick himself upon my wedding day—property in no way dependent upon the future success of my marriage—and jointly, his daughter and I would inherit additional lands and funds. Which I would administer, because, as I was told, she had no interest in business transactions. Meanwhile, old Merrick would achieve his goal of seeing his daughter gain unimpeachable social status—and my father would benefit from Merrick's gratitude, in unstated but lucrative ways that were not explained to me.

"I was eager for the union, but I stalled a week or two, pretending I had to think things over. I did not go to Wesleyan-Imrae to meet my intended bride. I did seek out the family name on the StellarNet, and find her picture, and consider it acceptable enough, and read the official information presented in the family history. I did not search for the Merrick name in the old news services, for why should I? It did not occur to me there was any mystery to this girl. Just as there was no mystery to me.

"Finally, having given my father and brother enough time to become impatient, I agreed to the arrangement, and the three of us traveled to Wesleyan-Imrae to have the wedding performed. Here I met Beatrice Merrick for the first time. She was a strange and yet alluring girl, quite quiet in the company of her family, but almost giddy on the few occasions we managed to get free of them. She had a way of moving that was hypnotic, because it was so fluid and almost balletic. She was constantly in motion. Her hands were never still, her head was always turning from side to side to gaze at something, and yet she moved with such grace that she was a delight to watch. Like observing a waterfall or a strand of brightly colored seaweed in a wash of tide—ocean metaphors kept coming constantly to my mind.

"And she was elusive too. I kept thinking—if I can pin her down, make her stand still, I will get to the heart of her, I will dissect her seductive charms. For I could not do it during that brief courtship phase. I would say something—she would look at me sideways, and laugh, and skip away—I don't believe she ever fully met my eyes while we stood face to face. I don't believe we ever gazed at each other, as even the most casual acquaintances will do if only for an uncomfortable moment. And there was something damned attractive about her unapproachability—she led me on with those backward glances and those little trills of laughter floating back to me from wherever she had run ahead.

"So—call me a fool—I *was* a fool, and not just because I was young and greedy. I knew little about women, little about love, little about anything except the injustices that I perceived had been done to me. So I flirted with Beatrice Merrick for two weeks while her mother finalized the plans for the wedding, and then the day arrived. Hundreds of people were invited to the event, for the Merricks wanted to be sure that all their acquaintances saw the coup they had scored. The ceremony was held outdoors on an oppressively hot day, and Beatrice was dressed in the most lavish, multilayered dress I had ever seen, and veiled with yards and yards of lace. I felt certain she must faint from the combination of heat and inappropriate clothing, but when, during the ceremony, I took her hand, it was cool as ice water. It occurred to me then, for the first time, that I had not touched any part of her body before this.

"The ceremony was endless, the following reception about as you would imagine, and I was impatient for the night to come. Well, this was my shy bride, and this was my wedding night! Of course I was impatient! And the hour finally came, and someone brought us to the spaceport, to the fancy hotel where we would stay until our commercial cruiser departed in two days' time."

He paused, and put a hand to his forehead. I was trying to understand, without being undone by sympathy, so I noticed with a rather clinical detachment that his hand was actually shaking. This story must be difficult to tell—not that I was surprised. I could already guess at the denouement, which was harrowing enough to make the buildup chilling.

"Our first few nights together," he said, in a voice that seemed steady only through iron determination, "were ecstatic. Beatrice was not, in this situation, shy—for which I was grateful, for my own experiences had been limited and not particularly fulfilling. I did not let myself wonder how she had learned what she knew. I merely appreciated it.

"We left on our honeymoon, taking the cruiser for the pleasure ports of Hyverg and Corbramb. But once we arrived on Hyverg, Beatrice began to change. She became fretful and erratic, and her beautiful, graceful motions grew spasmodic and jerky. I was alarmed, I was frightened—I was afraid that she had developed some neurological disorder that was wreaking all sorts of havoc inside her skull. But every time I pressed her to seek help, or at least go to our hotel's PhysiChamber, she adamantly refused. I began to scheme to find ways to get her, all unawares, to a doctor, because I really was quite frightened. And I had, during these weeks, imagined myself to have fallen in love with her—though now, looking back, I realize it was more a combination of desire and possessiveness that made me believe I was deeply attached to her.

"Things got worse. Sometimes when we were out in public, she would exhibit the most bizarre behavior. In the middle of an ordinary conversation, she would begin screaming, and could not be quieted, and I had to forcibly remove her from shopping centers and restaurants before the guards were summoned. A few times, in the middle of the night, she slipped out while I was asleep, and when I woke and found her gone I would leap up in a pure stage of panic. Once I found her swimming quietly—but completely nude—in the hotel pool. Once I found her walking through the streets of Hyverg Major, accosting strangers in a pitiful, incomprehensible voice—in a language that sounded foreign if not completely invented. Once I found her—well— she was negotiating a price with a tourist who believed she planned to reward him with sexual favors, and when I dragged her away from him, the curses she spewed at me were mortifying and terrifying to hear."

He stopped again, as if to compose himself, though his voice still sounded absolutely steady to me. "During what period of time did this transpire?" I asked.

"The events I am about to relate occurred within two weeks of our arrival in the city of Hyverg Major."

"So it was a rapid deterioration."

"Very. Clearly, things could not be permitted to continue as they were. One afternoon while she slept, I made arrangements for a prominent local doctor to come to us at the hotel. He warned me that, without his neurological equipment, there would not be much he could tell me about her condition, but he agreed that her behavior might be explained by some kind of tumor of the brain. He arrived, with a satchel full of tools, and I admitted him to the sitting room that I shared with my wife. The minute I introduced him, she began shrieking like a disordered child, hurling objects at him from across the room, and trying to escape out to the hallway. I grabbed her from behind and exerted all my force to keep her in check—and she nearly flung me across the room with one furious gesture of her arm. I had never felt such strength in anyone before—woman *or* man—and I was shaken in spirit and body when I scrambled to my feet. The doctor was busy readying some chemical compound, and when I dove for her again, wrestling her to the ground and rendering her momentarily still, he administered it. After a few moments of thrashing, she lay quiet.

"The doctor commenced his investigation while I hovered nearby, dreading to learn what news he might have to impart. He pulled apart her lids to examine her eyes, he dug out various instruments that he held over her pulse points, he touched her skin with some strange pad and drew out a few droplets of blood. And then he looked at me and said, 'I am sorry, Mr. Ravenbeck, I don't believe I can help you. I was under the impression that your wife was a human, which is all that I am qualified to treat.' "

Again, Everett stopped speaking, but this time I had been able to detect the tremor in his voice—and this time, despite all my resolution not to be melted by his recitation, my heart nearly unraveled itself in its desire to slip from my body and wrap itself protectively around his.

"I said, 'Excuse me? But my wife *is* human.' The doctor was putting his tools away. 'Half human. If that much,' he corrected. 'The android quotient is high in her. Though the reconstruction job was superb. I would not have suspected anything merely by looking at her, and I normally have a good eye for a cyborg.' I was too stunned to think of pretending ignorance and so preserving some of my own dignity. I cried, 'Cyborg! My wife is not a cyborg!' And the doctor looked at me very gravely and said, 'Indeed she is. And a malfunctioning cyborg at that. If you do not get yourself immediately to a robotics center, she will no doubt experience complete meltdown. She will—well, I don't know *what* she'll do. Things much worse than those you have already described to me.'

"Once he finished speaking, we stared at each other a moment in silence. He realized—he had to realize—that I had not, until this moment, known the truth of my wife's condition. Which he no doubt found incredible in the extreme! Yet his face was compassionate, and he looked as though he sincerely pitied me. I finally spoke. I said, 'Doctor, I do not know what to do or where to take her. Is there a place you can recommend?' And he wrote down the name of a nearby clinic, and wished me luck, and refused to be paid for his services. And he left."

Everett was now staring down at his folded hands, or at the carpet visible beneath them, but I was sure he was seeing instead that bridal hotel room, that sleeping girl, and the ruination of all his dreams.

"I could have contacted my father at this point," he said slowly. "I could have contacted *her* father, and demanded—well, at some point demanded explanations, but first demanded what it was I should be doing for her, for clearly there were ways to keep her imbalances in check or she would never have appeared as an ordinary woman. But I was too proud. I understood now, completely, how they had betrayed me—deliberately, maliciously, even gleefully. Old man Merrick had wanted his troublesome half-human daughter taken off his hands, and my father had known I would be fool enough to sell my liberty for a few plots of land. But I was not the only victim in their trap. They had treated Beatrice just as cruelly, for they had given an unstable creature over into the hands of a man who did not know how to care for her, and they had risked her utter destruction.

"I was not willing to be as cruel as they. I called the number the doctor had given me, and I had Beatrice taken to a local robotics center, and I had her stabilized. It was the saddest thing I had ever seen, Jenna, the morning I arrived to check on her and found the girl I had thought I loved lying in her hospital bed, strapped in place. For days she had not known me or anybody else, but finally they had discovered the flawed circuit, and repaired it, and the neurons in her brain were again firing in the patterns of recognition. I came in to see her, and her face lit up, and she exclaimed, 'Everett! Where have you been? I woke this morning and you were nowhere in sight, and there were only strangers here. I was so afraid.' "

"She did not remember the preceding days?"

"No. Not only that, she did not remember her own history—in fact, she did not *know* her own history. I had had time to do a little research, and I found the old news accounts of Fordyce Merrick's daughter and the spectacular aeromobile crash that nearly killed her when she was eleven years old. She had been saved, though it required a high percentage of robotic reconstruction to make her whole. But Beatrice refused to believe me when I repeated that tale to her. She started weeping so hysterically that I had to call in the technicians, who sent me from the room and sedated her. Later, one of the technicians told me it was a wonder she could remember anything at all—even her own name—let alone any of her bizarre behavior. For it was his theory that the human portion of her brain was rejecting some of its electronic implants, and the implants were damaging the brain. There was no way to reverse the process, he said, and no way to stop it, and over time her mind would totally degrade. So I was told by the specialists on Hyverg Major, and so I have found to be true."

He paused again and seemed to review the following months and years of his life, editing them down into a concise few paragraphs with which to conclude his story. "I did what I could for her, even so," he said. "The head of this institution recommended that I take Beatrice to Dorser, where they have the most advanced cyborg research facility in the universe. And so we went, though I had to conceal from her the precise nature of the institution we were visiting and our reasons for visiting it. And they did manage to—to upgrade the implant—some such thing—to make her more stable for a relatively long period of time. By that, I mean nearly two years, during which time she seemed an almost normal human being who was gradually deteriorating into a form of madness. She had happy, lucid days, and she had days of raging panic, and I never knew from day to day or hour to hour whether I would be dealing with the rational or the manic Beatrice. I just did my best for her as long as I could."

"It sounds—it must have been completely dreadful," I stammered, the words sounding so inadequate I almost wished them unsaid.

He nodded. "And the worst of it—truly the worst—was the fact that Beatrice herself did not understand what was happening to her or why I had ceased to love her. On her good days—and, at the beginning, there were many of those—she thought we were still lovers, honeymooners, ready to fall affectionately into each other's arms at a moment's notice. But I . . . I could not do it. I was so repulsed and horrified by what she actually was that I could not bring myself to love her, or even to pretend to love her. It broke her heart—and her heart, at least, was quite human. I can still recall the hopefulness with which she would approach me, in those early days, and the hurt and rejection on her face when I would turn away from her. But I could not love her. I could only be kind to her, and care for her, and wait for the moment of her absolute disintegration."

Now a peculiar feeling came over me—a selfish, unworthy emotion at such a place and such a time!—and yet it suffused me and made me speak when I should not have. "There are many people who cannot love synthetics," I said in a hollow voice. "My aunt, for one. I believe it is the reason she could not love me. And I wonder how—feeling as you do about created life and knowing my history—I wonder how you could have brought yourself to love someone such as myself. For I am in many ways as artificial as your wife."

He looked up at me quickly and keenly. "Yes, but you are the exception to the rule, Jenna," he said. "Manufactured—synthetic—even virtual, if that is what you turned out to be—I would love you. There is about you, at your core, such a bright fire of will and passion that I would want to warm myself at it no matter how that blaze had been ignited. It is *you* I love, your habits of thought and your strictness of soul and your serious face, and it is you I would love if all your systems were to turn out to be metal and rubber, and all those systems were in turn to malfunction. I would guard you close on your bad days, and on your rational days, I would walk with you through the grounds and delight in the observations you would make. Generated human—half-cit—cyborg—whatever you were would be precious to me, because it would be *you* in the heart of your body, and it is you I love."

I turned away, because such an avowal made me want to weep, and I could show no such weakness during this interview. "I am sure you would care for me, in such a situation," I said in rather choked tones. "For I see how you have tried to care for Beatrice."

"Yes—you do see that, do you not, Jenna?" he asked eagerly. "Because Merrick believes I use her cruelly, but I do not. I cannot leave her unwatched, and I cannot allow her to roam freely, and I have done everything in my power to assure both her comfort and her safety. But Merrick thinks I abuse her."

I composed myself and shifted face-forward again. "I think you treat her much more kindly than would most men in your situation," I said. "But I do wonder one thing. Why remain married to her? I would not have expected you to abandon her—I would condemn you if you had—but could you not have continued to care for her while freeing yourself from your matrimonial bond?"

He shook his head. "I looked into that very circumstance and no, I could not. At the center on Dorser, I learned that her robotic compound was so high that, were she to come to the attention of the legal community through such action as a divorce, she would immediately be declared nonhuman and devoid of rights. And you know as well as I do that malfunctioning androids are destroyed and recycled. And though there have been days—many, many days!—that I wished her circuits would overload and destroy her, I could not bear to be the agent that led to her dissolution. I could not do it. I had promised, during that fateful bridal ceremony, to give her my name and cover her with my honor, and I could not, because of its great inconvenience to me, renege on that promise.

"So once she deteriorated to the point that she seemed to have no humanity left, I installed her at Thorrastone Park, in the remotest of my properties," he continued. "I found a watcher for her, and a place she could be comfortable, and a setting where she could cause very little damage. I was not particularly well-known here, and my employees and the society people I met on Fieldstar would only know my history if I chose to tell it—which I did not."

"But any man's history can be discovered on the StellarNet!" I cried. "Even my own, insignificant as it is, can be looked up by anybody with an interest."

He nodded. "Yes, and I am sure the Ingersolls and the Taffs and the others did check me out in that electronic Debrett's," he said sardonically. "But there I am listed as a widower, though my machinations to achieve that status are not something I want to go into now. I consider it ironic, however, that although I could not divorce Beatrice Merrick, I could kill her."

"And yet she is not dead—and you have a wife—and thus you are not free to marry," I said in a low voice.

He made a brushing motion with his hand. "Until today, only two living souls knew that fact—myself and Merrick—for his father is dead, and the rest of the world believes her to be as well. Now a handful of my employees know the truth, but their interests lie with me and they would not repeat the story—and who would believe them if they did? We have a safe secret, Jenna. We can proceed in confidence."

"A truth that no one knows is still the truth," I said quietly. "You cannot eliminate it merely because you do not publish it."

He seemed, all of a sudden, irritable and sulky. "Well, this one I do not intend to publish," he said. "I do not wish to proclaim to the world that Everett Ravenbeck has chosen to live in sin—or attempt bigamy!—with a young half-cit girl who is supposed to be under his protection. The world will see us cleanly wed, and that is all that anyone needs to know or understand."

"But, Mr. Ravenbeck—"

"Everett, my love. You have called me that so sweetly for days!"

"But, Mr. Ravenbeck," I said steadily, for so I would address him aloud though I continued to call him more familiarly in my heart, "I cannot pretend to marry you. I cannot live with you as your simulated bride. I must leave Thorrastone Park—I must travel as far from here as my resources will allow."

He seemed not to have heard me—or, at any rate, not to have understood. "Yes, both of us must leave Fieldstar, and the sooner the better," he said. "It has always been, for me, a place of grim responsibility and despair, and for you it has become a place of betrayal and horror. I do not wonder at your desire to flee! My cruiser is still in the spaceport. We need only wait until it is light, and we will return to the city. We will be gone tomorrow, and we need never return here."

"Mr. Ravenbeck," I said as gently as I could, "I cannot travel with you. I cannot live with you, or be with you, under any circumstances. I love you too much to stay beside you, tempted always by the mere fact of your presence to do what is wrong. Unlike your wife, I am only human, and I am not strong enough to resist loving you. And I will not love you unless I am your wife."

"My wife!" He leaped to his feet and began pacing the room. "But you would be my wife, in every sense except the most formal! You would have all my affection—every dime that I owned would be lavished upon you—every society in the civilized universe would accept you with courtesy and honor—"

"Legally I would not be your wife, sir."

He rounded on me, rather menacingly standing over me where I sat in my straight-backed chair. "What! All you care about is your legal status? All you want from me is full citizenship—a chance to vote in meaningless elections and have your name recorded in a fancy registrar? I mean nothing more to you than the title I can give you? My love is not enough for you unless it comes with accoutrements?"

Now I was as stirred as he was and I too came to my feet, forcing him to back away a step by the warning in my expression. "Titles—status—money—none of these mean anything to me, and you know it," I said hotly. "What matters to me is my honor and my integrity and my very survival. If I let you take me with you now, who knows how long it would be before you tired of me, a half-cit girl who has no claim on you, whom you could abandon with impunity in any port on any planet across the settled galaxy? Who would care for me then? Or if you died? If I had no legal status as your wife, and I had lost all reputation by running away with you, how would I work? How would I live? Where do you suppose Janet Ayerson is at this moment, a young woman who eloped with a man who said he loved her? How can I give up the few things I have—and they are so few!—my unblemished reputation and my ability to care for myself, for a man who risks nothing for me? I do not care about your money. I do not care about your position in society. I would love you as well, or even better, if you did not have these things. But I cannot be your mistress, because I cannot throw away my life. I am too valuable for that. I am worth more than a rich man's whim."

"Jenna—no—you are wrong—" he exclaimed, coming forward with arms outstretched as if to take me into his arms. "How could you think I would tire of you or abandon you—"

I evaded him and stepped away. "I do not think it! I do not wish to believe it! But I cannot risk it."

"I will write a document, then! I will legally give over my property to you, avaricious and suspicious girl that you are—"

Again he reached for me, and again I sidestepped. "I do not want your property! I want to be able to rely upon myself, to know that *I* am still as good as my word, that *I* have not been compromised—"

"But you have not been compromised! You will not be! Jenna, I will love you till the suns burn down and the stars rotate out of their positions! With my heart, my mind, my body, and my soul, I love you. You can trust me to the limits of your life—as I trust you to the limits of mine—"

He had moved more quickly than I had; he had caught me around the waist and brought me, none too gently, into his embrace. I struggled, but in vain. He drew me closer, he crushed me against his chest. He bent over me with all the madness of a man who has been momentarily thwarted in his desire and is determined to achieve it or die.

"Say you love me, Jenna," he said, and his voice was both pleading and threatening. "Say you will come with me tomorrow—or even tonight—we could fly into the spaceport this instant. Say, 'Everett, I love you, and I will be yours—' "

"I will not."

He shook me, hard, and his face grew even more desperate. "Say, 'Everett, I understand all and forgive all. I love you and will live with you forever as your wife.' "

"I understand, and I do forgive, but I will not relent. I will not live with you, and you cannot force me, and if you do force me, you will not have me—not the me you want, not the part of me that loves you still—or would, if you did not kill it—"

My words seemed to snap some final civilized cord that kept his despair in check, for he uttered a short, agonized cry, and snatched me closer with a ferocity that made me gasp. He rained kisses upon my face, my eyes, my mouth, my hair; he sobbed my name over and over again, then began again with the desperate kisses. I could not breathe or struggle. I felt in peril of being ripped apart, devoured, consumed, and for a blind unreasoning moment I was tempted to give in. To exclaim, "Everett Ravenbeck, I adore you! I will be yours!" for so much I loved him, and so much was I moved by his love and grief. But the moment passed; sanity reasserted itself. With a great violent effort, I tore myself from his arms.

"I will not submit to you!" I cried. "I will not sacrifice myself to you! Do not make me hate you as much as I have loved you! Do not!"

My words were not even necessary, for my mere action of wrenching away from him had caused him to stagger back and shrink away with despair. He had covered his face with his hand. It was not impossible to believe that, behind his sheltering fingers, his eyes were awash with tears. "Jenna," he moaned, his voice broken and hoarse. "Do not depart from me like this. Do not turn away from me so harshly, leaving me abandoned and alone—without friendship, without love, without hope. I cannot live without you, truly I cannot. You are life to me now. Without you, there is only darkness and death."

I had prepared to flee from the room, now that I was free of his hold, but his words stopped me. I knew he spoke literal truth, for I felt the same way exactly. Once I left this place and his presence, my days would be dark and dreary—insupportably so, I feared.

"For what light it affords you, Everett Ravenbeck, I will love you till I die," I said softly. "Wherever I am and wherever you are, there will be that bond between us, that I love you, and believe you good. But I cannot stay with you," I added quickly, as his face lifted, hope written all over his countenance. "I cannot so put us both at risk."

"Jenna," he said, again in that pitiful voice.

I crossed to the door, and once there, put my hand with some determination on the knob. "Good-bye, Mr. Ravenbeck," I said, and I could not keep my voice steady, though I tried. "Be strong. Be good. I will attempt to be those things as well."

And I left the room.

Behind me I heard one last heartbroken wail, and then a dreadful silence. I did not stay to listen, to learn if he composed himself, or abandoned himself entirely to an uncontrollable frenzy. I went to my own room, and locked the door, and flung myself on my bed, and passed some of the bitterest hours of my life.

Chapter 15

✦

I must have slept, for a few hours later, I woke. I felt strange and haunted, as if I had endured unbroken decades of nightmares only to find, upon waking, that every morbid dream were true. The air about me felt so close, so unbreathable, that for a moment I feared the forcefield had been sabotaged again and that all inhabitants of the manor were about to suffocate in their beds. But slowly, as I pushed myself to my feet and glanced unseeingly around, I realized it was not the security system that had been breached, but my own inviolable wall of sanity. It was not the room that was surreal, but my senses that were unreliable. I must work on touch and memory, for neither my perceptions nor my calculations were likely to aid me now.

I must leave this place immediately.

I crossed to the closet and again looked through my pitiful assortment of ragged clothes. These would see me through a day or two, so I bundled them up and thrust them into a cotton carrying bag. I turned on the computer monitor to check my credit status—woefully low, for I had splurged so joyfully on my bridal trousseau—but it was enough, I hoped, to cover some part of a passage off-planet. If not—well, I did not know what I would do if it did not. If I stayed at Thorrastone Park one more day with Everett Ravenbeck, I would yield; I would not be able to resist either his love or his woe. I would forget my own needs in the overwhelming desire to alleviate his unhappiness.

I crossed to the door and reached for the knob, but I could not open it. I leaned my head against the frame and tried to summon up the strength to cross the threshold. Oh, what were my own requirements in the face of his despair? So long as he did not suffer, what did it matter that I threw away everything—every principle, every ethic, every personal belief—that had kept me strong through so many perils? If I could save him one moment of wretchedness, should not my whole life be forfeit? Who would care if I faltered, strayed, or disappeared?

A great rush of relief and anticipation washed over me as I thought, *I can stay. I do not have to leave him.* I lifted my head as this great burden of my own morality was lifted from me. I felt pounds lighter— giddy with hope—I would rush down the hall this minute, wake him from his bed or rouse him from his grief-induced stupor in the library, and I would promise to be his for all this life and eternity beyond. . . .

But I could not open the door.

The weight of my conscience descended on me again; the clear, cold eye of reason opened inside my mind. Who would know if I transgressed my own personal ethical boundaries? *I* would know. *I* would care. *I* would have to be answerable, for the rest of my life, to the stern inner guiding voice whose implacable division of right from wrong would not alter for circumstance or supplication. I might for days or weeks be blissful in my surrender to love, but I knew myself, and my reliance on that inner voice, too well. That bright glittering joy would turn to soot and ashes in my hands. I would grow resentful and appalled; I would cease to love or respect Everett Ravenbeck—worse, I would cease to love or respect myself. I would become spiteful and mean, accusatory and hard. He would grow bewildered, then angry, then brutal. Our great love would grow small and pointless—the greatest loss; and heaped upon that tragedy would be material loss, that could result in me being homeless, penniless, and alone.

Even that you can endure! my defiant heart cried out. *For those few weeks of happiness as his pseudo-bride, you can accept a lifetime of bitterness and drudgery! Live those few precious days, and when he no longer loves you, take your life. It will be worth nothing by then any-way.*

I was tempted. Oh, Reeder, so sorely tempted! But as I stood there, frozen to the spot, torn between desire and duty, I heard a great voice speak to me in sonorous, echoing syllables; I heard the compassionate, motherly tones of the animating spirit of the universe.

"This course holds only thorns and tears. Child, be strong and flee."

And I whispered in response, "Goddess, I will."

And I picked up my forlorn bag, and I opened the door, and I crept down the stairs and out onto the lawn.

There was a predawn shuttle that passed by Thorrastone Park every morning, and if I hurried across the field, I would be in the airlock in time to catch it. Thus, I did not tarry for anything—not a last, heart-broken look at the stones and windows of the manor; not a farewell to the fallen oxenheart tree; not a glance at the security field that had been my main occupation for so many months. Nothing held me, nothing detained me. I practically ran to the airlock and quickly dialed it open, then closed; and I waited, panting, for the shuttle to pull into view.

It did, not five minutes after I had made it to the rendezvous. I boarded, gave little attention to my fellow passengers, and found a seat to myself. And there I sat, bolt upright and apprehensive, for the entire slow journey into town.

Everyone would know where I had gone, of course. It was too much to hope that Mr. Ravenbeck would not come for me as soon as he dis-covered my absence. I must be safely off Fieldstar within hours of my arrival at the spaceport. My only margin lay in his probable reluctance to enter my room without an invitation. He might knock on the door, but he would suppose me sleeping, or impervious, for a good many hours yet. Or so I believed. I did not know how quickly he would breach the limits of courtesy and burst into my chamber—or send in Mrs. Farraday to perform the same service. Upon his tolerance for enduring uncertainty I must place my dependence now.

We arrived at the spaceport as sunrise was beginning to send its frail, unpromising streaks of light across the sky. Disembarking from the bus, I headed directly to the main passenger ship terminal, a great gray hulking building of bustle and impersonality. There was, I knew, within this building a ticket window expressly designed for the impecunious and desperate. Here, the impoverished traveler could offer to work off part of his passage on a ship needing extra labor, and here some of the commercial cruisers agreed to take on passengers at half price at the very last moment if their billets were not entirely full. A traveler could not be choosy about his destination or accommodations at such an office, of course, but since I was neither, I had some hope of finding a ship off Fieldstar that left before noon.

It took me some time and many inquiries to locate the window I wanted, for the building was huge, and echoing, and completely disorienting. When I did at last fetch up at the station I desired, at first I thought I was in luck, for there was a man behind the counter and no one in line before me. The small clerk was all-over brown—hair, face, clothing—and he was involved in a desultory conversation with two rather villainous-looking men who lounged against the pillars behind him. I set down my little bag and took a deep breath.

"Sir," I said. "I wish to travel off Fieldstar as quickly as possible. What kind of accommodations are available?"

"What kind of credit do you got?" was his reply. His voice was not exactly surly, but it was not particularly friendly either. His companions glanced at me once, then resumed their own conversation.

"Not much, I'm afraid," I said, handing over my credit slip avowal which I had printed out earlier. He took it and snorted.

"That won't hardly get you a pleasure jaunt circling Fieldstar for the day," he said. "You'll need more."

I swallowed. "But I don't have more. I'm willing to work, though. I'm a technician, specially certified for nuclear reactor maintenance, but I have other skills that a ship overseer might find useful."

The clerk shrugged and tapped a few sequences on his keyboard. "Well, there's the *Sallie Mae*. She leaves tomorrow morning, she's looking for sanitary crew," he said. "But it's dirty work—"

"I don't mind dirty, but I must leave today," I interrupted. "This morning, if possible."

"Leaving today I've got *Horatio* . . . naw, that's a commercial cruiser, she's not hiring. *Ojo*'s military, they won't take you on. *Macklin*'s an agricultural scow, they're always looking for hands, but that's not till late tonight. Other than that"—he shrugged—"no other choices."

I felt my blood drain from my face and pool in my knees and elbows. "What! Nothing else! But I must leave today! I—it's—surely you could check again, surely there must be something—"

He shrugged and played his hands once again over the keyboard. I stood rooted to the spot, but my mind was working furiously. Perhaps I could find someplace to hide in the spaceport, someplace Everett would not think to look for me, and sneak back to the landing field in the morning to catch either the *Sallie Mae* or the *Macklin*. This was a plan so fraught with risk I hardly dared consider it, but if I could not book passage today, I did not know what my other choice might be.

The clerk looked up at me, uninterest plain on his face. He did not even care what my extreme circumstances might be, that would cause me to flee a place so precipitously that I did not even ask the destination of the starships on which I was willing to book passage. "I don't see nothing," he said.

One of the men standing behind him had started listening to our conversation a few sentences back, and now he strolled forward with his hands in his pockets. He was large and rather ferocious-looking, for his wild hair and wilder beard were both black and uncombed, and his face appeared to be crisscrossed with scars where it was not hidden by hair. Yet his eyes were alive with intelligence, and it was with some shrewdness that he looked me over. Also—or perhaps it was just my dire need for it—with a trace of sympathy.

"What's the lady need? Quick passage off? We've got a berth open if she wants it," he said in a warm, rumbling voice. "And we're out of here this morning."

I nodded at him, gratitude making my eyes brim over, but the brown clerk objected before I could speak. "She's only got a few levels of credit," he said. "Won't cover the cost, even."

The big man shrugged. "We've got to run the equipment whether there's somebody in that slot or not. All the other bunks are taken, and everyone else has paid full price. We can take her with us."

"Yes, but will she want to go with you?" the clerk asked with some humor. He turned back to me and jerked a thumb at his friend. "Barkow's with the *Anniversary*. They're traveling out toward Appalachia. And 'cause she's a refitted scow that can't make standard speeds, the journey takes twice as long as it should. Like, a year."

I felt my eyes fly wide. "A *year!* But—but—I surely don't have enough credit—and I cannot—and I would need food and provisions— a *year*—"

Barkow grinned. "Cold storage," he said helpfully. "Only the crew's live. All the passengers go in suspended animation for the trip. Once you're strapped in, you just sleep the time away. We wake you up about two weeks outside of Appalachia."

I stared at him, his ugly, kind face, and I felt myself turn to ice without benefit of his equipment. I had heard stories of space travel by suspended animation, which was relatively new and highly controversial—and sometimes unsuccessful. More than one ship had arrived at its destination and attempted to revive its cargo only to find every passenger a corpse. The equipment had malfunctioned, the monitors had failed, the intravenous lines had delivered insufficient quantities of food; all these things could and had gone wrong. Even on the more numerous occasions when the passengers had all arrived more or less intact, some had suffered ill effects from the voyage—oxygen deprivation that caused severe brain damage, quasi-starvation, illness. The only reason suspended animation was still used at all was that the price of a yearlong space journey was prohibitive for any except the most wealthy—five or ten times costlier than the journey under hypothermic conditions—and the planets along the outer rim of the settled universe were still looking for colonists. Appalachia was even farther from Fieldstar than Billalogia, where Everett Ravenbeck had once proposed to send me. It was so far away my mind almost could not comprehend its distance. To travel so far would be to sever forever any physical or emotional bond to Fieldstar.

"When do you leave?" I asked through lips that felt already frozen.

Barkow glanced at his watch. "Less than two hours. If you're coming with us, you'll have to decide now, because it takes a little time to put you in place."

Almost without conscious volition, I nodded my head. "Yes. I will go with you."

Barkow laughed, and slapped the clerk on the back. "Feed her credit into our account," he said, and came around the edge of the counter to pick up my bag. "So what's your name, new lady passenger? Or should I not ask, seeing as how you're so anxious to get away from here?"

If I lied, Mr. Ravenbeck might not be able to track me. I glanced at the clerk, who had swiped my information through his terminal. "It's a double transfer," he told me. "To my general account, then from my account to his. Nobody's going to untangle it."

I thanked him with a nod of my head. "I would prefer to travel without a name," I said to Barkow.

He laughed and strode forward so quickly I nearly had to run to keep up. "Fine with me," he said. "But you'll need a name again sometime. Better be thinking of that while you sleep." And he laughed again.

We had not covered more than a hundred yards in the terminal before Barkow hailed a man driving a small loading cart that was conveniently empty. We climbed aboard this and took off at dizzying speed across the great space of the hangar to one of the dozens of shuttle ports that ringed the building. Here, we boarded a twenty-seat tug that looked only slightly more sophisticated than Everett's Vandeventer, and which appeared to be the personal ferry of the *Anniversary*, for it had the ship's name stenciled on the exterior and interior walls. Barkow spoke in an intercom radio to an invisible pilot, and minutes after we had strapped ourselves in, the vehicle took off.

"We're the last ones to board," Barkow said amiably, looking out the window as first the spaceport, then the landscape, and then the great round shape of the planet fell away. "I'll get you set up all nice and tight in your bunk, and we'll be on our way."

"I can't tell you how much I appreciate—"

He grinned and waved away my thanks. "See how much you appreciate it when you're on Appalachia," he said with unexpected insight. "If you have no credit left to you—well, we'll see. They're looking for settlers and people with skills, and they're not asking too many questions. Heard you say you were a technician. You ought to do just fine."

After that, we had no conversation. The journey on the tug out to the main ship took about forty-five minutes, but soon enough we were snapped onto the airlock, and Barkow was carrying my bag on board. I did not get much chance to assess my surroundings as he hurried me through the corridor, not bothering to explain the various doors and hallways that opened off this main route. From what I could determine, the *Anniversary* looked like an older model modified star cruiser, perhaps once used as a commercial passenger liner and now adapted to its specialized mission. The ticket clerk had called it a scow, but that really just meant it did not have the recent improvements that would give it enhanced speed and efficiency. But it was serviceable still—merely slow.

Eventually we made our way to a largish chamber deep in the heart of the ship. I cast one quick glance around, noting the low ceiling hovering close over the long, narrow room, and catching the antiseptic smell of medicinal chemicals. White-coated technicians moved methodically through the room, inspecting rows and rows of coffin-shaped black receptacles lined up in neat ranks across the floor.

"Hey—Colyo—I've got a passenger for the last berth," Barkow called out to one of these technicians. A middle-aged woman standing very near us immediately left her post, where she was bending over one of the caskets and checking an electronic readout. Her graying black hair was pulled back in a severe style and her face looked completely humorless, but there was a crispness to her movements that impressed me with a sense of her competence.

"Good," she said, looking me over thoroughly. I imagined she was judging my weight, health, and physical endurance, though I did not know how evident those would be upon cursory visual examination. "I prefer an even distribution. Has she been prepared?"

"Not at all," Barkow said cheerfully. "I just found her, looking for quick passage off."

Colyo's brows arched, but she made no comment. "All right. I'll finish everything. Thanks."

At that cool dismissal, Barkow smiled and handed me my own bag. "See you in a year or so," he said. "Enjoy the trip." And he exited.

Colyo was surveying me again. "I'll have to ask you a few questions and do a quick assessment of your condition," she said. "I suppose you expected that?"

"Yes. I don't know—I know very little about suspended animation but I would guess you must adapt your IVs to the individual, and I assumed you would need to examine me," I said. "I will be happy to cooperate with everything."

"Of course. We'll leave your bag here at your berth while I take you back to the lab for tests," she said, walking me forward through the rows of coffins and depositing my bag at the foot of one of them.

I could not resist, as we strolled through this strange field of dormant life, trying to peer through the smoked-glass lids of the receptacles to get a glimpse of the sleepers inside. But the tops were too opaque; I could see nothing. All I could observe were the monitors attached to every repository, blinking with green and amber lights in mysterious combinations. Yet I could *sense* the life-forms lying so still, so patiently, beneath their protective caps. I felt as I once had, visiting a crypt whose central ornament was the sarcophagus of a mighty king. It had not taken the hushed words of the superstitious guide to convince me that a spirit walked in this mausoleum. I had stared at the molded form of the regent's face, and I had *known* he was still alive, trapped in his bejeweled tomb, awaiting merely the most propitious moment to burst through stone and mortar and reclaim his existence. I felt the same implacable sense of waiting in the storage room on the *Anniversary*. This was a haunted place indeed.

"Are you coming?" Colyo asked me, her tone of irritation jerking me back from speculation. "We don't have much time."

"I'm sorry. I'm quite ready," I said, and hurried after her as she threaded her way to the back of the room.

Eventually we ended up in a small, sterile chamber with a PhysXam arm hovering over a narrow table. I disrobed and allowed Colyo to wrap the gauge around my wrist. Immediately, the PhysXam monitors began chirping with their incomprehensible comments. Colyo watched lines of type begin to scroll across a monitor, and occasionally fired out a quick question to me.

"Your age? Your occupation? General health status? Any standard immune shots you've missed over the past five years? Any particular allergies that haven't been eradicated? Other intolerances?"

I answered as comprehensively as I could, though I knew the PhysXam could fill in most of those blanks for her. Then I added, "And, if it matters, I was gestated in a gen tank."

She looked up at that, obviously intrigued. "Really? On what planet?"

"Baldus."

"I've done some work there. The facility closed recently, you know."

"No, I didn't know that. Do you know why?"

"Funding problems, political problems, a disagreement with the director. I was gone by then, so I just heard the rumors. I heard they were looking for their past crops, though. Trying to put together an alumni list of some sort. I can't imagine why. I didn't get the details."

I winced at the word "crop," though she clearly spoke without intent to wound. I supposed the technicians who worked at such sites *did* see their projects as a sort of produce to be harvested, though the bales and bushels of human flesh and spirit might not view themselves in just such a vegetative light.

"Will my origin affect my stay in cold storage?" I asked.

She had returned her attention to the screen, and now she shook her head rather absently. "Shouldn't. Might even be helpful. I'd think you would have been inoculated in the gen tank with every possible vaccine, and loaded with all the healthiest DNA." She glanced back at me appraisingly. "Which does make me wonder why you're so small. Most of the gen tank babies are bred like amazons. The adults are usually almost offensively strong and healthy."

I spoke in a rather constricted voice. Now I was not only dehumanized, I was inadequate. "The woman who commissioned me was small-boned herself, and she wished for a child who matched her description."

Colyo nodded. "Oh, yeah. Had that happen when I was working there too. Strange, because you'd think with all the advantages you could give your child . . ." She shook her head again. "Well, everything checks out. You're in great shape physically. You should withstand the trip quite well. Come on, now we've got to get you cleaned up."

I had considered myself reasonably hygienic when I arrived in the spaceport, but I soon learned Colyo's standards were fanatical. I supposed it only made sense that if you were to be unable to bathe again for an entire year, you would want to make your last ablutions thorough, but this bath was actually chemical. I was completely immersed in a cleansing tank for a period of about twenty seconds; I could feel the outer layer of flesh literally being eaten away from my body, exposing the uncontaminated second level of skin. When I burst up from the solution, I was red and gasping, and Colyo bundled me into a sanitized gown.

"Quickly," she said, and hustled me back into the main room and to my waiting bed.

On her instructions, I climbed into the casket and sat there dumbly while she attached all manner of tubes and trackers to my body. A catheter, three IVs, an emergency oxygen tube, a blood monitor—I could not even guess at the uses of some of the equipment she patched into place.

"All right. Now I want you to lie down and get comfortable," she directed. "I'm going to activate the anesthesia, and after that has taken hold, I'll begin the hypothermic sequences. People have found it less terrifying," she added, "to already be sleeping before the cold is injected into their systems. We always tell people they can't detect it, but in fact they can, and it's not a pleasant sensation. This way seems simplest."

"One more request—if possible," I stammered, for I was beginning to find a certain panic tightening my throat and constricting my breathing. How had the Great Goddess led me to this place—what fantastic confluence of events had brought me to this situation, at this hour, to be gambling away a year of my life in this bizarre and uncertain fashion? "If you could not lower the lid until I was actually anesthetized. I would feel better, I think."

Colyo nodded. "Many people make that request. Not a problem."

"And," I added. "A question. What will happen when I wake up? Who will recover me? What will I remember? Will I know where I am and how I got here?"

"You will be weak and disoriented at first. You should remember who you are soon enough—within a few minutes, an hour at most. We will wake you from suspension two weeks or so before planetfall so that you have some time to recover use of your limbs. You will be thinner. At first you will find it strange to speak. You might remember dreams of surprising detail and complexity. You might remember only an absolute emptiness. Your brain will recover more quickly than your body, but within a few weeks on-planet, you will feel exactly as you do now. If all goes as planned."

I did not remark on that caveat; what could I possibly say? "Thank you," I said, and lay back in my yearlong bed.

"I never did ask you," she said. "And Barkow didn't say. What is your name?"

"Will it be registered anywhere?" I asked.

"Not if you would prefer it was not. But I have found that, when they first are wakened, suspension patients recover more quickly when they are reminded of their names."

I nodded, for this made sense to me. "Jenna Starborn," I said.

Colyo clicked a switch and I heard the soft chugging sound of a motor engaging. "Well, Jenna Starborn," she said, "sleep peacefully."

Again the panic welled up, more fiercely this time, but its duration was short. I could feel my body relaxing perforce with the injection of the anesthesia. I could feel my limbs disconnect from my conscious control and my mind's bright perception grow dim. I had one last clear thought—*From the gen tanks to the sleep tanks; surely my body must remember this*—and then my eyes closed. It was a complete and utter dissolution; and for a year, I knew nothing at all.

Chapter 16

✦

"*J*enna Starborn. Miss Starborn. *Jenna.*"

"You mean, she still hasn't responded?"

"Obviously not."

"Have you injected her with BioJazz?"

"Yes, yesterday and today. No effect."

"But her heartbeat—her vitals—"

"All good. Well, within the acceptable range. Actually, on the low side, but nothing to be concerned about."

"Muscle condition?"

"We strapped her into the automatics yesterday and exercised her arms and legs. Everything reacted well enough, and we'll do it again today. And we're getting visual response—she can open her eyes, and blink, and look away from a bright source of illumination—but I can't tell if she's taking anything in. There seems to be no cognitive process going on."

"Have you done a neural scan?"

"That's next."

"Ten more days before planetfall. Do we have someone to contact if she arrives on Appalachia in this condition?"

A long silence.

"*Do* we? Have someone to contact for Miss Starborn?"

"No."

"No one? No contact at all? What's it say in her contract?"

"She was a last-minute addition. Barkow brought her on right before takeoff. We didn't learn anything about her. We didn't get a contract. I don't even know if this is her real name."

"Why is she going to Appalachia?"

"I didn't ask."

"Who brought her on board? Barkow? Maybe he'll know something more about her. Let's bring him in."

A silence of several hours. Perhaps days.

"*W*hat did you say her name was? Jenna what?"

"Starborn. You mean you didn't ask her name when you picked her up on Fieldstar?"

"I asked. She didn't seem to want to share. I let it go."

"Did she tell you why she was going to Appalachia?"

"I got the impression she just wanted to get off Fieldstar."

"Marvelous. Probably a criminal."

"Not the first one we've transported."

"Yes, but the first one in a catatonic state."

"Wonder what caused that. Everyone else has come out of cold freeze just fine, haven't they? Why didn't she?"

"Colyo's theory is that she had an emotional trauma and that her brain refuses to engage again because she doesn't want to suffer more pain."

"You'd think she'd have worked through all that in a year."

"Barkow, you're not helping."

"Well, what do you want me to do?"

"Talk to her. See if you can get her to respond to you. She might remember your voice."

"Davis, I only knew her for a couple of hours! I don't know a damn thing about her!"

"Try, anyway. Otherwise, I don't know what happens when we arrive on-planet. I'm not sure they have a social services program on Appalachia. You think we can just leave her in the spaceport—like this? I don't think so. And since you're the one who brought her on-board—"

A soft laugh of complete exasperation. "I'll do what I can. Somebody bring me a beer or something."

Scraping noises as if a piece of furniture was being dragged across the floor. "So. Your name is Jenna, they tell me. That's pretty. Jenna. Well, Jenna, I guess you don't remember much about your life. Let's see, what did you tell me when we were on Fieldstar . . . Oh, I know! You're a technician! Specializing in—now what did you say—nuclear science applications, I think that was it. So that means you can—what does that mean you can do . . . Service generators, sure, that would be one thing. I guess you could work on a ship, if you wanted, or at a utility company. Appalachia's got two, three big power stations that supply most of the energy to the settled parts of the planet. Bet you could get a job there, if you wanted. I'm assuming you want a job. Got to take care of yourself somehow.

"Let's see—I guess you don't know much about Appalachia, do you? Well, it's nothing like Fieldstar. See, I know how much you wanted to leave Fieldstar, so you can just relax about that. Appalachia's very different. Big planet, only a fraction of it colonized. Oh, and it's got an oxygen atmosphere too, so you don't need all those domes and force-fields like you did on Fieldstar. That's good, right? Breathable air. You'll like that. It's mostly aggie-based, so the colonists are setting up these huge tracts of land and starting to farm. Trouble is, they haven't quite figured out the best crops for the native earth, because the standard grains and legumes don't do so well there. They're still analyzing the soil makeup, trying to figure out what will grow. 'Course, some people are approaching the problem a different way and importing shiploads of premixed dirt with all the nitrogen and what all in it that your basic cash crop requires. I don't know too much about it. If you were a biol-ogist or agriculturist, now, you'd be in high demand here.

"But, you know, I think you could get just about any kind of job. Just have to be willing to work hard. And—hey!—if you're an *engineer*-type tech, well, there's all sorts of equipment here that needs constant maintenance. Somebody would snap you up right away if you could fix things. Got a whole mess of sophisticated machines out here, doing some of the farm work—and cyborgs too, if you know robotics—"

A long wail of heartbreak and distress that seemed to go on for hours. The sounds of running feet, sharp questions, disclaimers, med-ical equipment beeping at a more urgent frequency—and behind all this, the endless forlorn sobbing. It seemed to creep closer, grow sharper, become more localized until at last—with great suddenness—it turned both internal and external and I realized not only who I was but that I was the one screaming.

The next ten days passed in such a painful blur that more than once I wished that I had died during my yearlong voyage. The effort of walking from my bed in the monitoring room to the gym a few hun-dred yards away exhausted me so much that I could scarcely perform the exercises that Colyo and the other technicians demanded I attempt. Eating was a nightmare, for the scent of the meals prepared in the vast cafeteria made me want to vomit, and my stomach refused food the first three or four times I actually chewed and swallowed. The other passengers from the cold storage facility had been relocated to utilitar-ian but rather more inviting accommodations, but I returned every evening to my bunk in the observation unit so that I could be hooked up to medicine and nutrients. I had never felt so weak. I had never felt so ill. I could not imagine ever regaining my full strength of body and mental focus. Had I known how to do it, I believe I would have locked my glass lid from the inside and curled up in my little coffin to die.

But I was not allowed this luxury. Each morning, Colyo roused me, ruthlessly prodded me to the gym, strapped me aboard various exercis-ing machines, and forced my muscles to perform. She also bombarded me with a series of questions about math, science, literature, current events, and spatial geography which caused my head to hurt as I attempted to answer. Yet I did answer—I dredged from some remote spot in a long-disused portion of my brain the information she required: calculations, definitions, politicians, historical sequences. With each successful response, I felt my synapses grow more energetic; I could almost sense the electric buildup like an aura around my head. When I closed my eyes now, I saw pictures of star charts and public edifices and powerful dignitaries, whereas for so many months now I had seen only a blank whiteness. Slowly, with infinite anguish, I was remembering what it felt like to be alive.

I was having trouble communicating this anguish, as I was having trouble communicating anything. My speech was slow and scarcely coherent; my mouth had trouble forming the words that my brain remembered. At first, only Colyo could understand me, but gradually the other technicians, and a few of my fellow passengers, could catch the drift of my conversation. Not that any of these talks were extensive. I shunned the company of the others until Colyo forced me from my bed into the communal areas. I felt stupid, clumsy, embarrassed, alien and terrified. Although I remembered the events that had led me to this place, I still had trouble understanding why I was here and why I had suffered so greatly. I could not summon any of the courage or strength of will that I remembered I had once possessed. And so I cowered, and fretted, and very slowly improved.

I was not nearly recovered by the time we fell into orbit around Appalachia ten days after I had come to my senses. This was a fresh terror, for Colyo had made it plain that I had no haven here on the *Anniversary*. I had signed up to be delivered to this planet, and this was where I would be left, no matter how ill-equipped I was to navigate a completely foreign environment.

"For we have a full passenger list signed up for the next schedule, and no extra beds—not that I'd put you back in storage again after what you went through this time—and we've no need for more technicians, I'm sorry to say. But you'll do well enough on Appalachia. These remote colonies are always the best place for people like you."

"People like me?" I repeated faintly, for I could scarcely catch my breath. I was pumping my legs on the gravicycle, and the effort was using up every ounce of strength I possessed.

"People who don't have anywhere else to go," she amended, seeming a bit embarrassed. "The colonies always need bodies and they need every kind of skill. And nobody asks too many questions."

"I will—hope to—fit in, then," I panted, and she made no other observations.

It took the better part of a day to deboard the ship, because the tug could only handle twenty people at a time, and the round trip between the *Anniversary* and the docking bay on the spaceport took several hours. I was in the last group to climb aboard the tug, and it was with great trepidation I seated myself on the little shuttle in the company of fifteen complete strangers with whom I had shared the most bizarre voyage of my life. One or two I recognized from the cafeteria or the gym, but I had not exchanged a word with any of them before, and I could not think of an observation to make now. I sat there—freshly washed, holding my pitiful little canvas bag on my lap, and owning not a single scrap of credit—and thought dread would shatter my heart.

It did not—and neither did the intense gravitational pressure that weighted my head and all my limbs as we dropped closer to the planet's surface. After we landed, I came shakily to my feet and staggered down the ramp behind my fellow travelers. I emerged into a huge echoing dome of a building that served as the spaceport's hangar. Just so did hangars look in docking ports all over the universe, and for a moment I had the eerie sensation I had not left Fieldstar at all, but merely slept away a year in orbit above that planet. Surely not—surely not all this harrowing travail had been for nothing.

I took a few steps forward, into the bustle and the crowd, and wondered what in the name of the Goddess I should do next. It was midday, as evidenced by the sunlight pouring in through the skylights overhead, and so employment offices stood a reasonable chance of being open. My first priority would seem to be to find a post of some sort, preferably one that came with lodging—and that could not be accomplished by standing in the middle of this noisy dome, assaulted by the aviation noises above and buffeted by the human current below. I must take charge and move forward.

I therefore spent a wearying few hours inquiring the direction of an employment office, receiving conflicting information, wandering about the crowded streets of the spaceport in confusion, and fighting off an overwhelming despair. Even the mild, springlike air and the flirtatious afternoon sun could not lift my mood—and the oncoming night merely darkened it.

By the time I found the Appalachia New Transfer Job Opportunities Office, it had been closed for the day. A sign on the door proclaimed that it would open in the morning, twelve long hours away. I had no money to buy an evening meal. I certainly had no money to pay for a night in a hotel. I had nowhere to go at all.

I stood for a few minutes, stupidly trying to decide what to do. I did not think I would starve, at least not right away, for Colyo had rather brusquely handed me a few wrapped packets of food with the gruff admonition to eat carefully for a few more days. I just needed a place to sit and wait, where I would be reasonably safe from both human and environmental peril.

Back to the spaceport hangar, then. I knew it would be open and full of activity around the clock. There would be little real rest there, but I could find a place to sit, perhaps to sleep, before I tried my luck on the following day. I trudged back to the dome in the gathering dark, and wondered if I had finally reached the lowest point in my life.

The next morning, having tidied myself as best I could in one of the public rest rooms at the hangar, I made my way back to the Job Opportunities Office. This time, since I knew the way, it did not take nearly so long, but at the office itself, I suffered a series of checks. First was the long line that moved as slowly as I had feared. Second was my impaired speech, which made it difficult for my assigned clerk to understand me. I had been directed to the room of a pale, heavy, exasperated man who was barely visible behind his computer terminal and a stack of manuals, and I had attempted to inquire for work.

"Your name is *what*? What's your citizenship status? Did you come to Appalachia for a job or on spec? What are your credentials? Lady, I can't understand a word you're saying."

Eventually I took a piece of paper and a pen and wrote my name and my educational background on a piece of paper, and handed it to him.

"Oh. Nuclear *technician*," he said, as though he thought I had claimed to be a nuclear *reactor*. He turned to his monitor and typed in a few codes. "Well, you'd think there'd be something, but I don't have any listings—now, chemical technicians, I've got a few slots open—"

"I only have a little educational background in chemical reactors, enough to fill in my class requirements—"

"Say *what*? You know, I speak half a dozen languages, but you're just not being clear in any of them."

Despair washed over me. What would I do, what could I do, in this place where I could not even be understood? I jumped to my feet, intent on rushing from his presence before I burst into tears, but the move was completely ill-advised. The blood sang in my ears and I felt my body crumple. I could not stop my faint or my fall, and I felt myself land heavily on the floor.

I did not quite lose consciousness, for I heard the clerk's cry of alarm and the sound of footsteps running to the room. There were questions and sullen replies, and then someone administered a cold patch to my face. Some sort of adrenaline jolt, for I felt the ragged panic surge through my veins, and I struggled to a sitting position.

"Who is she? What happened to her?" a dark-haired woman was demanding from her post at the door. She looked severe, serious, and completely in charge. I guessed she was the top official at this facility.

"I don't know! She stood up and then she fell down! You can't hardly understand her—got a speech impediment or something—"

"She looks like she's half starved," said the voice of a woman who was out of my range of sight.

"Says she's looking for a job. A nuclear technician," the clerk said.

"Well, we can't have her lying around on our floors, no matter what skill level she possesses," the official said coldly. "Call for Public Aid and have someone come get her. If nothing else, maybe they can give her a meal or two."

"Thank you—I think I do need some aid—" I tried to say, but the dark-haired woman merely rolled her eyes and disappeared from the doorway. I heard the large clerk behind the desk speaking into a transmitter of some sort, asking for a transport for a displaced person. Heedless of the official woman's acid comment and my own considerable pride, I lay back on the floor and waited for someone to come fetch me.

*A*n hour later I was seated in the most hospitable environment I had seen since leaving Thorrastone Manor. (Must not think of that; close your mind; must not, must *not*.) It was a small, rather worn waiting room furnished with battered chairs and rose-colored walls, and the late-morning sunlight came dancing through the open windows like a blonde girl in a blue dress. I was sitting, quite exhausted, in a high-backed chair, watching a smiling young woman set up a tray of food on a table at my left hand.

"The people at the Job Op Office said you fainted from hunger, so let's feed you before we try to do anything else, shall we?" she said in a soothing and pleasant voice. She looked to be a year or two older than I was—in her late twenties, perhaps—and she had gorgeous auburn hair caught back in a very businesslike bun. She was dressed almost as plainly as I was, in natural-fiber coveralls that were so faded they might originally have been any color. Her hair was her only true ornament; her face, though open and friendly, was quite plain—but somehow more trustworthy because of that. I liked her instantly, though I was usually more guarded with my approvals. Or perhaps I needed her so desperately at that moment that I was prepared to like her no matter how crass or cruel she might turn out to be.

"I'm not sure I can eat," I said, enunciating as clearly as I could. "I'm not sure I can keep food down."

She looked at me sharply. "You can't—eat? Is that what you said?" she asked.

I nodded. "I'm not sure. I've been—" It was too complicated to explain. "Sick," I finished lamely.

"Well, I brought you some tea and some soup," she said briskly. "Very easy on the stomach. Let's try it and see how you do."

Indeed, the bowl of soup looked more like broth, though it smelled wonderful, and tea, of course, was an invalid's mainstay the universe over. I ate cautiously at first, then more ravenously as my stomach did not reject my offerings, and I finished every ounce of food on my tray.

The woman watched me with a face half pleased and half wondering. "Gracious, you must truly have been starved," she said. "Would you like more? Or perhaps we should wait a while and see how well you handle that much."

"Yes, let's wait," I said.

She had settled in a facing chair while I ate, and now she studied me with frank curiosity. "Do you feel better now? Can we try to talk?" she asked. "I'd like to help you, but I think I need more information."

"I'm Jenna Starborn," I said right away. "And you?"

"Your name is Jenna? Is that what you said?"

I nodded.

"Starrin? Jenna Starrin?"

I shrugged, then smiled. It was a manufactured name anyway; that was close enough. "Yes," I said. "And your name?"

"I'm Deborah Rainey," she said, seeming to understand my question with ease. "My brother and sister and I run the Public Aid Office here on Appalachia."

"Public Aid Office?" I repeated, for I had not heard of such an institution. In many of the larger cities, there were facilities for taking care of the indigent and the outcast, but these were referred to by such unattractive titles as Half-Cit Rehabilitation Center and the Welfare and Reform Office, and only the lowest and most desperate creatures would think to seek shelter there.

Though I was a low and desperate creature, and at the moment, I would not scorn any help at all.

Deborah Rainey was answering my half-articulated question. "Yes, my brother, Sinclair, founded this facility three years ago when we first relocated to Appalachia from Newyer. Our goal had been to purchase a tract of land and begin farming, though none of us had any experience with agriculture. We were just looking for a hopeful new start on life! But Sinclair had friends who had set up businesses here in Cody—"

"Cody?" I could not form a complete sentence, but Deborah Rainey seemed to catch the drift of my one-word question, for she answered this one easily as well.

"Yes, the name that has been bestowed upon the major spaceport here. It has grown to be so much like a city that we have given it a real city name. Anyway, Sinclair had friends here who were already established, and who knew Sinclair from our days back on Newyer, where he also ran a charitable institution. And they persuaded him that Cody needed such a facility right away, for it was growing so fast and receiving such an influx of would-be settlers that there were any number of people getting lost in the shuffle. The Job Op Office does what it can," she added in a careful tone of voice, "but the personnel there don't have the time and patience to deal with people who aren't instantly prepared to take up the rhythms of a new life. So we have found ourselves very often taking in travelers who need a period of adjustment before they can accustom themselves to their new world."

"I cannot pay you," I said instantly. "I have no credit."

"No, no, we are entirely funded by the business owners of Cody," she said quickly. "We provide a service to the city by keeping wanderers off the street and helping displaced travelers recover their senses. And most often, after a stay of a few days or a few weeks, these travelers become the energetic, productive people they were when they left their home planets, and they take new jobs, and they are quickly absorbed into the economy of Appalachia. It is very satisfying work."

"Then I can stay?"

"Yes, Jenna, you can stay. As long as you need to."

I could not help myself. I started crying. Deborah Rainey leapt to her feet and came around to hug me, patting my disheveled hair and murmuring reassurances into my ear. It did not matter that the reassurances were generic, for she did not know what my sufferings were and how to allay my true fears. Her words seemed genuine, and her embrace felt sincere, and I felt safe as I had not felt in over a year.

That night at dinner, I joined Deborah Rainey, her sister, her brother and their other temporary boarders in a communal dining room. Maria Rainey looked much like her sister, except that her face was several years older and her hair not quite so lustrous. Still, her expression was just as warm and welcoming, and I immediately liked her as much as I had liked Deborah.

Sinclair Rainey, on the other hand, seemed to have been constructed from an entirely different set of raw materials than his sisters. His face featured fine modeled cheekbones and a firm, determined chin; his oak-blonde hair formed soft curls that he had cropped as short as he could, though nothing could entirely subdue their gaiety. His eyes were such a brilliant blue that I would have sworn they were enhanced, except that five minutes in his company led me to believe he would scorn such personal embellishments. For he had the expression, attitude, conversation, and courtesy of an aesthete—a fanatic—a man called to a mission that he would serve with so much passion he would forget the needs of himself and the ones he considered that he loved. I did not know what his mission was, but that he had one, I was willing to swear that very first evening.

The other guests were, like me, rather beaten-down and disoriented casualties of a long space voyage and no clear plan of action. Three of them formed a small, miserable family—father, mother, and son—while the fourth was an older man of somewhat rakish mien who spoke wistfully of his days on some planet I could never definitively identify. The family members I assumed had come to farm, but I was not certain what the older man's claim to employability might be. In any case, I was not required to converse with him. Maria Rainey spent most of the evening listening to his rambling talk with every evidence of interest on her good-natured face. The rest of us made short, hopeless attempts at discussion, but mostly applied ourselves to our food. Which was very good and caused no rebellion in my stomach at all.

After the meal, Sinclair Rainey disappeared and the sisters invited the rest of us into a small parlor where, they said, there were books, games, monitors, and other entertainments. The others gratefully accepted this possibility of a few hours' distraction, but I excused myself, and went up to the small bedroom I had been allotted. Within a few minutes, I had washed my face, breathed a prayer of heartfelt thanks to the Goddess, and fallen deeply asleep.

The next morning, I presented myself in the kitchen as soon as I was awake and sensed the house astir. Maria and Deborah Rainey were already there, moving in comfortable silence from the freezecase to the bakeshelf as they put together ingredients for a morning meal.

"Is there anything I can do to help?" I asked.

Maria almost dropped a bread knife, for she had not seen me come in, but Deborah smiled and motioned me forward. "You may come and keep us company," she said. "Are you hungry?"

"Yes, very."

"That's an excellent sign!"

Maria asked, "And nothing you ate last night disagreed with you?"

"No, it was a wonderful meal. Thank you both so very much. But I would like to do something to prove my gratitude—or earn my keep."

Deborah laughed. "I told you, nothing like that is required. We are funded by the city."

"Yes, but I am not accustomed to sit back idly while others work to take care of me," I said, noticing as I spoke how much clearer my words sounded today. And, indeed, neither sister seemed to have trouble understanding me, for they both smiled.

"Very well, then, you may mix up this batter if you wish. Do you like to cook, Jenna?" Maria asked.

I obediently took a bowl and a spatula and began folding in ingredients. "I don't know. I've never done it."

"Never!" Deborah exclaimed. "Why, where have you lived that you have never had to cook for yourself?"

And, the unspoken question hung in the air, *how have you fallen on such hard times that you now must work like a servant girl?*

"I have not enjoyed a luxurious life," I assured them. "I have lived in grand houses, but they were not my own. I grew up as the ward of a lady with much wealth but very little heart, and then I lived at an educational institution where all the food was prepared for us by cafeteria workers. From there I went to work in a great manor where all the meals were served by a cook who did not like others to meddle in her kitchen."

"I cannot decide if such a life sounds adventurous or sad," Maria commented.

I smiled somewhat bitterly. "At times it has been both."

"Here, when you have done with that, you may chop these into the finest pieces you can manage," Deborah said, setting a knife, a chopping board, and a mass of small vegetables beside me.

I was bemused by the sheer volume of work laid before me. "All these, for just the eight of us staying in this house?"

The sisters laughed. "Oh, there are only five of you who are our guests here, but we run another small facility nearby," said Maria. "At the moment, I believe there are ten others staying at the dorm house."

"Eleven," Deborah said.

"Eleven, then. They have been here a few weeks and are really in transition—most of them have found jobs already, but they do not have places to stay yet, so we provide beds for them—and breakfast. Everything else they are responsible for on their own, though Sinclair is instrumental in helping them find both housing and employment."

"It must keep all of you quite busy, running two households and what is essentially a job placement office," I observed.

"*Quite* busy!" Maria said with a smile. "But we all enjoy the work."

Deborah handed me another bag of vegetables and turned the conversation back to me. "So what did you do at this grand manor where you used to work?"

"I was a nuclear technician," I said.

The sisters exchanged glances. "Really! But that's excellent!" Maria exclaimed. "Can you repair systems? For ours is most unreliable and Sinclair simply *will* not take the time to call in a repair team."

"You have your own generator?" I asked in surprise, for normally all the buildings in a city would draw on the energy from one or two central power plants.

"Well, we do, but it's a long story," Maria said. "It's very small, and it hardly ever works, and when it doesn't, we rely on city power. But someone offered to sell the system to Sinclair for a very low price, and he bought it thinking *he* could then sell extra power to nearby businesses as a way to raise additional money for our programs, but since the day we've owned the generator, it's been broken more often than not. Of course, no one will contract to buy from us, because they don't trust us to supply power on a regular basis—and they're quite right!—but Sinclair refuses to sell it because he keeps saying it was an excellent investment. But if you could repair it for us—"

"I should be able to, unless some complete systems breakdown has destroyed its usefulness."

"Oh, this is wonderful!" Deborah said. "Right after breakfast, I will take you to the access area. First we will feed you, though, or you will faint of hunger before you can do us any good at all!"

She was clearly joking, and all three of us laughed, and I felt sustained by a warm glow of companionship that was more nourishing than the breakfast that I helped served a half hour later. The other four boarders were in the dining room, patiently awaiting food, but Sinclair Rainey was nowhere to be seen. I imagined he was often absent; he seemed like a man so preoccupied with larger issues that he would rarely remember to feed his body with food or refresh his soul with conversation.

After the meal, Deborah escorted me to a cramped, poorly lit room tucked off of one utilitarian hallway (where laundering equipment and a multitude of storage boxes also had made their homes). It seemed astonishing to me that the equipment worked even intermittently, so poorly organized were the fuel leads and generator cables, but a cursory examination of the items on hand led me to think there was nothing irreparably wrong.

"Though I may need to replace a few parts," I said, looking doubtfully at some worn connectors. "Is there any budget for that?"

"I would imagine Sinclair would be happy to drop some of his credit on machinery, if you could ensure it would function in the future," Deborah said. "Perhaps, if you could get an estimate—"

"And there are supply stores in Cody where I could get parts?"

"I'm not sure, but you could check with the power companies and see if they would be willing to sell you items."

"Yes—that's a very good idea—well, first let me take a thorough look at the setup and see what might be missing."

"I'll check back with you at lunchtime," she said, and left me.

I spent the next few hours happily enough, absorbed in work that I understood and that seemed to render me valuable to people who had been kind to me, which made it twice as satisfying. I kept a growing inventory of parts that needed immediate replacement, parts that should for future reliability be replaced soon, and parts that were so outdated that it would be better just to upgrade them now. I also scoured down a few encrusted connectors and checked safety levels and investigated the toxic dumping hoses (which, I was glad to see, appeared to be in excellent condition). It was, or would be, a tidy little system which could supply enough power to run a couple of city blocks; I was sure Sinclair Rainey would be able to realize his dream of selling enough energy to his neighbors to make his facility self-supporting.

I took a quick lunch with my fellow residents, told Deborah I thought the job would be relatively simple, and returned to my task. By dinnertime, I had climbed over enough wires, cables, tubes, and protuberances to get my coveralls filthy, so I returned to my room to shower and change before I joined the others for the evening meal.

I had barely seated myself at the table before Deborah turned to her brother and exclaimed, "Sinclair! The best news! Jenna Starrin is a nuclear technician who is able to repair our generator! She has been working on it all day and compiling a list of the parts we will need to make it operational again."

Sinclair turned his solemn, considering gaze my way with such intensity that I found myself blushing for no good reason. His eyes were so remarkably blue, and so completely unwavering, that I felt transfixed by his attention; I did not believe I would be able to move or speak until he gave his permission. "Has she," he said in a light, calm voice, and the force of his personality made the simple words seem invested with drama. "Well, Jenna, and what will be required to achieve this goal?"

My lips moved soundlessly, and for a moment I feared I had resumed the incoherence that had hampered me when I was first released from cold storage. But I swallowed and tried again. "Many small parts," I said in a quavering voice. "One big one, but I do not think it will be too expensive. And some cables. Deborah thinks we might be able to buy them from a power company."

Sinclair flicked that calm, lethal gaze at his sister, who went on serenely eating her food as if his glances held no terror for her. "Good idea, Deb," he said; and again, such was the deliberate and impressive power of his speech that his words sounded like a divine pronouncement. "I shall call Leopold in the morning and tell him we are coming over. You will have this list by the morning, will you not?" he said, returning his attention to me.

"I—certainly—I might check it over once before—but it is all but complete now," I said, stammering like a schoolgirl.

Sinclair nodded majestically. "Good. The sooner it is functional, the better. So where did you learn such technology, Jenna?"

A personal question from this imperial personage! I had not expected it, and continued stammering. I was sure he believed I was fabricating a history even as I spoke, so nervous and uncertain did I sound. "On Lora. At—at the academy there. I was a student and then—then I was a teacher for several days—I mean, *years*."

"Lora Tech. That is partially a charity school, is it not?"

I nodded. "Yes, and I was one of its charity students."

"Did you like it?"

I considered, and tried to recover some of my habitual calm. "My classes were hard at first, but grew easier. I learned a great deal. And I acquired skills that I can use anywhere in the universe, so that I have assured myself of employment wherever I go. So I liked the results I achieved."

Sinclair nodded, as if this answer pleased him. "It is good for anyone—man, woman, citizen, half-cit—to have useful skills that can be translated to a variety of environments. One never knows when one's circumstances will change, drastically or for the worse. Self-reliance is a cardinal virtue."

"I have always believed so," I said.

"Yes, well, I believe human kindness is an even more cardinal virtue, if one thing can be more cardinal than something else," Deborah said saucily. "That shall be the skill I cultivate."

Sinclair bent his lancet gaze on her, a reproving look on his face. "Human kindness will not always see you employed and able to care for yourself," he said repressively.

"No, that's the point. It is something you spend on *others*, not on *yourself*," she retorted.

"It is a valuable commodity," he conceded, "but you must arm yourself with more practical ones as well."

Maria laughed. "Let it go, Deborah, you will never convince him."

"Yes, but I cannot agree with Sinclair's values! What do you say, Jenna? Which is more important? To fortify yourself with a strong head or a strong heart?"

Oh, this was a fine question to be asked, indeed! How should I answer, I who had trampled on my own heart because of the very principles Sinclair Rainey espoused? "My head and my heart give very different answers," I said at last with a rather painful smile. "In my *heart*, I believe we would all be better off if everyone led from emotion. But my head has often dictated tougher choices than my heart would prefer, and I have always believed the head must be protected before the heart can be hazarded."

"Very well put," Sinclair approved.

"Yes, but how dreary!" Maria exclaimed.

"A full life teaches you dreary scenarios," I said.

"You must tell us about that life sometime," Deborah said. My face must have showed a look of alarm, for she laughed merrily. "I didn't mean *now*," she added. "Sometime when you're more comfortable with us."

"Yes, I shall be interested to hear how one so young could have formed such decided opinions," Sinclair said gravely. I thought to myself that I would never be comfortable enough with *him* to feel like making confidences. "I would not have expected it."

I made some inconsequential answer, and the talk turned to other topics, for which I was profoundly grateful. Someone else at the table then spoke up to ask about a game that had been played the night before, when I had retired early to my room.

"Yes, that was fun. Shall we try that again tonight?" Deborah replied. "Jenna, you will join us this night, won't you? It will be so much fun."

I understood, of course, that she wished to rehabilitate me—body *and* soul—and that she would not consider me quite healed until I was able to indulge easily in playful human interaction. So I agreed, and spent a pleasant enough evening with the other residents of the house playing mindless space-battle games. I must admit, having won two of the three games we played, that I was feeling rather cheerful by the time I at last ascended to my bed; and perhaps it was the various triumphs of the day that led me to the best night's sleep I had had since I had woken on the *Anniversary*.

The next day, however, my first waking thought was one of dread: I was to make an expedition in the company of the august Sinclair Rainey, and hope to appear professional and competent before him. It seemed a singularly daunting task, but I reminded myself sternly that I had faced more severe challenges in the past and always managed to emerge relatively whole. I donned my last clean pair of coveralls and joined the others for breakfast.

Sinclair was already awaiting me, having eaten his morning meal at some impossibly early hour. "How much time will you require to go over your lists and make a final assessment?" he asked me as I hurriedly swallowed my meal.

"An hour, perhaps. I do not want to be careless."

"Very well. I will be working on my computer when you are ready."

Deborah had pulled me to my feet and appeared to be measuring her body against mine. "It is a shame you are so small, because I could lend you some of my clothes if we were closer in size," she said. She was not a large woman, but both taller and more amply endowed than I was, and the idea of me in any item she owned was laughable. "I think you would make a better impression if you were more suitably outfitted."

"That is certainly a trivial preoccupation," Sinclair observed. I winced, but Deborah ignored him.

"I know!" she exclaimed. "I shall ask Rianna if she has anything she's outgrown. She's almost as small as you are."

Sinclair's head whipped around at the mention of the other woman's name. "Rianna!" was all he said, but his voice vibrated with deep emotion.

"Yes," Deborah said, quite unmoved by his tone, "she often donates linens and other small items to our houses, and I'm sure she'd be happy to help Jenna out. Unless you object to charity," she added to me.

"I am living in your house on charity," I said, smiling. "I am happy to take whatever anyone is willing to give me."

"You should not be troubling Rianna," Sinclair said in a low voice.

Deborah shrugged. "She will tell me if she cannot help. But I'm sorry I can't do better for you today, Jenna. Unless you'd like to wait a day or two?"

"I think not," Sinclair said.

I smiled and shook my head. "Your brother is impatient," I said to Deborah. Then, to Sinclair, I said, "Give me an hour and I will be ready. I will come to you."

Soon enough I was finished with my final examination, and Sinclair Rainey and I were on our way. I had spent such wretched hours wandering Cody's streets that I had not realized the spaceport contained an underground transport system that was fast, clean, and efficient. Sinclair shepherded me aboard this, kept fairly close track of me when strangers pressed in at each new stop, then escorted me back aboveground when we had reached our destination. Eventually we entered a tall, sleek building that appeared to have been constructed from a single seamless sheet of black glass. Although Appalachia was not yet sophisticated enough to sport much technology, it was clear to me that the power companies were in advance of most of the other planetary businesses. Sinclair spoke a name into an automated teller; a small, self-propelled, floating car popped up beside us, and we climbed aboard. Within minutes, it had whisked us up circular hallways and through narrow, spiraling shafts at a breathtaking pace. I was quite overwhelmed by miracles by the time it deposited us at the office of a man whose name on the door was given as Leopold Joester.

He turned out to be a large, jovial, red-faced man, dressed casually (though not as casually as I) in a black tunic and cotton pants, and he seemed delighted to see Sinclair. They talked a few minutes of business plans that had no relevance to me, and then Sinclair rather abruptly introduced our mission.

"This is Jenna Starrin, a nuclear technician who has just arrived on Appalachia. She is going to repair my generators, which you know have been malfunctioning for months, but she needs some additional parts. I thought you might be willing to sell them to me at a reasonable price."

"Repair it! Really! I was beginning to think that was a hopeless task. What sorts of parts do you need, Miss Starrin? Before I commit myself to any kind of transaction."

I took out my list and read it to him. I could tell that, though he had had his doubts when Sinclair first introduced me, he was impressed by my basic understanding of key nuclear components. He nodded a few times, took notes, then looked up with a smile.

"I don't see a problem with any of that. When would you like it delivered?"

"Today, if possible," Sinclair said. "As you know, the less time wasted, the happier I am. Tell me what the cost will be, and I will write out a transfer right now."

Leopold Joester waved one large-knuckled hand. "Count it as my contribution for the month," he said negligently. "It will cost me less in the long run."

Sinclair smiled faintly. "Very well," he said. "I appreciate it. Let me know next time there is something I can do in return for you."

The men talked a few more minutes, and then Sinclair rose to his feet to say good-bye. I quickly followed suit, murmured my thanks to Leopold Joester, and followed Sinclair out the door. We reversed our modes of transit, and in a short time were back at the Public Aid Office telling the Rainey sisters our success. Everyone seemed jubilant, but my happiness, though the quietest, was by far the greatest. For I had again, at least briefly, a task and a purpose; and I did not know any other way in which to make my life endurable.

Chapter 17

✧

The next few weeks, for me, passed in an atmosphere of ever greater comfort and contentment. I spent the bulk of my days working in the generator room, repairing and replacing machinery; at mealtimes and in the evenings, I interacted with a circle of friendly and undemanding acquaintances, some of whom I became fond of very quickly; and at night, I slept with serenity. Most of the time. It was true that I had my greatest mental and emotional struggles at night, before I fell asleep, when visions of Thorrastone Manor and its many beloved residents rose before my eyes and would not be banished.

What had been Everett Ravenbeck's reaction the morning—more than a year ago!—when he rose and found me vanished from his home? How long had he searched for me, how long had he mourned for me, and what desperate measures had he taken to assuage his grief? For that was my greatest fear, that the man I loved so deeply had, through my behavior, come to terrific harm. I knew his past propensity toward numbing his troubles through a reckless pursuit of hedonism, but I could not think such a course would be anything but disastrous now. I could not be sure there would be any checks on his behavior; I did not know how far he might fling himself down the road of self-destruction.

I was afraid to search for news of him on the StellarNet, because I believed him fully capable of mining his name references with codes that would alert him to my inquiries. I did occasionally, when the house computer was free, browse through general news and society reports, hoping to come across a mention of his name, but I never found it. I did accidentally discover that Bianca Ingersoll had married Harley Taff and settled at the Taff family estates, but no list of guest names was provided in the article and I was afraid to query the computer for more details.

But it was not only Everett Ravenbeck whose fate troubled me. What had become of Ameletta since Janet and I had both disappeared? For that matter, had any news of Janet Ayerson ever been discovered? What of Mrs. Farraday, who had considered both Janet and myself to be under her care—and balancing on the border of respectability? Would she blame herself for my defection? Or her employer? Would she resign her post? What then would become of Ameletta—and Everett Ravenbeck?

Oh, I wanted to know everything, and I knew nothing, and a full year had passed. They could all be dead or scattered or struck down by madness, and I could not learn a thing.

So these were the doubts and fears and apparitions I wrestled with, every night, before exhaustion overtook me or I was able to will myself to sleep. My dreams, oddly enough, were bare of the distresses that kept me awake so long. It was as though, having suffered so bitterly every night before sleeping, my brain or my body cut off those impossible questions and allowed me a few hours of peaceful rest. I woke each morning feeling stronger, more determined to make a life for myself here on Appalachia. And gradually it began to seem as though I would succeed.

It also began to seem as though I had found a more or less permanent home in the Rainey household. That is, while my original fellow boarders moved to the nearby dorm within a week of my arrival, and new ones came in to take their places and then also moved on, none of the Rainey siblings seemed to expect me to relocate. In fact, every day I seemed to be integrated more fully into their lives—in ways that, when

I was first deposited on their doorstep, I would not even have dared to imagine.

Our first bond was formed over religion. I had not been there a full week when, one night as our group separated for bedtime, Deborah drew me aside.

"Please do not think there is any obligation involved," she said to me as the others filed past us to their various bedrooms. "But tomorrow Sinclair and Maria and I will be attending services at a local sanctuary, and we always like to invite our boarders to join us. Many of them do not," she added quickly, "and there is no offense to us at all! But you strike me as a woman who sees a sense and majesty in the universe, and I thought perhaps you would be interested in joining us."

Not since I had been in school on Lora had I had an opportunity to attend regular worship services, and I admit I was intrigued. "I would gladly consider coming with you," I said. "May I ask what church you belong to?"

Deborah smiled. "Well, perhaps when you know a little more of our background, you will understand our religious affiliations, but we have always associated with the PanEquists."

"The PanEquists!" I exclaimed in a state of great excitement. "But I am one as well!"

"No!"

"Yes! I became a convert when I was still a child, and nothing I have seen of the settled worlds has caused me to question for a moment the spirit of the Goddess or the great constant communion of the universe."

"But that is exactly how we feel! The marvelous brotherhood of people and planets has just served to strengthen our conviction that we are all the same, every one of us, and we are all equal . . ."

We continued in this fashion for a few moments, trading the basic doctrines of the faith, and growing more pleased with each other by the moment. Naturally, I agreed to accompany all three Raineys the following morning, and when we parted that night, I was almost too elated to sleep. I had not known that Cody boasted any religious facilities at all, but that it did—and that my hosts had chosen to worship at the only church in which I could feel entirely comfortable—gave me an almost superstitious chill. It was as if I had been predestined to immigrate to Appalachia and fall into the hands of these kind and gentle people; it was as if they had been fashioned to suit me, and to answer all the needs that I had at this particular moment of my life.

We went to the sanctuary the following day, and I thoroughly enjoyed the rational speech and well-reasoned argument presented by the leader of the congregation. There were only about fifty other people present, so the flock was small, but I could not help noting evidences of intelligence and thoughtfulness on the faces of those I could see well enough to study. I realized, of course, that I had a predisposition to think well of those who adhered to a philosophy that had so completely defined my life, and yet they truly did seem to me to be a superior sort as they listened, applauded, and, later, made comments of their own.

At the conclusion of the service, there was a small reception, and the Rainey sisters introduced me around. Sinclair had immediately fallen into conversation with a rather stern-looking older man, but Deborah and Maria made sure everyone else in the hall learned my name. I was shy among so many strangers, and made very little attempt at conversation, but I smiled a great deal and hoped that I appeared pleasant.

One of the last people to whom I was introduced was a small, frail, blonde woman with an otherworldly countenance and a sweet-tempered smile. "Oh, Jenna, you must meet Rianna Joester," Deborah said as she and her sister led me over to the ethereal beauty. "She is one of our greatest friends—both to us personally, and to the Public Aid Office in the guise of a benefactress. Rianna, this is Jenna Starrin, our *new* friend. She's the one repairing our generator."

The name Rianna chimed in my memory, but I could not recall why. The young woman held out her hand and gave me a smile that seemed almost wistful. "Oh, yes—Sinclair has talked of you to me," she said in a soft and lovely voice. "He seems to admire you greatly."

I laughed a little nervously. "Really? Sinclair always seems a little too aloof to experience much admiration of mere mortals."

Deborah and Maria laughed, and Rianna smiled again. "Yes, Sinclair's attitudes and ideals make him hard to fathom sometimes," Rianna said, "and harder to reach. But he is an excellent man."

"Of course. I completely agree," I said hastily.

"Rianna, you will join us for dinner one night next week, won't you?" Maria asked. "It has been so long since we have seen you, but it has been so busy at our house!"

"I will be happy to come over," Rianna said. "And I know my father is curious to see how—Jenna?—has proceeded with the generators. He too spoke well of you, after your visit to his office."

This was said with absolutely no malice at all, and yet I had the curious feeling that Rianna Joester had not been entirely delighted to hear my praises sung by two of the men in her circle, and I could not help but wonder why. The mystery was cleared up a few minutes later, however, as Maria and Rianna went off together to greet another acquaintance. Deborah, always more inclined to share secrets than her sister, drew me aside with an impish smile.

"She's pretty, isn't she? Sinclair is just enraptured with her, and I am certain she has feelings for him as well. But they are very different creatures and they find each other complete and unsolvable mysteries. It is funny and a little sad to watch them together—as you shall see, when she comes over next week. Maria and I just love her, for she is so good-natured, but she is quite the materialistic girl! And Sinclair, you know, cares for very little except whatever dream he happens to be entertaining at the moment. So they watch each other and—and—circle around each other, and never get even very deep in a conversation. I wonder what she thought when Sinclair told her about you! She must have been consumed with curiosity!"

Indeed—and now I remembered where I had heard her name before. Deborah had thought Rianna might lend me some of her cast-off clothing, and Sinclair had been incensed at the suggestion. Oh, yes, I could see why Rianna Joester might be just a little perturbed to hear the name Jenna Starrin spoken of with unalloyed approval!

A few nights later I was able to observe for myself the truth of Deborah's remarks. The boarders (there were six this night) had all been served in the kitchen, while the Raineys, the Joesters, and I had a late meal in the formal dining room. It was still a casual affair. Maria, Deborah, and I had cooked everything, and we served everything too, though for the most part serving dishes were handed around the table family-style. Leopold Joester and his wife, Tasha, were both outspoken and high-spirited individuals who seemed to feel an equal zest for every topic introduced, and it was clear that Deborah and Maria liked them very much. Their son, Harmon, did not have quite their force of personality, but he had a pleasant face, an engaging smile, and a great deal of common sense, which made every one of his contributions to the conversation worth listening to. Rianna, who seemed to resemble neither her brother nor her parents, was much quieter—indeed, much of the time she seemed to be lost in her own thoughts and not even conscious of being in the same room with the rest of us. Sinclair Rainey alternated between adding his measured arguments to the discussion, and watching Rianna with such intense and brooding concentration that I wondered she did not faint from the attention.

I did not offer much to the general conversation until Leopold Joester dragged me into it. "Here, now, Miss Starrin, you seem like a sensible creature," he said. "Do you not think that we as a society, and people as individuals, require some sort of systematic form of classification and government if we are to operate in any kind of coherent fashion at all?"

I glanced from him to Rianna, who sat toying with her food at the far end of the table. "I take it you are not, as your daughter is, a member of the PanEquist faith?" I inquired.

"No! It is not without its attractions, I admit—though I think its attractions would loom largest to the impoverished and the unemployed—but I cannot accept some of its basic precepts. I don't have trouble with the idea that we're all equal at a cellular level, but I don't think you can discount the evolution and accretion of those cells into beings of greater and lesser importance."

"Hence your desire for a society in which everyone is assigned a class and adheres to the standards for that class."

"Exactly. Doesn't that make sense? If we are all part of a whole, which I *do* believe, isn't that whole served best when each limb or organ carries out the duty that it best knows how to perform?"

"But that doctrine leaves no room for personal growth," I said, for the moment abandoning the tenets of PanEquism to address this challenge. "Assuming we all have a role to play in the universe, and I am born to be a—a foot and you are born to be a head, that does not allow me the chance to learn and improve and achieve a better station in life."

"Ah! But you are assuming that a head is a preferred station! Perhaps it is not—perhaps it is just different, not better," said Leopold Joester.

Harmon spoke up in his quiet voice, smiling slightly. "Hierarchy is implicit in the argument," he said. "If you are to assign roles, one will inevitably be superior."

"And that is the human condition, anyway," I added. "Everyone desires to improve his lot and gain some ascendancy over his peers. No one desires to take a lesser position. And thus, when you divide people into categories, everyone will be measuring his worth against his fellows', and discontent is the only possible outcome."

"Whereas, if you begin with a premise of universal equality," said Sinclair, unexpectedly entering the fray and voicing the PanEquist principles, "you erase envy, and you erase strife, and you create cohesion."

"But there is no such thing as equality! Not in the real, actual world—which none of you zealots appears to be living in!" Leopold Joester exclaimed. "Even if you obliterate class and monetary privileges, you cannot discount the hierarchy created by intelligence and ability! Miss Starrin can repair a nuclear generator, and so can I. But my daughter cannot, and no one else sitting at this table can do so. That gives me and Miss Starrin the edge in that particular talent. Can you claim equality with us? No—or if you did so, it would be disastrous when you attempted to repair the failed connector!"

"Yes, but differences in ability should not be allowed to determine differences in worth to society," Rianna said, speaking up in her quiet voice. "It should be because of her very existence that Jenna is valued, not for her technical skills. Those are the qualities she offers to the general good, and we all have such qualities, but they should not determine whether or not society deems us worthwhile to live."

"Well, I don't see why not," Leopold Joester said, and instantly every voice at the table was raised against him in friendly mockery. The big red-faced man laughed, held up his hands for silence, and then plunged back into his argument the minute he had the floor again.

It was, for me, a wonderful evening of rare intellectual excitement. My mind had not been so stimulated since the days of my early debates with Everett Ravenbeck—and, oh how I wished he could be sitting at this table with me this night! How much he would have loved the quick repartee and the refusal to concede a single disputed point!

But I must not picture Everett beside me in my new life. I must not think of Everett at all.

The conversation continued well into the night and appeared to please everyone as much as it pleased me. Everyone except Rianna Joester, perhaps. For though she spoke up from time to time, and usually appeared to be following the argument at hand, she never seemed wholly engrossed in the discussion. That wistful look that I had remarked upon before appeared almost a permanent fixture on her fine features, and it deepened every time she glanced in Sinclair's direction. Which was often. It was obvious there was some kind of bond between them, though of a troubled nature, and I could not help wondering exactly what the obstacles were that would keep the two of them apart. Perhaps on some future date Deborah would again feel inclined to gossip, and then I would learn more.

At any rate, the mystery was not to be solved this night. Eventually, Tasha Joester glanced at her watch and cried, "How late it is! Leopold, we must be going home! Oh, thank all of you so much for a perfectly delightful evening."

The general good-byes took another fifteen minutes, and I noticed with interest that Harmon Joester managed a few moments of private conversation with Deborah while the other members of his family made more public farewells. I wondered if Rianna and Sinclair were the only two members of these families to have formed tendres for each other—but of course, it was not the sort of thing I would ever bring myself to ask. But it did make me eager to see more of the Joesters so that I could continue to judge for myself just what sort of impact they might have on the family that I had adopted for my own.

𝒜s the weeks passed, and I grew even more settled in the Rainey household, our lives began to intertwine in still more ways. Now we attended PanEquist services on a regular basis; the sisters and I worked together constantly in the kitchen and consulted over menus and household chores; and Sinclair and I developed a mutually respectful relationship that centered around business and power. He had contacted the tenants of various nearby buildings to offer them access to our energy, and, once they had been assured that the system was now reliable, many of them accepted his deal. This required me to regularly reconfigure currents to direct it to the new customers, and to keep Sinclair apprised of any new equipment I might require to meet new demands. He also liked to be informed of any problems I had encountered during the course of the day, and gradually we fell into the habit of having a short meeting every evening after dinner to review sales he had made or troubles I could foresee.

"You have a very clear way of explaining things, Jenna," he observed one evening as he and his sisters and I sat sipping tea in the comfortable family room shortly before bedtime. There were no boarders this week, and the house seemed extremely peaceful and homelike. "I always understand exactly what you mean to convey."

This pleased me, for—though I was beginning to become more at ease around Sinclair—I still found him a rather austere and awe-inspiring presence, and his approval meant a great deal to me. "Well, I was a teacher for four years, so I have some experience in trying to explain ideas," I said.

"You taught nuclear physics?"

"Yes, on the theoretical level, and generator maintenance on the more practical level."

"Do you suppose you could teach me the same curriculum?"

My eyes widened a bit; this was not the direction in which I had expected the conversation to tend. "I don't know. I don't see why not. I do not have any of my books or teaching materials with me—"

"Those might be obtained, do you not think? They could be ordered over the StellarNet."

"Yes—in fact, the majority of texts can be transmitted electronically."

"Well, order them as quickly as possible. Tomorrow, if you can. I am eager to learn this new science. I think it will be valuable to me. We shall study together every night once your materials arrive."

I nodded gravely, though inside I was marveling somewhat. I could not imagine that Sinclair Rainey would *not* be able to master the intricacies of the complex science, for I could not picture anything that determined young man could not accomplish once he put his mind to it. But I had never heard of anyone asking to be taught nuclear theory over the tea table during his free evenings, and the whole thing seemed just faintly preposterous.

I glanced over at his sisters to see if either of them shared my opinion. Maria was absorbed in a book and did not look up, but Deborah caught my eye. The look on her face was a bit rueful, though she smiled at me, and then she shrugged. So she thought it was strange too.

The next day, when she and I were alone in the kitchen, Deborah explained it to me.

"Sinclair is not happy here on Appalachia, you know," she said, and again her expression was a little pensive and a little sad. "I think he expected much wilder country when he persuaded us all to immigrate here. I told you, he had wanted us to start a small farm, and live off the land and what we could sell of its crops. And when he arrived here and found Cody so much like a settled city, and his old skills so much in demand, he was quite disappointed. He pictures himself as a sort of pioneer, you know, going off to tame unconquered land, creating some kind of personal empire purely through his own will and physical strength."

"He certainly seems to have too much passion for the position he currently holds," I said rather cautiously. "I can see how a broader canvas would be more suitable to his personality."

Deborah smiled again, still sadly. "Yes. And Maria and I are sure he will agitate to relocate again in a year or so. He feels a duty to the Public Aid Office here, and I don't believe he will leave until it is completely organized and self-supporting—but you have made that last condition, at least, very nearly a reality! Lately I have heard him speaking of a planet called Cozakee which has just recently been surveyed by scientific teams for habitability. If it indeed is found to be livable, anyone who agrees to homestead there is guaranteed a substantial tract of land and two full citizenship upgrades. I am sure he will go. If not to Cozakee, somewhere. It is just a matter of time."

"You do not sound as though you would be willing to follow him this time," I said.

"No—I don't know—no, I don't think I would." She smiled again, a tight, painful smile, and there was a world of unspoken loss in that expression. "You see, when we came to Appalachia, all of our lives improved so much! We had all lived on Newyer, sharing the smallest quarters imaginable and laboring every day just to get a little money ahead. We were all half-cits, of course, and Newyer is such a crowded planet that featureless, ordinary people like ourselves had almost no value. Neither Maria nor I had any special skills, so I worked in a kitchen and Maria worked in a child care facility, and the hours were long and the pay was terrible.

"Sinclair had done much better than we had, for he had been discovered to have a gift for administration and he had been given the task of running a social services office. In fact, he was doing so well at it that he had been offered a pay and status upgrade to level-five citizenship. We were ecstatic, as you might imagine, but Sinclair said he would only accept on the condition that Maria and I also be given such citizenship status. His employers refused, and Sinclair resigned.

"Well, we were in dreadful straits then! We could not afford to live without Sinclair's income. But he had already been investigating emigration at this point, and he had done a great deal of reading about Appalachia. We knew that the planetary government was looking for colonists, and we knew that if we could come here, work for five years, and make any kind of reasonable contribution, all of us could eventually earn citizenship. Maria and I still had grave doubts—for we are not, as you can tell, adventurers!—but Sinclair was very persuasive and we really had no other options. So we applied for admittance, sold our few major possessions, and came here."

She was silent a few moments while I waited to hear the rest of the story. "In fact, Appalachia was not Sinclair's first choice," she said slowly. "He wanted, even then, to go somewhere wilder, riskier, somewhere that we could earn citizenship in a year or less and where our very presence would be almost the only mark of civilization on the planet. He fancies himself—oh, almost a missionary in this regard. He wants to be in the vanguard of humanity as it spreads across the universe.

"But Maria and I would not agree to go someplace so—so barren. We had to have some amenities, some social structures in place, and so we compromised on Appalachia. We have now been here three years, and, as I say, Maria and I are as happy as we have ever been. We have food, space, employment, friends, a purpose in life—everything we ever had wanted, everything that for so long we had been denied. For us it is enough—it is more than enough—it is a rich bounty. But for Sinclair . . . he will not be content to stay here long."

She had fixed her eyes on her folded hands during much of this last part of her tale, but now she looked up at me again. "All that by way of explaining to you," she said lightly, "why Sinclair wants to learn nuclear generator maintenance from you. If he really emigrates to a desolate and unsettled planet, he will need every mechanical skill he can master. And he knows it. You will do him a great service if you can teach him what he needs to know."

"I will be happy to do so. I would like to in some small way repay the many favors he and his family have done for me. But what of you and Maria? If he leaves, will you be able to survive without him?"

"Yes, I think so. Maria and I can run this institution ourselves, especially if we are able to generate some income by selling energy, and the city officials have been by recently to discuss expanding our services. We may soon be in the position of needing to hire more help! Plus it is not beyond the bounds of possibility that one or both of us might marry—" She stopped abruptly and looked away, blushing. I hid my own smile.

"So you have no fears for your own welfare, should Sinclair decide to move on," I said gravely. "But you are not happy about the possibility of him leaving."

Still not looking at me, she shook her head rather violently. "No! For as long as I can remember, Sinclair has looked after us. He is only three years older than Maria, but he is ten years my senior, and I do not remember a day of my life that I didn't feel was made more secure because of Sinclair's presence at my side. When I was growing up in Newyer—in such poverty! I cannot describe it—he was my physical protector. He made sure I was safe when I had to travel from one destination to another, and he made sure I always had food to eat, even if there was not enough of it. I knew that no real harm could ever come to me as long as Sinclair was in my life. And even though I know that now, situated as I am, no real harm will come to me if he is gone—still I cannot imagine such a circumstance. It has never existed for me before."

The next question had to be delicately put, but I was really curious about the answer. "You say that Sinclair cared for you," I said. "Then I take it your parents were not much of a factor?"

"We had no parents—no real ones," she said bitterly. "I suppose you might not be familiar with the gen tanks on Baldus, but that is where Sinclair and Maria and I were all conceived."

I hid my amazement, as there was obviously so much more she had to tell me, but I could not wait to reveal to her some of my own mysterious origin.

"We had been commissioned, one by one, by a wealthy couple who were unable to have children of their own," she said, seeming to keep her voice steady only with great effort. "You may have remarked how different Sinclair's appearance is from mine and Maria's. That is because he was sculpted from entirely different genetic clay. Maria and I came from very similar gene pools, for they liked her looks when she was a baby and they wanted her sister to match. But they did not spare much thought for us once we were all in the household. They were not cruel to us, they were just neglectful. They did not bother to send Maria or me to school, so Sinclair—who had had basic educational classes—taught us language and math in the evenings. No one was assigned to watch us, so we ran in and out of the house and ate when we wanted and slept when we wanted and outgrew our clothes and lived like wild creatures half of our lives. And then they died, and we learned that not only had we not been formally adopted, we had been left only the paltriest sums in their wills. And that their home was no longer our home, and no one had a claim on us, and no one had a care for us, and we were truly on our own."

"How old were you?" I asked sympathetically. I was appalled but not surprised; this was a common story among those who had been harvested from the gen tanks. I was very familiar with it myself.

"Sinclair was eighteen, Maria was fifteen, and I was eight. We went into the city and used our small legacy to pay a month's rent in the smallest apartment we could find. Sinclair and Maria got jobs within three days. I started working as soon as I was old enough. And that was our life until we came to Appalachia." She took a deep breath and released it. "So you see," she said, on a small laugh, "why we all became PanEquists! It has been called the religion of the forgotten man, and no one could have been as forgotten as we were!"

I could contain my excitement no longer. I was almost bouncing in my chair as I leaned over to take her hand. "Deborah," I said, and such was the tone of my voice that she was instantly alerted to something unusual, for she looked up at me with wide eyes. "You know how glad and surprised you were to discover I too am a PanEquist?"

"Yes," she said.

"And you know how well you and Maria and I understand one another—how well we work together, how we at times seem more like sisters than companions?"

"I have often thought it," she said.

"Well, listen! When I first came here and you asked my name, you thought I said Jenna Starrin, but I did not. I have called myself Jenna Starborn for years because—"

"Starborn!" she cried, for she too knew the common name taken by children of the gen tanks. "But then—does that mean—"

"Yes! And not only was I conceived, gestated, and harvested as you were, but all this happened on the same planet! On Baldus! And I would not, at this point, be surprised to learn we were grown and harvested in the same facility, for there cannot be that many facilities in the civilized universe, and certainly not on Baldus—"

"Oh, Jenna! Oh, I cannot believe this! You *are* a sister to us, I have always sensed it, but even so, this is wonderful beyond belief!"

And we both leaped from our chairs and hugged each other like twins long separated, and we wept like people to whom joy is so rare that it sometimes feels like sorrow.

"I cannot believe it," she said, over and over again, first drawing back to study my face for kinship, and then renewing her fervent embrace. "Jenna, we *are* sisters—in spirit, and in history, and perhaps in some kind of true genetic fashion—"

"Oh, would that it were true! That some of our cellular material is the same!"

"We can pretend it is, in any case—"

"And I *feel* as if it were so—"

"If nothing else, we must consider ourselves cousins," Deborah said at last. "For we are at least as close as that."

Nothing would do, of course, but that we must go immediately to share the glad news with Maria and Sinclair. Maria reacted much as Deborah had, with exclamations of wonder and many affectionate hugs. Sinclair's gladness was more tempered, but appeared equally genuine.

"I have so few relatives that I am always happy to claim one more, particularly one who has made herself such an intrinsic part of our family already," he said, crossing the room and taking my hand. "I agree with Deborah—we shall call you cousin and be done with it. Welcome to the family, Jenna," and he bent down to plant a chaste kiss upon my forehead.

That night we celebrated with a special meal, and the next few days were gilded with a sort of lingering euphoria, but nothing else about our routine changed drastically. The women and I still maintained the house and the dorm and cared for the boarders, while Sinclair spent his days engaged in administrative tasks. In the evenings, we usually gathered in the family room to read, talk, counsel our new residents, play games—or study.

Sinclair had purchased the textbooks I had directed him to buy—for I still had no credit of my own—so very soon I was ready to begin teaching him the basics of nuclear generator maintenance. We sat in one corner of the large room, quietly going over theorems, while the others sat scattered in their various positions in chairs throughout the room. It was not, perhaps, the best possible situation for teaching, but I preferred it to working alone with Sinclair in some more sterile environment. I still found him a formidable figure who was easier to take when diluted by his sisters' presence.

He was a quick learner, for his mind was very agile and his will to understand was extraordinary. He retained every stricture, turned in faultless lessons, and studied on his own in his free time. More than one morning, after I had made my way to my work station in the generator room, I found him there before me, examining the equipment and preparing new questions.

"I begin to think that, very soon, you will need a teacher with greater skills than mine," I told him one evening. "Perhaps your friend Leopold has a technician on his staff who could take up your training once you have learned all you can from me."

"I do not think I will need to learn more than you know," Sinclair replied. "And this is how I wish to acquire knowledge."

I wondered if this had been intended as a compliment, but I was fairly certain it had been a simple statement of fact with no positive or negative connotation attached to it. And, indeed, if I could truly teach Sinclair everything I knew about generator maintenance, he would be well-equipped for the life Deborah had outlined to me. There might be more he could learn from someone, but he would know enough to survive.

During this period of time, only one event transpired to disturb my equilibrium. It came late one evening, after everyone else had gone to bed and Sinclair and I had spent an extra hour working on a stubborn calculation. When he finally solved it, Sinclair pushed his chair back from his desk and rewarded me with a rare smile.

"Well! If there are not too many problems like that in our next few lessons, I think I shall acquit myself tolerably well," he said. "I am more impressed all the time at the layers of knowledge that you keep locked up so demurely in your head. To look at you, one would not suspect that the greater part of your brain spends its highest percentage of energy solving mathematical dilemmas that the rest of us cannot comprehend."

I smiled. "No, indeed, I do not perform math functions for my amusement. Only when I am required to."

"Speaking of problems, I am faced with one that is not centered around arithmetic," he said, speaking so calmly that it did not even occur to me that I should be experiencing a sense of panic. "Perhaps you can help me with it."

"Surely. If I have any knowledge at all, I will be glad to share it."

He rummaged through the homework papers lying before him and pulled up a sheet that had apparently been printed out from his computer terminal sometime recently. "There is a general notice that has been circulated among the governmental and social services agencies of Appalachia," he said, still in that ordinary, unalarming voice. "Indeed, I assume it has been sent out to most similar offices on all the outer worlds where colonization is under way. There is a man, a high-grade citizen, who is looking for someone who has disappeared. He seems to think she may have taken refuge on some world which does not look too askance at half-cits without a work history."

I felt myself growing colder by a degree with every word that left his mouth. He spoke with complete dispassion, so that I could not tell if he expected his words to have any effect on me or not. Did he believe I was a runaway—this runaway—or did he merely think this little tale might have some slight interest for me, a half-cit whose own life had been difficult?

"Who is the man engaged on this quest?" I said, trying desperately to keep my voice steady.

He glanced at the printout. "An Everett Ravenbeck. The notice was issued from Corbramb, but he says the woman disappeared from Fieldstar." He paused and frowned down at the paper. "Fieldstar. That is quite some distance away from here. A terraformed planet, I believe."

"Yes, that sounds right," I managed to say.

He looked up at me again, and his fathomless blue eyes could have held all knowledge or no inkling whatsoever; they were that clear, that unreadable. "He says here that the woman he's looking for is named Jenna Starborn, so you can see why I thought it might be you."

There was a long silence while I tried to think of a reply. I could not renounce the name that I had so recently claimed; and I could not—I simply could *not*—bring myself to say aloud "I know no one by the name of Everett Ravenbeck." Nor could I imagine what course Sinclair Rainey would take if I did admit to being this hunted creature. Would he betray me, would he continue to shelter me, would he demand to know the tangled story of my life before he made his judgment? I merely stared at Sinclair, my face showing I could not guess what despair, and waited.

He dropped his eyes, shuffled his papers together, and laid the notice on the top of the pile. "Well, I suppose there may be any number of women in the settled universe who have the name Jenna Starborn," was his next unexpected remark. "Just the other day I went onto the StellarNet to search for Sinclair Raineys, and I found ten without even looking very hard. There are probably a dozen or so of you Jenna Starborns traveling through the star systems, and it's likely he will never find the one that's missing."

I felt as though I had surfaced after a stay too long underwater; I could feel myself struggling to catch my breath. "Yes—no doubt—both given name and surname are quite common," I said, stammering a little.

"I shall not contact him, then, and raise his hopes," Sinclair decided. "And everyone else here still knows you by the name Starrin, so I do not think they will be alerting him to your presence. Just as well. We would not want this Everett Ravenbeck to think he has found the woman he is searching for when she most certainly is not on Appalachia."

Again I was overcome by so much emotion that I could not speak. I did not know how to express my gratitude, for I was not in the habit of giving Sinclair the easy embraces I so often bestowed upon his sisters, and I absolutely could not utter a word. Besides, I was not entirely positive that he was playing a charade just to simplify my life; he might actually believe that I was the wrong Jenna. Sinclair was so guileless it was hard to tell.

"Well, it's quite late, you know," he said, glancing around the room as if for the first time realizing that everyone else had vacated it. "You have worked doubly hard today, first at your chosen vocation and then at teaching me. Go to bed, Jenna, and sleep well. We shall continue with our studies in the morning."

And that was the only time he mentioned Everett's name to me; and if he spoke of the incident to his sisters, they did not repeat it. They had called me their cousin, and cousin I had become to them, someone to whom the shelter of the family would be extended for whatever protection it could offer against whatever threat materialized. I wished with all my heart there was some way to pay them back for every kindness, every gesture of affection. I knew I would be as unsparing as they had been if my opportunity arose.

Chapter 18

✦

*I*n fact, just a week later, I was presented with the most unexpected opportunity to repay my bottomless debt to the Raineys—a way I would not have envisioned if I had spent my life imagining ways I could enrich my own life and the lives of those I loved.

It was evening of a day that I had spent mostly absent from the house. I had journeyed by underground transit to the Joester power company building to invest in some additional parts. I needed these to make minor repairs to the existing equipment, but I also wanted Sinclair to begin handling the actual connectors and cables, and I thought these would be an excellent training tool for him. I rather enjoyed myself, traveling around the city that I had rarely crossed on my own, and taking my time before returning to the house. I did walk by a few shops and think, rather wistfully, what I might buy if I had even a small income. But I was just fantasizing, not repining; I was very well content with what I had in life.

When I returned to the house, I found all three Rainey siblings clustered in the family room, reading a notice on the computer monitor. Sinclair was seated before the computer and scrolling through the text, while his sisters stood behind him, watching the words skip by. They were so engrossed that they did not turn to greet me when I entered, and I instantly sensed that something was amiss.

"Is there news? Bad news?" I asked in some concern.

They all glanced back at me, but only Deborah left her station to come and give me an absentminded hug. "Hello, Jenna. Was your day productive?"

"Yes, very. But you all look so discouraged. Has something untoward occurred?"

Now Maria turned to give me a faint smile. "Oh—not really—we were rather foolish to get our hopes up in the first place. It is just that we have been left out of a legacy we thought we had a chance at. We don't really want for anything, of course, it's just that—well—it's always nice to have a little extra money!"

"But, Deborah! Maria!" I exclaimed. "I have no idea what you are talking about! What legacy? What hope?"

Sinclair, who was still watching the screen, shrugged, and swiveled around to look at me. "Deborah has told you some of our history, I know," he said. "It is, after all, how we discovered our connection. But perhaps you did not know that the founder of the clinic where the four of us were conceived has recently died."

"No," I said, in some bewilderment. "I do not even know who the founder is—or why I should care if he lives or dies."

Sinclair smiled faintly. "He died a wealthy man—and, strangely enough, a childless one. He was a quirky individual who had trouble forming relationships with anyone, and although, through his efforts, thousands of people were brought into this world, it appears he could not call a single one of them a friend. He did not want his inheritance to go to the tax courts or his only blood relatives—to whom, it will not surprise you to learn, he has not spoken in decades. So he determined his heir by lottery."

Maria took up the explanation. "About two years ago, when he knew he was getting ill, he began a systematic search for all the individuals who had been harvested at his clinic. He posted notices on the StellarNet and encouraged everyone to send in their current locations and announced that he would choose his heir by drawing a name at random. Naturally, the three of us replied at once, and we have been following the news ever since, wondering when his choice would be made known."

"It sounds ghoulish, I know," Deborah said. "But this was the route he himself chose."

"I understand perfectly," I said.

In fact, my mind was racing as my memory replayed for me that final bedside watch at my Aunt Rentley's side. She had told me repeatedly that someone had wanted me; I could still hear her fevered voice crying, *"They asked me for you, but I would not give you over to them!"* It must have been the officials of the clinic, even then, trying to round up addresses of all its creations and descendants. I added, "So I suppose today the announcement was made, and none of you are his beneficiaries?"

"We really could not have expected to be," Maria said wistfully. "Out of so many thousands of possibilities, it was unlikely that one of us would answer to the name that was drawn."

"But who is the lucky winner?" I asked. "Someone's life has just undergone a material change! We should congratulate this person!"

Sinclair pivoted back to the screen. "For a moment, I hoped it was you," he said to me over his shoulder, "for the heir's name is also Jenna. Jenna Rentley."

I felt the floor shudder under my feet, and for a moment the room went black. I must have flung my arm out, seeking a handhold, for I felt Deborah's fingers close over mine as she drew me quickly to her side. "Jenna! Are you ill?" she asked, and as if distantly, I heard the echoing voices of her brother and sister.

"No—I—let me sit a moment," I gasped, and staggered to an unoccupied chair. Deborah knelt before me, chafing my wrists, and Maria hurried over with a glass of water. I took a few sips and exerted all my will to focus my mind, and then I looked up to encompass them all with a glance.

"*I* am Jenna Rentley," I said.

There were the expected exclamations. Deborah actually fell back onto the floor; Maria pressed her hand to her mouth as if to hold back more cries of wonder. Sinclair stood a few paces behind his sisters, an aloof blonde god, looking down at me with an expression very hard to decipher.

"You, Jenna?" Deborah said at last, the first one out of all of us to muster a coherent sentence. "You are the founder's heir? But if your name is Jenna Rentley, how is it we did not know it?"

I swallowed some more water and set the glass aside. "I did not mean to keep secrets from you," I said. "I have not used the name Rentley since I was a child—in fact, I never officially used it at all. Like you, I was commissioned by a woman who decided, once I was in her care, that she was not so certain I suited her after all, and she never formally adopted me. I left her house when I was ten years old, and from that time on I chose to go by the name Starborn. It is the name under which I graduated from Lora Tech, and the name under which I sought employment. Jenna Starborn is who I am. But Jenna Rentley is the name by which the clinic would know me."

"So you are the founder's heir!" Deborah exclaimed next, excitement thrilling through her voice as she began to realize what my confession meant. "You must contact the clinic immediately!"

"But if she has never gone by the name Rentley," Maria said, "will they believe her? Will she be able to prove her identity?"

"A simple DNA test will establish that," Sinclair said, speaking for the first time. "There are lawyers here who can make sure you are properly identified."

"And—Jenna! Do you realize? You are now a wealthy woman!" Deborah said. "I truly rejoice for you!"

"Rejoice for all of us," I said, sitting up straighter as I regained some of my strength. "For we are cousins, do you not remember? Whatever is mine, I will share equally with you."

"Oh, Jenna, no!" Deborah said, and at the same time, Maria cried, "Jenna, you must not! That money is for you!"

"Nonsense," I said firmly. "Why, you three have shared your home with me for these past months, and asked nothing of me in return. You gave me a home when I had none—hope when I had none—family when I had none—and I have prayed to the Goddess so often for a chance to pay you back. We have *all* inherited the founder's money. Oh, what a day this is for celebration!"

They argued a few more minutes, even Sinclair advising me to think over my decision for a few days, but I was adamant. Once I heard the sum of money involved, I was more than adamant—I was almost terrified. "I could not possibly spend so much in three or four lifetimes!" I declared. "I must split it into quarters, or it will go completely to waste!"

Once they accepted that my offer was sincere—indeed, immutable—the Raineys also began to rejoice on their own behalf, discussing in excited voices the improvements they could make to the house and the possibility of buying additional property. Indeed, we all soon realized that, even split among the four of us, our legacy was substantial enough to allow us all to purchase citizenship, and we debated whether that would be our best use of funds—for the Raineys, at least, had only two more years of residency on Appalachia before they would qualify for level-five citizenship on that planet. It was something to consider, we all agreed, but we would think it over long and hard before spending the money on something we had all lived for so long without.

During our discussions, more than once I caught a contemplative look on Sinclair's face. His sisters noticed it too, for now and then I saw them casting grave looks in his direction. I guessed that he was thinking how he could use his inheritance to fund his homesteading expedition to Cozakee or some other frontier planet, and that his sisters were not happy to realize that his dream had suddenly become a much more likely eventuality.

"Well, we should not spend every last credit before we actually have the money in hand," Maria finally said decisively, reining us all in. "For I suppose there may be some problem, after all, and the authorities might not recognize Jenna without a legal battle. We must, for a while at least, continue as before—but with a white glimmer of hope before us, a ray of the brightest sunshine!"

This made sense to all of us, and we soon realized that we were exhausted from joy and speculation. It was very late, and none of us had eaten dinner yet, so we all trooped into the kitchen and munched on leftovers and now and again let the forbidden topic creep back into our conversation. Then someone would put a hand to his or her mouth, and we would all laugh and look guilty, and someone else would strive to introduce a more mundane subject. In this way, we ate our scrambling meal and ended the evening in the highest of spirits. As soon as we had consumed our food, we made hearty and affectionate goodbyes, and we all went up to our bedrooms to spend the night in dreaming wonder.

I, Reeder, felt the greatest sense of wonder of all. For here I was, an orphan in every sense of the word, a creature recently so close to total obliteration that even now I sometimes could not believe I was safely back among the living. And I had—through some unimaginable combination of luck and fate—been thrown in the path of three of the few individuals to whom I could claim some connection, however remote, and we had developed an emotional bond so fierce that I did not believe it could be severed. And now—again, through some strange, impossible twist of fortune—I had been placed in a position to better myself and honor them beyond my wildest hopes. Jenna Outcast, Jenna Friendless, had become Jenna Beloved and Jenna Blessed. Who could doubt that there was a Goddess who ordered the machinations of the universe? She had tested me severely, but she had rewarded me magnificently, and I knelt beside my bed for a very long time and offered up heartfelt prayers of thanks.

As Sinclair had foreseen, identifying myself as Jenna Rentley was a task for which I needed the help of the legal community. Leopold Joester, not surprisingly, was the one who directed us to a lawyer, who put into motion all the necessary activities. I had to go to a health center and submit to a series of tests, and the results of these were transmitted to the lawyers at the Baldus clinic. Meanwhile, on my behalf, my new legal advisor contacted the lawyer who had served my aunt Rentley when I was a child, and he readily confirmed the basic background facts of my adoption. The officials at Lora Tech outlined that I had been admitted as Jenna Rentley and graduated as Jenna Starborn.

Since there had been no other name change in the interim, I did not need to call in any witnesses to account for the intervening years of my life.

"And the best part of all of this," Sinclair observed to me one evening when we were supposed to be studying but were in fact, once again, discussing how we might dispose of our new income, "is that the news services that are carrying this story are only referring to you as Jenna Rentley, for that is the official name of the heiress. I have not yet seen any of them post the addendum of your altered name."

I looked up a moment, discomposed, for it had not previously occurred to me that my good fortune would also result in my complete exposure. He smiled as reassuringly as he was, with his austere face, able to do, and patted my hand. "Do not worry," he told me. "As I said, your identity is so far still protected. I think you will not be found."

"I hope not," I said. "But I never realized till recently how a name might make your fortune—or betray you."

"You could change your name again," he suggested.

"I don't know that I have any desire to do that," I said.

He shrugged. "You might marry. If you took your husband's name, Jenna Starborn might be eliminated altogether."

"I rather like her," I said, laughing. "I do not know that I want to see her eliminated."

"Very well, then. If you took a husband's name, you would be less likely, perhaps, to be found."

"It is true that I have no wish to be found," I said. "For I have come to rest in the place I will want to stay."

"Stay forever?" he asked, almost idly. "I confess, the idea of a relocation appeals greatly to me. It does not to you?"

"I have relocated three times in my life, and each time the change resulted in a great improvement," I allowed. "So if I were to move a fourth time, I suppose I could expect to, once again, affect my life in a positive way. But I must say, I would need a strong inducement to make such a change."

"Change itself I have often found a strong inducement," he said. "If

I were you, Jenna, I would be thinking very hard about what I might do with my life, now that I might do anything with it. There are opportunities before you that I do not believe you have even considered. Keep your mind open, and I think you will see the universe is a much larger place, full of so many more opportunities, than you are used to believing."

This was all very bewildering, especially as he spoke with such passion that it was clear he wanted me to be profoundly moved. I did not know what to say, so I nodded dumbly, and in a few minutes we returned to the lesson I had planned for the evening.

But it was not to be expected that Sinclair would not return to this topic. In the days that followed, as we got our daily updates from our lawyer keeping us apprised of the legal tangles we must unknot, Sinclair often found a chance to speak to me in private. He began to tell me, in quite vivid detail, of the beauties of the world Cozakee, which had just been opened up for colonization. He spoke of the advantages of homesteading, the exhilaration of wresting a new life out of foreign soil, of creating an empire from an empty, unused world. Most often these conversations occurred rather late at night, while we were still studying and everyone else had gone to bed, and I was often so fatigued by this time that I wondered if I was imagining how much pressure Sinclair was beginning to exert to make me consider emigration. It seemed as though he wanted me to share his sentiments, but perhaps he merely wanted me to understand them; and my confusion on this point made me respond more cautiously to his enthusiasm than I could tell he wished.

I did not say anything to his sisters about our conversations. With them, I talked of the furniture we would buy, the clothes we would purchase and the luxuries we would indulge in as soon as we received our money.

"Which should be any day now," I finally had the chance to tell them when I had gotten the good news from our lawyer. "For I have been confirmed as the heir! All the tests were approved and I have been officially named! We should have our money by the end of the week!"

Of course, that was a cause for jubilation, and the arrival of the credit transfer—which was instantly divided into four portions and deposited into our four separate accounts—gave us another reason to celebrate. We had a veritable feast that night, catered by the finest restaurant in Cody, and attended by the Joesters and various other city officials who had shown an interest in our progress. Maria, Deborah, and I were attired in simply marvelous dresses of outrageous hues and construction. Mine appeared to be made of cobalt-blue synthetic feathers and came complete with a hat that added four inches to my height. The Rainey sisters were dressed with equal flourish. I could tell that Sinclair did not feel we had made our first purchases wisely, though he did not, as I had expected, spend his time at Rianna Joester's side to complain of our frivolity. In fact, he did not speak to her once that I observed during the whole evening, though everyone else mingled with great liberality.

This was so unusual that I whispered of it to Deborah when I got a chance. "What has occurred to cause a coolness between your brother and Rianna? Usually they are talking all night—or at least staring at each other, trying to *think* of things to talk about."

"They have had a falling out, I believe," she whispered back. "A couple of weeks ago. He was telling her about Cozakee, and she told him nothing would induce her to leave her family, and ever since then, he has not had two words to say to her. I believe it has caused them both unhappiness—but there is a pair I cannot decide whether I want to see matched up or separated, so I take no hand in their quarrels."

"There is another member of the Joester house who seems eager to be upon good terms with the Raineys," I teased, for Harmon Joester had not been able to keep his eyes off Deborah tonight. Indeed, her gold-and-flame-colored dress, which revealed far more of her bosom and thigh than Deborah was used to exhibiting, was a perfect choice for her. It set off her lustrous auburn hair and her full, inviting figure, and it was so bright that it was almost impossible to look away from.

She laughed, blushed, and lowered her eyes, but she did not seem at all offended. "Well, fine clothes do make a fine lady, no matter what our sermons might try to teach us to the contrary," she said. "I do feel beautiful enough tonight to attract the attention of any number of Joesters!"

I leaned closer and whispered in her ear, "I do not believe it is your dress that draws him. I believe it is your soul." And she laughed again, and blushed even more deeply, and I abandoned the topic, but she did not speak a disclaimer. Indeed, rather late in the evening when the larger group had broken into smaller gatherings for more intimate discussion, I saw Deborah and Harmon in close conversation, by turns looking so serious and so merry that I could not imagine they were discussing anything less comprehensive than the idea of a future spent together. I hoped with all my heart that it were so.

If it were, the announcement was not to be made that night. It was so late that it might almost be called early the next day before our party completely dispersed. Our guests made sleepy farewells, and we host and hostesses called out responses through our yawns as we saw them out the door.

"Great Goddess! I have never been so tired!" Maria exclaimed as we climbed wearily up the stairs to our bedrooms. "I believe I will sleep the whole day through—as any leisured lady might be expected to do."

And being reminded again of the fact that we were all rich made us laugh even as we made our final drowsy good nights. I crawled into my bed and whiled away the minutes between closing my eyes and falling asleep by wondering if Deborah and Harmon Joester might really decide to marry, and soon. Nothing but news of a bridal could top the excitements of the past few weeks, I reasoned, and I had become so addicted to good fortune that I did not want to see the trend reversed.

But talk of a wedding, though it did arise a few days later, came from a most unexpected source, and threw me into much more turmoil than joy.

Chapter 19

✦

The weather being exceptionally fine for the past few evenings, as Cody melted into a rapturous spring, Sinclair and I had developed the habit of taking our books and studying outdoors on the small rooftop patio that surmounted the Raineys' house. For some reason, though the Raineys used the patio often during the spring and summer months, this rooftop retreat had never been wired for electricity, so if we wanted light to read by, we had to supply our own. I had found a small battery-operated lamp and I usually carried that upstairs, while Sinclair brought an industrial strength flashlight and balanced it on a pile of books so that it shone on the papers before him.

Although there is nothing even remotely romantic about the steady beam of an electronic bulb, somehow the small, private pools of light created an atmosphere of intimacy this night. The soft night wind blew around us, gently ruffling our hair; below us, the city made its muted but purposeful noises, too distant to worry us, but musical enough to add a pleasant counterpart to our quiet conversation. Sinclair's face was imperfectly lit, so I could not watch the play of his features as he spoke. I merely listened to the fluid, hypnotic rhythms of his voice and thought how lovely his speech was. Lovely enough that, from time to time, I lost the sense of his words and only listened to his cadences, measured and confident. He could have been reciting from the Pan-Equist's Creed or the Nuclear Technician's Field Handbook, and I would have found his voice equally pleasing.

But he did not, for the moment, appear to be reading from either. I had been listening only idly when a change in his tone brought me to complete attention. "But you have heard me speak such praises before, have you not, Jenna?" he said, and it was the serious note that caused me to sit up straighter and comprehend the individual words. "There must be nothing about Cozakee's attractions and advantages that, by now, you are unfamiliar with."

"No, indeed," I said, smiling in the dark. "I believe I could recite for you its discovery, exploration, status, and projected population growth in a few succinct sentences."

"You realize," he said somberly, "that I intend to emigrate there, though the notion displeases my sisters."

"I knew you had seriously considered it. I did not know you had decided."

I saw the shadow of his head nod over the flashlight's unwavering beam. "Yes. I have made my reservations today on a ship that leaves in two months' time, and I will spend the interim buying all the items I will need to take with me on such a life-changing expedition."

Clearly, his inheritance had speeded up the possibility of his relocation, and for that reason I was a little sorry to have received my legacy; but it was, after all, his money and his life, and he could do with either what to him seemed most urgent and gratifying. "I do not know what to say," I said a little hesitantly. "Having found a cousin at such an unexpected juncture in my life, I am loath to lose him—but I truly believe you must follow the course designed to bring you the greatest happiness. And you have fixated so firmly on this course that I would not even try to dissuade you from it, but merely wish the Goddess to guard you in all you do and smile on your endeavors."

Whether or not the Goddess smiled, he did, a ghostly expression in the insufficient light. "You do not have to lose me at all," he said. "You could come with me to Cozakee and we could homestead together."

I felt myself jerk backward from surprise, and I am sure my face showed every variety of astonishment, though mercifully the night cloaked at least some of my expressions. "Go with you—to Cozakee?" I stammered. "I have no thought of leaving Appalachia—I have no desire to uproot my life again."

"But consider it, Jenna, I beg you most sincerely," he said, though his tone was more commanding than pleading. "It is true that any of the four of us could now buy our citizenships, but think how much more valuable such status would be if we could earn it by honest labor and sheer dedication to a task. Think of the rewards of taking an untracked, untouched planet—an entire world!—and remolding it into the landscape of our dreams. We who have had nothing for so long will have everything. We who have been outcasts in our society will now make our own society—we will become pioneers, leaders, creators. It is intoxicating, Jenna! Does it not make you breathless with excitement?"

Indeed, the ardent conviction of his voice had its own exhilarating effect on me, but I was by nature too cautious to be caught up in any spell of the moment. "You are passionate about your cause, Sinclair, and it moves me to hear you, and so I do not doubt that you should go to Cozakee and immediately," I said, choosing my words with care. "But I have no reason to believe my place is there. I am happy here with what remains of my family."

"But I wish you to come with me," he said stubbornly. "I do not wish to settle Cozakee on my own. I want a lifetime companion to stand beside me—to labor beside me at the selfsame goals—a lover and a wife to fill the loneliness that will inevitably hover around such a strange and unpopulated planet."

If I had reared back at his first suggestion, these words almost caused me to fall from my chair. "A wife!" I exclaimed in the faintest voice. "But—do you mean—you wish to marry *me*?"

He nodded vigorously. "Yes, of course that is what I mean. Why, what else could you suppose? Two unrelated individuals of the opposite sex, no matter how they might style themselves 'cousin,' cannot be expected to live unchaperoned together without falling into habits of physical intimacy that can only be sanctioned by the institution of marriage. I wish to sire my own dynasty on Cozakee—it is part of the world I envision creating—one that is stamped with my bloodlines and imprinted with my brand of intelligence through the centuries that follow. Personal achievement can be spectacular, but if it dies with the individual, it has no lasting power. And that, if you have not understood, is what I want—to make an indelible mark on this society that would have seen me live and die without the least acknowledgment."

"An understandable goal—a laudable goal—but I do not know that I am the bride who can help you accomplish your aim," I said, stammering again. I was completely in shock. It had never occurred to me that Sinclair would either ask me to accompany him, or require such a commitment from me if he did.

"But I believe you are," he said rather impatiently, without allowing me time to put forward any formulated objections. "We come from such similar backgrounds that we can be considered absolute equals with no thought of trying to take precedence over each other. Our fortunes are identical, and we inherited them precisely the same way—and we can invest them to their grandest purpose in undertaking this new life. On the personal side, you are everything a man could want in a wife. You are neat, inoffensive, helpful, and quiet—you do not have inexplicable emotional rages, nor do you attempt to punish anyone in your circle through your moods and attitudes." *Who are you describing here?* I wondered, but did not get an opportunity to ask, as his list of my virtues continued. "You are not materialistic, and would be happy to go years without acquiring fashionable new clothes or furnishings for your home. And you are young enough and sturdy enough to be capable of filling our new house with sons and daughters who will carry on our homestead after us."

"Flattering as this assessment is," I said, though I knew he would not detect the edge in my voice, "I cannot help but point out the obvious: You do not love me."

He shrugged. "That is not important."

"I disagree," I said firmly. "A lifetime spent on an unpopulated planet with a woman you do not love may become a sentence of misery more profound than the life you led on Newyer."

"Love is a popular romantic notion that leads to nothing but its own brand of misery," he said rather bitterly. "What is important between a man and a woman is respect, affection, and common ground. Those things we have."

"Indeed we do," I said cordially. "And those things, perhaps, last longer than the violent romantic emotions which you seem to distrust so greatly. But I do not know that I am prepared to marry for respect and affection, especially if those sentiments will carry me so far from the place I have come to feel is home."

He had listened carefully, for he seemed to pounce on my words the instant I stopped speaking. "You do not *know* if you are prepared to marry me," he said. "Does that mean you will consider my offer?"

"I will consider it." My own words surprised me. I could not believe I did not reject him out of hand. I knew I did not want to marry Sinclair Rainey; I knew I did not want to leave Appalachia; I knew that the delights that *he* saw in Cozakee held no appeal for me. And yet there was about his cold-blooded, practical proposal an element of adventure—and even romance, in the most old-fashioned sense. To set off for an unexplored world and make it a place of your very own—! Like Sinclair, I could hear the siren call of that ambition. I could feel the centuries-old desire for ownership stir in my disenfranchised blood.

And once married to Sinclair Rainey—to any man—I would be free forever of the fear of one day succumbing to my attraction for Everett Ravenbeck. Or—dear Goddess—so I would like to believe.

"When will you decide?" Sinclair asked next. "We do not have much leisure to contemplate, for, as I told you, I have reservations on a ship leaving here in two months. If you come with me, we will have much to do to prepare."

"Give me a week to think about it," I said.

"So long!"

"A week seems a short period to consider consequences that will last a lifetime."

He nodded curtly. "Very well. If you do not object, however, I will take my opportunities during that week to discuss with you advantages of the proposed match."

"I do not imagine that by objecting, I can forestall you from sharing such advantages with me," I said, unable to resist a smile. He did not smile in return, but merely nodded again.

"Good. We will meet again tomorrow night to finish our studies—for, if you do not come with me, I shall need to know as much as I can. And if you do accompany me, it will still be valuable for me to have such knowledge as you can impart, so that when you are busy with children, I can manage the equipment on the estate."

I had a sudden disquieting vision of myself overseeing a household of ten or fifteen children, stairstepped in ages and sizes, while Sinclair gravely studied technical manuals and went off to repair broken cables. I had to shake my head to dispel the image, and then I had to speak up quickly so Sinclair did not think I was giving a negative response to his last statement.

"Yes, indeed, I believe it is best that you continue to learn what you can," I said. "We will resume our studies tomorrow. In the meantime, I am tired and I have much to think about. It is time for me to retire to my bed."

We stood simultaneously and gathered our books, papers, and electrical lights. With more ostentatious concern than he was wont to show me, Sinclair ushered me through the rooftop door and down the winding steps to the story where all the bedrooms were located. He even accompanied me to my own door, something that he had done only rarely in the past.

"Good night, Jenna," he said gravely, looking down at me for a long, unblinking moment. I could not tell if he were debating making another observation or merely attempting to read my face for any signs of reaction to the evening's central conversation. In any case, he did not speak again, but leaned down to plant a kiss very deliberately on my left cheek.

The feel of his mouth was warm and heavy and entirely pleasurable. I was astonished at the way my nerves leaped to attention, frantic to assess the texture and placement of his lips. I had forgotten what a kiss felt like, even such a chaste one; I had forgotten how much promise was implicit in the remotest physical contact with a man. Or I thought I had forgotten—my body all too clearly remembered its elemental rhythms and most primitive desires.

Covered with confusion, I did not speak again, but rushed inside my room and closed the door too hurriedly behind me. I was shaken and distressed, not so much by the kiss but by the memories the kiss had evoked. Oh, Goddess, if a man were to touch me, I knew the man I wanted! Loving Everett Ravenbeck, could I ever marry Sinclair Rainey? Would Sinclair's kisses always remind me of another man's? Or did the body, after all, really care who stirred its senses and caused its brief, glorious moments of madness? The body could be tricked—this I knew instinctively—but I was not so sure about the gullibility of the heart.

I stood in the middle of my room, and I trembled.

The next six days passed for me in a sort of tightening noose of apprehension. I had made several momentous decisions in my life, some of them quite painful, but few of them had involved a step that literally was irreversible. And so I viewed the prospect of marriage to Sinclair Rainey, for I was not the kind of woman to undertake such a task and then, if it became too onerous to me, shirk it. If I gave the man my word, plighted my troth to him, I would become his wife and I would stay his wife though hell itself awaited us in our life together. I did not expect hell, of course. I did expect, on Cozakee, long hours of labor and many high-caliber frustrations; I expected setbacks and disappointments and worries. But I envisioned triumphs as well—first crops, first neighbors, first exports, first babies—a parallel line of joys to march alongside the unending difficulties.

I must admit that many of Sinclair's arguments carried great weight with me. I understood his dream of proprietorship, and it reverberated against my own desolate memories; I too would like to create a place of my very own that would be inviolate and completely imprinted with my desires. And to pass that along to the heirs I had never allowed myself to believe I might have.

And yet such a life, such an estate, might be abandoned if the conditions eventually proved too intolerable or if my own wants materially changed. Now that I had what for me amounted to unlimited credit, I could walk away from any failed venture and start anew; my life would not be ruined by a single bad investment. I could attempt Cozakee and, if it did not suit me, I could leave it. But I could not so easily dissolve a marriage to Sinclair Rainey.

Once or twice, late at night as I mulled over my opportunity, I considered giving Sinclair this answer: "I will homestead with you on Cozakee, but I will not marry you. I will be your fellow laborer, and I will be your best friend, but I will not be your wife." But then I remembered the kiss in the corridor, and I knew he would not accept that compromise, and I knew that his refusal would be the safer course.

But could I marry Sinclair Rainey?

My thoughts were so taken up with this question during the next six days that I grew a little withdrawn from all three of my so-called cousins. Sinclair, who knew the reason for my abstraction, made no comment on my behavior, but Maria and Deborah more than once asked me if something was amiss.

"For I worry about you, Jenna, I truly do," Deborah said to me one morning as we worked together in the kitchen. "You are so strong and solitary! I believe, if you thought it necessary, you could tear yourself away from your closest friends without a word of good-bye, and then we would be left wondering forever after what had caused you to leave and what had become of you."

I smiled rather sadly, for this truth struck too close to home, but I shook my head. "I shall make you this promise, Deborah, that when I *do* leave your household, you shall know why I go and what my destination is."

"But, Jenna, are you contemplating leaving us?" she cried. "You must not! Wherever could you be thinking of going?"

I was sorely tempted to confide in her, because, of the three Rainey siblings, I felt the deepest bond of affection with Deborah, but I did not like to betray her brother's confidence or let her know that I might reject him. Sinclair could share that information if he wished; I did not like to be so careless.

"It is you who might leave me," I said, managing another smile. "For if I am not mistaken, Harmon Joester was here again just last night, and it was you alone he cared to speak to."

Now Deborah was the one who looked as if she had news she could not contain—and she was finally unable to suppress it. "Oh, Jenna, he asked me to marry him, and I accepted! I am so happy, but I am in such turmoil! It changes everything—and who will run this house?—and I know Sinclair is making plans to emigrate—and I do not want you to think you will not have a home with me forever, no matter if or when I marry—"

I laughed at this, though my first reaction had been to take her into a delighted embrace. "Oh, no, you don't! Don't you even consider turning down such an offer because you worry about my well-being!" I teased her. "I would be very happy renting a small house of my own, or sharing it with Maria if she finds herself at loose ends, and finding some useful employment to pass the time. That is, if I was not up at your house at all hours of the day and night, helping you raise the children I am sure you plan to have immediately—"

She blushed and disclaimed, but the rosy red of her cheeks was more credible than her disjointed statements about "intending to wait."

I added, "And if you fear I will be lonely in any solitary home of my own, let me tell you what a pleasure it will be to have an entire house to myself and not be sharing it with whatever unfortunates have disembarked off the latest starship, disoriented and stupefied, who consider themselves free to wander the hallways at will."

"Yes! I confess that I am looking forward to a little privacy as well! But then what becomes of the Public Aid Office? For it is very useful, you must agree, and I would hate to see it disbanded altogether once Sinclair is gone and I am out of the house."

"You and Leopold Joester and your other high city officials will hire someone to replace Sinclair and everything will go on as before," I said. "Your kindness and good nature will be hard to duplicate, but your physical presence will be easily replaced, I promise you."

"Yes—that is what Maria says—but I do worry—"

I reiterated my belief that all would be well, then pressed her for details on her betrothal. She was happy enough to talk of Harmon Joester, and their plans to move outside the Cody city limits and homestead a small tract of farmland. Once again, I saw that my inheritance had made a long-held dream shape up into a practical reality, and I rejoiced for her. If ever anyone deserved good fortune, it was Deborah Rainey.

But later that night, as Sinclair and I studied after dinner, I reflected that Deborah's marriage made my own more plausible. It gave me one more reason to accept Sinclair, for it gave me one less reason to stay in Cody, attempting to continue living the life that I found so agreeable. True, it would be hard on Maria to lose me *and* both of her siblings in a few short weeks—but Maria too had her suitors, and I did not see her living for long alone.

Did I not want to marry too, with everyone I loved stepping into the bonds of matrimony?

I was quieter than usual this night, which was obvious to Sinclair, and I had declined the opportunity to resume our studies outdoors on the grounds that a spring storm was moving in and the winds were too disruptive. So we sat in the library, while his sisters read, and we went over a few tangled equations. The last five nights, once our lessons were over, he had spent some time outlining for me again the various attractions of Cozakee, but this night I was not prepared to hear one more word in praise of that distant world. When Deborah and Maria rose to seek their bedrooms, I came to my feet with alacrity and proclaimed my own exhaustion. Sinclair nodded to me with his usual somberness.

"I will read a few minutes longer on my own," he said. "But we will talk again tomorrow, Jenna, will we not?"

Tomorrow, of course, was the deadline I had fashioned for my decision, and so I knew what he referred to. "Yes, Sinclair, we will talk then," I said, and followed his sisters from the room.

But once I was in my own bedchamber, I found myself too restless to sleep, or think, or pray. In less than a day, I must announce my intentions, and I was not much closer to certainty now than I had been the night Sinclair first made his proposal. I knew that I was inclined to accept him, but for reasons that did not bear close examination—not because I loved him, not because I was interested in the life he had to offer, but because such a course would free me forever from any need to think again about my own future. I would have to work, but I would not have to worry and wonder. My choice made, I would have no options but to go forward. Such inevitability appealed to me; I felt my battered heart could use some constancy.

But still I was not sure I could bring myself to marry him.

"Goddess, I need a little guidance from you this night," I whispered under my breath. But my small, comfortable room seemed too close and confining to admit of her expansive presence; I thought I might have a better chance of hearing her whispers of wisdom if I stepped outside and stood in the windy dark. Accordingly—fervently hoping that I did not inadvertently encounter Sinclair on his way to bed—I crept from my room and up the back stairs to emerge on the rooftop patio.

A storm was indeed building up from the plains that lay west of the city. Against the blackness of the heavens, I could see a more forbidding darkness mounting in that direction. It was as if Night herself had drawn her features together in a scowl and, like a distempered baby, was about to vent her ill humor on us in one long howling wail. The wind was even stronger than I had anticipated, and it whipped around me with such force that I staggered back against the door once I had shut it behind me. The very air smelled of sulphur and fury—it crossed my mind that it might not be the Goddess who communed with me this night, but something altogether darker and more devilish.

Nonetheless, she was the one I had come here to consult, and I pushed myself away from the door with some determination. Fighting the bickering wind, I made my way to the center of the patio, and lifted my face to the manic skies. A few angry drops of cold rain splashed across my cheek and were scrubbed away by the wind. I did not mind; I almost hoped the heavens opened up, a great shower of purification, washing me clean of my cluttered thoughts and leaving me empty, scoured, and serene.

"Goddess!" I cried, flinging my hands out as wide as they would go and appealing to that faceless, furious sky. "Goddess, command me! I am your obedient child, I am your willing daughter—where would you send me that I might do the most good in your name?"

A distant roll of thunder answered me, and a spray of rain for a moment blinded me, but there was no clearer directive. I shook the water from my face and asked again.

"You have spoken to me twice in the past—you have shown your love for me, you have not allowed me to set a foot wrong. I am lost now, I am confused. Tell me what you would have me do—show me what I should know."

The wind blew so fiercely for a moment that the door rattled violently on its hinges; I dropped to my knees on the hard stone of the roof to be somewhat out of its way. There was a live quality to that wind, a sentience. I felt it palpitate with the hands or heartbeats of all the creatures it had whistled past on its blistering journey to me. There was sound in it too, mutters and whispers and muffled cries, and I strained to separate out a single voice, a single sentence, of sense and coherence.

And I heard one word, in that voice I had heard twice before in my life, and that voice said, *"Listen."*

"Listen for what?" I cried, but the wind answered only with its indistinguishable moans. "Listen for whom?" But this time there were no human voices at all, just the rough shrieking passage of the wind.

I stayed where I was, now folding my arms about me and settling back on my heels, and prepared to wait. The night grew blacker; the clouds piled in the west drew closer and closer, gradually obliterating the shaken stars overhead. Rain began to fall in good earnest, soaking me through in a matter of minutes, and not for a moment did the wind cease its game of chase and follow. And still I knelt, and still I waited, and still I strained with all my senses to hear what the Goddess bade.

The storm grew so rough that I could hear nothing except the lashing rain and the roaring wind and the things that came crashing down because of them. It was as if I had been transported back in time, to the violent birth of the universe, or forward, to its turbulent death—so primitive did the tempest seem, so full of rage and incontrovertible purpose. I would not have been surprised, upon staggering to my feet, to find I had been hurled to another time or another dimension; such was the force of that gale that I felt it could have launched me to any place real or imaginary.

I have no idea how long it lasted, though it seemed as though hours passed while I knelt there, buffeted by the most elemental forces at the Goddess's disposal. At last—a break in the rain, a faltering in the wild air—and then, with an ominous suddenness, complete and utter stillness.

I lifted my head, for I had drawn it close to my chest for protection, and listened to the profound silence around me. Nothing in the whole city appeared to move or function. The stars themselves seemed to have halted in their courses and stood, dumb and motionless, overhead. This was the silence at the dawn of the universe, before the planets knew men or men knew speech; this was the breathless advent of time itself.

All the corridors between all the worlds were open. If a single man spoke, every creature would hear him. If the Goddess blinked her eye, every star would tumble. Every atom was connected, across the unbridgeable distances of space, and every living molecule was contracted into one small dense core of matter.

And at the precise moment I had this revelation, I heard my name spoken aloud.

"Jenna!" The syllables rolled across the glittering trails of starlight. "Jenna! Jenna! Jenna! Jenna!"

Nothing more—my name, over and over again—but I leaped to my feet, panting like a wild thing. "Everett!" I cried. "Where are you?"

"Jenna!" The voice came back, but fainter now, as if receding across some unimaginable horizon, or as if the speaker himself did not have the strength to go on. "Jenna—Jenna—Jenna—"

"*Everett!*" I shrieked, as panicked as if I could actually view him, slipping across the boundary of life and death before my very eyes. "Everett, I am coming! Wait for me!"

Chapter 20

✧

Three months later, I disembarked at the spaceport on Fieldstar. It took me some little time to adjust myself to the shapes and scents of the place I had left a year and a half ago. The shuttle hangars were the same huge, bustling, impersonal spaces I remembered, full of too many people and too much noise. Outside the hangars, the streets of the city wound sleepily away. The quality of the air immediately caught my attention, and I glanced up at the faint metallic dome arching overhead. On Cody, I had become used to vagrant breezes and the playful touch of the sun, but I instantly remembered how on Fieldstar, such amenities did not exist. All was filtered, artificial, recycled. I took a deep breath and stepped purposefully down the road.

What I wanted now was to hire a conveyance to take me to Thorra-stone Park. In the past, I had never made the trip between manor and town in anything except the public bus or Everett's aeromobile, but today I knew the latter would not be at my disposal, and I had no patience to wait for the former. Vehicles and their drivers could be hired, I knew from overhearing the conversation of Joseph Luxton and Harley Taff, but until now I had never had the need—or the resources—to put such knowledge to the test.

In fact, I was finding I quite liked the advantages to being a woman of substance. My credit account had allowed me, three months ago, to book passage on a fast, commercial liner that would take me between Appalachia and Hestell in one sixth of the time it had taken the *Anniversary* to cover the same distance. On Hestell I had purchased another expensive ticket on the cargo ship heading toward Fieldstar by the fastest route. Its accommodations were spartan, to say the least, but I did not care about furnishings; I cared about speed.

I had to get to Fieldstar and Everett Ravenbeck as quickly as I could.

The Raineys had protested, of course, and I had considered myself obligated to tell them the whole story on the following morning. They had been, I think, shocked to discover yet another twist in my history, though this time at least no name change accompanied the revelation. They could not believe Everett Ravenbeck could still have any claim on my affections after his lies to me, and they greatly doubted my sanity when I described what had transpired on the rooftop patio.

"We must investigate," Sinclair had declared, and stalked away to the library monitor, all of us following behind. But after he called up news services and narrowed down his search to Fieldstar, it became clear that something disastrous had occurred at Thorrastone Park. There had been a compromise in the forcefield. Several people had been injured, and one had been killed.

"Killed?" I repeated in a strangled voice, for Sinclair read these words in a detached way, and his head blocked the screen. I could not see the monitor to read the words for myself. "But who—does it say—but what else happened—"

"There are very few details," he said, seeming to skim ahead in the news item. "Oh, but here—it quotes your Everett Ravenbeck as saying he intends to make full repairs to the house. So he at least was not the one to die."

One great fear assuaged! But dozens of others instantly swarmed in to replace it. What of Mrs. Farraday—Ameletta—any of the staff members I had come to know and respect? Such names would be of less interest to the media services, which cared only to report on the activities of high-grade citizens, but to me the import of their deaths would be almost as grave.

"No other news?" I demanded. "Nothing?"

Sinclair swiveled around to face me. "Nothing," he said.

Deborah laid a hand on my arm. "You were right, then," she said quietly. "He does need you."

Sinclair looked contemptuous. "The fact that he has suffered a tragedy in no way changes what he has done to her in the past and the fact that she is better off free of him and galaxies away. The most the situation requires is a note of sympathy—though even that, in my opinion, would be ill-advised."

I was looking at Deborah. "I will pack immediately and leave as soon as I can." Maria and Sinclair exclaimed against this, but Deborah only gave me back a solemn stare and nodded with complete understanding.

And the next day I was on my expensive cruiser, and then I spent three months in a state of exquisite torture. Wretched as the first experience had been, I almost wished for the oblivion of cold storage for this voyage back to Fieldstar, to spare myself the strain of constant and helpless worry. I hourly checked the media postings but found no news of Everett Ravenbeck's death. More details of the disaster I could not discover.

So when I landed on Fieldstar, I was in no mood to brook delays. I marched down the spaceport streets, inquired of the first sensible-looking person I saw where I might hire an aircar, and followed his directions until I fetched up in a slightly seedy-looking office not far from the Registry Office that I had visited once so long ago. Three youthful drivers slouched around the office, debating the merits of some brand of automotive circuitry, and they all glanced rather indifferently in my direction as I strode in.

"I need to hire a car to take me to Thorrastone Manor immediately," I announced.

A slim, long-haired youth whose shapeless clothes did not entirely conceal the fact that she was female, though that seemed to be their intent, was the only one to respond. "No such thing as Thorrastone Manor anymore," she said.

I felt hands clutch upon my heart; I am sure I staggered. "Gone!" I gasped. "But—the news reports—I thought the park had been saved—"

"Oh, sure, the park's still there, and some of the mining buildings," the girl replied nonchalantly. "But the house—it hasn't been fixed up again. Can't nobody live there."

"So—then—the people who lived in the house—where have they taken up residence?" I asked, stammering a little.

The girl looked at her fellow drivers and shrugged. "I don't think there were too many people living there. An old lady, a couple of servants."

"And Mr. Ravenbeck," one of the other drivers said.

"Oh. Right. He got hurt, didn't he?" the young woman asked.

"Mr. Ravenbeck. That's who I'm interested in finding," I said, making my voice as steady as I could. "Where might he be located?"

The girl shrugged and, as if that did not convey enough ignorance, spread her hands. "Don't know. Don't know who could tell you."

I remembered something she had said a moment ago. "But the mining compound is still functional? Is it still being used?"

She nodded. "Sure. Dropped off a fare there two or three weeks ago."

Then Mr. Cartell or Mr. Soshone could tell me where Mr. Ravenbeck could be found. "Take me to the park," I said as imperiously as if I had had money my whole life. "From there, I will decide what to do next."

It was the young woman who elected to be my driver, and she talked easily and rather vapidly for the whole flight. Although at first I thought her senseless chatter would drive me mad, soon enough I became grateful for the mild distraction it offered, for the two hours of this leg of the journey seemed to stretch as long as the three-month star voyage had. I sat beside her on the ripped faux-leather seats, my hands clenched tightly in my lap, and tried to keep from shrieking.

How many times had I made this journey between Thorrastone Manor and the spaceport, and how many times had the trip been almost unendurable?

At last, at last, we arrived within sight of the familiar enclosure. But how unfamiliar it looked now! Even from some distance away, I could view the damage to the once proud manor, every window shattered, a few shingles and shutters hanging at rakish, negligent angles. All around the house and throughout the great yard, weeds took a rapid ascendancy.

"Dear Goddess," I murmured, "it looks like a desolate place."

"That's a fact," my driver said, slowing down so we could enter the airlock. "Guess all the windows blew when the forcefield went down."

"How was the forcefield torn? Was there any damage to the mining compound?"

She shrugged, as I was beginning to believe she often did. "I didn't pay that much attention, you know? Didn't know anyone who lived there. Didn't really matter that much to me."

I had already established that she did not know the identity of the single person killed in the calamity, and I knew it was pointless to ask her more questions now. We paused for a moment inside the airlock, then activated the door that would allow us onto the park grounds themselves.

"Now where?" she asked.

"The mining compound," I said, pointing away from the house. "I'll find someone there who can help me."

It was another twenty minutes or so, however, before this goal was accomplished. I had never actually been inside the compound, so I was not certain how it was laid out, and we maneuvered our little vehicle past several very dreary and abandoned-looking buildings before we found any sign of human occupation. Then we spied a cluster of workers who greeted our arrival with some surprise but who willingly offered to go fetch Mr. Soshone, "being as Mr. Cartell is not on the premises this afternoon, miss."

"Yes, Mr. Soshone, I will be happy to meet with him," I said, feeling a great sense of relief that I would now *finally* be able to speak with someone who could give me some concrete information. I turned back to my driver—whom I had been reluctant to release until I had some assurance that the park was indeed inhabited—asked what I owed her, and paid her. She drove away while I stood there, two small suitcases at my feet, and awaited the arrival of the assistant mine supervisor.

When he came on the run a few minutes later, I could read the astonishment on his face. The last time he had seen me had been under conditions of such excruciating humiliation that I could not wonder that he had never expected to see me on Fieldstar again.

"Miss Starborn!" he exclaimed, a little winded, as he pulled up beside me. I remembered his plain-featured, good-natured face and the awkward courtesy that made him hold out his hand as though I might not be willing to accept it. But I was.

"Mr. Soshone," I said warmly, shaking his hand as though he had been a dear friend instead of a virtual stranger. "I know my appearance here must be an odd thing—let that go—but I *must* have information from you. I learned only recently of the horrors that occurred here, but I have no details at all. Tell me, please, what exactly happened—and who was killed in the disaster."

"How it happened is still not entirely clear," he said, and a shadow fell across his face. "But all of us have our guess as to how the field was violated—and it was done by the same individual who died because of it."

I put my hand to my throat as if to block the exit of my leaping heart. "Beatrice Ravenbeck," I whispered.

Mr. Soshone nodded soberly. "I never even knew of the lady's existence until—well, until that day. You know. But we had all heard tales about some strange woman who wandered the grounds at night. Some even claimed to have seen her, though I never did. I thought—some places have ghosts, even mostly fake places like Fieldstar. Who knows what kind of creatures they uprooted and destroyed when they came in to terraform? I thought she might be one of them, come back to make us all sorry. It never crossed my mind that she might be—what she was."

"And then one night, she escaped from her keeper," I prompted, for that much of the story I could guess.

"Yes, she slipped out while Gilda Parenon was sleeping, and she made her way to the manor house. And it seems she went to the basement, where all the equipment's kept, and she fiddled with the controls till she shut down the forcefield around the house and grounds."

"But the mining compound was still intact?" I asked, for I knew it was protected by a secondary failsafe.

"Mostly," he said. "We lost some air, but it was a slow process, and Mr. Cartell was able to get everyone in an oxygen mask before anything went too wrong."

"But at the manor—"

"At the manor, it went quick," he said. "All the windows shattered at once. The alarms must have gone off right before the glass broke, because everyone had time to get an oxygen mask—Mr. Ravenbeck, Mrs. Farraday, and those women who worked there. The only one who wasn't protected when the house blew was the lady crouching down in the basement."

He had omitted a name. "What about Ameletta—the little girl—Mr. Ravenbeck's ward?" I asked urgently. "Was she safe too?"

"Oh, Miss Starborn, she's been gone for months now. Shortly after your—after you *left*, Mr. Ravenbeck sent her off to school on Salvie Major. She wasn't in any danger at all."

I filed that information away for future examination, but continued to press for details about this most critical night. "So once the windows broke—what then?"

"Some of us from the mine came running over to see if we could help. Somebody even thought to get the airbus and fly it over there, which was a good thing, because oxygen or no oxygen, pretty soon Mr. Ravenbeck and all the others would have been exploding too. So somebody flies the bus over there, and they all climb aboard, and then somebody else notices that Mr. Ravenbeck's wife—that is—the lady—"

"His wife," I said steadily.

"That she's not to be found. And Mr. Ravenbeck insists on climbing back out of the bus, though Mr. Cartell did convince him to put on an airsuit, and he goes on down into the house to try to find her. Down to the basement. I don't know how he knew that's right where she'd be. I thought she'd have been dead anyway, so why bother, but Mr. Cartell explained that she might not need oxygen the way the rest of us do, but that she might be hurt and someone really did need to go after her. And Mr. Ravenbeck found her, and he carried her upstairs and out the door, and we could see him taking puffs on his oxygen tube then holding it up to her mouth, so I guess she did need to breathe after all, and she was actually still alive. And then—it was so strange, Miss Starborn, you should have seen it. She suddenly pulled herself from his arms and started this—this screaming. You never heard anything like it."

"I have," I said.

"And she started fighting with Mr. Ravenbeck—wrestling with him—and she was so strong, she knocked him to the ground when he reached for her again. And then she ran away from him, back into the house, panting like an animal, and I thought, 'Well, that's it, let her suffocate up there.' But Mr. Ravenbeck, he went up after her. We could see them through the broken windows of the landings, running up the stairways. And then they disappeared, but we could still hear her shrieking. And then suddenly—horrible, it was horrible—we saw them at an upstairs window, fighting again and shouting. And then they—together they—just fell. Right through that broken glass, three stories down."

He shook his head, seeming as affected in the retelling as he had been at the actual event. "She was dead. Broke her neck. Mr. Ravenbeck, he got all cut up by the glass, his right hand especially. Tore a bunch of muscles and broke the bones. It's still a terrible mess. And when he fell, he hit a rock or something with his head, or else something just got knocked around in there, maybe started pressing on an optic nerve, because he's basically blind."

"But he survived?" I said urgently.

"Oh—he's alive, more or less. He doesn't do much these days—doesn't say much. Of course, it's only been, let's see, a little over three months since it all happened. My wife says it might take anybody a year or so to take an interest in life again after such a thing, but I don't know. I think it's more than the accident and losing the manor. I think—well, there isn't much he wants to live for these days. And a man who doesn't really want to live doesn't usually live a long time."

I brushed aside the philosophy with a quick hand, though it struck me to the heart. "You speak as though you see him often," I said.

"Where is he? Can you take me to him? Or can one of the workers fly me to wherever he's taken up residence?"

"You don't need to fly, miss," Mr. Soshone said in a tone of surprise. "He's right here. My wife and I have been caring for him since the accident. Mr. Cartell and I, as the mine supervisors, we have our own cottages," he added in a confidential tone. "Now, Mr. Cartell's house, it's a bit bigger than mine, but he's got the three kids, and Evelyn and I thought Mr. Ravenbeck might find it more restful at our place. It's not like he hasn't done a lot for us in the past—Evelyn was glad of a chance to do something for him in return, though she says it's dreadful that he'd be in a situation where he'd need our help. But we've got the room, and it's not like he's any trouble. He eats with us, and sometimes one of us flies him into town and takes him wherever he wants to go, and other than that he pretty much keeps to himself."

Alone—blind—wrapped in his own bitter thoughts! My heart, already sore, felt bruised by the immediate picture I conjured up. "I must see him," I said. "Now. Where is your cottage?"

He looked doubtful for a moment—and I wondered whose well-being he was thinking of, mine or Mr. Ravenbeck's, that he considered our reunion ill-advised—and then he bent to pick up my suitcases. "This way, Miss Starborn," he said.

I followed him about a quarter of a mile through the drab mining buildings to a rather more pleasant cul-de-sac which consisted of a variety of buildings that appeared to be communal barracks interspersed with individual homes. They all looked onto a grassy common area that sported a few untended flowers and a couple of wrought-iron benches; three young children were chasing one another through the blooming bushes with great energy and complete disdain for our arrival. Mr. Soshone led me to the smallest of the houses, a two-story bungalow with lace curtains at the window and bright red flowers along the walk. It was a near-perfect facsimile of a country cottage, though if you looked closely, you could tell the brick was simulated and the roses were a strange hybrid with a rather hectic, unhealthy color.

"Evelyn!" Mr. Soshone called, pushing open the door and setting down my bags. "Evelyn! There's someone here to see you."

A few minutes later, Mrs. Soshone came bustling in, then stopped short at the sight of me. She was a small, fine-boned, dark-haired woman who appeared quite fragile, though her no-nonsense expression and intelligent eyes led me to suppose she had great strength of character.

"Why, it's Miss Starborn," she said, quickly recovering from whatever astonishment she might feel and coming forward to shake my hand. "I expect you've heard of our recent troubles here and come to see how everyone is."

Trust a woman's instinct! She knew that, to have planned to marry Mr. Ravenbeck, I must have loved him almost beyond sanity; and she knew that no revelation, no tragedy, could have mutated that love into anything approximating hatred. She knew why I was here the minute I walked through the door. And I knew that that knowledge, that sense of complicity, would help me through the next difficult hours and days.

"Your husband has told me some of the tale," I said, releasing her hand. "He told me that Mr. Ravenbeck is staying with you. I am grateful for whatever you have been able to do for him."

"Which has been very little," she said. "I feed him and make sure he stays alive, but beyond that, he has very little interest in me or any of us. I suspect, however," she said, giving me a long, considering look, "that he will respond with more energy to your arrival."

I smiled painfully. "Perhaps so. I would like to see him immediately, if I may. Where is he?"

"Upstairs. There is a sitting room next to his bedroom, and he has taken that as his main retreat. It has windows on three walls, so it is filled with sun, and we have set it up with all his electronic equipment, so that he can listen to music or cruise along the StellarNet. The computer has voice-command activation and read-back, and he is often up there, talking to the monitor or having it talk back to him. I found it a little eerie the first few times I came upstairs and heard him, but now I rather like to catch some of the conversations. At least I know he is participating in something."

"Yes—that is good news—I rather thought he might be brooding in silence and darkness," I said.

"There are days he does that as well," she said quietly.

Mr. Soshone touched his wife on the arm. "I must get back to the mine," he said. "You will take care of everything here? Make sure everything is all right?"

He spoke rather elliptically, but with some seriousness, and I was certain now he was a little concerned for Mr. Ravenbeck's reaction to my arrival. But Mrs. Soshone patted his arm and smiled, and in her expression I could read no such apprehension.

"Everything will be fine," she reassured him. "We will see you tonight at dinner." And she kissed him on the cheek and gently pushed him toward the door.

When he was gone, she turned and smiled at me. "Generally at about this time every day, I go up and bring Mr. Ravenbeck an afternoon snack," she said. "He does not eat much at dinner, so I try to make sure he takes small meals all day. Would you like to carry the tray up to him?"

"Yes, very much so," I said. "But—first—I need a few moments to refresh myself—"

"Of course. You can wash up down the hall, and I'll fix a plate of food for Mr. Ravenbeck."

In fifteen minutes, we were both prepared. I had needed the interval, as much as anything, to calm my nerves, which felt skittish and strange under my skin, and to regularize my erratic pulse. To see Mr. Ravenbeck again! Under such circumstances! I must have been made of steel and synthetics to be able to face such a prospect with utter poise.

But now I was ready—I was in control of myself—I was carrying the light tray up the wide stairway and breathing as naturally as I could. Mrs. Soshone had told me to turn into the second door on my left, but I could have found the room without directions. As she had warned me, words were emanating through the half-shut door, a stranger's sentences engaged in a dialogue with a most well-known, and well-beloved, voice.

"The population of the outer desert is scattered and thin, for the sere soil supports almost no plant life and the underground water tables have been severely depleted. Even scanning devices that can detect water several hundred feet below the surface crust find no promise of additional moisture in this sector of the planet, so that the native tribes face the grim prospect of relocation to a more habitable spot on Clobak or another world. Terminate or go on?"

"Go on," Everett said.

I pushed the door open, then stood motionless on the threshold.

"There are three possible venues on Clobak where location would appear to be an option, although each venue has its own drawbacks. The first, the western continent, offers a more moderate temperature and adequate water supplies, yet the terrain is almost nothing but solid rock and will not, without extensive terraforming, support human life. Terminate or go on?"

"Go on," Everett said, but there was a questioning, uncertain tone in his voice. He was facing away from me, as he sat in a high-backed chair that looked out toward the green common ground, but I could tell that he had cocked his head at my entrance and that he was straining to discern if there was a presence at the door.

"The second is a string of islands located along the equatorial line of the planet, which offer both adequate water and arable land. However, each island is so small that it can only be expected to support a handful of families, and the islands are widely enough separated that easy congress between tribes would be difficult, if not impossible, to sustain. Terminate or go on?"

"Go on," said Everett, who had now half turned in his chair. The sunlight fell rather harshly on his harsh face, illuminating the prominent nose and strong cheekbones, but that was not what made me swallow a gasp. A long, narrow scar cut a furrow from the bridge of his nose to the corner of his jaw, and a smaller one crossed it from his ear to his mouth. His eyes looked my way, but blindly and helplessly; I thought I saw a shade of desperation in their impossible seeking.

"The third option—"

"No, terminate," he said abruptly. "Evelyn, is that you?"

I could not reply.

"Evelyn?" he asked, a shade of impatience in his voice, but also a shade of uncertainty. "Have you brought my afternoon tray?"

I made myself take a step into the room, and the simple motion freed me of my moment's paralysis. "It is not Evelyn," I said, "but, yes, I have brought your tray."

An indescribable expression crossed his face. He half started from his chair, gripping its arm with his one good hand and focusing what senses he had remaining on the apparition at the door.

"Speak again!" he commanded, fear and excitement twining through his words. "I know that voice—surely I know that voice—"

"Where would you like me to put the tray?" I said, coming closer but seeing no likely surface near his chair. I spoke with an almost superhuman calm, for I had resolved to make this reunion as quiet, as far from hysterical, as possible. I did not know how he would react to my appearance at his door—I did not want to presume. And so when I spoke again, my voice was still serene, though my heart was not. "Shall I set the tray on the table by the window or do you balance it upon your knee?"

"Dear God," he whispered. "Or dear Goddess, as she herself would say. Every accent is so familiar—" And then, falling back in his chair, he addressed me with most unexpected and sternly spoken syllables. "Begone, then! I have had enough of you for one week—indeed, for one lifetime!"

My heart for a moment stopped beating, but his agitation was so great that I realized he was as wrought up as I was, though I was not sure why. So I said, as mildly as I could, "Why, sir, I have not been here to trouble you this twelve-month and more. I do not know with whom you have been speaking this past week, but it was not I. In fact, I just this instant arrived at your door."

He covered his face with his hand. "Dear God, dear God, it has got her very inflection perfectly," he moaned into his palm. "Just so would she seem to give the most complete and reasonable answer, and just so would she tantalize by saying nothing at all—" He uncovered his face and glowered at me, rather impotently, from those sightless eyes. "Begone, I say! I want no more spirits haunting me and taunting me. I welcomed you once, twice, a thousand times, but each time you melted away into insubstantial air, leaving me more pitiable and alone than the time before. Begone, I say! Mock me no more. I prefer quiet, and solitude, and despair."

Ah! In a moment I understood the problem, and I was instantly exuberant, though I hid it. I set the tray on the table by the window and crossed to stand right before him. "I am no ghost," I said. "I know you cannot see, but can you not at least tell that a shadow has crossed your face? That is because I am standing between you and the sunlight. Could a ghost achieve such a feat? Would a ghost stand here and argue with you about its very existence? Would a ghost"—and here I leaned down to very gently take his hand in mine—"feature true flesh and blood?"

His hand closed with such energy on mine that I had to bite back a cry of pain. "Her fingers—her delicate little bones—her own skin, which I studied so long I knew it better than my own . . .." he murmured, turning my hand this way and that, now lacing his fingers between mine, now running his thumb along the join of my wrist and thumb. Suddenly he pressed my hand against his mouth, then turned his cheek into my palm; I felt the dampness of a solitary tear melt between his skin and mine. "Jenna," he whispered. "If it were only, really, truly you."

He still doubted! He still thought himself visited by specters of the past! I jerked my hand away, causing him to sit up in astonishment, looking aggrieved at the behavior of this particular wraith. "I see I have much to do to convince you that I am real," I said in a voice of decided exasperation. "Is there another chair to be had? I want to sit and make myself comfortable while I explain myself. Also, if you are not going to eat the excellent snack Mrs. Soshone has made up for you, I think I will help myself, for I have traveled far today, and not stopped for so much as a drink of water, and I am famished."

He stared up at me with blind, marveling eyes. "I—but if you—how could you have—"

"A chair?" I reminded him. "Where might one be found?"

He gestured vaguely toward the hallway. "The room across the way—I think—but—Jenna? Jenna? Is it—"

"Just a moment," I said, and disappeared through the door.

I could hear him calling out questions attached to my name for the next few minutes as I checked the room across the hall and found a nice, sturdy high-backed chair. I carted it back into the sunroom and set it close to Everett's, though at an angle that would allow both of us to sit in sunlight. Then I dragged over the small table which now held the tray of food, and situated this so it was convenient to both our hands. All this time he continued to pelt me with questions; all this time I refused to answer.

"Now!" I said, when I was finally comfortable. "How about a little of this bread? I will butter it for you, if you like."

"Jenna? How is it possible? Where have you been? Are you really returned? How have you survived these many months?"

"I will answer every question, but first you must swear I am not a ghost, and then you must eat at least a piece of bread, and probably a slice of cheese too, before I will give you any hard information."

"Oh, it is really you, all-too-human Jenna, I believe that now!" he exclaimed, and though he attempted to imbue his voice with the mock scorn he had always used with me, I could hear the trembling in his speech. "No ghost would saunter in and force me to consume a meal before proceeding to break my heart again!"

"No, I assume that eating and drinking are activities that the dead might wish to engage in but cannot," I said around a mouthful of food. I knew I was being uncouth, but I did not care. For so many days I had been unable to summon up an interest in any meal—but now, suddenly, face-to-face with the man I had crossed the universe to find, I was starving. "I, on the contrary, intend to make a most hearty meal. Here, try one of these—grapes, I suppose they are. Some kind of fruit, though it's a little pinker than any grape I ever saw. Quite good, though."

He took the item from my hand, put it in his mouth, then returned his hand quick as a flash to take hold of my wrist. "If I must eat, then you must allow me to touch you," he said when I pulled back as if to free myself. "I must have constant reassurance that you are real, or I shall falter again—I shall slip into my old ways and accuse you of possessing merely a spiritual nature."

"You may hold my hand, then, if you choose, but you must continue to eat."

A moment's silence. "I cannot," he said at last.

"Oh? And why is that? You have two hands, I suppose."

"Two," he said, "but only one that functions."

I knew this, of course; it was not the dread revelation he expected it to be. "Oh? Well, let me see it. That shall be the hand I hold while your other one scoops up food."

"You will not want to hold it once you see it," he said, and withdrew it from its hiding place between the arm of the chair and his seat cushion. It was truly a wretched sight, a mangled mess of ripped, scarred flesh, and bent, ill-healed bones. It resembled a monster's claw invented to scare children, and it was clear, from the way he held it, that his range of motion was either severely limited or nonexistent.

"Do you have feeling in it still?" I asked in a very nonchalant voice.

"Yes—not extensive, but I can tell if it is touching silk or leather, and if I have plunged it into water hot or cold."

"Good," I said, and reached out to take it between both of my own. He started; I felt the maltreated fingers twitch in their highest degree of pain or ecstasy. "Can you feel my hand?" I inquired.

"Yes," he whispered.

I sat forward on the edge of my chair, and brought his hand to my lips. I kissed each broken knuckle, each separate scar. "Can you feel that?" I asked.

This time he merely nodded dumbly.

I sat back in my chair, retaining my hold on his hand and letting it lie in my lap. "Good," I said briskly. "Now let us finish our meal."

"Jenna," he said, and nothing else.

"Were you going to ask me something?" I said politely.

"No—so many things, but—no—"

"Then let me ask you something," I said. "Why have you not had the hand repaired?"

This, like so many of my observations this afternoon, seemed to catch him completely off-guard. "What?"

"The hand. And the scars on your face—and your eyesight, which I understand is nearly ruined. Why have you not had them repaired? You know as well as I do that there are doctors throughout the galaxy who could make each of these perfectly whole again. Why have you not had the treatments done?"

For a moment he looked completely stunned—then, slightly embarrassed. "I—the wounds are relatively new—I have not had a chance yet to investigate—"

"I think you like sitting here feeling sorry for yourself," I said, taking a bite of a rich chocolate pastry. "Mmm, this is very good. I think you like sitting here, wounded in the dark, and remembering all the dreadful things that have happened to you. I think you are a man who has gotten addicted to grief."

He snatched his hand away from me and looked angry enough to take a shove at me too, if he could have been sure of my exact location. For a moment I thought he might knock the tray over, so furious did he appear. "That is *not* so!" he declared. "I have suffered worse wounds than this in silence—wounds to my soul, wounds that I did not ever expect to heal—and I did not mope around looking for sympathy. I have not addressed these broken parts because—because there seemed no reason to do so. There was nothing I particularly wanted to look at, nothing I particularly wanted to touch, and so I did not care if I could see or feel."

"Good. Then you will have no objection to me doing a little investigation on the best surgeons to be had for your condition," I said brightly. "Unless—oh, but perhaps I misunderstood—there may have been another reason you hesitated—"

"*Now* what will you say?" he demanded, sounding so exasperated that I almost laughed aloud.

"You may have some distaste for the results of any operations you undergo—that is, the synthetics that will have to be incorporated into your body to make you whole again. That is a sensitive subject to you, I know."

"Not that you would care if it was so sensitive it made me weep merely to have it addressed," he muttered, and I could not help but grin at the irritation in his voice. "Banish that thought, you provoking girl!

I would let myself be remade, every bone, every blood cell, if it would please you. My only condition would be that they not exchange my heart for something artificial, for it is my own that I would want to love you with, and not something cobbled together from rubber and metal and electric wires."

I smiled again, and reached for the hand he had jerked away from me. The broken fingers stirred and tried to return my grasp, then lay quiet inside my own. "That was very pretty, sir. Thank you."

His good hand came up to cover mine with an urgent pressure. "May I speak now, Jenna? Have I swallowed enough morsels to earn your permission to ask a question or two?"

"Yes, you have done quite well. Ask me what you will."

"How did you come to be here? Why did you leave? What have you heard of the disasters that have befallen Thorrastone?"

"I saw news of the tragedy on the StellarNet, but I could not find the details. I had to know what had happened—to you, to everyone. And so I journeyed back."

"You could have sent a stel-letter," he suggested. "Contacted some-one at the spaceport who could have supplied the information. Hired an investigator—though that would have taken money, I suppose."

"I have money now, sir," I said, smiling.

"The devil you do! How did that happen?"

"It comes at the end of a very long story," I objected. "And this has been a long, tiring day—"

"Oh, no, you don't! Some of the details you may skip, but I expect the outline now. Tell me what has transpired in your life during the eighteen long months since I saw you last. Begin with the night you left here, in stealth and sorrow, leaving me so terrified for your well-being that I became, for a time, almost a madman—"

"Do not dwell on that, I beg you," I interposed swiftly. "It hurt me to leave you for your own sake almost as much as it hurt me for mine, but I could not stay. My reasons you know. I need not outline them again."

"You took nothing," he said, disregarding my prohibition. "A few items of clothing—a pair of shoes—nearly everything you owned was on my cruiser, and you had scarcely a note of credit to your name—"

"Yes, but I managed quite well," I said, instantly deciding to edit the greater number of horrors from the tale of my escape. "I went to the spaceport and found an outbound ship that was willing to take on a last-minute passenger to fill up an available berth, and I traveled practically to the end of the universe."

"Where did you go, Jenna? I looked for you everywhere. I sent messages out to every planet and outpost for which I could find a general address."

"To Appalachia, sir. Have you heard of it? It's a frontier world, and still growing, so there is a great deal of opportunity there for someone who is willing to work hard."

"Yes, that's one of the places I sent my messages. Did you like it there? Did you apply for a farming license and learn to grow beets?"

"Not exactly. Upon my very first day there, I was introduced to people who had need of my technical skills, so I found a home right away among people who valued me. And then, the most astonishing thing! We soon discovered that we were cousins—of a sort."

"This does not surprise me at all," he assured me. "You are constantly producing relatives that you had never mentioned before."

"One time only," I corrected him. "My aunt Rentley. And these people were not related to me by birth, but by conception."

"I don't understand, Jenna."

"They too were created in the gen tanks on Baldus, though they were raised on Newyer, and they had an upbringing not unlike mine. We were so amazed at the connection that we called ourselves cousins thereafter, and felt as close as I believe true kin could ever feel."

He was frowning now, remembering something. He had a very quick mind, so I was sure he would soon put the pieces together. "Wait a minute, I remember a news story from—oh, four or five months ago. Before the accident here. The founder of some clinic on Baldus was looking for his harvested offspring, wanting to leave a fortune to one of them—"

"Yes, sir," I said simply. "That was me."

"Why, Jenna!" he exclaimed. "Then you are a wealthy woman! Congratulations! For his estate was considerable."

"Well, I split it among my cousins and myself, but still I am left with a handsome sum," I said. "And that money enabled me to hurry to your side as soon as I heard of the events that had transpired here."

He seemed to speak with some difficulty. "Did you know then—before you set out on that long journey—what had happened—and who had died—"

"No, sir," I said quietly. "I came not knowing if your wife still lived."

"But then—as I asked before—why come at all? Why not find out by other sources how I fared and how matters stood?"

For a moment I did not answer. Sinclair Rainey had asked me the same thing, more than once, in the day I had spent packing for my trip. I had had no ready answer for him either. "Because, like you, I had to see and touch for myself," I said at last, squeezing his bent fingers with a gentle pressure. "I could trust only the evidence of my own eyes and senses to know that you were alive and well. No other report would do."

He had another question prepared to ask, I could see by the expression on his face, but just then a knock sounded on the door and a hesitant voice spoke. "Mr. Ravenbeck, I am sorry for interrupting," said Mr. Soshone. "But there's been a small problem—"

"Can it wait?" Everett snapped, but I had already come to my feet and picked up the food tray.

"You confer with Mr. Soshone. I know he would not seek you out for some trivial reason," I said. "Now that I have assuaged my hunger, I am so exhausted I do not think I can see straight! I will beg Mrs. Soshone for a room, and I will meet with you again at dinner."

And I escaped through the door while Everett rather testily argued behind me. Mr. Soshone mouthed an apology at me, but I smiled it away. I really thought this was the better plan, to allow Everett time to get used to my existence before we delved into the fresh issue confronting us: Now that his wife was dead, now that I was returned and he was free, could we reconstruct the future that had once seemed so bright before us? I did not want to take him by storm and surprise a declaration from him. My own heart was unchanged, as faithful as ever, but time and tragedy might have twisted his to the point where love was no longer possible. I hoped not; I believed otherwise; but I thought a few hours of separation and cogitation might help both of us understand more fully what we truly wished.

Accordingly, I did not see him alone again until the following morning. In the interim, Mrs. Soshone showed me to a small but charming room on the first floor, and I immediately fell into the soft bed and slept for several hours. I woke in time for the dinner meal, which was pleasant, though slightly strained, as Everett spent nearly the entire hour addressing random comments to me merely to force me to verify my continued existence. After the meal, I hurriedly retired to my chamber again, though I heard the others move around the house for another few hours before they all finally sought their beds.

In the morning, I did not emerge till I smelled breakfast cooking down the hall, and then I came out fully dressed and braced for whatever joy or disappointment the day might have to offer. Like dinner the night before, breakfast was made both uncomfortable and amusing as Everett focused all his attention on me. The Soshones exchanged frequent glances of hope and hilarity, and I could see that they, like I, thought one specific outcome would be most guaranteed to bring everyone happiness.

"Miss Starborn, why don't you and Mr. Ravenbeck take a nice long walk?" Mrs. Soshone suggested as her husband left for his day in the mines and I offered her help cleaning up the kitchen. "I'm so used to working in the house by myself that it will be easier on me if you two take yourselves off somewhere for a few hours. Mr. Ravenbeck does quite well walking as long as someone's there to guide him."

"Do you like to walk?" I asked him.

"On my less belligerent days," he replied. I smothered a laugh, though Mrs. Soshone looked quite surprised at his humor. I realized he had probably not indulged in it much during the past eighteen months, and I rejoiced that he was able to show that side of his personality to me.

"Then let us go for a stroll. You can set the pace, but I know the course to follow."

"And what is that, Jenna?" he asked me. "It is not like there are a variety of nature walks here in the park confines."

"No, but there is a monument I would like to see. I know the oxen-heart tree was felled more than a year ago, and I am sure it is nothing but a rotting stump by now, but I would like to visit it again. It was an important place to me in the past—I cannot, because it suffered misfortune, consider it inconsequential now."

"Let me pack a light luncheon for you," Mrs. Soshone suggested. "That way, you can stay out as long as you like."

Soon enough, we were on our way. I had, as a matter of courtesy to the blind man, taken Everett's arm so I could lead him across the lawn. That he clutched my hand with a rather extreme pressure I took for no more than the agitation of a man who could not see the path and feared he might fall. As for myself, the first few minutes of our stroll were occupied with remembering: the stale, still quality of the enclosed air; the filtered sunlight, which seemed so insufficient and artificial; the coarse grass that sprung up so instantly once my foot was lifted that I could not help thinking it resented my very presence on its planet. After Appalachia's fresh air and soft breezes, this environment seemed stilted and strange—and yet, for how many months had I longed to be back on this very world, in these few connected acres!

"Did you sleep well, Jenna?" Everett asked. "Your voice sounded so tired yesterday. Are you more rested?"

"Quite rested, thank you. And you?"

"I don't believe I slept at all, but I feel both rested and bursting with energy today. Usually it does not matter to me if it is noon or midnight, but I could not wait for dawn to come this morning."

"Yes, I was looking forward to the day as well."

Neither of us said why, and we spoke little more until we arrived at our destination. The oxenheart tree, which had been shattered by a mystical fireball the night Everett had declared his love, I had now expected to find a grayed, rotting hulk stretched full-length on the grass. But, "Look at that!" I cried as we approached, and Everett glanced at me with a smile.

"I cannot see it," he said. "Describe it to me."

"It has not been destroyed, as I thought. The bolt cleft it in two, but only partway down its trunk—it still stands, as firmly rooted and fiercely stubborn as it ever was. Some of its higher limbs are leafless and dying, but its lower branches appear stronger and fuller than ever. In fact, the whole trunk seems even more massive than I remember, as if it has bulked itself up after this latest assault and is determined to dig itself in place even more incontrovertibly."

"And this pleases you?"

"Oh, yes! I am happy any time any creature is able to defy the fates—can face them down and say, 'You cannot destroy or even harm me. You cannot bend me or uproot me or make me cease to flower. Come storm, come disaster, I am who I am, and I will never change.' "

Everett reached out a hand to give the rough bark of the trunk a friendly pat. "Very well put, Tree," he addressed it. "I might almost think your philosophy is the same as my friend Jenna's. You two must have a great deal in common."

I laughed. "And, look! This is new. Someone has placed a bench under the branches in just such a place to receive sunlight in the chilly morning and shade in the warm afternoon."

"I wonder who could have thought of such a thing?" he asked in such a tone that I was convinced the idea had been his. "Let us sit there, shall we? I'll wager it is a comfortable spot."

And so we settled on the rustic bench, and twined our fingers together, and talked quietly for a good hour. This time, step by slow step, Everett led me through the weeks and months of my recent adventures, learning names and relationships and events so well that I was sure he could recite them back to me if I asked.

Naturally, Sinclair Rainey's name came up a number of times during this recitation, and when I had finally finished with my story, Everett immediately returned the conversation to my cousin.

"This Sinclair Rainey. You lived in the same household with him for three months?"

"With him and his sisters, yes."

"Ate dinners with him, passed him in the hall on your way to bed, that sort of thing?"

"Attended church with him, met his friends, knew his fondest dreams and wishes, yes."

"I can't recall if you described him, other than to say he did not much resemble his sisters. He was not as attractive as they were?"

"On the contrary, he is quite a handsome man. Tall, slimly built, and yet fairly muscular, with strong cheekbones and pretty hair. Yet his eyes are his best feature, I would say, for they are so blue they are sometimes hard to look at, and they always send me groping for poetic comparisons."

"Ah. And yet—what—there was something about him you did not like? Perhaps his standards of intelligence were not particularly high or his public manner was embarrassing?"

"No, Sinclair is quite a well-read, well-spoken man who handles himself extremely well in social settings. Indeed, the few times he spoke at our worship services, his voice nearly electrified the audience—we all went home feeling as if we had been visited by the Goddess herself."

"But he was a busy man, you said. Ran the office, solicited donations from outside sources—you probably did not spend much time with him because he was always away at some function, is that right?"

"At first I saw very little of him, that is true. But once he discovered my technical skills, he became extremely interested in spending time with me. He wished to learn those skills, you see, and so he asked me to tutor him in the evenings."

"You taught Rainey nuclear physics?"

"Yes."

"Did you also teach his sisters?"

"Oh, no. They had often gone to bed in the evenings before our studies began."

"Did you offer to teach him?"

"No."

"He requested that you become his instructor?"

"Yes."

"What was his motive for learning?"

"He wanted a skill that would benefit him if he decided to emigrate to an even less settled planet than Appalachia."

"Did he learn his lessons well enough to apply them in such a situation?"

"When I left, he was, theoretically at least, nearly as proficient as I am."

"Did he, in fact, decide to take his newfound knowledge to some environment where it would be of use?"

"Yes, he has already emigrated to Cozakee, though his sisters were not happy at his decision."

"He went to Cozakee without them? Alone?"

"He wanted me to accompany him."

"To Cozakee? In what capacity? Nuclear advisor?"

"He wanted me to go as his wife."

"As his wife!" Everett exclaimed. "This is the first time you have mentioned that particular request!"

"It was not germane to the story. I turned down his offer."

"And why? For this well-read, well-spoken, quick-learning, electrifying, and handsome man seems like the answer to any woman's prayers. And he had, by your own account, recently inherited a sizable fortune, so he was a good catch in the monetary sense as well."

I could not help smiling at the ill-tempered jealousy that Everett made no attempt to disguise. "I had no interest in emigrating to Cozakee," I said. "And besides, Sinclair did not love me. I found the idea of being tied for life to a man who did not love me to be unappealing in the extreme."

"Are you sure about the state of his heart? For you are easy to love, after all, though you give yourself little enough credit on that count."

"I know whom he loved, and it was not me. A pretty, sweet, materialistic girl named Rianna, who was not at all the sort of woman you would take to rough, unsettled country. She fascinated him—whenever she was in the room, he could not take his eyes off her—but she was not strong enough to take into the wild. And so he asked me instead, for he thought I could work hard and bear children and keep my complaints to a minimum."

Everett digested this comment in silence for a moment. "Well! If that is the way he phrased his proposal, I am not surprised you turned him down. Were your feelings hurt, Jenna? I would not for the world have you wounded."

"No, for I understand Sinclair and I feel a great affection for him. But I am unwilling to be bound to him—or indeed, anyone—unless he feels true love for me, and I feel the same for him."

"But you have a soft heart, Jenna—you might mistake pity for love, or tenderness for love, or any of a dozen other kind emotions. You might confuse the memory of love with the reality of love—you might love the ghost instead of the man."

"I am not like you," I said calmly. "I do not confuse flesh-and-blood beings with their otherworldly counterparts. I know a specter when I see one—and I also know a living, breathing, real, and beloved man if I am so lucky as to encounter him as well."

I had put my hand to his cheek as I spoke, and he lifted his own hand—the scarred and mangled one—to cover mine. "And you could still love me, Jenna? You could forgive all, forget all, my perfidy and your own struggles? You could go back to those happy, innocent days when you believed in me and I swore no action of mine could ever bring you a moment's pain?"

"We cannot go backward. We cannot erase time and events. But we can go forward, hand in hand, hope in our hearts and love lighting our way. These are our choices, as I see them—to go forward alone, apart from each other, in grief and darkness—or to go forward together. For either way we must go forward—and as for myself, I would rather take that path with you by my side than attempt to walk it in silence and solitude for so many weary miles."

Now he drew me against him, wrapping both his arms around me and murmuring my name over and over into my hair. I could tell that he was weeping, but I was not. Joy had gone scalding through my veins and was radiating out through the pores of my skin with such a white-hot fervor that it burned away any tendency toward tears. I had not known you could be this happy and not alchemize into something lighter, less substantial; I clung to him as much for the delight of it as the fear that otherwise I would waft away toward the iridescent ceiling overhead. I smoothed back his hair, and I kissed his forehead, and silently I laughed.

"I love you, Jenna," he whispered, and I kissed his forehead again.

"I love you too, Everett, with all my heart."

Epilogue

✦

*R*eeder, I married him.

Quiet as we had planned that first ceremony to be, this one was even quieter. Two days after my arrival on Fieldstar, we took the public bus into town, because he could not see and I could not fly his Vandeventer, and we walked into the Registry Office and were married. Afterward, we had sandwiches at Ameletta's favorite pastry shop, and talked about where we would live and how quickly we could schedule surgery for his hand and his face. We talked about Ameletta too, and Mrs. Farraday, and all the beloved people with whom I had lost contact on my precipitate flight from Fieldstar.

Ameletta had been sent away to school on Salvie Major, but Everett admitted he was not sure she was content there, and I resolved instantly to investigate. We had pretty well determined Fieldstar would not be a happy home for us. Since Everett had several other estates on more hospitable worlds, I thought we should choose a location where we could be close to a good school that Ameletta could attend. He agreed to this, and suggested Brierly, which was reputed to have a fine educational system; and so that problem was easily disposed of.

Mrs. Farraday seemed more happily settled than Ameletta, for she had taken up residence with one of Everett's elderly cousins who required very little more than pleasant conversation over the breakfast table and a few errands run in the afternoon. "But I believe she would be willing to join us in any household we set up," he added, "especially if it included Ameletta."

"Then by all means, let us contact her at once. There is no one I would rather have by me as I run a new home than Mrs. Farraday."

He also, to my great comfort and relief, had obtained news of Janet Ayerson. "As we all expected, Joseph Luxton abandoned her within a few months of seducing her, but she never did apply to me for help," he said with some regret. "But, like you, she instinctively sought out a frontier planet, one of the last places in this society that an outcast can find hope of a useful life. She is homesteading on a place not unlike Cozakee, I think—she tells me that in three years she will become eligible for citizenship. She has refused all my offers of aid, but once she established herself, she began a regular correspondence with me, and I know she will be glad to hear from you. She has asked me often about your circumstances. She does not know the whole story—or, if she does, she did not learn it from me—but she does know you have been missing and she will be overjoyed to hear of your return."

I did not think we could convince Janet to join us in our cozy new household, but just knowing that she was alive and well suffused me with great peace. "I will write her immediately as well," I promised. "Oh, how it lifts my heart to see how all our sorrows can be turned through gradual degrees to happiness again!"

"That does not erase the sorrows. They are still behind us, to be dragged along whether we like it or not. Before us too, no doubt," he warned me.

I smiled and took his hand. "But the sorrows do not erase the joys either, nor do they cancel each other out. They alternate, perhaps, like sun and shadow, but the dark always gives way to the light and the impossible becomes possible again."

He smiled. "You lift my heart, Jenna, with your indomitable spirit."

I kissed his fingers. "And you lift mine with your mere existence."

* * *

A year later, all had changed. Everett's injuries had been repaired; his hand would never be quite as supple as it had been in the past, and his eyesight was, after a long or tiring day, unreliable, but he was virtually whole again, and profoundly grateful to be so. By that time, we were also living in a spacious, light-filled mansion on Brierly, where neither of us had to do a day's work because Mrs. Farraday kept the household running so smoothly.

Ameletta, though she lived half a planet away, came home on regular visits and continually delighted me by her worldly wisdom and her sweet nature. She had grown even more beautiful and self-assured in the intervening years, and it was easy to tell that she would be a stunning woman of great poise and beauty; but either she did not realize this or she was not spoiled by her own radiance, for she was as unaffected and friendly as ever. She lavished on me all the affection a child might give a favorite aunt—even more so when she learned that I was carrying the child who would become her adopted cousin. The whole period of my pregnancy consisted of Everett worrying over my health and Ameletta covering me with kisses, so that, for more than the usual reasons, I could not wait for my child to be born.

Everett was more moved by this event than by anything I had ever witnessed, and as he held his son in his arms, he seemed struck mute with ecstasy. It was half an hour or so before he could bring himself to look away from his son's dark face and meet my eyes again.

"I do not know whom you thank for happiness so profound as this," he said quietly.

I smiled. "The Goddess, of course. For it is she who creates the cycles of our lives and she who has woven us into this pattern."

He shook his head, as if my answer was not sufficient, and gazed down at his son again. "A year and some months ago," he said, still in that quiet voice, "I did not want to go on living. I had, in fact, determined to take my life. It was a week or so after the accident at Thorrastone Park, and it seemed to me that I had lost everything I had ever cared for in my life. I was, at that time, living in the cottage with the Soshones, but one night, in secret, I crept out of my room and groped my way down the stairs and managed to get outside. I had brought a bottle of pills with me, which I intended to swallow, but some compulsion had made me leave that kind house so I did not taint it by such an unforgivable act.

"I took a few careful steps along the pathway toward the common green—that far I could get on my own by daylight, and naturally I had no reason to care if it was dark now—and I made my way to the middle of the grassy area. There, I fell to my knees, and looked up at that blank Fieldstar sky, and I wondered aloud why there was no peace or love or justice anywhere in the universe. And since you were the one to whom I had been unjust, and you were the one whom I loved, I called out your name, over and over and over again."

He was silent a moment, motionless except for the flicker of his eyes as he watched his son's changing expressions. I said nothing. I had caught my breath and did not believe I would be able to release it till this tale came to an end. "And after—in the blackest moment of despair in my entire life—I had called out your name, I held up the vial of pills that I intended to swallow, and removed the cap. And in that instant, before I could place the first tablet in my mouth, I heard a voice—your voice, or so it seemed—calling out to me. Just a few words—first my name—and then this phrase: 'I am coming. Wait for me.' And I waited. I put away the pills, I staggered back into the house, I lay in my bed that night. And I waited."

Now he looked up at me, and his eyes were full of a fresh wonder even at so old a tale. "And three months later, you appeared on my doorstep. I have never put much faith in this Goddess of yours, this spiritual entity who collected every ounce and atom and laid them into a mosaic of souls. But I have no other explanation for what occurred that night, except divine intervention and the complicity of the universe. If it is, as you say, the Goddess who has brought me this degree of happiness, then I will give over to her what portion of my heart does not belong to you. For she is capable of miracles indeed."

He seemed still so awed by this evidence of the Goddess's existence that I hesitated to tell him my own part in that unearthly conversation, but a few days later, I recounted the tale to Deborah in a long letter. We had become regular correspondents, and she was even now planning a visit to Brierly to see my son, bringing her husband, Harmon, and her own daughter with her. Through her I learned most of my news of Maria, who was planning a wedding, and Sinclair, happily laboring away on Cozakee—and to her I told all the secrets I would tell a sister.

"There have been times I myself doubted what occurred that night," I wrote her, "for I know that the human imagination is creative and willful and the heart can always be trusted to construct its own reality. But if it was a delusion, it was a shared one, and so powerful that it leaped across more miles than the mind can comprehend. But I think it was real, and I think it was love that gave us the voices to speak and the ability to hear words that no rational person would either entrust to the wind or pluck from it. He called me to his side, and I am content to stay here till I die, surrounded by more joy than I knew the universe contained.

"All of us are looking forward to your visit. Ameletta speaks of you already as if you were a long-lost relative, and she has posted a calendar counting off the days till your arrival. Everett frets that you will not like him, but I have no fears on that score. You have the happy ability to love upon the smallest encouragement, and certainly there will be no shortage of encouragement here! As for myself, I cannot wait to see you again, my closest kin and my dearest friend. Until then, know that I think of you daily and with the greatest fondness. Your loving cousin,
Jenna Starborn."